The Com

The Committee

by

P. M. Nugent

Copyright © 1999 by P. M. Nugent

All rights reserved. No part of this book may be reproduced, stored in a retrieval system, or transmitted by any means, electronic, mechanical, photocopying, recording, or otherwise, without written permission from the author.

ISBN 1-58500-910-5

About the Book

Senator Walter Mossingame froze in his chair. McAdams started to rise, in slow motion it felt, to his feet. The gun was pointed straight at them. The gunman's mouth dropped into a toothy grimace and then sparks of fire and puffs of smoke erupted from the black metal. The chamber echoed with sharp, painful explosions as three quick rounds plowed with sickening thuds into the head, neck and back of their witness, Professor Tidback. Pieces of his skull and chunks of his brain sprayed in the direction of the Senators' dais. McAdams felt the awful mist hit his face and hands. Mossingame reared back in his seat, recoiling from the bloody rain.

The brutal execution of a witness testifying before a Senate committee looking into the assassination of Martin Luther King leads chief investigator John McAdams on a treacherous search down the dark corridors of this country's past. The missing 18 pages of John Wilkes Booth's diary provide shocking clues as McAdams unlocks a 200-year old conspiracy responsible for a chain of political assassinations through the years.

* * * * * * * * * * *

Coming in 2000 is another John McAdams' political thriller, **The Witness**. Senate investigator McAdams must find out who is behind a secretive US government operation in Cuba that leaves over 400 foreign terrorists dead. And he must come up with answers fast, before the President is indicted and convicted for war crimes. America teeters on the brink of political upheaval in turbulent times. Its only hope, McAdams' only ally in a macabre underworld of political intrigue and secret government fronts, is a notorious outlaw from American justice hiding out in Cuba who has witnessed the bloody raid, a woman from McAdams' past.

Dedication

**For Patty,
who believed from the beginning,
and for
Liz, Claire and Patrick,
who prove that the best is yet to come.**

Acknowledgements

I want to thank a select "Committee" of great people who gave me the gift of their valuable time, who actually read earlier drafts of this work, and who delivered enthusiastic and helpful, detailed comments. Thanks to Tom Hemnes, Robert Gibbons, Dan Henninger, Mike Schiffres, Duncan MacDonald, Clint Walker, Toni Galardi, Paul Shay, Joe Markoski, Toby Solberg, Rich Edlin, Tom Cirillo and Liz Nugent. Special thanks must go to Patty Nugent, Elly Gustafson and James Adams who have read so many drafts they know the book better than I. And, finally, my gratitude goes to agents Kevin Lang and Nina Ryan who guided me along the way, to Michael Paxton for his word processing rescue skills, to Don Sigovich and his Image Works for a beautiful book cover and to Tim Romero of Definitive Stock, Inc. for the front cover photo. Of course, the errors and inaccuracies within are all mine.

Chapter One

Tuesday, April 7 -- Washington, D.C.

"The Committee will come to order!"

Senator Walter Mossingame discharged three loud bangs with his heavy gavel and then held it aloft, glaring into the cavernous hearing room for any challengers. "This is the last day of hearings for the Senate Select Committee on the Assassination of Dr. Martin Luther King. It will be a long one. Let's get started."

Mossingame, Committee Chairman and Vermont Democrat, sniffed his approval as the spectators settled down. He lowered the gavel and nodded to the man to his left, Taylor Brock, a Republican who hailed from Virginia. Brock and he were the only Senators present from a special Select Committee that numbered eleven - six Democrats and five Republicans. The rest would show up at the end of the day, he knew, when the CNN and C-SPAN cameras were scheduled to start rolling. They would come waving closing statements chock full of grand words and lofty sentiments.

"Now," murmured Mossingame, his eyebrows arched, "where is our first witness?" He looked out into the hearing room and eyed the empty witness table. "It would be nice if we had a witness, wouldn't it, Mac?"

Behind the two Senators and off to the side, alone in a row of staff seats against the wall, sat John McAdams, chief investigator for the Committee. McAdams was Mossingame's right hand man. Sixteen years ago McAdams came out of law school and found a job with Mossingame on Capitol Hill - that complex of House and Senate buildings overlooking Washington, DC. Together, over the years the Senator and the investigator took on all sorts of liars, extortionists and thieves, through one Committee or another. Together they were always on someone's shit list, hit list or enemy list.

This morning McAdams sat with his elbows on his knees, wringing his hands as he waited for the testimony to come. His pale brown eyes scoured the hearing room. His thick, wavy brown hair, still wet from his shower, fell over the collar of his tired, dark blue suit jacket. Years of New England boating had left his Irish skin rugged and ruddy, exuding the false impression of regular and recent leisure and sport. A three-inch long, wishbone-shaped scar marred his left cheek, its longest, thin pale line pointing menacingly up toward his eye socket.

"It would be very nice to have a witness, Mr. Chairman" McAdams replied. He followed Brock's gaze into the hearing room to spot a man getting up from one of the spectator seats. The man lowered himself into the center chair at the witness table below the Senators' dais. A folder, presumably his, waited on the table in front of his seat. He shifted his weight back and forth, looking for the cue to begin.

Mossingame nodded to the witness and then summoned again his deep, resonant voice. He had to cough and hack a few times to get it going.

"This Select Committee was created by special act of Congress. Responding to new evidence in the case, the Congress gave us broad investigative powers to review the King assassination of 1968 and to settle unanswered questions that have come to light. We have uncovered disturbing new evidence over the past two years, some of which suggests that there were multiple conspirators in the death of the late Reverend Martin Luther King. It has been an ordeal for me to preside over this process. I think it fair to say this has been an ordeal for each of us on the Committee. Our witnesses today will elaborate on what we have heard. And, perhaps, Senator Brock, they will suggest a course of action for us to take in the future."

The courtly Virginian nodded at his colleague's perfunctory introduction. "Ah hope so, Mistuh Chairman," he replied, staring into the hearing room.

McAdams noticed that Brock's thick knuckles bulged as he gripped the edge of the table in front of him. A fly landed on one of the old Senator's liver-spotted hands, and waited for action, some morsel. Fed up, it flew off and languidly buzzed McAdams before it settled on Mossingame's right shoulder.

Mossingame squinted at a typed page in his hand. "Our first

witness today is Professor David Tidback. He's from the University of Mississippi. Welcome Professor."

"Thank you, Mr. Chairman," blurted the nervous little man. His small eyes were locked onto the microphone in front of him, which reached as high as the bridge of his nose. Tidback had to be 65, but looked energetic and fit. He was dressed in clothes a decade old. The professor slowly opened the folder before him and peered inside. He looked up, his eyebrows knitted in puzzlement, his eyes darting back and forth. He spoke, haltingly.

"Senator Mossingame, Members of the Committee, I ...." Tidback scanned the row of empty Senators' chairs fanning out from either side of Mossingame and Brock. His sponsor, Senator Richard Charlton from Mississippi, was nowhere to be seen.

"Senators," Tidback continued, "I ... I come before you to testify about new evidence relating to the assassination of President Abraham Lincoln. President Lincoln ...."

"Professor Tidback ...," interrupted Mossingame, "Professor Tidback. Just a minute." McAdams recognized fatigue and a hint of uncharacteristic impatience in the Senator's voice. He watched the fly spring from its perch on Mossingame's shoulder and zip off into the hearing room, looking for better fare.

"Professor Tidback," continued Mossingame, "I am truly sorry to cut in here, but this is the *King* Assassination Committee, not the...."

"Please, let me continue," pleaded Tidback, " ... I beg you. ... Senator Mossingame, President Lincoln was the victim of a conspiracy of the Confederate Secret Service and a cabal of others. This conspiracy continues to this day, it is alive and it threatens to start a second Civil War in the United States. I have evidence, Mr. Chairman, and I can and I will produce it for this Committee."

The room fell silent as Mossingame furrowed his brow at Tidback. Low, embarrassed murmurs rose up from the small audience. The five conspiracy buffs that always filled the back row craned their necks, their noses in the air flared with the scent of secrets and sin.

A bald reporter in the back stood, as if to leave, jamming his notebook inside his leather jacket. He reached under the press table and hauled up a gun that looked to be the size of a small cannon. He held it out in front of him with two hands, one hand steadying the other, and aimed at the front of the room.

Mossingame froze. McAdams started to rise, in slow motion it felt, to his feet. The gun, that gun, was pointed straight at them. The gunman's mouth dropped into a toothy grimace and then sparks of fire and puffs of smoke erupted from the black metal. The chamber echoed with sharp, painful explosions as three quick rounds plowed with sickening thuds into the head, neck and back of Professor Tidback. Pieces of his skull and chunks of his brain sprayed in the direction of the Senators' dais. McAdams felt the awful mist hit his face and hands. Mossingame reared back in his seat, recoiling from the bloody rain.

McAdams reached out and grabbed Mossingame. He pulled him under the dais by the time the screaming began. He did not see the erstwhile reporter turn the gun to his own mouth and fire two more shots in succession. The killer fell on the table in front of him, pumping blood from what was left of his neck over the notes and astonished looks of his companions.

Chapter Two

The explosions of the gunshots echoed off the high ceiling, becoming somehow faint while still resonating powerfully within McAdams chest, competing with his thundering heart. He heard a sudden, mad screeching of chairs as the reporters at the table backpedaled desperately away from the carnage before them.

McAdams lurched up from behind the dais in time to see one veteran word jockey retching. His painful heaving was punctuated by an old woman in the audience screaming "Oh God, oh God, oh God..." as she rocked back and forth in her chair with her hands placed tightly against her ears. The old man with her was trying to pull her hands away and speak to her. Seeing assassination at work, the conspiracy boys sat erect like owls, silently, joyfully taking it all in. Their day had come.

The uniformed officer at the hearing room door clutched a radio in one hand and a pistol in another, looking left and right for more assailants. "Shooting in 1-5-2 Dirksen!" he cried by chance into the correct hand. "I need assistance!"

McAdams slowly took in the hearing room. Clumps of skull and flesh gleamed everywhere in the bright lights. A pink spray covered the Senators' dais, dappled with thick chunks of gray brain and pale white shards of bone. The fly had returned, joined by a mate, and they wallowed in a small, crimson pool of thick blood that had ended up in front of Brock. The professor, a skittish witness only moments ago, lay with what was left of his head slumped over his folder, as if taking a short nap. Off in the back of the room the assassin was splayed sideways over the reporters' table. Except for the sick one, the reporters were bent over the body, studying it and taking notes like they were coroners. They wished for their cameras but Christmas was too far away.

McAdams finally breathed. He inhaled the terribly sweet, heavy smell of blood mingled with the acrid odor of burnt gunpowder. He shook his head and felt a deep ache. The witness had been begging to be heard when he had been killed, begging for everyone to hear, begging for a few moments. McAdams pulled Mossingame gently from the floor. "Walt," he whispered into the Senator's ear, "let's get out of here before what's left of the press comes after us."

Mossingame nodded and staggered to his feet. "Macky", he said, as McAdams steered him to the door behind the platform for Senators and their staff, "How could this happen in my hearing room? That poor man there..." His hand fluttered in the direction of Tidback's body.

McAdams spotted Lewis Shephard, Brock's chief of staff, coming into the hearing room through the back door. Shephard's pudgy faced bulged out of a shiny blue suit and a dingy shirt that must have been white - once. The shirt buttons were straining to get free and pop onto the floor where they might get lost.

Guiding Mossingame, McAdams passed in front of Shephard. "Had to see it for yourself, Lewie?" he hissed. Shephard sneered his reply. McAdams noticed a thin veneer of grease bubbling on Shephard's forehead.

Suddenly the reporters behind McAdams noticed the attempted escape. They rushed forward, shouting. "Senator?" "Mr. Chairman? ... Mac?"

As McAdams disappeared through the door, he glanced over his shoulder. Shephard was heading out the other side of the hearing room. Brock, stunned, was sitting by himself, something red, wet and large dripping down the front of his expensive, new Hermes tie. The Virginian stared beyond the killing ground before him, out of the room, to some other place.

Braying reporters turned on Brock. The Senator managed to pull himself into a standing position and began walking as if in a trance out of the hearing room. He started climbing the stairs across the hall, not hearing the reporters' pleas and shouts. They gave up and ran as one for the phones at the other end of the building. The stairwell echoed with their footfalls.

Brock floated through the anteroom of his office, ignoring the "Good morning, Senator" from the unknowing young receptionist. He veered toward his stately, wood-paneled office. It was his sanctuary - with 20 foot ceilings and photographs of the Virginia Shenandoah mountains, good ol' pols like him from back home, and groups of smiling voters pleased as punch to be with him. He lurched inside, slapping his arm absent-mindedly behind him to close the door.

Lewis Shephard came out of his office looking pale. He caught Brock's back retreating into his office, and then the door swung shut. He looked down at the receptionist's office phone. Brock was on his personal line.

He turned away and went into his office, quietly closing his own door. A second light flickered on the receptionist's phone set as she looked up to see a gaggle of reporters comically squeezing all at once through the door.

"He found the gun," Shephard whispered hoarsely into the phone, his hand cupped around the speaking end of the receiver. "They're dead." A deep voice grunted acknowledgment and hung up. Shephard sunk into his chair and with the back of his bulbous hand wiped away the thin ribbon of sweat that curled over his upper lip.

Chapter Three

The 7 o'clock TV news that night had five full minutes on the story.

Tom Brokaw told the country that David Tidback was the "first witness ever to be assassinated in mid-sentence in the history of the United States Congress." Tom had said so, so it had to be true.

McAdams shook his head, his eyes closed. It was his witness who got shot, testifying in front of his Committee. He sat powerless while his witness got shot in front of the whole wide world.

He held his wrist to stop it from swaying before his eyes and squinted at his watch. He was getting close to whirling drunk, that stage before the eyes and the memory record nothing. Whirling, whirling, ready to fall down. Ashes, ashes, all fall down.

It was ten minutes until closing time. Time, he figured, for one more. He whipped his hand in the air. "Garcon!"

The bartender three feet away stood drying a glass with a towel. He lifted his eyes to glare at McAdams. "Hey, Mac, you're sitting at the bar. On a barstool. I'm right here, right across the bar from you, OK?"

McAdams put his fingers to his lips. "Quiet! OK! Quiet! Got it!"

"Bones" Jones, so called because he rolled the biggest joints in Washington, D.C., shook his head. It was a bad day for his favorite customer. There was a whole lot of crime on Capitol Hill, but he couldn't remember gunfire inside the hearing rooms for Christ's sake.

"Mac, I'm feeling bad for you, I have all night. But no more. You finish the one in front of you, if you can see it." Bones suddenly let out one of his famous belly laughs that levitated the beard from his chest. "I'll walk you home after I finish up."

"You're all right," nodded McAdams. "All right." He needed his friends right now.

McAdams sat back and reached for a cigarette. He lit it and blew a long plume toward the street light on the other side of the bar's large front window. He marveled at how the light outside projected the neon sign on the window onto the empty dance floor. The words "EJ O'Riley's" shimmered underneath the window as if there were some cause for excitement.

He stared into his glass and suddenly saw thick hands, others' hands, clutching glasses of whiskey and cups of steaming hot coffee. He *was* drunk. He was again in Bridgeport, Connecticut, in the back rooms of its labor halls, VFWs and waterfront restaurants where his father had plied his trade. The old man was a powerful city councilman and then Bridgeport mayor over a span of 30 years and the king of local politics in a falling empire of urban decay. It was hard to believe now, but once upon a time the McAdams family was a rising political force in Connecticut society and politics, with elected positions and powerful party posts going back over a hundred years to when the first McAdams barely clawed his way out of starving Ireland to America in the late 1840s. Once upon a time his father, John McAdams Senior, was the proud heir to that noble legacy, a legacy shaping up to be a small-scale version of such New England political dynasties as the Lodges and the Kennedys in Massachusetts, the Pells in Rhode Island and Connecticut's own Bailey clan. That was before his father fell into the bottle, and into the arms of too many women. It was before the bad times hit, and before his father's conviction for taking a little too much money, a little too much free lunch, a few too many expensive women, even for the local judiciary who always had a hand in someone's pocket. A massive heart attack took his father in jail, just before he, Mac Junior, turned 18.

Before that, when the old man was riding high, his father had brought him along on his runs so that his oldest boy and namesake could get "educated" on "how the world worked." One such time thrust itself upon him now.

His father was city councilman, running for mayor for the first time. He remembered sitting off to the side in a straight-back chair in the rear of a darkened restaurant. His father sat at a large table shoved into the corner, huddled with a group of swarthy men under a cloud of smoke. The table had a dark maroon cloth and the flames in several cheap candles in red glass containers flickered like wild snakes. The table was covered with bottles and glasses of beer and whiskey, and cups of coffee, and there were loaves of bread, chunks of cheese and pepperoni and kielbasa scattered about. His father exchanged envelopes with one man, then pointed a finger in another's face.

Voices were raised, chairs screeched as one man went for the other. His father pounded the table loudly and shot a glance in his son's direction. Others followed with sullen looks. The commotion stalled and he followed his father out of the restaurant into the night.

That was it, democracy at work according to his father's strictures - greasing the skids, pumping the flesh, passing the bucks, that's what it was all about in this US of A. McAdams shuddered on the barstool, a blast of cold air from nowhere passing over him. He left that town as soon as he could, at 18, and came to Washington for college and then law school, and hooked up with Mossingame. He became the son the Mossingames always wanted and never had. They never forgave him for it, the family back home, never really invited him back either, except for baptisms, confirmations, weddings and funerals. He took a mouthful of Dewars, swished it around and swallowed. It landed with a searing burst in his stomach.

He wondered about what he had been doing these last 16 years with Mossingame, and why. All it amounted to was stable cleaning, and chasing down bad guys, fixers and takers. He did it with such a vengeance and a dedication that it scared people, and made them wonder what devils haunted him. It got them guessing why there wasn't more to life for a guy who looked good, talked smooth, and had tons of connections. Maybe, in going after the corrupt and the crook, maybe he was trying to punish his father, or get his chance - finally - to rebel, a chance denied him by his father's death. Maybe that's all it was. He took a long drag.

He hated these moments of clarity, badly. They usually did no one any good. They reduced grand motivations and ambitions, a life's work, to some twisted, infantile reaction to unfortunate or accidental past events or parental hang-ups. A vision of a rat in a cage with electrodes and bells and feed bottles tried to nestle in his mind.

He shook it off, for now. With three bullets into the head of David Tidback this afternoon, McAdams knew, the fixers and the takers were back with their own brand of vengeance. They came to kill. And they were coming after him. This was for real.

He looked for Bones, who was still drying the damn beer mugs. Around the bar there were last acts being played out. There were a few stragglers with their heads back, trying to suck the alcohol off the last of the ice in their glasses. A couple, tangled in one final, anxious exchange of words, sat at a huge round table that was littered with standing and fallen empties and smudged glasses. A guy snored with his head on his arms at one of the corner tables, a threatening circle of skin on the top of his head betraying his outer display of peace. And the same table of young Congressional staff sat in the corner looking fresh, earnest and convinced they were about to make some major contribution to law and society.

The table of youngsters pissed him off. They were, plain and simple, from a whole new era. They were part of that new wave on the Hill, political scientists with serious jobs to do, with appointments, agendas and deliverables that required sensible doses of diet seltzer, wine spritzers, light beers, de-caf lattes, unsalted pretzels and butterless popcorn. At 41, he already was the old guard, the guy who goosed and guffawed and politicked and drank too much. Suddenly he and his kind were the defilers of democracy and freedom. Maybe, in their eyes, maybe he and his kind had become the fixers and the takers.

Fuck 'em. They couldn't have saved Tidback today. They couldn't have done shit. What the hell was a latte, anyway?

He spun around on the barstool. "Take me home, Mr. Bones, take me home." He poured the remains of his glass down his throat and grimaced. It had been a long, long day.

Chapter Four

Wednesday morning, April 8 -- Harpers Ferry, West Virginia

A white, wrinkled face under a wild thatch of mottled gray hair pressed up against the window. The old man's mouth hung open as he concentrated on what was going on inside, dark teeth and ragged gaps outnumbering the eroded and yellowed chips that punched up through rust-colored gums.

The face disappeared and then the door opened. Chief Charles Jackson of the Harpers Ferry police department waited behind his desk wondering if the old codger in his haste was going to fall down the three stairs that led to Jackson's large one-room office. It wouldn't be the first time.

Jackson's coal black eyes twinkled as he ran his hand through ringlets of tightly curled gray hair. His mud brown, fleshy cheeks bulged with splashes of tiny black moles under each eye. You wanted to talk to that face, everyone said. You wanted to get it all off your chest. A perfect face for a cop.

"I found their car, Chief! I found it! It's way up there on Blueberry Hill outside town! It's..."

"Now slow down, Orville." Jackson pivoted back and forth from side to side in his comfortable dark green swivel chair, its ample seat cushion and widely spaced arm rests cradling his well-rounded body perfectly. Jackson personally had commandeered the chair from the office of a defrocked Harpers Ferry sewer commissioner caught up in whiskey and graft.

"Slow down, old man, or you'll catch a coronary. Now, whose car you talkin' bout?"

"The boys'! The god-damned missin' boys!"

Jackson stopped his back-and-forth and squinted at Orville to see if he was drunk yet. It would have been a bit early for him, but that happened from time to time too. But not today. Orville was winded, excited and stone cold sober.

"I'm telling ya, Chief, that damned ve-hic-kil has been a-sittin' up there on Blueberry Hill since the end a' January when the big snows started. It's only been since the last few weeks it's gotten warm enough for the snow to melt and the car to come to the top. I've been wondering what the mound was all this time, thought it was a stack 'a wood or something. Anyways, first a patch of green peeked through and then a whole lot more. Tha's when the wife started gettin' spooked that there was somethin' wrong."

Emma. Everyone knew about Emma. When something was bothering her, poor old Orville was bound to move heaven and earth to figure it out and fix things right. She'd run him to his grave soon enough.

"No one's touched it," Orville continued, breathless. "I know 'cuz I've been watching it ev'ry day since it first started showing from under the snow. Listen, Chuck, it's really riling my Emma. Ya gotta go up there and move it. It's the boys' car. It hit me in the face this morning when I looked out the winda'. It's the boys' car ...."

The "boys." Jackson felt, by now, as if he knew the five of them personally. They were slightly retarded boys, young men really, in their 20s and 30s. They'd been missing from several towns over since late January. They were last seen in a faded green 1973 Dodge Custom Coronet, a beaut of a car whose picture had been plastered all over the papers and the police reports for weeks along with the sad, fuzzy dime store photos of the smiling men in happier times.

"You sure it's the boys' car? You look inside? Touch anythin'?"

The old man vigorously shook his head. "I looked inside it, but tha's all. Sure enough it's their car, it's the same one I seen in all the newspapers. Emma swears it, too, she checked it out with her binoculars ..."

Emma's binocular's ..., thought Jackson. The ones she uses to spy on all the neighbors, inciting them to call the office, complaining. Orville stopped when he saw the flash of recognition shoot across Jackson's face. Emma's binoculars .... He started shifting back and forth on his feet as his eyes found the floor.

"All right, Orville, all right. I won't get into that again. Let's go. I'll follow your truck. If that car belongs to those boys, I got my work cut out for me and you got one big story to tell tonight down at the American Hotel bar."

"You got that right!" Orville exclaimed as he looked up. And it would be sooner than tonight too, Chuckie boy. And, yes sir, the story telling - and the free drinks - would be his for a good long while. He licked his cracked lips.

Jackson hauled himself out of the chair with a grunt and headed for the hat rack near the door that hoisted his cap and belt and holster. He plucked the patrol car keys off the hook on the wall and surveyed the office.

His secretary was off getting a root canal and Deputy Landry would be away most of the day transporting two overnight prisoners to the federal penitentiary in Morgantown. Crime would just have to slow down while he was off in the woods with Orville. He locked the office behind him.

They reached the green car after a half hour's drive, including a bumpy ten minutes along a rutted dirt road made muddy and sloppy by the melting snow and the spring rains. Patches and mounds of snow still dotted the landscape in the small valleys and in the heavily treed areas. They found the abandoned car sat along the side of the road, looking for all the world like someone had just stopped and hiked off into the woods.

It was the boys' car all right. He turned to look over his right shoulder. There, about a half-mile away near the top of a short rise, stood Orville and Emma's single story ranch cabin. Beyond that but out of sight from his vantage point would be three or four additional, ramshackle cabins scattered over the rolling foothills.

"Orville, you ever hear or see any cars coming and going up this excuse of a road?"

"Not during the day time, Chuck. But we's sound asleep by 9 o'clock at night."

You mean dead drunk, corrected Jackson as he nodded in response. "What's up the trail?" Orville followed Jackson's gaze along the vague continuation of overgrown road that went on beyond the abandoned car of the missing boys.

"Beats the hell outta me," he replied with a shrug. He

scratched his dry scalp as if to emphasize the point.

Jackson studied the position of the car. It was parked along the trail and, if Emma and Orville had their wits about 'em, the car was sitting exactly where it was now since late January when the first big snow came - the night the boys disappeared.

They had gone to see a basketball game some 20 miles north of Harpers Ferry, Jackson recalled. A couple of hours before midnight last January 24, when the contest ended at Shiloh College, the five young men climbed into this bomb belonging to Ted Samuels, one of the boys. They drove out of the parking lot right after the game according to some students there who had noticed them.

He had tracked the students down simply by going to the College sports office and finding the season-ticket holders. They didn't take the old, black man seriously at first. The brightly shining badge flashed in their faces got some of their attention. His insistent questions got some more. The stabbing, absorbing black eyes got them to answer very carefully. So did his threats of a night in a cold Harpers Ferry jail cell for the uncooperative ones. It was good enough for college kids.

After the game the five boys stopped a mile away from the basketball arena at Anderson's Market. They delayed the clerk who was about to close up early. They bought a bunch of junk food, plastic-wrapped sandwiches and sodas. Had someone, someone not noticed, been with them that night? Had someone met them, perhaps at Anderson's?

Jackson put on a fresh set of surgeon gloves and tried the car doors, carefully touching the handles to avoid smudging possible prints. Locked. Inside a pile of four maps, including one of West Virginia on top, lay neatly in the middle of the car's front bench seat cushion. On the floor in the back were the discarded wrappings from Anderson's. He was going to have to come back with the forensics team from Morgantown before going any further.

"As long as we're here, Orville, let's take a walk up this road." Jackson removed his gloves and started down the trail. Orville looked nervously back at his home and could swear he saw a glint of sun off Emma's binoculars. He turned reluctantly and followed Jackson.

After nearly twenty minutes of exertion and a couple of miles up the trail Jackson suddenly moved to the side of the road behind a tree. He motioned Orville to come behind him.

Up ahead, settled under a dense patch of high trees, was a large, stationary trailer home about the size of a bus. A radio antenna rose out of the top and two wooden storage sheds stood on either side of it.

"You ever seen this before, Orville?"

"N-o-o-o sir," came the cracked whisper.

Jackson pulled his service revolver, released the safety and headed for the trailer. He moved along the patch of trees as low to the ground as his big belly and gravity allowed without toppling over. He took off his cap and peeked inside one of the windows and saw nothing. He moved to the door to the trailer. His gloves back on, he turned the handle and opened the door with an explosion of painful, raucous squeaking. He cast a quick glance around the area behind him, hoping Orville hadn't hightailed it back down the trail. The old man stood paralyzed in wide-eyed wonder in the bushes.

He stepped inside.

The stench of decay and foul, dead air hit him like the time the local morgue got backed up after that terrible highway accident back in '86. It was so bad he stumbled back against the half-open trailer door, a dry heave forming at the pit of his stomach.

He saw it, lying on a bed in the corner. There was no mistake about the shape. It was a body. A sheet was tucked tightly around the dead man's head, as if something might crawl out. He stepped over to the bed, softly as if he would waken someone, and gingerly pulled back the sheet.

Back in late January, when he and his four friends disappeared after seeing that basketball game, Ted Samuels had weighed about 210 pounds and was 5'11". He looked maybe 150 pounds now, wasted away. Terrible frostbite had taken over his feet and hands. The dead man had no shoes. The growth on his once chubby face indicated he had lived for about a month, in what would have been bitter cold, wracking starvation and pure, horrible torment.

He noticed it then and his stomach lurched. The skin on Ted's fingers had been chewed away straight down to the major knuckles. Those terrible, gnarled finger bones crawling their way out of Ted's mummified hands were cupped under his chin as if he had been feeding on them to the end. Jackson shivered and put the sheet back down over the body.

Neatly arranged on the table next to the bed were a man's ring with "Ted" on it, a wallet with green dollars showing, and an ancient, military gold watch with its crystal missing. There was also a necklace - a gold chain with a very small copper circle hanging from it. The medallion was stamped with a depiction of Lady Liberty's head.

Chapter Five

The same day – Washington, DC

The wind-up alarm clock clanged harshly, like a freight train coming through a darkened town. McAdams awoke with a start and violently stabbed the off button. The pain in his forehead jabbed back.

He pulled himself into a sitting position and eyed the clock ticking belligerently on his nightstand. Eleven thirty, a.m., he read over open bottles of buffered aspirin and extra-strength antacid. Bones had poured him into bed less than 8 hours ago. He had 45 minutes to get ready and meet Mossingame for lunch.

Crowded before the round face of the alarm was a collection of framed pictures staring back at him. Behind an aging photo of his mother and father Anne leaned back against a tree, one foot up with the heel against the bark, her arms folded contentedly, her wide smile lighting up the day, and now the room. He still spoke to her in the picture, still marveled at the sparks in those blue eyes. He tried to remember the last time that he saw those eyes, that way. He wondered, again, when he would break down and toss the photo out, when an errant wind might come and knock it off the table, shattering the glass.

In front of her, in a discolored photo, his parents sat stiffly on the uncomfortable white wrought-iron bench that had dominated the front porch of his family home in Connecticut. Don't get too close now, he warned his mother, slightly moving his head back and forth as he exaggerated the conversation in his head. Don't worry, she smiled through clenched teeth.

He shook his head. Frozen in time where they sat, his parents were never close. His mother of the perpetual beatific countenance, her hands demurely gathered in her lap. His father - The Uncomfortable One - at "home," a lit cigar in a beefy hand that rested on the bench beside his leg. The glowing hot end of the cigar came perilously close to his mother's elbow but she didn't seem to notice. It was the last picture of them together, before the charges of corruption brought them all down. The old man died six months later; it took three months after that before she decided to let go.

From the back of the nightstand his two older brothers beamed at him. They were caught in Christmas card photos of happily together families of sedentary husbands, contented wives and numerous kids of extraordinary promise and poise. The brothers held jobs that were paybacks from some of the beneficiaries of their father's largess. The jobs were pay-offs from the past, really, materializing out of nowhere and certainly out of no talent. John Senior's version of life insurance proceeds for the family.

McAdams escaped the reverie by looking out the window next to the bed to the corner of 4th and East Capitol Streets four stories below. Rain. Again. It was gathering in puddles, which percolated like coffee as the heavy drops fell. The distortion of the old windowpane gave a surrealistic cast to the dismal scene. His head throbbed.

He turned away from the window and threw on his well-worn, red-plaid robe. He headed down the hall to the kitchen. The flip-flop of his feet on the floorboards echoed off the bare walls.

He lived in a suite on the top floor of a three-story federal townhouse dating from the mid-1800s. It had been converted into a six-suite cooperative and was near the familiar domed Capitol building where the House and Senate met in session. He was only a few minutes walk to the Dirksen Senate Office Building where he had an office along with about a third of the Senators and hundreds of staffers from other Committees and offices.

"I'll rarely be home anyway," he remembered praying as he signed the lease and put out two months' rent for security. The cockroaches were kind enough not to move back in for a couple of weeks; he had stayed over five years now, the last two without Anne's constant banter and her exhaustive bubble gum music collection playing at all hours of the day and night.

He filled a chipped soup bowl with corn flakes and milk, good for the stomach after a night on the town. He downed it, and a glass of orange juice, you needed Vitamin C too after a bender, while he waited for the teakettle on the ancient gas stove to bring the water for coffee to a boil. He stared out the only window in the kitchen to the dancing pools below. The coffee scalded his tongue on its way down.

"Ahh, a brand new day," he cursed as he placed the dishes in the sink with a small crash. A chip newly liberated from the bowl careened around the sink and ended up in the drain trap.

He hurried out of the kitchen and down the hall to the bathroom. In and out in 10 minutes, he dressed in another 10. He surveyed the living room before he left.

Newspapers, magazines and Congressional Records were strewn everywhere. Tapes and CDs were piled high on the coffee table. Books lined the walls of shelves and others were piled horizontally over those properly shelved. The National Gallery poster from last year's Cherry Blossom Festival tilted at an angle on the wall.

All was well, he thought. Everything was right in his comfy little world. He burst out the door and took the three flights down two stairs at a time. He'd just about make it to the Rayburn Cafeteria on time.

Chapter Six

McAdams stood in the middle of the Senate cafeteria, a lunch tray in his hands. Mossingame, sitting at a table for two in the back, waved, trying unsuccessfully to get his attention.

Mossingame noticed that McAdams looked pale and wan. That horrid scar under his left eye seemed darker than usual, almost crimson red. It had been a bad night. Mossingame waved again and this time the younger man spied him. He nodded his head, managed a thin smile and took long, purposeful strides across the cafeteria.

Mossingame watched his protégé, over six feet and lean and lanky, navigate the crowded room. He smiled. McAdams had worked his way in, out and through many a jam. They both had, for that matter. They had gone after defense contractor collusion in the production of M-16 rifles and had exposed price-fixing in the Army's tank program. They had taken on Mafia penetration of dozens of unions as well as consumer product defects galore. During Iran-contra, they had exposed White House lies to Congress and abuse of Agriculture's foreign farm credit subsidy program.

Their investigations led to new legislation, and sometimes what they dredged up started or stopped federal funding for key programs that touched millions of people. Some folks went to jail as a result of the evidence they had produced and relayed to federal prosecutors. Some of their targets, and informants, had been killed or taken their own lives. Not a few careers and family lives had been thrown on the garbage heap. There were some good moments, for sure, but mostly it had been many years of hand-to-hand in the trenches.

"'Afternoon, Honorable Senator." McAdams put his tray on the table and sat. His brown eyes floated in a pool of bloodshot.

"Tough night?"

"Hmmmm, there've been tougher. Or so I've been told."

"Read the newspaper yet?"

McAdams shook his head as Mossingame passed the Washington Post to him. On the bottom, right-hand side of the first page McAdams saw a two-column banner - "Assassination Witness Murdered - Assailant a Mystery." He read the headline aloud.

Mossingame winced and nodded. "Read the story."

McAdams skimmed it as he sipped his coffee. Their dead witness, David Tidback, had been a visiting professor at the University of Mississippi. He was also, until last fall, a full, tenured professor at Randolph-Macon College in Virginia where he had taught for close to a decade. Tidback started his academic journey over 30 years ago, as an American history teacher at St. Louis University. He was born and raised in St. Louis. The assailant, with his fingerprints expertly chiseled away and his teeth obliterated by his own gun blast, remained unidentified. There were no leads, but the FBI had wrested control of the investigation from the Capitol Police, the DC Police and the Executive Service. Washington was lousy with cops fighting each other for turf and headlines.

A quote from Mossingame showed the Senator's pain at what had transpired in his hearing room. He had no idea if the murder was related to the Committee's work. Not a peep from Brock.

Joyce Thompson, the reporter, had done a good job given the time she had. She regularly got inside news, and occasionally a dinner invitation, from McAdams. She always took him up on the former, and on the latter once or twice had caved in to what she called his sad-assed routine. McAdams preferred to call it "working the press."

Mossingame wiped his mouth and watched McAdams pour too much pepper and then a mound of Tabasco sauce onto his greasy cheeseburger. "You've got a stomach of steel," Mossingame remarked, "and one day you'll regret it." McAdams shrugged and started wolfing down the burger.

"Mac, how'd this witness get before my Committee. Who in God's name referred him?"

McAdams chased a mouthful with coffee. "I checked with Charlton's office. They claim one of his staffers who does constituent service - she's all of 19 years - put Tidback on the witness list. It looks like the good professor called her and pleaded to be shoehorned in on the last day of the hearings. He said it would be all right with his former student - Senator Charlton. It was all a lie, of course. But she bought it, gave him a spot, called the Committee's secretary to re-type the witness list, and that was it. He walked in and got shot."

Mossingame sprung a puzzled look. "Well ..., if Tidback appeared suddenly out of nowhere, how'd the assassin know to be there in time to get off a shot?"

"I haven't figured that out." McAdams flew back to the moment Tidback emerged from the spectator seats right before the hearing began. The worried man had not wanted to be seen, or recognized, until the last possible moment. But recognized by whom? McAdams couldn't shake the desperate, anguished look on the man's face when he finally opened his folder on the witness table.

"The only people who got the witness list were the members of the Committee and their staff, and the witnesses of course," explained McAdams. "They had it the night before Tidback was killed. And ..., well, ... we do post the list outside on the door of the hearing room."

McAdams' brow furrowed as he settled back in his chair, his coffee cup cradled in his two hands. "Gustafson - the cop at the door - told me that Tidback's written statement was missing from his folder. It was missing from the start because, as Gustafson so eloquently informed me, a 'river of blood' from Tidback's head ran clear across the folder. The river was not diverted or disturbed in the least, as it would be if someone had removed the testimony after the shooting. It had to be taken between the time Tidback had shown up, put his folder on the table, did his best to hide out, and then return to the table. And we never got copies delivered in advance to the Committee for distribution and Web posting, like the rules require."

Mossingame shook his head. McAdams' face darkened as the Tabasco fought back. "Maybe this WILL be the death of me," he conceded. He stared at the red bottle standing defiant on the table.

"Or maybe it'll be our damned investigation. All the leads that go nowhere - or point everywhere. All the people who wanted Martin Luther King dead - but knew, saw, heard, did nothing. All the official silence. ... And now Tidback, dead. Where does he fit in?"

"You're the chief investigator ...." replied Mossingame with a wink. "You tell me."

"Yeah, yeah," laughed McAdams as he piled his empty plate and silverware on his tray. "People keep telling me that. Maybe the FBI will give me something. They must have some clue about Tidback. There has to be a connection to the work of the Committee."

Tidback's last words echoed in his ears for about the fiftieth time. A Lincoln conspiracy, one that continued today, one that threatened another Civil War. And the professor had proof he wanted to give the Committee.

"Where are we with the Committee's Report, Mac?" The Senator drained his coffee cup. "Or should I ask, where are YOU with the Report?"

"Not finished, that's where. And I'm getting worried. The resolution setting the Committee up says we have to issue a Final Report to the Congress by May 1. That's three weeks from now. The only authority we have after that is to wrap up loose ends."

"Mac, we have to meet the deadline. There's enormous pressure to get this over and done with. Some think what we're doing is destructive. Some think it flaky." Mossingame nodded in the direction of the exit sign and the two men got up from the table. They walked out of the cafeteria and back to the Senator's office. Mossingame frowned as he spoke.

"You and I believe what we're doing is healthy, Mac. But we're dismally out-voted. We are not going to get authorization to take additional time. Senator Brock, in particular, is adamant about this. He's told me he'll call in old chits to bring this 'unholy disinterment' as he calls it, to an end."

They stopped in front of Mossingame's office. The younger man's features clouded up.

"Our Report will disturb a lot of people, you know."

"So? When was the last time we heard applause? We've angered so many in our day. I've stopped taking names."

"Yeah, but think about it." McAdams started pounding the

rolled-up Post into the palm of his hand. "We're the first official government body to look at the King assassination since the FBI and Memphis police probes. We're a Special Committee of the US Congress. We're about to say to the American public that we think that James Earl Ray was doing the bidding of others when he killed Martin Luther King. We're going to say the government, at best, was incompetent in preventing and then investigating the assassination. And, at worst, that some in government may have helped Ray out.

"This is going to piss off some folks, Walt, and rile up a bunch more. This is bigger than other things we've peeked under the covers at. Listen, I remember all the hatred, the riots, when King was killed. I was riding a bus with my brothers in Bridgeport, the only white folk on it, when news about the assassination hit the radio. We were going right through the black park of town. Some angry people saw us through the window and started stoning and rocking the bus, shouting for our heads. Thank God the driver got us through. If they ever got on the bus ...." He shook his head. "This could be one hot summer in the cities."

Mossingame watched McAdams, in reflection, study the blotches of brown and white marble clustering on the floor around his feet. He noticed for the first time that the younger man's hair was showing a few ornery strands of gray. One day it would resemble his own distinguished mane.

A bubble of pride gushed in his chest, followed by a pang of concern. From time to time, he would breath a prayer McAdams would be lucky enough to live to a grand old age. The young man carried around with him a lot of worry and skepticism, and a fiery fervor to make things right, to undo the corruption and thievery he grew up with. A man can burn bright that way, yes, but he burns briefly, too.

Pamela, his wife, could see things others missed. Mac was alone, something that came out even in a crowded room, even when he had some young thing on his arm, the both of them laughing and teasing each other. He could grow detached and sad, she said, at the most joyous or spontaneous of times. But he hadn't always been like that. Just since that terrible incident with Anne. That terrible, terrible time not so long ago.

Mossingame sighed heavily and leaned back against the wall. Dark bags hung under his eyes. "I woke up last night. ... Pamela says I was talkin' and thrashin', tryin' to wipe something from my face. In my dream, my nightmare, it was a chunk of Tidback's brain."

Mossingame sighed and then continued. "Now you know there's not much that gets to me. Not McCarthy in the 50's, not General Westmoreland, not Dita Beard and ITT in the seventies, not Richard Nixon and his 'enemies list,' not even that nutty old Bill Casey. But there's something wrong here, Mac .... Real wrong."

Mossingame looked up and down the silent, poorly lit hall. "It's not just Tidback's murder I'm talkin' about, either. That was the coup de grace, but there's something else out there, something terribly dark that we've come across - or that's found *us*. Whatever it is ..., we need to unearth it."

They stood in silence. McAdams studied the old man. He was a kind patriarch usually sporting an easy smile in a wrinkled face. His bright white hair and grand manner acknowledged his wisdom and fairness. He always made sure witnesses were comfortable, and was often visibly moved by the compelling personal stories that citizens brought to Washington, stories he would fashion into the fodder of law and legislation. Mossingame, after a hearing, alone would step down from behind the dais to rest a comforting hand on the shoulder of the young girl who had just testified about parents lost in an unsafe car that crashed or to thank the middle-aged whistle-blower with kids in college who had lost his government job saving the taxpayer some bucks. That was the way Mossingame was, more concerned about the little person lost in the big picture than the other way around.

"We'll find it," said McAdams, almost in a whisper. "You and me. We'll pull the right levers, punch the right buttons, grab all the right lapels. We've done it before. And I'm going to find out why David Tidback came to the King Committee ranting about a Lincoln murder conspiracy." McAdams turned away, this morning's newspaper still rolled into a club in his fist.

The old man watched him walk away and then trudged into his office.

Chapter Seven

Wednesday -- Harpers Ferry, West Virginia

Jackson glanced at his gnawed fingernails and cringed when he imagined Ted Samuels' blood-caked stubs. Some 20 miles from his office, that poor, damned kid lay eating his fingers just to keep alive or maybe, in some sort of advanced dementia, to end the stinging pain of frostbite. Jackson thought about how it must have felt to die like that, his regulation boots propped up on his desk, his arms now behind his head.

His mood grew as black as the boots before him. The bright sunshine dared to waste no more than a few tentative rays through the blinds in his office. Another thing ate at him.

"Ted Samuels' car worked just fine," he mumbled under his breath as he brought his feet down and pounded the desk in front of him. "And it had a quarter of a tank of gas."

Jackson's deputy, George Landry, looked up from the file cabinet that stood before him. "Huh? ... Whadja say, Chief?"

"Ahh, nothing," Jackson barked. "Nothing!" He glared out into the street between the spaces of the Venetian blinds, squinting as he tried to piece together the action outside by the parallel snatches he glimpsed from his desk.

He had been busy since he and Orville found Ted Samuels' emaciated body only 24 hours ago. He could move quite rightly and quite sprightly when he wanted to. He could get the job done, despite his 67 years and a cascading paunch that hung over his belt like a dangerous Appalachian precipe. Especially when a case got to him - like this one was beginning to do.

Jackson grew somber. The first thing he did after finding Samuels was talk to the boy's mother. It wouldn't be right otherwise. All she could do was go on about the night they disappeared, a ridge of tears sparkling above reddened lids and smeared mascara. Her words haunted him.

"There was a full moon that night," she said, her washed-out silver hair scraggly and frizzy, her eyes seeing another place and time. "A winter moon. Sharp and bright. Almost hurtful to the eye. And it was so cold. But they went out anyway." Her head and shoulders had dropped, burdened by memories.

"I woke up early - 5 in the morning. It was snowing hard. Not big flakes that starts you to dreamin'. No sir, it was a hard-driving snow that blinds you, the kind that forces cars off the road and makes school buses crash. Killin' snow."

She had started sobbing then. Jackson could still see the wrinkled mouth, the eyes almost swollen shut with pain. The quiet in her house woke her, she said in a low moan that came from somewhere in the bowels of hell.

"Teddy's bed was empty. Empty ...," she cried, the pain forcing her down into a torn and rumpled living room chair.

The burning pain of a lost son .... He had lost one too. To Vietnam. The pain hurt, came up in his chest like acid stomach, like it happened yesterday. For a brief moment, his breath would not come. And, then, he found it again, like he always did. But sometimes it got so bad he wondered if it wouldn't come at all. He took a handkerchief out of his back pocket and wiped his face and eyes, his chest heaving.

Imogene Samuels had said she couldn't figure out why, but something told her to do something that morning. She said she couldn't sit around and wait, with her fears staring back at her from the dark corners of her bedroom. She phoned Jack Hughlette's mother, Caroline. Caroline had been up since 2 a.m.

"Jack didn't come home neither," the other mother had whispered. She told Imogene that she had already called Jack Murphy's and Bill Sterling's mothers that morning and was about to call her. "The boys are plain gone!" Caroline Hughlette had shrieked between sobs.

Samuels' mother told Jackson that she hung up right then and there and marched down the street to see Geoffrey Larcher's stepfather. He told her his boy was nowhere to be found.

"He was meaner than the son," she told Jackson. "Never, ever, did I understand why my Teddy took a liking to that Larcher boy. Of course, you won't ever find him. Mark my words. He's off somewheres ..., and I bet our boys paid for it, with their lives." Her voice had fallen again to a low, rasping moan, her face by then a flushed red mask of grief and loss.

Somehow, Jackson figured, Ted Samuels' body ended up in that trailer, two miles from his abandoned but working car. He might well have been led to the trailer, or taken there against his will. And there he had frozen to death.

Samuels had a key to the trailer in his trouser pockets. There were matches, books and wood furniture in the trailer for a bonfire. They lay, unused for that purpose, in the same likely spot they sat during Samuels' final hours.

Over two dozen empty C-ration cans from an outside storage shed were piled high on one of the trailer's kitchen counters. They had been opened with a can opener. Someone had eaten, but surely not the wasted Ted Samuels. The shed where the C-rations came from also had a locker filled with enough dehydrated meals to keep a half-dozen men alive for a year. Samuels had a key to the shed. And the locker.

"He had a key to just about everything," snarled Jackson out loud to nobody.

Landry looked up again but knew better than to ask another question. He returned to his filing. Jackson listened to the folders of paper smacking lightly against each other as his deputy rapidly flipped through them.

Jackson went back to his mental inventory. Left unused and still full was a propane tank in another shed outside. No one had turned it on to supply heat to the trailer. All it took was a twist of the hand. No one had bothered to use the ham radio. That took but a twist of a knob. And the radio worked, like Samuel's car, like nearly every other darned thing in that trailer-tomb.

Jackson shifted back and forth in his chair, agitated and angry. The county searchers he had dispatched had come back a couple of hours ago. Just after dawn broke this morning they had come across three more of the boys. The grisly discoveries lay on both sides of the road to the trailer site, at varying distances up to a mile into the woods. The dead men either couldn't make it to the trailer or they had died trying to get away.

Jack Murphy's body had been chewed to the bone by wild animals. In the feeding frenzy, the scavengers must have dragged the carcass some twenty feet to a stream. Murphy was just lying there when they found him, with what remained of his face pleading to the heavens. The packed snows of winter had conspired to leave the right side of his face intact, freeze-dried and wide-eyed. During the dark of some wide-awake, lonely night, Jackson knew the younger members of that search team would remember the awful look of that staring, solitary eye. They would think again and again about what it was that Murphy was looking at when he drew his last breath.

Jackson felt a pang of regret for the younger searchers. They had wanted to help, and all they would get for their efforts would be a lifetime of bad dreams, maybe even a few that would wake 'em up in the middle of the night, sweating and flailing. Maybe even screaming.

Jack Murphy's right hand was curled around the watch on his left wrist. Odd how those body parts survived, odd how they stayed in position. It was like Murphy was waiting for someone to show up, said Landry. He died waiting, thought Jackson.

Nothing much remained of Bill Sterling but white, brittle bones and an ID bracelet that circled the right wrist bone. Landry said the bones were so white when they found them that they gleamed, almost vibrated, in the first rays of the sun. Landry swore a sunrise would never look the same again.

The third body they found this morning probably belonged to Samuels' best friend, Jimmy Hughlette. Jimmy's father had rushed to join the searchers when news of the trailer discovery circulated through his hometown. It was the father who found what was likely his own son's backbone and skull in a hollow just off the road and only 1/2 of a mile from the trailer. Looking at X-rays of Jimmy Hughlette from when he broke his back in a car wreck on an icy road several winters ago, the coroner was already saying that the backbone found in the woods was Jimmy Jr.'s. A few other bones were found scattered 100 yards downhill. The remains came up northeast of the trailer, like Sterling's and Murphy's. South of the trailer by almost 2 miles was Ted Samuels' car that Orville and Emma had discovered.

On, around or near each of the carcasses and skeletal remains the searchers found the same necklace laying on the table next to Samuels' body in the trailer - a gold chain with a small copper medallion stamped with an image of Lady Liberty's head.

They hadn't found yet any sign of Geoffrey Larcher, the fifth member of the group who had ventured out on that bitterly cold January 24 night. Larcher's worn combat boots were inside the trailer where Jackson found Samuels. Larcher might have taken them off, Jackson thought as he tapped his teeth with the eraser end of a pencil. He just might have taken them off to put on his friend Samuels' larger boots, which were missing.

"Just right for someone eager to move on but hung up by feet swollen with frostbite," he mumbled as he took his own throbbing feet off the desk and planted his elbows where his feet had been.

Larcher had disappeared. No trace of him anywhere in the woods within a five mile radius of the trailer. They'd expand the search, of course, but Mrs. Samuels probably was right about Larcher. He got off and the others met the big man above.

Jackson scratched the stubble on his chin. Why did those boys press on through miles of cold, empty midnight and deep snow to enter a heated trailer with a ham radio and plenty of food, only to die an agonizing death?

When Jackson took on the job after lunch of telling Jack Murphy's mother about finding her son, she just stared. Her immobile black eyes stabbed straight through him. Gertrude Murphy had her own ideas of what happened that night the boys disappeared.

"It was some force that got 'em to go up there," she had said through clenched teeth. "They wouldn't have run off up into those woods like scared rabbits. I know somebody forced them - led them - to do it." He left her half-whimpering, half-begging in her tired living room.

What Mrs. Murphy didn't know, what Jackson couldn't tell her, made him grit his teeth hard until they hurt. Lining the shelves of the tidy trailer where he had found Samuels were books on guerrilla and small arms combat and the penal codes of the 50 states. There also were several editions of a White Aryan Resistance publication called "WAR" and some editions of an Aryan Youth Movement newspaper. The papers had cartoons of bleeding Jewish women with long, chiseled teeth protruding from hideously receding gums and others showing burning black children running from a fire-bombed church, their mouths and eyes wide open in pain and shock.

One of those children looked just like his own son when he was a boy. Jackson could not lose the image. He fidgeted and reached down into his bottom right drawer where he had put the loose physical evidence from the trailer. He pulled out the marked plastic bag containing the things from the table next to Samuels' deathbed. Jackson studied the watch that turned out to be from the Civil War period and the odd copper necklace with the golden medallion and Liberty's sculpted image. He stared at them for several minutes trying to put them like puzzle pieces into the right place. With a sigh he threw the collection back into the drawer.

He pulled himself out of the chair, switched on the answering machine and grabbed the patrol car key ring off the wall to the left of the front door. Looking back, he saw that everything was in its place. He slammed the door and headed for the patrol car in the lot in front of the station.

"Yeah, OK ..." said a smiling Landry. "I'll take care of things here. I'll be fine, don't worry about me. You go about your business." He shook his head and went back to work. The boss was in a funk about those boys in the woods. He'd feel bad and apologize later.

Chapter Eight

Jackson sat in his parked patrol car in front of the trailer. He wanted to get the feel of the crime scene, to sit and absorb the air, and the secrets whispered by the walls and the furniture. It was time to feel the vibrations from the last desperate gasps, the last agony and thoughts of the dying Samuels. Every once in a while he'd get lucky and a vision would come. And the vision would show him the way.

He got out and waved to the state police officer patrolling the cordoned-off area. Jackson inhaled deeply before entering the trailer.

Once inside, he let his eyes run over everything. The place was neat, organized. The books and magazines on the shelves were arranged in orderly fashion. He visualized again how tightly the sheets had been folded around the emaciated body of Ted Samuels.

It was a large trailer, with sleeping accommodations for four, maybe five. There was a nice sitting area next to a roomy kitchen. It had a table as big as the one he and his four brothers and sisters and his mother and father had crowded around, elbow to elbow, when he was growing up.

But there was no laughter and story swapping around this table. This place was used for serious meetings, not for living. There were corkboards, chalkboards, and legal-sized pads of paper everywhere. There were markers and pointers and pens scattered about on the table and the shelves. He made a mental note to see why the paper pads weren't taken for examination. All the food, the military requisition kind, was probably used to feed those who came to the trailer meetings. How many meetings had there been? How many eager participants, rapt and open-mouthed? Where were they now, the ones still living? Where was Larcher? Were there other trailers, and other bodies, buried in the woods?

He could sense that the boys had come up here more than once. Maybe for big meetings, staying for a few days at a time. There might have been one the night they came up here to die, something they had to get to, even with all the snow and the dark. They were laughing that night in Anderson's, excited. Maybe thinking about the big event up at the trailer in the woods.

His eyes narrowed. He stood up and examined again the many cabinets and cubbyholes built into the walls. While the racist newspapers had been taken into evidence, the combat intelligence manuals and law books still lined the shelves opposite the entrance to the trailer. There must have been almost 70 or 80 of them altogether.

"Damn their hides," he muttered. The state police should have seized these books. They had been called in to supplement the Harpers Ferry force since Samuels and the others came from outside his jurisdiction and this thing looked bigger than his small force could handle anyway. They should've done a better job and seized all the books.

He thumbed through the combat intelligence manuals. Some were from the Vietnam War era - Green Beret type of stuff. An impressive array of detonation devices, silenced guns, miniature knives and injection devices unfolded before him in black and white etchings and dot matrix print. He marveled at how many of the devices could be fashioned out of ordinary materials and natural resources.

The books were well worn, but gave up no identifying information. On some of the pages, Jackson saw scribbled notes and underlined text. This extraneous writing was found only in the margins of sections dealing with lethal weapons; the parts of the books dealing with strategy, intelligence, codes, and survival techniques were virtually mark-free. He placed two combat books with writing on the table.

He turned to the state criminal codes. They were current to the end of last year. Some of the code sections - the statutory definitions of murder, manslaughter, public mayhem, maiming by force, malicious mischief and felonious assault - were marked and underlined.

It suddenly came to him that he was reviewing a primer for those wanting to inflict serious harm and fear on the public without exposing the perpetrators to overly long prison sentences. A chill shot through him. He was dealing with something cold-blooded and smart. Something organized. The boys had been someone's students, students of hate and hurting.

He noticed that one of the law books was carved out. Someone had taken a razor and sliced through clumps of pages at a time, until a square hole emerged from the pages of the book. The hole was empty.

He pushed his cap back on his head and started examining all the books. By the end he had discovered five similarly carved out. He placed them on the table along with the marked-up books he had set aside. The largest of the carved-out books must have been 10" wide by 18" long and almost 500 carved-pages deep. It was a terrific "safe."

When he sat down to examine the books, the rusted chair creaked loudly. He grunted his disgust at the flimsy arrangements as he opened the largest book and studied its empty interior. He squinted and turned quickly to the back.

Taped to the bottom, on the back cover, was an 8" by 10" envelope that matched the size of the carved-out space exactly. It was arranged so that when you opened the book you couldn't see the envelope, even with the carved out space empty. You wouldn't see it unless, of course, you knew it was there or were looking, like Jackson, for a miracle revelation.

His hands trembled as he carefully peeled the envelope off the back cover. When he pulled the envelope away, some yellow flecks of paper drifted to the tabletop from the slightly jagged edges of the carved-out pages. He reached into his pocket and pulled out a plastic sandwich baggie. With his penknife he scraped the remains into the baggie.

The envelope was sealed so he slipped his penknife between the gummed edge and the envelope to open it. Inside were yellowed papers similar in composition to the flecks he had scraped into the baggie.

Three pages slipped out of the envelope onto the table. They were unfolded now but had been open and closed many times. They were antique pieces of paper sliced out of some sort of journal or binder. They were journal pages, half the size of a sheet of typewriter paper, with space for three days per page.

Tuesday, June 7, 1864 was printed at the top of the first page, with Wednesday and Thursday, June 8 and 9, 1864, underneath. The second page began with Friday, June 10, 1864, and the third with Monday, June 13, 1864. There was a penciled slash mark through each printed day and date.

He scanned his discovery. Regret tore through him as the pages crumbled at the edges and along the folds. He heard a step on the creaky stairs into the trailer. Praying the sudden impact would not tear them, he slipped the antique pages under the books on the tabletop.

Jackson looked up to see the state police officer patrolling the perimeter now standing in the doorway. Had he seen what Jackson had been doing?

"What ya got there, Chief? Doing a little library research?" The voice was disdainful. Jackson's heart accelerated with abrupt thumps against his ribcage. The officer eased over to the table.

"Yep, you can say that," replied Jackson, perhaps a little too quickly. "It looks like you boys missed some evidence here. I noticed handwriting in the margins. Nothing intelligible, but who knows?" Jackson shrugged nonchalantly.

The officer shrugged back. He looked over at the book open on the table, peered into Jackson's eyes, then walked around and behind him to cup of steaming coffee from a thermos on the kitchen counter.

Jackson ventured nothing. The chair squawked as he shifted. Suddenly it felt stuffy and hot. The lingering, rancid odor of Ted Samuels' decayed body seemed to squeeze the air out of the place. Slowly the officer drank, staring out the window only a few feet behind Jackson's back. He finished, crumbled the Styrofoam cup and tossed it into a paper bag on the floor. The officer came back into Jackson's left peripheral vision and then passed him. As he stood in the door on his way out, he spoke over his shoulder.

"Don't be takin' out those books now, Chief, unless you got yer libr'y card. 'Cuz if you do, Ah guess ah'll have to report yuh to the 'thorities!"

"Ha!" smiled Jackson, sharing the weak joke. The officer let loose a guffaw and disappeared from view.

What had he seen? And why didn't he seize the books for the State Police? The three pages quickly went back in the envelope that gave them birth on the tabletop. He picked up the five books taken from the shelves and walked briskly out of the trailer, being careful to lock it up behind him.

As he lowered himself into the car, Jackson waved to his new-found friend on the other side of the clearing. "Good bye, you shit-eating lard-ass," he mumbled. The officer obligingly waved back with a flourish and a grin. When the car was out of sight the officer headed quickly for his car and picked up the handset to his radio. He turned to a little used frequency and reported Jackson's departure with an armload of books.

Driving away, Jackson's mind was on his discovery. He wondered about the yellowed, fragile pages. On the first was a sketch, crudely rendered. Although smudged, the image was that of a wide, four-story house built, like those all over downtown Harpers Ferry, over a hundred years ago. On the second page was a similarly rough sketch of a two-story building with nine small windows evenly spaced across the front on each level; bushes or vegetation were etched in on the top of the structure. It looked like a fort. Directly in front of the walls was a rocky coastline, which fell away to a churning sea. Underneath the drawing was the word "Maine."

The last page from the trailer had names on it. On the left side of the page were six names under the caption "C". On the right side were five names with no caption. Underneath the names was a drawing of Lady Liberty. He hadn't recognized a single one of the names, although he recognized the lovely lady's profile.

He passed the spot where the boys' car had been found. On the way out he had intended to stop and look around the area. That was forgotten. The ancient pages absorbed him now.

Chapter Nine

Friday night, April 10 -- Washington, DC

McAdams parted the bushes and emerged on the sidewalk. Slightly out of breath from his run across the US Capitol grounds from his office, he stopped and looked around. Nothing stirred under the streetlights. Traffic had called it quits for the night. He crossed the road and headed up the stone stairs to the Jefferson Building of the Library of Congress. His calls to David Tidback's haunts, at the University of Mississippi and Randolph-Macon College, did not shed any light on why Tidback came to Washington, DC, to get shot talking about a Lincoln murder conspiracy. Tonight he would have to do a little digging of his own.

Built in 1897, the Library of Congress was a grand domed edifice, a smaller and darker version of the nation's Capitol building glowing behind him. To his left, across East Capitol Street, was the Supreme Court Building. Three blocks away, at the corner of East Capitol and Fourth Streets, was his town house. Familiar territory, but not tonight, not since Tidback's execution a little over 72 hours ago.

"You're here late for a Friday night, ain't you Mac?" Frank, the wrinkled Library guard, flashed a lascivious grin. "Whatsa matter, boy, can't find yourself none 'a them dee-lightful little in-terns that sashay around here all day?"

McAdams smiled despite himself as Frank licked his lips and pumped in slow motion his creaky old hips. Frank had been the night guard at the Library of Congress for most of the past decade and a half and knew just about every staffer on Capitol Hill. He was a good ol' codger with seven grown children and a solid marriage to a battle-ax of a woman named Mabel. Everyone figured the night job kept old Frank married to the unseen but much talked about Mabel; how he produced the seven kids was anyone's guess.

"Fuck off, Franklin." McAdams wiped the perspiration from his brow. It was a close, muggy night for April. "Here's your turkey on rye, apple pie, coffee and a diet Pepsi. That OK?" He had called ahead to take his order, like usual.

"Yes sir. And thank you kindly. Now don't stay too late. All right? Or you into little librarians now?" Frank shook with laughter, enjoying his randomly generated, one-man show foisted upon any one who walked within fifteen feet.

"Tell me, Frank, you've been around. Did you ever wonder why you do things? Even if they're good things that you do, do you wonder if you do them for the wrong reasons?"

"Ya got me, Mac. And if that's why you're here tonight, son, you ain't gonna find any kind of answer in any one of those books inside."

"D'you ever wonder if your kids do the right things because they're scared of you or mad at you or hateful, whatever? D'you ever wonder if what you do is really what you want to do, instead of some reaction to your parents, your upbringing, whatever?" He couldn't get over his moment of clarity at EJ's the night Tidback died.

Frank eyed McAdams. "Who gives a shit? … As long as they are doing the right thing, it doesn't bother me at all. Hell, if they try to be smart so they don't have to be dumb like me, I don't care. If they try to love their wives and husbands because they don't want to be like me - lonely, fat and working the night shift - damn, that's good enough for me. That's what us fathers are for - to show our kids what to avoid."

McAdams laughed. The wisdom of Guardian Frank. "I'll think about that," he said as he passed through the great doors into the building. "I'll think good and hard." He made his way down the hallway to the center room of the Library, wondering if he'd ever come to know what fathers were for. The lights were off, as befitted the hour. From the end of the corridor, however, there came a soft, warm glow.

He stopped when he got to the hallway's end and stood viewing the expansive chamber spread out before him. The central reading room was illuminated for the night by low-light bulbs implanted in the majestic, painted ceiling some 200 feet above him. In the middle of the room stood the reference desk, looming like a gargantuan hotel registration desk from another era. Three concentric circles of polished oak desks surrounded it. Green-shaded reading lamps shot up from the desks at three feet intervals.

Aisles from the reference desk ran to dark book stacks at the outer edges of the grand room. Beyond the desks, in alcoves lined with bookshelves, were computers enabling on-line access to the card catalogues and the some 100 million items of raw information held in the Library of Congress. He headed for one of the computers.

The Library held a copy of every book, article, software, map, and other works registered by authors in the United States. In the early days of the government, McAdams was once told, the Library was based on private collections and libraries in New York and Philadelphia. When the US government moved to Washington, DC, in 1800, Congress began buying its own books.

The story went that, during the War of 1812, the British raided the White House and the Congress and burned the 3000 books that had been compiled in the Library of Congress. Thomas Jefferson was said to offer his own private collection to replenish the Library -- six or seven thousand books. It was rumored now and then that some in Congress engineered the purchase of Jefferson's books to provide him an off-the-books pension for his old age. It was a smooth, inside deal Mac's father might have dreamed up.

The notion of cheap, petty corruption dissipated the stillness that had settled over him. Tidback's execution roared back, filling the yawning silence. The professor had reached back into the past and uncovered something, something big and corrupt. Whatever it was, it was big and bad enough to draw out unknown assassins over 100 years after Lincoln's murder. Whatever it was, it was important enough for Tidback to risk his life. Maybe that's what was on the professor's face that morning - not worry, but resignation in the face of doom.

McAdams remembered what he came to do. He found the records of two Congressional committees charged with investigating Lincoln's assassination. The first was the House Judiciary Committee which, in 1866, looked into charges that the

Confederacy was behind Lincoln's murder. The second was a special House Assassinations Committee, created in 1867 to investigate claims that President Andrew Johnson, Lincoln's successor, and others in and out of the US Government were involved in the assassination. Good places to start.

The daily record of the proceedings of the House and Senate as a whole, called the Congressional Globe back then, would provide some information. He found the index. The soft blue light from the computer cast changing patterns and shapes on his face as various screens came and went a foot before him. The clicking keyboard echoed faintly in the silence. The pages of the past unfolded.

July 11, 1867. The day the House voted to create the Lincoln Assassination Committee. A Massachusetts Congressman was named to head it up. He scrolled back a few months to catch more of the preliminary debate.

Feeling something move, McAdams lifted his head. His eyes came to a squint as he peered into the dark surrounding him. The shadowy book stacks loomed silently beyond the rows of desks in front of him. After a few seconds of black silence he looked back into the comfort of the blue screen.

March 26, 1867. Massachusetts Congressman Butler was ranting in the daily journal of proceedings about the role of the White House in the assassination. It was the Andrew Johnson administration that caught his wrath. McAdams could see the irate Butler leaning over his desk in the House chamber, pointing towards the White House as his bitter words of incrimination rang out.

Butler raved about a diary, John Wilkes Booth's diary. "Who spoliated that book," he said, "after it got into the possession of the Government, if it was not spoliated before?"

McAdams' brow furrowed. Butler was claiming that pages of Booth's diary were missing, that the missing pages would tell the world why Booth would leave a cryptic note for then Vice President Andrew Johnson at Johnson's hotel only two weeks before Lincoln's assassination. A cryptic note asking, in familiar terms, if Johnson were ready to meet with him.

The existence of Booth's diary was a well-known fact. But

this was the first time McAdams had heard about someone removing diary pages after it had been taken from Booth the night he had been tracked to a flaming barn and shot down.

Butler raged on. "If we had only the advantage of all the testimony, we might have been able to find who it was that changed Booth's purpose from capture of Lincoln to assassination; who it was that could profit by assassination who could not profit from the capture and abduction of the President; who it was expected by Booth would succeed to Lincoln if the knife made a vacancy!"

McAdams knew that some historians had continuing suspicions that the Lincoln assassination was really borne of a Confederate conspiracy launched and supervised by Jefferson Davis himself. In this regard, David Tidback's testimony -- or his attempt at it -- was nothing new. A good number of historians believed that the conspiracy that ended in Lincoln's assassination was, in the beginning, no more than a Confederate kidnapping plot. Booth and his cohorts may have had plans to spirit Lincoln out of the city across Washington's 14th street bridge, to Virginia.

Booth's frustrated mind may have tired of the kidnapping attempts and turned finally to assassination in the final days before Lincoln was shot. Some thought that the Confederate Secret Service, and its sympathizers, had set up an escape line that ran south from the District through Virginia to Richmond. It was to be used by Booth after Lincoln was kidnapped. When plans for kidnapping changed to assassination, the escape line still came to Booth's aid.

The diary found on Booth the night he was shot now stood in a protective display case in the Ford Theater museum. But missing pages? "Spoliation?"

McAdams froze. He leaned forward and stared into the darkness. He felt unseen eyes playing over him. Someone was out there, in the great room somewhere, staring back. He stood up and walked hurriedly to his left, out of the alcove, and down the aisle to the reference desk in the center of the reading room. He stopped and then walked past the desk, pausing in the shadows. His ears echoed with his own heartbeat as he saw that, back in the alcove, he had been out in the open with the computer's blue haze like a street lamp shining over him.

There was a rustle of movement behind him. He twisted around and lurched down the shadowy aisles between the tall bookcases. Something, someone, had been there, and was now gone. He came upon an exit door at the end of the stacks. It was closed, but for how long?

The door opened without the piercing scream of an alarm. It had been disabled. He stood looking both ways on Second Street. He was on the other side of the Library from where he had entered. To the left, a half block away, was East Capitol Street. To his right were Independence Avenue and the beginning of a short and brightly-lit stretch of bars. The street was empty, the glass in the pavement glistening in the dim light cast by flickering street lamps.

A chill from the damp night went through him. He felt in the heavy and menacing air the residue of something, someone, that had come this way. He backed into the Library, then walked hurriedly in the direction of his alcove. His shoulders tensed, waiting for a shot to ring out like that morning in his hearing room.

He saved the pages of the Globe onto a disk and placed it in his jacket pocket. He turned off the computer with damp, clammy hands. Going back the way he had just come, he pushed through the back door in a hurry and came out on Second Street again.

His footsteps echoed as he race-walked home. He dared a backward glance but once or twice. Before entering the townhouse, he stepped into tall bushes to the right of the stair stoop, and looked back the way he had come.

He stood still, his chest heaving. The street was empty and silent, lined with dark shadows thick enough to hide a man.

The cigarette didn't get lit until he had run up the three flights of stairs and made it inside his darkened living room. He closed the door behind him, fumbled for a smoke and leaned with his damp back against the solid door, exhaling sharply.

Chapter Ten

Saturday morning, April 11 - Harpers Ferry, West Virginia

George Landry jumped up from his desk when Chief Jackson came through the door of the station. Landry's face was flushed.

"Well, out with it Georgie. What's got you so excited?"

"We just executed the search of Larcher's house. I mean the stepfather's house."

"And ...?" Jackson flung his cap, like always, onto the pole protruding at the top of the hat stand. It landed on target and spun several revolutions before it came to a stop with its gold badge facing him. Jackson grunted at the achievement; it was going to be a good day. He hitched his expansive rear end onto his desk and faced the deputy who had hurried over.

"Larcher's medicine for his schizophrenia 'ain't where it should be,' according to the stepfather. Mrs. Hughlette was right, that guy is a mean son of a bitch. Couldn't care less if his stepson ain't got his medicine, if he walked away from the trailer, or if he's dead somewhere out in those woods."

Jackson finished the thought. "But the medicine being gone suggests his stepson wasn't comin' back the night he left for the basketball game. Right?"

"Yup. You got it, all right. The medicine had to be taken every day. Two kinds. Stell-o-zine and co-gen-tin." Deputy Landry carefully stretched out the syllables to get it right.

"Larcher had been taking the medicine about three years. I called up Doc Edlin and he said that if a patient didn't take that stuff, depending on the severity of his schizophrenia," Landry paused to look down at his notes, "the patient could lapse into a ... disoriented, uh, psychosis."

Jackson smiled at Landry's careful and painstaking labors. The boy had to be careful to make up for God's gift of mediocre brains. George knew his limitations and exceeded them through diligence, detail and his little notebook.

"Was Larcher in the Army, George, like we heard?"

"Yes siree." Landry walked back to his desk and picked up a folder. "He had a history of violence in the Army. There was a lot of aggravated assault charges filed against him."

"Good work! Anything else?"

"Oh yeah." Landry stood taller, puffing out his chest. The bright morning sunlight coming through the windows shone off his well-worn patrolman's uniform.

"Ted Samuels followed Larcher around like a puppy. All those guys were like brothers - helping each other get through the day-to-day with their, you know, their mental limitations and all. Well, everyone says only Larcher could have led or taken them boys through several miles of snow to the trailer. They wouldn't 've gone otherwise. Only Larcher could have told them to keep their hands off the food, the radio, the propane, even thought it's pretty clear he stuffed himself before he took off for God knows where."

"And I looked at their car again, Chuck. It didn't have a scrape on it. How could they have gone up that rutted road up to the snow line where we found it, late at night - even with a full moon - without at least some scraping underneath? Five big men in a car with bad shocks. Come on ..."

"What do you think?"

"I think they had to be really lucky or they knew that road really well. But the mothers, and Larcher's kin, say the boys didn't know the road, had never been up there before. You know what I think? ... I think they didn't know their boys so well. That's what I think."

A long pause. Landry's face grew pink. "And now, for the big news ..." Jackson sat and waited, his patience ebbing.

"I found something in Larcher's bedroom, at the bottom of his dirty magazine pile on the top shelf of his closet. It was more of that Nazi stuff we found in the trailer. And I found copies of a whole bunch of articles written by Professor David Tidback."

"Huh?"

"Tidback ... He's the guy who got shot a few days ago in D.C. after goin' on 'bout a Lincoln conspiracy. Remember?"

"Yeah ..." Jackson remembered. He had too many bodies in his woods the day the news broke to think too much about one in

Washington, D.C. He remembered the strange story on the news that night, and how Tidback went on about a Second Civil War.

"What kind of articles?"

"Right here." Landry handed over nearly three inches of paper.

"Georgie, you'll take my job yet." Jackson put on his reading half-glasses. " 'The Influence of the Confederate Secret Service on Modern Day Intelligence.' ... 'John Wilkes Booth: The Confederacy's Secret Weapon' ... 'Guerrilla Warfare during the Civil War' ... Dang! These are some heavy-duty pieces. You read any yet, George?" Jackson winked.

Landry shook his head, looking embarrassed. "Nope. I ..."

"Do you think Larcher could've read 'em?" Jackson interrupted. "I mean he wasn't retarded, even though he had his problems."

Landry scratched his chin. "Yeah. He was in the Army wasn't he?"

Jackson pondered the logic in that answer. For an instant he saw in Landry's face his beaming, pimply son on the day he got inducted into the Army. The 1968 Tet offensive wasn't too far off then. Tet ... He breathed once, deeply, and then looked down at the lengthy paper in his hands.

"Looks like I'm gonna have to look at this stuff myself," he said as he fell back into his chair. "But, first let me tell you what I found when I went up to the trailer this morning ..."

Jackson gave Landry the full story, showing him the books with the writing and markings in the margins, and the yellowed pages containing the etchings and the list of names.

Landry sat wide-eyed throughout and whistled long and loud when Jackson finished.

"Maybe those etchings were of buildings from the Civil War, Chuck. Maybe those lists of names, too. You think that guy who runs the John Brown center can help?" Landry meant old Marcus Henninger who ran the local historical society's memorial of the John Brown raid. Henninger was a history teacher up at Yale who came to Harpers Ferry on sabbatical research ten years ago and never left.

Jackson crossed his arms and leaned back in his chair.

"Mebbe. Couldn't hurt." He rocked back and forth, thinking.

"You know," he continued, "I should contact someone in Washington about Larcher's interest in Tidback."

Jackson ran his eyes over the faded green walls of the station house as his mind played with the case. He watched the secretary in the corner smoking a cigarette bonded to her lower lip and lining up a long form in her typewriter. The fan above her whirled like a slow helicopter blade. Landry reclaimed his desk chair.

"George, tell me something. What has Tidback, these etchings, and all these names on yellowed old paper, what do they got to do with our dead boys and Geoffrey Larcher?"

Landry knew Jackson wasn't really asking so he sat mute. Jackson picked up one of the Tidback articles from his desk. He flipped through the pile of scholarly material for twenty minutes as Landry wrote notes and filed papers. Jackson slapped the last article on his desk and fished through papers for the Washington Post with the story of Tidback's murder. The morning train that came the 90 miles from Washington, DC brought it in every day.

"Tidback goes to DC," Jackson said aloud at last, "to testify 'bout how the Confederate Secret Service killed Lincoln and 'bout how the conspiracy continues and threatens a second Civil War. And he gets his brains blown out."

"Now,' he continued, "our boy Larcher has copies of some of Tidback's scholarly articles hidden in his bedroom closet - under his girlie magazines for God's sake. Larcher, our Civil War student, belongs to some God-awful group that reads Aryan garbage and studies state and federal criminal law to exploit the sentencing loopholes in our grand system of justice. Now, this group meets in a trailer that's lost in the woods, and it looks like they're all wearing these Liberty medallions. And the trailer gives up hidden lists of names and drawings of houses and forts over a hundred years old. And this God-forsaken group of Larcher's just leaves these poor boys with their feeble minds - just leaves 'em out to die horrible, horrible deaths in the moonlit freeze of winter."

Jackson stopped, looking at the top of Landry's head as the deputy furiously scribbled notes. Landry looked up.

"Larcher's a suspect in our case, Chief. No doubt 'bout it. He may have even killed Tidback hisself ..."

Jackson grunted his agreement as he picked up the phone to call Washington information. "There's so many cops involved with that killing in DC, I'm just gonna call the local boys. That's gotta be the Capitol Hill Police according to the papers."

He got the number and dialed it. Waiting for the connection he leaned down to the drawer in his desk with the physical evidence from the trailer. He reached into an envelope and pulled out the four gold chains with the copper medallion engraved with the picture of Lady Liberty.

He looked at the yellowed pages found in the trailer library. The Lady Liberty on the medallions exactly matched the circular sketch on the bottom of the yellowed list of names.

"Judas Priest," mumbled Jackson as the earpiece echoed the ringing of the phone of the Capitol Hill Police. A voice finally came on the other end, interrupting his thoughts.

"Uhhhh, yes ...," he stumbled. "My name is Chuck Jackson, Chief of the Harpers Ferry, West Virginia, police department. I got information that's relevant to the murder of that Professor Tidback a few days ago. Put me through to the officer in charge, would ya?"

"You mean the officer in charge today or the officer in charge of the Tidback investigation, sir?"

"Investigation," sighed Jackson.

"Just a minute, sir." Jackson's eyes danced back and forth among the Ladies Liberty.

"Lieutenant Welch here, Chief Jackson. I'm helpin' run the Tidback investigation. I understand you have information?"

"Helping? Are the Fibbies bossing you around too?"

Welch laughed. "Oh, yeah, you got that right, Chief. What I'll do is relay what you give me over to Agent Shay just down the hill from us a few blocks at the FBI."

Jackson paused. "Well, why don't you give me that name, and I'll just call him myself, Lieutenant."

"Very well. It's Paul Shay, with an A. 626-6634."

"Isn't it unusual to give everything over to the FBI so early in the investigation?"

Welch's voice tightened. "That's how things go sometimes. You know?"

"All right, then, all right. Thanks for your help. I'll call Agent Shay right away."

Screw them, he thought as he hung up. No way was he gonna call Agent Shay. He never trusted cops who give up their cases too easy. Something stunk about this whole damn deal. He shook his head. He wasn't giving up on this case yet. No, sir. Those poor, dead boys deserved better.

In Washington, Lieutenant Marty Welch - 30-year veteran of the Capitol Hill Police Department - dutifully made a note of Chief Charles Jackson's inquiry from the Harpers Ferry, West Virginia police department. He stuck the note inside his brown, marbled legal-size envelope labeled "Tidback." He closed up the envelope with satisfaction and turned back to the business of arranging for parking for an entourage of labor leaders coming to lobby the Hill.

Chapter Eleven

Saturday afternoon -- Washington, DC

"Where is he on the Report?"

Brock rubbed his eyes as he spoke. He had not slept well since Tidback's murder. The thick, sweet smell of blood, the horrible, wet sounds of the bullets' impact, were too fresh.

"I've been trying to reach McAdams, Senator. I've stopped by his office. I've called time and again. I cannot reach him." Lewis Shephard sat in a cushioned chair in front of Brock's huge mahogany desk, looking uncomfortable in his new blue jeans and a polo shirt.

"McAdams and Mossingame are ignoring us," Shephard continued. "You must force their hand, or go to the Senate leadership. Perhaps Chairman Mossingame thinks he will be authorized to extend the Committee beyond our May 1 sunset date." Shephard sniffed his contempt at the notion.

"He will NOT!" Brock pounded the table as he shouted. His features quickly softened as he realized he had startled Shephard. "Ah'm sorry, Lewis. Ah'm not myself lately."

Shephard nodded, his lips tightly pursed, as if in disapproval. He watched Brock slump deeply into his chair. Behind Brock on the bureau stood two mounted Confederate pistols and a replica of a three-masted tall ship, sails billowing in an unseen wind. Next to these were perched framed medals earned by Brock's ancestors in the Civil War, the War of 1812 and the Revolutionary War. In front of Brock on his desk was a photograph of him and his now dead wife sitting hand-in-hand on a wooden bench under a weeping willow on a misty hot, summer day. Another one had them on the porch of a stately mansion, leaning over the railing and waving happily at the camera.

Brock bent forward, defeat and betrayal weighing down the normally haughty, upward tilt of his face. His eyes dimmed as he measured Shephard. "Why was Tidback killed?"

Shephard squirmed in his chair. "I shouldn't have the

slightest idea."

"What was the Professor gonna say? Do you know?"

"We don't. He was a surprise." Shephard wiped a handkerchief across his greasy brow.

Brock studied his chief-of-staff. There were all kinds on Capitol Hill, but Lewis Shephard fell into a unique group of staffers you could spot a mile away. They were highly capable, smart and influential but, at the same time, they were a little off, a little too hunched up, a little too much in overdrive. They were simply too fired up by some blinding cause or political passion to care too much about the latest fashion much less matching socks, pressed pants, combed hair or seeing a skin doctor now and then. And, to top it off, Lewis Shephard was changing. He was growing more secretive. There was more of an unholy gleam in his beady little eyes. Frankly, Brock concluded, Shephard was becoming an odder and odder duck, even by Capitol Hill standards.

Brock exhaled loudly in frustration. "It's all a shame..." He shook his head slowly. "It's all such a shame. But Ah'll tell you what, Lewis ...." He gestured to a wall filled with dim daguerreotypes of his ancestors and ancient parchments documenting his legacy.

"Ah'll tell you what. We've lost our sense of where we've been, where we've come from. We're no longer guided by the principles that gave us birth. We're no longer the beacon on the hill that is our country's true guide."

Brock grabbed hold of the desk and pulled himself up. He walked over to his picture wall, his hands clasped tightly behind his back as he studied them one by one. Shephard waited, gripping the armrests of his chair with his two hands.

"Now, Lewis, Ah've done some extreme things in carrying on our noble traditions. But these new boys, YOUR boys who brought you to me, well ..." Brock walked to the window behind his desk.

He gazed out at the Capitol building dome. "This new crowd of ... *professionals* ..." The word came bitterly to his tongue. The old man grew silent and then suddenly stood straight, as if he were drawing strength and sustenance from the expansive government buildings laid out before him.

Brock's chin lifted. He and his family had given much over the years. Honors had been heaped upon them. Their destiny was not one of defeat. He turned, his eyes flashing.

"Ah will not let Mistuh McAdams get away with this secrecy of his. We must know what he has. Ah will put pressure on Senator Mossingame to get that early draft. Ah will start getting my colleagues to make some calls as well. That will force open our Mistuh McAdams' carpetbag."

"Senator, you know McAdams. He will manipulate us until the bitter end. He will play the rules to the hilt. He's got almost three weeks to do his damage ... We may need to try other, firmer ways of convincing him to ..."

"Enough!" Brock slapped his hand on his desk as he glared at Shephard. "There are ways to handle everything. People - yo' people - must realize this before they go too far! ... Ah'll see what Ah can do. In the meantime, go on about yo' business." He dismissed Shephard with a sweep of his hand.

Brock watched the odd duck waddle out the door before punching some numbers on the phone. He didn't want to make this call. They could not be trusted to handle sensitive problems with finesse.

The phone picked up at the other end. Brock leaned back in his chair, his eyes closing as he spoke.

"It's McAdams," he said in a low voice. "He's delayin' the Committee's Report, and so far keepin' us from seein' what's in it. We need access to his work. You said once you could produce this access. How would you propose doin' it?"

"We will start on it immediately," came the terse reply. "You should have alerted us earlier if things were this bad. Why didn't you?" There was no wait for an answer. "Is there anything else, Senator?"

"Ah want to know what you gonna do before we jump into anythin'."

"Taylor, if we want results, we must move now. We have searched McAdams' office, down to the computer disks and the trash cans. We've gone through the files and desks of the Committee staff. We have nothing - no notes, no rough drafts of the Committee Report, nothing. We have to take other courses of action before McAdams' Report sees the light of day. Certainly before May 1. We'll handle things, Senator."

"Ah said Ah ..."

"The group shall meet on Friday. We'll talk then."

A dial tone filled the line. The old man sat with the phone to his ear, rubbing his forehead with long, bony fingers. The new boys, the professionals, were flexing their muscles.

Chapter Twelve

Saturday evening -- Washington, DC

McAdams eyed the phone. He drained his glass of Dewars straight and picked up the phone again. He lit a cigarette between the third and fourth ring. She answered.

"Hello?"

"Hi, Anne." His breath stopped.

"Mac ..." Anger, maybe regret at answering, lowered her voice. "What is it?"

"I wanted to catch you before you headed out for the evening."

She said nothing. Classical music played in the background. He didn't know when she had made the switch from the Turtles to Tchaikovsky. In fact, he didn't know she had made the switch at all.

"Can we get together? Next week some time?" He inhaled.

"Why would I want to get together with you?"

"To talk, maybe ..."

"Give me a reason."

"To talk." The explaining sound like begging, and he hated it. "Because I need to."

"Mac, what's going on? Are you hitting the bottle a little early tonight? Is this about your witness getting killed this week? Did you bring him out into the open, too? Did you leave him unprepared? Unknowing? Vulnerable? Exposed? Like you did with me?" Her voice grew more ragged with each blast. "Are you looking for fucking sympathy, Mac? From ME?"

Like a punching bag he took the flurry of questions, accusations really. He choked down the anger that erupted in his chest. "Maybe I am."

One, two, three beats of silence pounded through the phone lines.

"Christ!" she said at last. "Jesus Christ. ... Where?"

"Top floor of the Washington Hotel." Her favorite.

She paused, slowed down by some memories maybe. He waited.

"The Washington Hotel," she began softly " A lot of coincidences today …"

"What do you mean?" McAdams lit another cigarette, thinking he might actually finish the smoke before the conversation went down the drain.

"Remember the house, Mac?"

He hesitated, puzzled, and exhaled. "You mean 'our' house?"

"Yeah, where we all lived - you, me, Ed O'Connell, the Honorable Nelson Wilkins. … Well, I saw his eminence, Deputy Defense Secretary Wilkins, today. He spoke at a function I put together for my law firm's military-industrial clients at the Army-Navy Club. I was hoping to get the Secretary herself but in walks Nelson as a stand-in. He insisted out loud in front of everyone that he had to bail out an old housemate. Of course all my clients now think we, he and I, lived together - and that he was fucking my brains out."

McAdams winced. "He probably felt he needed to kiss your ass," he managed, "what with all the clout you've got these days. … Amazing. Only in Washington could your bum housemate from long ago end up the number two guy in Defense."

For the first time McAdams heard ice in a glass on the other end before Anne spoke again. "We were all lowly Congressional staffers back then, Mac. Me handling military intelligence for the Senate Foreign Affairs Committee. You doing procurement fraud with Mossingame over at Senate Government Operations ..."

"Yeah. O'Connell was in defense appropriations in the House. Wilkins the terrible took on military readiness and conventional warfare for Senate Armed Services. They introduced us, remember?"

"Of course! At the house's first Christmas party. I moved in with the New Year."

It had been snowing heavily in Washington that night they met. Capitol Hill, as if by sheer dint of his wishing it would happen for so many years, had finally taken on the mantle of a Christmas card. Anne and he took a break from the raucous party and walked. They strolled, soon arm in arm, watching the snowflakes flutter in the streetlights and peeking into the homes aglow from within. Bundled-up adventurers, neighbors for a night, would call out "Merry Christmas" as they wandered the snowy streets. The Capitol dome wore a white cap of snow to ward off the cold, and white drifts clogged the windowsills and doorways of century-old, Federal style townhouses.

"What a magical night," she said dreamily, ice clinking. "The street lights and the house lights were like twinkling Christmas bulbs. I can remember the lamps at the far end of the streets practically shimmering within halos in the falling snow."

"We kissed under the street lights, pretending we were lovers on a stage."

"When we got back to the party Ed was wearing that cap with a rack of antlers, and he had Rudolph's glowing red nose perched over his crotch." She let out a laugh at the memory.

"Everyone was sitting around singing Christmas songs, trying to come up with something, anything, beyond a first verse."

"No one could do it, but no one cared either. Everyone was laughing. Everyone was drunk or high or both."

"God, there were empty liquor bottles and beer cans piled up on tables and in the sink. Smoke hung at the ceiling for days. It took a week for us to clean the place up. I think you moved in with me right after we finished the sanitation project."

"Nelson tried to get in my pants that night. He planted a big, sloppy wet one on me when we came back from our walk. Remember? He was just tottering in the door with a joint with a long stretch of unspilled ashes in one hand and a glass of his disgusting bourbon in the other. ... Glad the confirmation hearing didn't get into those particular weaknesses of the good Deputy Defense Secretary."

"I rescued you. I pulled you away to dance."

"Remember the song?"

"Uh ...."

" 'I Saw Mommy Kissing Santa Claus.' By the Ronnettes."

"Those were good years, Anne. Really good years."

"The best." She looked out of her window to see night had come. "They were the best."

"Remember how we would all just hang around over breakfast on the weekends at that long, rickety table that filled the dining room? ... Oh, man. All the coffee we'd drink ..."

"And those fresh donuts from the 7-11 down the street ..."

"The ones that practically rotted my teeth," he laughed.

He heard her swallow hard whatever it was she was drinking. "That," she blurted, her words becoming slurred, "was from all the Coke you drank and the packs of Snow Balls you used to wolf down every night after we got high!"

McAdams filled his glass with Dewars from a quart bottle on the table. He sat back. "No matter what the hour, someone would be awake, ready to talk politics or to trash you for your latest social miscue, or just share a joint or a thought or a chili dog. And the parties, Christ, sometimes they went on for days."

There was a long pause and then she spoke in a voice with all the air let out. "They were good years, Mac ...." More ice sloshing around. "... We were lovers then. We lasted a good four years, two of which we actually lived like husband and wife! Jesus! ... Imagine, four whole years as one! A near record for Washington. Certainly records for me and you."

He closed his eyes, waiting for it. Waiting for the big salvo.

"We could have had a lot more years together, Mac. But our chances died the night ... we lost everything. And now we avoid each other, until our work, this small town, brings us together and then all my nightmares come back. I'm sick of it, dammit!"

Her voice grew husky. "You should have told me what you were working on back then, Mac. You owed me a warning that we were in danger. You really should have ... protected ... me better. You should have protected ... US! But you didn't. And that scar on your cheek will remind you every day, just like my scars, of how you let me, us, down. ... I trusted you .... Now I don't trust any one. ... I can't afford to."

"Anne ...."

She wasn't listening. "We'll never be able to go back, will we Mac? We can't go fucking back ...." A glass hit a table hard on the other end. "Look, I don't want to continue this right now. And I won't. ... When?" She poured another drink.

"What?"

"When do you want to get together?"

"Uh…, I'm leaving tomorrow for Randolph-Macon College and then I head to Mississippi…"

"Where the paper said your dead witness came from, right?"

"Right, I want to do some digging around."

"When do you want to get together then?"

"I'm back Tuesday - late. How 'bout Tuesday night, around 9? Meet you there?"

"OK, Mac. I don't know why, but I'll see you in a few days." She hung up.

He listened for a while, hoping she would pick up or something, and then he put the handset in the cradle. He filled the glass again and lit a cigarette as he sank back in the chair.

Chapter Thirteen

Early Sunday afternoon, April 12 -- Washington, DC

They hadn't seen her like this in a long time. Anne Gardiner was sitting with a mysterious man. The two were clinking champagne glasses and leaning over the table. They exchanged long, lingering glances. And how she sparkled!

Four of Anne's former female cronies from the Senate sat, transfixed. They craned their necks from another table at Harry's, one of the best places for Sunday brunch in Washington. Everyone went there to be seen, or to see who showed up to get seen. Sports figures, politicians, bureaucrats, lawyers, tons of lawyers, and lobbyists, tons of them too, all clamoring for eggs, pork products, red steak, booze and danish.

This morning the cronies got more than they bargained for - power hitter Anne Gardiner, their own Anne Gardiner, caught cold. Anne - former Chief Counsel for the Senate Armed Forces Committee, former senior member of the White House staff and now managing partner for one of the most politically well connected law firms in town - Hardy, Dixon & Morton - Anne was at Harry's in all her glory.

Had she gotten laid the night before? The betting was 3-1 she did. Crude insults erupted from the table. But none of THEM had gotten any in months, the sudden and rueful recognition of which led to insistent calls for another round of stiff Bloody Marys and Mimosas, light on the OJ.

Mark Fisher cast a glance at Anne's watch as she put her etched crystal champagne glass on the table. Her bright, pale blue eyes pooled in a rosy complexion brought on by very expensive champagne. Her lean, smooth face with its signature, pointed jaw drew longing stares from lonely men at several tables around them. She tossed back her thick black, shoulder-length hair with a deep laugh and looked at him with pleasure. He was charming the pants off her. But there was work to do. Fisher smiled.

"Anne, what do you see of your ex, John McAdams is it?"

The buzz in her head popped and fizzled. She blinked as she eyed him up and down. Fisher was very, very hot looking, no doubt about it. He sported a brown tan that seemed to last all year long. Jet black hair moussed straight back from a perfectly shaped forehead. Intense, bright green eyes. Square jaw, with a deep dimple - in the middle of his chin no less. Beautiful hands with long, long, long slender fingers. And he was athletic, not an ounce of fat. A senior White House domestic aide, albeit in a different Administration and political party than hers, Mark Fisher was a serious power broker, one of Forbes' Top 100 young leaders. A rising star.

"Mark, why are you doing this to me? Where does this come from?"

"Just curious, " he replied. "I wanted to see where your loyalties lay."

"My loyalties? Where they 'lay'? What ever could you mean, Mark?" Her ruby red lips curled into a devilish smile as she slowly arched her back, leaning even closer to him over the table. She took a long, sensuous sip of champagne, eyeing him over the rim of the glass. She smiled and then turned coy, casting a mischievous glance around the restaurant. Not a few men got caught staring at her and had to look away.

She zeroed in on another table and spotted four sets of familiar fluttering eyelids above wide, leering smiles. "Oh shit ...," she muttered.

"I mean, do you still see him? Can you talk to him?"

She turned to meet his gaze. Concern draped his face. There was something going on here. She put her glass down.

"Yes, of course, Mark, I talk to him. We do move in the same circles. We have to." She wiped her mouth daintily with a napkin and put it on the table. Her hands folded together in a heap between the two of them. "To tell you the truth, this is not a great subject with me. I recoil, to be honest. Why are you asking about John McAdams? Trying to piss me off?"

"I'm worried about his work with the Assassination Committee. I don't want him to hurt the President with reckless claims in connection with the King thing. I want to be prepared should he have ammunition ... or innuendo."

"Why should you be concerned?"

"There may be ... supporters of the President, even some Cabinet figures, who were, shall we say, too much in the background back then. You know, back then they were in government agencies, or interest groups, that might now appear compromising if put in the wrong light."

"Can't you be more specific?"

"Let's just say, there may be a few folks affiliated with the President who could have blown the whistle on any anti-King stuff that went on back then - had they known. Or maybe they knew of a little anti-King stuff and thought nothing of it because King was thought to be a Commie back then. That kind of stuff. You know, nothing serious."

"Well, I don't know, Mark. I do know, however, that Mac does damage if he decides there is some blame to hand out. He can be quite ruthless." She felt a twinge of regret using the familiar 'Mac' in front of Mark Fisher.

"Can he really hurt the President? I mean, the King Committee is looking at events almost 30 years old!"

"The President has around him many men of influence from that era. Men who were key players in the CIA, the FBI, the Army, the Secret Service and other agencies implicated in the King death. These men are important policy makers now. McAdams taints them, he taints the President. We must know what he's up to, before he spills anything. ..."

She made a face and waited for the truth. She stole a glance in her friends' direction and saw they were back guzzling and gossiping, their foreheads almost colliding as they leaned in to share their crude comments.

Fisher's waved his hand back and forth in front of her face to get her attention. "OK, OK. Now listen to me, Anne. We think McAdams has some dirt. He may have found, if not a smoking gun, some smoldering piles - or files."

"I see," she answered. That was it. Mac had something. Something good enough to smoke Fisher out into the open.

"So, you'll help me?" Fisher asked. He flashed a brilliant smile. She smiled back, despite herself. He was extremely desirable.

"What can I do? Mac - McAdams - and I are old news. Way old, as they say."

"Find out what he's going to say in the Committee's Final Report. He must have made up his mind by now. Probe him. He has computer files. But where are they? Find out if he's raising any unusual claims or positions."

He kissed her hands now gathered up between his. "Please?"

"Mark, who do you think I am, H. Howard Hunt? G. Gordon Liddy? L. Patrick Gray? Ollie fucking North?"

He laughed. "You have ways. You have many talents. Many friends. ... Do this for me. Do it for the President. I promise a 'patriot's dinner' - you and me with the President and First Lady. IF you deliver, that is."

"Well..., why should I help someone from the wrong party?"

"I'll get you access in the White House. Promise! And that will be good for your clients, which, in turn, will make you richer. And remember, the President most surely will win a second term three years from now. That gives you a total of six years of access to the highest reaches of government."

"Hmmmm ... That presumes YOU stay 6 years."

"I'll introduce you to layer upon layer of decision makers. I'll embed you in the decision-making process."

"Oooooo!" She playfully licked her lips. "I like that."

"I'll give you sex on demand ..."

She shook her head with exaggeration, her hair sashaying provocatively in front of her face. "Not enough ..."

"I'll make sure the President names you to head his new Presidential Commission on Women. You might make the cover of Time!"

"Whoa, boy...! Talk to me. You can deliver on that?"

He nodded. "I can and I will."

"When?"

"By the 4th of July ..."

"This year?"

"Anne ...!"

"I said, 'This year?'"

"This year, you bitch."

She smiled and drained her glass. She smacked her lips. "Get me the offer from the President in writing next week and I will consider your proposition."

"I shall. But please get to work now, Anne. McAdams must wrap things up by May 1. ... Time is running out for us."

She smiled as she considered their devil's pact. A little quid for a little quo. That's what made Washington go round. She would be doing a service to the Administration if she alerted it to evil past deeds by some of its members. And if indeed Mac had stumbled upon something really serious, well ..., she just might have to fudge what she told Fisher. She had a reputation to keep. She wasn't a crook. No harm, no foul, and no skin off McAdams' nose.

She thrust her lips into a little girl's pout and waved her empty champagne glass at Fisher. He responded immediately with a hail of the waiter. They paused while a second expensive bottle was opened with a flourish on the table between them and poured expertly into fresh glasses.

"I'll be seeing him - McAdams - this week," she offered, taking in the intoxicating bubbles with closed eyes. She didn't want to let him know why she was meeting McAdams. "After he gets back from a road trip to Virginia and Mississippi to see what that dead witness of his was up to. Can you believe it? Here you are worrying about the President and John McAdams is off investigating the background of a dead history professor. ... Don't worry, Mark. That proves he has nothing. If he did, then he'd be holed up writing his Report."

Fisher's tanning studio tan barely covered up the blood suddenly draining from his face. A few minutes later he excused himself from the table. "That champagne just runs through me after a while ..."

"Wimp!" she exclaimed as she waved him away. She poured another glass for herself.

He was at the phone at Harry's reception desk in less than twenty seconds, speaking in hushed tones, his hand covering his mouth as luminaries of every variety continued to pour in through the front door. Some he knew, and he nodded and smiled to them as he spoke urgently.

Five minutes later he returned to the table. "Now where were we ..." he said into Anne Gardiner's sparkling blue bedroom eyes.

Chapter Fourteen

Sunday evening - Alexandria, Virginia

"Are you proud of me?"
Lewis Shephard gripped the phone and sat down at the table. He was at home. It was almost dusk and he had not yet turned on his kitchen light. The shadows in the corners of the room seemed to thicken. He strained to hear the sounds on the other end of the telephone line.
"What did you say?"
"Are you proud, Mr. Shephard? Are you proud of me?"
Shephard swallowed hard as static erupted in his ear. It was Geoffrey Larcher, using his cellular phone. "Yes, I am, Geoffrey. The execution went well. ... Where are you now?"
"Robert had to kill himself, didn't he." It wasn't a question. Geoffrey Larcher must have seen the news reports covering David Tidback's killing and the suicide of the assailant. He knew Robert had taken his own life.
"Yes, he did. That's the way it must be. You know that John Booth would be proud."
"Yes," came the robotic answer. "Very proud. It is a noble legacy we carry forward."
Shephard smiled. Larcher sounded OK, still in touch with the message drilled into the West Virginia campsite, and into every other campsite that Shephard had set up and visited over the last couple of years. "You're right, Geoffrey, it's a very noble legacy. ... It's good to hear you. We haven't spoken since before you found Robert."
"I told you I had the man for you. He came from the Baltimore campsite. I knew he would be very good."
"Did I know him?"
"He said you came to the campsite and spoke to them there. You invited them to cut up the face of that city council nigger woman up there, the one who wanted to give 'hate' crimes extra long prison time, the one who was trying to make a big national issue of it. You promised them money would be waiting for

them at the bank if they sent a message, if they hurt her so bad that others could feel her hurt and know it was because of what she stood for. They did what you asked and you delivered. ... Robert had great faith in you, and what you said. He believed in the Leaders who sent you."

For a moment Shephard felt the surge. The campsites had been his mission, yes, perhaps his own legacy. And he HAD done well. He wiped his wet forehead with the back of his hand. "Have you seen the news reports on the campsite in West Virginia?"

"I saw the nigger sheriff, or whatever he is, all over the TV news and the papers. I heard about the bodies they found. I heard that I'm missing." This was punctuated with a high-pitched giggle. "I gave them the medallions that night, you know, the night you didn't show. We had a big night."

He giggled again. "I brought big bottles of beer with me and we drank all night. Some of them started throwing up real bad."

"I tried to meet you but the snow was too much. I couldn't make it. I tried to call ... ."

"We drank in the snow, drank and drank. I told them to wait, that I was going to get you. I told them to not touch anything until you showed up. I told them everything might be poisoned, booby-trapped ...."

"Why did you leave?"

"I was pretty scared. And all the snow was making them crazy! I didn't want to stay up there with those fruit cases." He began to laugh in machine gun bursts.

"OK, Geoffrey, OK." Shephard swallowed again. Samuels, according to the reports from Harpers Ferry, had survived for weeks, only to die a gruesome death. The others must have escaped the trailer sometime during the first night or maybe the next couple of days, out of desperation or to answer some phantom calling to them. They each probably had staggered around for hours and hours and slipped into frozen sleep. It was all over the papers and the news, even in Washington, even with the Tidback killing.

"Where are you, Geoffrey? You must tell me. I have more work."

"I ..., I don't know. ... Will I get more money?"

"Of course you will. You do the bidding of the Leaders, you are rewarded. Just like I have instructed you. There are enemies out there and we are beginning to take them on, one by one. They are taking our country away from us, giving it to the women, and the minorities and the immigrants." He believed this, too. Like those in the campsites that he reached out to, he had been pushed out by the blacks and the women and the Haitians and the Mexicans and all the rest. Simply put - he had to fight to get what they got for free. And they got more respect, more status than he, without working for it. But not any more. Not for him, not for the boys - the men - who came to the campsites to listen and learn. They now had a mission, and the wherewithal, and the Leaders, to strike back.

"We need to take the country back, Geoffrey."

"What do you want me to do, Mr. Shephard?"

"Do you know where Richmond, Virginia is?"

"Yes."

"You'll have to find the airport there."

"OK."

"Let me describe the target. His name is John McAdams."

"Not the jigaboo cop from Harpers Ferry? I would like to do him."

"No," Shephard chuckled. "John McAdams is the one. He ...."

Chapter Fifteen

The same evening

McAdams ran out the front door of his building after a quick dinner of grilled cheese sandwiches and steaming hot coffee. It was a balmy evening and night had already claimed most of the horizon. The phone call with Anne last night, how it went from sweet to sour in a heartbeat, replayed in his mind. So did the sight of David Tidback's body stretched over that witness table.

He pulled open the door of his three-year-old black Ford Mustang and threw his overnight bag into the passenger's seat. As he slipped inside, he glanced up and down the street he had maneuvered the night he had been scared out of the Library of Congress. Today only a few bending boughs, caught in a gentle, rising breeze, were suspect. He brought the car to life and roared away from the curb.

First stop was Ashland, Virginia, home of Randolph-Macon College where Tidback was a tenured professor in the History Department. The University of Mississippi, his next stop, was for Tidback a visiting professorship since last fall. Ashland was 15 miles north of Richmond, Virginia, and 75 miles south of Washington, DC. After Randolph-Macon he'd hop a flight to Memphis, Tennessee from Richmond. He'd rent a car in Memphis, and head southeast for 70 miles, to get to the University. He'd be back Tuesday night in time to see Anne.

He drifted back to the morning Tidback was shot as he made the I-95 freeway south. Tidback's last words ... Ongoing conspiracy. Lincoln and the Confederate Civil Service. ... A Second Civil War. ... What had Tidback stumbled across?

Brock's face that morning showed more than recognition of Tidback. The Virginia statesman's comfy little world had been upended - plain and simple - when he saw Tidback. Brock looked like he was somewhere else, watching his life roll like a movie on a screen inside his eyeballs. Strange look. He played around with all the possibilities as he drove.

He almost missed the road sign glowing in his headlights. It was forty miles to the ramp off I-95 that would take him to a small highway that in turn went straight through Ashland. He turned on the windshield wipers as rain splotches, looking like cat's paws, appeared on his windshield.

He glanced in the rear-view mirror. The pick-up truck with the mountain boys was still there, about three cars back. Around Manassas, just south of DC, they had pulled up next to him and gave him a once-over they thought he hadn't seen.

The driver was a long-haired youth wearing a backwards white baseball cap. He had big gaps between his teeth and a ragged beard that spilled down over an ample stomach pressing obviously against the steering wheel. His passenger had a cap with the Confederate flag across the front. This man's hair was pulled back in a tight ponytail, his beard neatly trimmed. Tattoos took up most of his thick arms.

It was time to lose the Smith Brothers, McAdams knew, before they got too close on one of the back roads to Ashland. He visualized loaded shotguns spread across their laps.

His tires squealed painfully as he veered sharply across an empty lane toward the exit coming up on his right. Braking cars screamed behind him and several fishtailed to a stop on the wet highway, their occupants seized with sputtering venom and wide-eyed fear. The pick-up truck sped past. The pony-tailed passenger was pressed up against the window to watch where McAdams was heading, his mouth locked in an ugly sneer.

McAdams' car zigzagged down a hill, straightened out and then headed for a gas station at an intersecting four-lane thoroughfare. He pulled up to the gas tanks closest to the garage. He sat for a few moments, shaking. Inside a youth with long, dirty blond air and a faded red flannel shirt sat behind a gray aluminum desk. The kid stared into a small TV with bent rabbit ears. Smoke, blue in the light cast by the TV, drifted lazily from an ashtray on the desk.

McAdams got out and began filling his tank, looking over the top of the Mustang as he did so. The ramps leading to and from the highway were empty. No pick-up trucks careered around the corner. The rush of traffic on I-95 above him sounded almost soothing.

Paying for the gas inside the station, he said nothing. Back in the car, he steered for the on-ramp to the interstate, his heart still pounding in his ears. He drove, his eyes moving jerkily the entire time between the pavement unfolding before him and his rear-view. No more mountain boys joined him as he took the Ashland exit off the highway.

He lit another cigarette as he drove and took a long drag. Someone knew he was in the Library of Congress two nights ago. And now they were following him to Ashland. He arched his back and shoulders to relieve the tension gathered in knots, pushing his mind toward his appointment.

He was to meet the head of the Randolph-Macon History Department, Professor Rufus Crockett. Tidback's boss. They were to get together at 9:30 tomorrow morning, right before Crockett's 10:15 freshman introductory history class.

Up on the right appeared the Ashland Holiday Inn recommended by Crockett. McAdams pulled into the nearly empty parking lot and checked in. His room was on the fourth floor overlooking the unlighted two-lane state highway that led south to the school only a few miles away.

The "Taverna" on the ground floor was even slower than the parking lot. Its oak bar was on the opposite wall from where he entered. The bartender, leaning with his back against the bar, watched a color TV attached to a swivel arm in the upper right corner of the room. The faces of the characters from an Ironside episode were tinged with green and slightly unfocused. The bartender didn't seem to care.

McAdams sat to the bartender's left, on the short side of the bar so he could see who came in. The bartender didn't budge.

"Vodka, double, with a little cranberry juice to give it color."

The man looked him over, figured he could pay, and made him a drink. He slapped the glass on the bar and turned back to the TV. Chief Ironside had taken a tumble in his wheel chair, and lay on the ground glowering at three bad guys.

McAdams drank quickly and ordered another, paying just after the drink hit the counter. The bartender's red nose and eyes, however, betrayed him to Mac as the biggest customer that night.

"What do you know about Randolph-Macon down the road?" McAdams asked at last. "I got a job interview tomorrow."

The bartender's lips turned up in a slight smile. "Nuthin," came the rasping reply. "It's a school. About a thousand smart-assed kids, mostly from the state and the East Coast."

"Any professors ever come in here?"

"Don't ask what you do. Only ask you to behave and pay your money." Ugly threats against Ironside came from the TV.

"Didn't that guy, that professor that got shot up in Washington, teach here?"

The bartender reached under the bar and produced a newspaper. He slid it down the bar and turned back to watch his show.

McAdams picked Friday's 10-page Ashland Clarion off the top of the counter. In the upper left corner, next to the story about the commencement speaker coming in June was the headline "R-M Professor Gunned Down in Washington." Pithy.

The paper, last week's news, gave little information. Tidback was well-regarded, scholarly, quiet, a cog in the academic machine. No family life, no relatives, no big burial. A smattering of accolades from peers for his work on the Confederacy and the behind-the-scenes of the war in the South. There was no mention of Mississippi. No mention of why Tidback was in Washington. No mention of dangerous Lincoln conspiracies.

Another drink sounded good, but he decided against it. He left a reasonable tip and walked out without saying good-bye to his new friend. Ironside was OK, thank God, perched smugly back in his wheelchair.

Chapter Sixteen

Up in the room, McAdams settled back in the sagging bed and retrieved from his bag two sets of documents on the Lincoln Assassination. He began reading.

The short 1866 Judiciary Committee report concluded, over the dissents of prominent Southerners, that Confederate President Jefferson Davis probably approved secret attempts to assassinate Abraham Lincoln in 1865. The lengthy record of the 1867 Lincoln Assassination Committee hearings, there was no final report, gave him more.

The hearings were dominated by the testimony of Lafayette Baker. Baker had been a descendent of Remember Baker, one of the Vermont Green Mountain boys who included among their number the famous Ethan Allen. The Green Mountain Boys had gone down in history fighting the British during the Revolutionary War.

Lafayette Baker was an intimate of President Lincoln, meeting frequently with him on security and investigations. He also was head of the National Detective Bureau -- the first national crime-fighting agency that evolved later into the Secret Service and the FBI. As head of the Bureau Baker reported to Lincoln and Secretary of War Edwin Stanton.

Baker was a force. He exposed prostitution rings and corruption in the Treasury Department and the Quartermaster Corps. He fought against the corrupt sale of draft exemptions during the Civil War. He spied on Union generals during the Civil War to police loyalty. He was chief investigator for a House Committee and a Select Committee on government employee corruption. Baker exposed a plot right after Lincoln was re-elected in 1864. It involved Union generals, Treasury officials, US custom officials and the US Commissioner of Indian Affairs in a conspiracy to provide Northern food for the enemy army of Robert E. Lee in exchange for cotton from the South.

It was Lafayette Baker who assembled the search party that hunted down John Wilkes Booth. War Secretary Stanton got

Baker to help after the US Army had failed to find Booth in the hours after Lincoln's death. Baker looked into his J. Edgar Hoover-like files containing information on criminals, corrupt army officers, spies and Congressional informants, and turned up Booth's picture. The picture became plastered on thousands of "Wanted Dead or Alive" posters. The final clue leading to Booth's whereabouts came from tips Baker received from his spy network in Virginia.

The search party found Lincoln's assassin in a tobacco shed on a farm near Bowling Green, Virginia. A soldier who was part of the search party mortally wounded Booth. He died on the porch of the farmhouse alongside the flaming tobacco barn. Baker's protégé, Colonel Everton Congers, was with Booth when he died. He took from the body a number of items: a knife, a pipe, a pocket compass, a pair of pistols, a carbine with cartridges, bills of exchange issued by a bank in Montreal, about $100 in US Greenbacks, ... and a diary. Congers testified before the Judiciary Committee that he gave Booth's last remains to Baker who handed over everything, including Booth's diary, to War Secretary Stanton. Stanton said he passed Booth's possessions to the Judge Advocate General presiding over the trial of Booth's conspirators.

A curious thing then happened. The diary never was submitted as evidence in the conspiracy trial lasting from May to June of 1865. Everything else taken from Booth's body, however, found its way into the trial. It was not until the US House of Representatives began an investigation into Lincoln murder conspiracies in 1867 - almost two years after the assassination - that the diary faced public scrutiny.

Baker's testimony jumped out from the pages before him. "I think there was a great deal more of the original diary than appears here now," declared Baker. He testified that a good many pages of the diary, measuring 4" by 6", had been cut out during the two years since he had given it over to Stanton's War Department. All that was left, he said, were a bunch of empty pages and only two entries in Booth's handwriting, the same two entries you could see today, McAdams remembered, when you visited Ford's Museum in Washington.

One of these surviving entries had Booth deploring how "we" had tried to capture Lincoln but how, in the end, it had been left to him and him alone to act decisively. He would have to take up the gauntlet and kill the President in order to save the nation. Booth also said he wanted to come back to Washington, DC, "to clear his name." The second entry that could be seen in the Ford Museum diary was a rambling account of Booth's disappointment in his President and his country.

The diary with these two passages was not presented at the trial of Booth's alleged co-conspirators even though the passages would have been useful in showing the existence of a conspiracy as well as Booth's pre-meditation and motive. Had the diary been produced, of course, the missing pages would have been noticed. The absence of diary pages, especially in the hands of a good defender, could have been used to create doubt in the mind of the judge at a time when most wanted to punish Booth's cohorts and move on with national unification.

McAdams wondered how Booth planned to clear his name. Was it as Representative Butler said in the Congressional Globe pages he had come across in the Library of Congress, by implicating others? Perhaps others named in his diary? On pages now missing?

Secretary of War Stanton disputed, as did others, Baker's testimony about the missing pages. Stanton said that whatever pages were missing were gone when the diary was taken from Booth's body and gone when he was given the diary by Baker. Stanton testified that he had studied the diary for 30 to 40 minutes after Baker gave it to him.

"Stanton looked at the diary for thirty to forty minutes? To read two or three pages of Booth's scribbles?" McAdams snorted out loud, shaking his head. Whatever Stanton read over that period of time consumed a great many more pages.

He got up and walked over to the window to stare at the near-empty parking lot. It shone with a sparkling sheen from the night's rain. Why, he thought, would a man like Baker - responsible, a descendent of patriots, the first "Untouchable" - why would he jeopardize his staggering accomplishments and his proud ancestry? And why take on such a lost cause? Why not lay low, say nothing? Unless he could no longer keep silent after seeing what the intact Booth diary had revealed.

What could have been contained on those now missing pages from Booth's diary? What had Lafayetter Baker seen? Names of co-conspirators? Threats? Linkages to powerful puppeteers and maybe even the sitting President? What could have been there to motivate Baker to make such claims in the tumultuous and dangerous years in Washington, DC, right after the Civil War? Surely, Baker, no stranger to the corruption and insidious ways of Washington, knew the consequences of his allegations and the vicious retributions that would come.

Baker claimed he quickly scanned the diary after it was given him by Congers. The diary, he said, was really a calendar printed for 1864. It was used by Booth as a journal and was dated 1865 in Booth's handwriting -- the year of the assassination. Baker claimed in nervous, difficult testimony that there were pages in the diary, pages now missing, which contained extensive writing, some lists, hand drawn maps and ledgers, and drawings. The sparring between Baker and the members of Congress went on for pages.

McAdams stopped reading. Strong stuff, he thought as he went back to the bed. He picked up the House Judiciary Committee report. The Judiciary Committee was to look especially into charges that Booth's diary had been withheld, suppressed, and altered, but no findings ever were issued on the topic. The Committee eventually cleared Lincoln's successor, President Andrew Johnson, of complicity in the assassination and found no conspirators beyond those hung and those sent to a remote island off Florida.

McAdams closed his eyes and threw the report back onto the bed. How could the Committee fail even to publish a word on the Booth diary, if only to say there was nothing to report? He smelled another effort to stifle truth.

It was after midnight but O'Connell wouldn't care. He picked up the phone. The ringing ended with the sound of mad groping at the other end.

"What?" spat Ed O'Connell as he found the phone.

"Wake up, Eddie ... It's Mac."

"Mac, what d'ya want? Christ, it's Monday tomorrow. Gimme a break, will ya?" McAdams' old housemate lay flat on his back with the phone to his ear, his eyes squeezed shut, his mouth a tunnel of cotton. O'Connell forced his fingers to rub his forehead. He needed more aspirin.

McAdams smiled. O'Connell was all right. He was one of McAdams' oldest friends. The devoted hell-raiser would do anything for him, anywhere, anytime.

"Hey! Asshole!" McAdams replied. "Wake up! I need help."

"What? Are you fucked up somewhere?" O'Connell was chief counsel over at the House Judiciary Committee, twice divorced and most assuredly all by his lonesome right now. He was alone most weekends despite valiant, pitiful attempts to correct the situation.

"I need the records of the two House Committees that looked into the assassination of Lincoln."

"Oh, man, you ARE gone. You call me tomorrow and fuck yourself in the meantime." McAdams heard the rustling of bed covers as O'Connell rolled over. Dial tone would be the next sound he heard.

"Ed, wait! I need the records of those Committees. I have to see what evidence came before them. I have to see everything, even if it's sealed or confidential."

O'Connell's eyes fluttered open. He sat up in his bedroom across the river from Washington, in Rosslyn, Virginia. He ran a hand through what was left of his dirty blond hair.

"I can't do that, Macky-poo, they're sealed."

"Ed, that was over 125 years ago. Surely anything sealed that long is not required to stay sealed. It's an oversight, right? Can't my Chairman make a special request to yours?"

"125 years? ... Mac, what 125 years? I can't ..., I shouldn't even be saying this. Those records were opened and re-sealed about 30 years ago! By a special House Subcommittee order obtained by the FBI in executive session."

McAdams grew rigid. "Ed, these are the Lincoln files I'm talking about -- not the Kennedy files, not even the fucking McKinley files, for Christ's sake!"

"Mac", persisted O'Connell, "read my lips. No - can - do. Come over tomorrow and I'll show you the Committee order and the summary of what was sealed. That's the best I can do. OK? Good bye." He hung up before McAdams could tell him where he was, that he wouldn't be there for a few days.

O'Connell made a fervent wish as he fell back in his bed. "Stay away from this, Macky. Just stay away, you dumb shit." He stared up at the ceiling as sleep was no longer possible.

Why, McAdams wondered, would O'Connell be so conversant on FBI-Lincoln trivia at this hour? And what the fuck was the FBI doing in executive session with a House Subcommittee on the subject of the Lincoln assassination?

Chapter Seventeen

McAdams awoke thickheaded the next morning. His ears rang with the sound of footsteps and his own heavy breathing. Morning had revealed to him, finally, the exit from the alleyway he had groped along all night long.

He sat up, lit a cigarette and smoked it in bed, orienting himself before he quickly showered. He got into his jeans, loafers, no-name navy blue polo shirt and navy blue blazer, checked out and downed thick orange juice, strong coffee and a greasy breakfast at "Tammy's" next door to the hotel. Tammy was sweet and alive, all peaches and cream skin and dark brown eyes, peppering him with banter and free cups of coffee. He retreated as soon as he could for Randolph-Macon College.

The College dwarfed the town of Ashland. The campus of 100 acres had about 40 buildings. He found Crockett's without a problem. As he wandered down the academic halls, an eerie and familiar feeling came over him. He was missing class or had a report due that was three weeks late. He wasn't going to graduate! He moderated his breath and calmed himself. There was no problem, of course, he had already graduated, two decades ago.

"Mr. McAdams, pleasure to meet you, suh," boomed Professor Crockett in a loud, thick drawl. Crockett was a contemporary of Tidback - about 60 years old. He had wavy, white hair with random black streaks, stood over 6 and a half feet tall, and was lean and lanky. He had a wide, crooked smile as he stretched out his catcher's mitt of a hand.

"It's Mac. Please!"

"Well, then, fo'get the 'Professuh' stuff and call me Rufus. Now, did you know that the Confederacy used this campus to train its intelligence personnel in the clandestine activities for which the South was so famous during the war?"

"No, can't say that I did." McAdams took a seat in front of Crockett's desk. He felt like he would need a pad and pen.

"Yes, suh, it's true," replied Crockett as he lowered himself into his chair. "This place is steeped in history. It's why David came here and why he stayed. But enough of that. I can go on and on, and often do. Now, how can I hep you?"

McAdams got to the point. "I think that Tidback was on to something big, something terrible that took away his life."

Crockett sat back. "Well, the FBI and the Virginia State Police agree with you, I reckon. They have been most diligent in talking to David's colleagues. And they cataloged a number of his documents for shipment."

Crockett gestured toward the three boxes in the corner of his office. "Federal Express is to pick them up this morning."

McAdams glanced at the boxes. Three boxes each about three feet high and two feet wide were in the corner. He got up and walked over to them. They were headed for the FBI at the corner of 10th and Pennsylvania Avenues in Washington, DC.

A puzzled look crossed McAdams' face "Did you say State Police? I thought the FBI was in charge."

"I think the State boys were along just for the ride. You'd know if you lived in these parts for very long that the Virginia State Police often come along just for the ride." They smiled at each other knowingly.

"Do you have a subpoena, suh?"

"Yes, as I told you on the phone, I have a Committee subpoena duces tecum which allows me to examine the offices of Professor Tidback and "tecum" with me whatever I choose."

"Well, help yourself," Crockett chuckled. "I'll be glad to show you around. How 'bout some coffee first?" McAdams nodded eagerly and Professor Crockett pointed to a table in the corner with a drip pot, a tower of Styrofoam cups and a collection in a bowl of sugar and Cremora bags and stirrers.

McAdams got up and poured a cup for each of them. "I take mine black, thanks," said Crockett. McAdams delivered the coffee and took a chair.

"Rufus, why was Professor Tidback shot?"

"Mr. McAdams, I don't know." Had he a window in his office, Crockett would have walked over to it, scanned the horizon and run his fingers through his hair. Instead, he looked directly into McAdams' eyes.

"Mr. McAdams ..."

"Please," he held up his hand, "Mac..."

"Right. Mac it is. Sorry... Professor Tidback was a thorough, insightful and gifted researcher and teacher. He had a rather long list of publications - all dealing with the Civil War. In the last few years, he studied the clandestine side of the Confederate war.

"He did the best research to date on the Confederate Secret Service, the guerrilla activities of the South during the war, and the precedent these activities established for today's CIA and Defense Advanced Research Planning Agency. You know," Crockett winked, "the South waged a smarter war. You Yankees only won because of your superior industry and overwhelming numbers."

McAdams nodded wisely, conceding nothing.

"David produced a number of works on the Confederate Secret Service," continued Crockett. "He did a lot of research into the Copperheads, the Sons of Liberty, and other groups of Southern sympathizers in the north during the Civil War. He was beginning to hone in on the Lincoln assassination. He believed that the assassination was the result of a plan by Confederate President Jefferson Davis and his Secret Service, and others, and that Booth was chosen to execute the plan."

Crockett was warming up to the subject. "Professor Tidback was secretive about his work. I think he moved to Mississippi this school year to be isolated from others. I don't, for the life of me, know what he found there."

Crockett leaned forward. "Now, the FBI and the State Police didn't give a 'coon's hide what I think, but since you do, I want to tell ya that I think David came across something."

"Why do you say that?"

"Well, the damned US Justice Department came down here. They were lookin' for David after he had gone off to Mississippi. Seems David had sent in some Freedom of Information Act requests to Justice using this address. He was lookin' for government records on the Lincoln assassination. Recent records, having to do with the diary of John Wilkes Booth."

McAdams' hand twitched at Crockett's pronouncement. Coffee spilled down the sides of his cup. Crockett noticed.

"I thought you'd want to know about that, son. You see, the FBI investigators that packed those boxes over there didn't know the first thing about the Justice Department coming down here. Didn't have any inkling about any Freedom of Information Act requests. I wasn't gonna cue 'em in either."

"How long ago?" McAdams finally croaked. His throat had gone dry. "Justice ... How long ago did they come around?"

"Oh, I'd say January or February of this year. And ever since then the Virginia State Police has been coming 'round ev'ry few weeks poking their heads in to see if ol' David had shown up. They, like everyone else, thought he'd gone up to Canada on a private sabbatical."

"I have to tell you, Rufus, that kind of a response from Justice on a FOIA request is really, really unusual. ... Did they identify themselves? Do you have any names?"

"Oh, they flashed me something. They were government types."

"Do you have copies of Tidback's FOIA requests?"

"I don't. First I heard of 'em was from the Justice boys.

"I, I, don't have to tell you I miss David," said Crockett in a suddenly lowered voice. "I don't know what he got himself into. He was a gentleman, a friend. ... Excuse me." Crockett pulled a handkerchief from his rear pocket and wiped his eyes.

"No excuses needed," replied a subdued McAdams. He stood and walked over to the boxes in the corner, giving Crockett some space. "May I?"

"Please ... " Crockett threw him a letter opener.

McAdams crouched down, sliced into the plastic tape and fumbled through the first box. The second and third boxes contained the same as the first - copies of publications by Tidback, course syllabi, internal departmental correspondence, research books, and Tidback's research notes scrupulously recorded and indexed on legal size yellow pads and index cards. There was nothing that spoke from beyond the grave, yielding at last the secret of why Tidback was killed.

"Professor," he said as he stood, "could you show me Professor Tidback's office?" He moved to the doorway.

Crockett gathered himself up. "Of course." He picked up

his cup and downed a big gulp. "Here are the keys. You can look into his old cubicle too, if you want, but you'll find nothin' of his. It was cleaned out a long time ago and someone else has been usin' it since."

Crockett hesitated and McAdams waited. "You mentioned on the phone somethin' about Mississippi. I'd like to join you -- if I may intrude. I'd like to collect Professor Tidback's effects there - if anything's there, that is - and bring 'em back home. I need to get that over with before ..."

"Say no more. I'm on the 7:25 flight tonight on US Air out of Richmond. I'd love the company. I'll come for you about 6:30 and we'll take my car to the airport. How's that?"

"I'll be ready. In the meantime," he chuckled, "let me show you the way to David's den." His humor had begun to return.

Chapter Eighteen

McAdams and Crockett walked down a few corridors before Crockett stopped in front of a closed door. "This is it. Our recent visitors from the FBI and the State Police have ransacked the place. I haven't had the time to clean it up."

He pointed to the keys. "Try the round key."

Crockett winked before he lumbered down the hall. McAdams turned to the door to Tidback's old office, turned the key and entered. He flicked on the overhead light.

Books and papers were strewn everywhere in the mid-sized room. The desk was piled high with folders, magazines and blue-covered student composition books, some of which bore large letter grades in bright red felt tip ink. The floor-to-ceiling bookcases behind and to the right of Tidback's desk were packed with ponderous, dog-eared books. Whatever the FBI took didn't make a dent in the room.

He sat down in Tidback's swivel chair and looked around. He thumbed through the piles on the desk. He opened drawers and pushed things here and there, searching for anything that would give him a clue to the secret Tidback possessed. The bookshelves behind him held only Civil War books - the greatest titles and the most obscure. He recognized some from his history courses, others from his own recent look at Congressional inquiries into Lincoln's assassination.

The shelf on the side wall had more of the same. At eye level were titles dealing with the Secret Service of the Confederacy, the South's guerrilla warfare, and Lincoln's assassination. He took from the shelf Lafayette Baker's *History of the Secret Service* and placed the large book on the desk in front of him. On the bottom shelf were copies of Tidback's publications from historical journals. He had written a lot - over 20 scholarly articles besides his books.

McAdams leaned over to look at the books on the bottom shelf. There were a number on recent Presidential assassinations. Kennedy. McKinley. Garfield. He straightened up as too much blood flowed to his head, giving a surge of new life to the pounding in his left temple from last night.

A noise behind him froze McAdams. He spun in the chair and stopped abruptly. Standing in Tidback's doorway was a young woman. She hesitated on the threshold, tense, ready to spring off like a deer on long, slender legs. She had dark brown eyes that bore in on him from under black eyebrows and lashes. She had dark brown, frizzy hair that cascaded in thick waves to her shoulders from a part in the middle of her head. Somewhere between Hawaiian and black, she was regal in appearance with a delicate, slightly upturned nose, high cheekbones and perfect skin the color of light copper. She stood there in denim shorts, a brown, sleeveless vest sweater and work boots, poised, watching him, thinking, ready to bolt.

The quiet between them pounded in his ears. He smiled. "Hi."

"Hey," she replied. She jerked his head in his direction. "What are you doing here?" Suspicion clouded her face.

"I work for the Congressional Committee where Professor Tidback was testifying when he got shot." She winced and he instantly regretted his words. "You?"

"Well, he taught me last year. ... I liked him a lot. I was just walking past here." She gestured absently into the hallway. "And ... and I, uh, I saw the door open."

Sure .... He started reeling her in. "Maybe you can help me. Could you sit down for a bit, and talk?"

"Are you, like, a cop?"

"Not really. I'm an investigator working for Congress. Right now I am handling the Committee looking into the King assassination. I don't have jurisdiction over who killed Tidback, or why, unless it somehow relates to the work of my Committee. And since Tidback got himself killed testifying in front of my Committee, and I do mean right in front, then the 'who' and the 'why' behind Tidback's murder must somehow relate to what I do."

His eyebrows arched. "Am I making any sense?"

She let a small laugh slip, liking his directness. She breezed into the room, easing herself softly into the chair in front of Tidback's desk. "Yeah," she nodded. "Perfect sense." She flipped an errant strand of hair behind her left ear.

"So, what was Tidback like? Was he a good teacher?"

"Oh, the best," she bubbled, showing a flash of perfect white teeth. Realizing she was revealing too much, too easily, she settled back in the chair. "... All the students loved him. He liked to teach, he dug into new areas of research. His classes were really exciting. He's, he *was*, heading the team reviewing my graduate thesis. Actually, my doctoral thesis. I was about to finish up my P.H.D. in American history with him."

"I'm getting the impression that people liked him a lot."

He paused. She nodded.

"What did he come across in his work that would attract killers? He said something about an ongoing Lincoln conspiracy. Do you know what he was talking about?"

She shrugged.

"And now the FBI and the state police are all over this. They're gonna mess things up, lose the threads that may string us back to the killers. They don't care about Tidback, or what he had to say. I hope they're trying to bring his killer to justice, but I'm beginning to wonder. They blew it with the killers of Martin Luther King."

His words caught him by surprise. In trying to get her to talk, he was giving shape to his own unformed thoughts.

She studied him. He was straight. She could feel that. And he cared about things. Kind of like Professor Tidback. Maybe he could help, she mused.

He studied her face. She had something to say. What would get her going? What was the key? "The cops," he ventured as he looked around, "cleaned the place out this weekend. I can't find anything of any use. They beat me by a couple of days."

"They were here?" She moved to the edge of her seat and cast an eye at the file cabinet behind her. "Where?"

"Well, they checked out this office, his cubicle, what used to be his living quarters," he replied. He got up to look in the file cabinet she had eyed. "What's your name?" he asked as he moved behind her. "I'm John McAdams. People call me Mac."

"Linda Walker." Her head rotated as she followed him.

"Hello, Linda Walker. Nice to meet you. Excuse me while I

go through these file cabinets behind you." He started flipping file folders. "Hmmm ... Student files, departmental files, copies of exams, history association stuff."

She watched him over her shoulder. He stopped and passed behind her again and sat down again behind the desk. "Linda, what was he researching these days? Do you know?"

She screwed her pale pink lips to the side as she grew thoughtful. "Well, I was his researcher and graduate assistant the last two years, even though he was in Mississippi ..."

She saw his surprise. "Yeah, I knew he was at Mississippi. Just Professor Crockett and I knew where he was, although Crockett would never say. Anyway, Professor Tidback was hung up about the Confederate Secret Service. I helped him research his articles. It was so exciting finding out what the Confederates were up to."

Her enthusiasm lit up her face. She leaned forward as she spoke about her work. "You know," she said, "those guys were the first real government spooks in the country."

"What guys?"

She chuckled at his spaciness and sat back. "The Confederate Secret Service, Mac! Hel-LOOOO? ..."

"Oh. Right!" He smiled in embarrassment. "But where was his research taking him?" He pointed to the books on his left, on the bottom shelf. "Was he beginning to look into other Presidential assassinations? Ones since Lincoln's?"

"He started looking at the profiles of assassins in the twentieth century. Well, assassins since the Booth-Confederacy alliance. I know because, when he was in Mississippi, he asked me to get him books and articles."

"That's it?"

"Well, yeah. Right around that time, late last fall or so, he told me that he thought someone was watching him or following him. He was always very careful about when and where he would call me, and how I was to reply to him. All the books I took out had to be in my name, not his. He was real, real secretive. Real anxious. It frightened me."

McAdams sat up and rested his arms on Tidback's desk. "Why did he go to Mississippi?"

"He said he had to get away from here, from whoever was watching him. He said he had some researching to do that he could only do there."

"When did you last speak to him?"

"It was late in the week before he died. He called me." Tears welled up in her eyes.

"And...?"

"He was pumped. Said he was coming back east, real soon. That there was some big news I would hear about. He had found something real big that was going to put Randolph-Macon on the map. He never told me what he meant, never told me about his testimony. ... Nothing." Her face registered betrayal at not being included in Tidback's closing intrigue.

McAdams leaned back and tapped his folded hands against his lips. He turned and his eyes went back to the books on the bottom shelf. There were a couple dealing with the Kennedy assassination. Others that were general treatments of political assassinations and twentieth century assassins. Nothing on Martin Luther King.

Strange ... He bent over and picked the books off the bottom shelf and put them on the desk.

"No one will miss these, will they?"

"I don't think so." She stood up and moved to the doorway. "I should go," she mumbled.

He got up and hurried over to give her his card. "Call me if anything else comes to mind, or you just want to talk about all this. If you come to DC, I'll even show you the real city. Not just the tourist stuff."

She hesitated, not yet entering the hallway.

"What ...?" he ventured, throwing his last lasso.

"There's something else."

"What?"

"You didn't ask me where I delivered those books I took out for the Professor." She was intent, scolding. "I didn't mail them off, you know. I left them in a loft he kept above a garage about a half mile from here. No one knows about it. No one knows he stayed there often."

"No one?" he choked. "Not even Crockett?"

"No one. Professor Tidback wanted it that way."

"Can we go there, now? Time is very important ..."

"OK. I need to get the key." She lowered her head, embarrassed, and looked up at him under impossibly thick eyelashes. "I left it here."

She walked over to the file cabinet, opened the drawer with the student files, found hers and retrieved a key taped to the outside bottom rear of her folder. "I thought it would be safe here. I didn't think cops would come. I was lucky."

"You sure were. Listen, you head for the loft first. I'll meet you there. There's no use in us being seen together." He told her about the pick-up truck that followed him to Ashland and the two rough customers inside. If he were being watched, he didn't want her caught in the cross hairs. A spasm shot through the dead skin of the scar on his cheek. Maybe he should have been this careful, this thoughtful, long ago, when he and ... Anne .... He stopped, before he felt like too much of a shit maybe, and shook it off.

She rattled off the directions to the loft and again started to leave. "Linda ...," he said before she disappeared, "thanks for trusting me."

She wrapped her arms around herself and leaned against the doorway. She was alone and vulnerable. "I needed someone to help me with this," she said at last. She stopped and looked at McAdams for a moment.

"I'll see you there," she smiled. "Don't take all day!" And then she was gone. The room was suddenly empty.

Chapter Nineteen

It was easier to drive. He left the car on the street a few blocks away from the address Linda had given him, and then headed back in a circuitous route.

The loft was over an empty detached garage next to a vacant residence. He hurried down the length of the tree-lined driveway and through the garage door that swung up. He moved into the shadows inside the garage and looked back to see if there was anyone in the house or the street watching, or following. The street was silent but possessed the eerie air he always felt in suburbia, like someone unseen was standing sentry behind some Venetian blind or drawn curtain. The house was empty, with gaping windows that were unshuttered and undraped. It was black inside.

He walked over to the staircase to the loft and began to climb. The first step squealed like a stuck pig and a spike of anxiety shot up through McAdams' back. He kept going. Knocking twice quickly and lightly on the door at the top of the stairs, he twisted the doorknob and went inside. Linda sat in the middle of the room on a wooden chair, her bare legs pressed together and her hands on her knees. The chair looked like it would fall apart if she leaned too far in any direction.

She blew out a huge breath and smiled broadly at him. "Hi. I sure was hoping that was you down there. I was getting real nervous."

He smiled back and took in the room around her. It was a perfect little money-raiser for a family needing the income from renting out a small room so close to the College. From the outside there was no way the local property tax assessor could guess at the existence of what had to be called, technically, a property "improvement." But it did the trick.

The room had no windows and there were piles of books and papers lining the walls. A big, oak desk and chair sulked at the far, shadowy end of the room. Just beyond where Linda sat was a rickety dinette table and, next to it, a small refrigerator hummed noisily. A standing lamp leaned precariously over a lumpy, naked mattress, a single, to the right of the door he had used. Beyond that stood a tub with an overhead shower faucet mounted on a pipe that grew out of the floor. The pipe held up a large, rusty ring with a curtain on it that hung over the tub like an oversized basketball hoop. Next to the tub was a metal commode.

A lamp glowed on the desk behind Linda. She had turned on the standing one next to him, too.

"Cozy," he joked, trying to relieve the tension.

"I haven't been here in weeks," she answered. "Professor Tidback wanted privacy. I could only come and drop off these books and papers inside the garage below us. He ... he probably stayed here the night before he went to DC to testify."

"Let's see what he left behind." The papers and books were organized neatly in knee-high piles. Nothing was placed carelessly anywhere. "Neat guy, huh?"

She nodded vigorously. "Meticulous ..."

What surrounded them looked like a whole lot more of what was piled in Tidback's office. No written confessions, no highly incriminating evidence. Just more on the Confederacy, Booth, Baker, and a whole lot of original and published material on late 19th and 20th century assassinations.

Linda followed behind McAdams as he looked through the books and papers on Tidback's desk. Every now and then she would explain what was in his hands. After a while the room grew stuffy and his blazer came off and landed on the oak desk.

He moved to the floor and the walls, tapping them and sliding his fingertips back and forth across surfaces. When he opened the refrigerator Linda giggled. A jar of instant coffee and a pint of milk greeted him. The milk would expire next week. A hot pot and two-burner Coleman stove were on top of the refrigerator.

He sat down on the mattress, resting his arms on top of his knees. "Did you rent this place for Tidback?"

"Uh huh. I told the guy I wanted to garage my car. We both winked at that one. Especially when I wrote him a check in advance for a year's worth of water and electricity."

"Did Tidback have access to the empty house in front?"

"Nope."

The only place left to look was underneath the furniture. He lifted the mattress and pushed it away, exposing several loose floorboards. Deep scratches and groove marks around the edge of the boards indicated they had been pried up.

His eyes met Linda's. "What have we here?"

He went down on his right knee and slipped his car keys under the boards. Five were loose and they came up easy. Underneath the boards was an opening about the size of a case of wine. Resting in the compartment under the floor was a jumbo-sized, plastic freezer bag. It held old documents.

He pulled the bag out of the hole and looked at Linda. Her eyebrows rose in anticipation.

She followed him across the room to the desk. He moved his jacket and pulled the desk lamp closer to the middle where he placed the plastic bag. His mouth felt dry.

There were two old, yellowed pieces of paper arranged side by side within the bag. The first was a diary page from a small journal with a printed date of June 12, 1864 that was scratched through. The handwriting on the page began with a different date -- March 21, 1865. About three weeks before Lincoln's assassination. The signature was flowery and ornate.

"John Wilkes Booth!" McAdams whispered. He sat down, his breathing shallow. Linda leaned closer. "It's from Booth's diary," he said in a voice barely above a church whisper. "Holy shit!" she answered.

Scrawled on the diary page was a note to a "Secretary Nathaniel Brock and the Committee," without any other address. Taylor Brock's distant look the morning of Tidback's murder came to him now. Oh yeah, McAdams thought, Taylor Brock knew David Tidback all right. Real, real well.

McAdams read the short letter out loud, struggling to catch some light from the lamp as Linda crowded in.

Dear Sirs:

Last night we tried to abduct the President on the grounds of the Soldiers' Home in Washington. We must have been tricked, else a traitor is in our midst.

The lot of us approached the President's wagon as it made its way along the concourse of the grounds - its usual route. It was nighttime and no stars were out so we could not see well. We approached the wagon, prepared to take the President and kill his guards as we were instructed. But coming upon the wagon, we found no guards and only Secretary Chase.

The President was nowhere to be found. You can imagine our most profound disappointment. I beg your indulgence and your patience.

We are preparing to kill the President now -- I will take that bold stroke for our country. It is the only way. The others will take the remaining leadership, so to cut off with one stroke the head of the monster killing our brothers, our wives, our children, our nation and our future.

Sic semper tyrannis,
John Wilkes Booth

McAdams stared at the page, running a finger lightly over Booth's signature. "Sic semper tyrannis," he breathed. The words that some witnesses said Booth shouted out after he jumped to the stage at Ford's Theater, his evil act done, limping with a broken leg as he began the desperate escape that ended some two weeks later in a cabin in Virginia.

Linda shivered. "What's on the other page?" she whispered.

The second sheet was from the same diary. At the top of the yellowed journal page was the caption "O.A.K." scrawled in a thin line. Underneath was an oath of some sort. Beneath that was a drawing, maybe an impression left by a stamp, showing Lady Liberty's head.

McAdams read aloud the oath. He had to push Linda gently back from the already paltry light spilling onto the page.

> No free mason, minuteman, federalist, republican, judge or any false patriot shall be allowed to interfere with the enjoyment and pursuit of property -- either by constitution, law, plebiscite, referendum, military rule, imprisonment or taxation -- without answering to our punishment. By such work shall We the People secure the promise of our Revolution and our Nation.

McAdams gently turned the freezer bag over. They saw a 3" by 5" index card behind the two yellowed pages.

"It's his writing," gasped Linda, "... Professor Tidback's." The card held eight lines of his penmanship:

✓ 1865 - Lincoln - Booth
? 1881 - Garfield - Guiteau
   1901 - McKinley - Czolgosy
✓ 1912 - TR - Shrank
   1933 - FDR - Zangara
✓ 1935 - Long - Weiss
? 1963 - Kennedy - Oswald
? 1968 - King - Ray

"What is this?" asked McAdams in a hoarse voice.

Linda ran a finger down the list. "Professor Tidback has check marks next to Lincoln, Teddy Roosevelt and Long. ... Would that be Huey Long ... of Louisiana?"

McAdams nodded. "Must be. He was assassinated ... in Baton Rouge when he was a US. Senator poised to beat FDR in the next Presidential election. Shot by a doctor named Weiss."

She screwed up her face. "What about TR - Teddy Roosvelt? He wasn't assassinated ..."

"No, he wasn't, but he was wounded in an attack as I recall. By this 'Shrank' on the Professor's list. I know all this history because, when I got ready for the King hearings, I checked how the government handled other assassination investigations "

"But what do the check marks mean? That there's some sort of relationship between the three assassins or assassinations?"

"Well, when I check something off on a list it means it's been done or that there's a connection between the things I have checked. And when I use a question mark ..."

"Like the Professor did next to the names of the assassinated Garfield, Kennedy and King ...,"

"... it means that I don't know what the hell the answer is!"

"I wonder," Linda breathed, "what the question was."

McAdams burst from the chair and lurched to the center of the room. The index card bothered him more than the Booth letter or the OAK creed. He even forgot for a moment that Booth had reported on his assassination attempt to a "Secretary Nathaniel Brock." He looked at her with eyes pulled into darkened sockets.

"He wanted to know whether Booth's 'Committee' was connected to all these assassinations and assassination attempts. His answer was 'yes' in the case of Lincoln, TR and Huey Long. His answer was 'don't know' in the case of Garfield, Kennedy and King. He hadn't even gotten to McKinley and FDR yet."

Linda looked puzzled. "I know McKinley was assassinated. Did someone go after FDR?"

"Sure did," he answered. "Zangara tried to shoot FDR as he passed by in a motorcade. He missed and hit the Mayor of Chicago instead."

Linda felt the room envelope them in the silence that hung in the air after he spoke. The air grew warm and palpable in the yellow light cast by the wobbly lights. McAdams watched her as she fell back into her chair. She brought her feet up to the seat and wrapped her arms around her knees.

"This is Tidback's conspiracy, Linda, and his research plan." McAdams pointed to their discovery on the desk. "He came to Washington to talk about all this."

Tears boiled up in her eyes. "This is too ..."

"Bizarre? ... Frightening?"

"It ..., I don't know. It just doesn't make sense, Mac. I mean, how's this 'Committee' that Booth wrote to involved with the assassination decades later of Huey Long? And Kennedy? And Martin Luther King? ... What's the connection?"

She looked at the simple note card and the yellowed papers

nestled neatly in an everyday freezer bag. "Something's missing, Mac."

He walked to the desk and put the bag inside one of the books he had taken from Tidback's office. He crouched down in front of her and placed his hands on her shoulders.

"Linda, think out loud with me. We have to find out if Tidback had more research like this." She nodded and waited for him to continue.

"... Just before he was shot, he said he had 'proof' of a present day conspiracy that threatened another Civil War. Now, unless he was prone to exaggeration..."

She shook her head emphatically.

"... then he had other documents hidden somewhere. Or he was hot on the trail of something promising. Maybe something that could explain the index card."

"Maybe that was why he went to Mississippi ...," she offered.

"But why did he pick up and come back to Washington?"

"To testify in front of your Committee. Because - at long last - he had something to say, to show ..."

"... That might be it. Tidback had what he needed, maybe not everything, but what he needed. And he came to Washington to shove his findings up Senator Taylor Brock's ass - the descendent of John Wilkes Booth's pen pal. And he wanted to do it right in front of the national press and TV. Where else could he reach so many, and so many of the right people, without someone distorting his message? The final hearing of the King Assassination Committee. ... Maybe even live, on TV. He probably thought he'd be safe, too ..."

"What ... what do you think he was going to say?"

"I don't know! But someone knew what he had on his mind. And they knew he was coming to Washington. The Virginia State Police and the Justice Department knew Tidback was on to something. They hounded him about his Lincoln research for several months before he came to Washington. Brock knew who Tidback was. No doubt about it, you could see it on Brock's face that morning. And Lewis Shephard, Brock's chief staffer, showed up out of nowhere, right after the shooting, to see if the job was done. I'm sure of it. Yes, indeed, Tidback had something and someone knew it. Someone knew enough in time to find a hit man, plant a gun and steal his testimony. And someone knew enough to have two thugs follow me here to Randolph-Macon to see what I might dig up in David Tidback's backyard."

He glanced at his watch and stood. Time to get Crockett and head for Mississippi.

"What'll we do now?" she whispered, her eyes darkened with worry.

"Time to split. This place feels like a tomb. Ours." McAdams looked around. The walls were closing in. He reached for the book and freezer bag on the desk.

She placed her hand on his arm. "But what do WE do next? What do you want ME to do?"

"You keep low." He watched her eyes widen in protest. "You got to promise me that, Linda. Whoever wanted Tidback dead did a good job. You don't want to be next."

"But I can't back out now. Mac, you got to let me help!"

He wondered - and hoped - if there were any way to keep her out of this. She had so much going for her, so far to go. Biting her inner cheek nervously, she watched him, waiting.

"OK, OK," he said at last. "Maybe you can keep your eye on this place and on what happens here at Randolph-Macon. You're still Tidback's research assistant, wrapping things up. Use that to see what he was looking into, to see if he had any more of these hideouts. Contact the University of Mississippi and follow up on his work there. Use my card to call me at my office once a week. Or call Mossingame's office through Capitol Hill Information. But call from a public payphone."

He paused and looked at her, a small smile playing out on his lips. "Is that enough?"

She nodded.

"And listen," he said, "no one - including Crockett - can know or suspect what we've found here. No one can know this place exists. OK?" She shook her head again.

A noise came to them from below, from the garage under their feet. They looked at each other and waited. The first step squealed. McAdams looked around for a weapon, anything. He saw books, paper, lamps, a chair. "Jesus," he breathed.

Treading lightly, he stepped over to the refrigerator. It was a good thirty pounds in weight. He pulled the plug. He picked up a lamp from the desk and swung it back and forth, testing its heft, and then he unplugged it as well. He stuck the book and freezer bag into the back of his pants under the waistline and put the lamp beside the doorframe. "When I count three," he whispered to Linda, you yank that door open and I'll heave ho." He nodded to the refrigerator.

A look of disbelief crossed her face.

"Now!" He bent over to pick up the fridge. With a loud grunt he hoisted it above his head, his arms unsteady, his mind telling him he could do it despite all the missed work-outs, all the late nights hunched over papers and computer screens. He tottered over to the door to the garage, and took a deep breath.

"... Three!"

She yanked and he stepped out into the landing at the top of the stairs. His eyes met a startled white face below, halfway up the stairs, a face obscured by a long, bushy beard and a dirty baseball cap pulled down low over blood-shot eyes. It was one of the rednecks who had followed him in the pick-up truck, the young one with the backward baseball cap. The man's sneer suddenly disappeared, replaced by a look of raw fear as his eyes moved above McAdams' head to the square of steel and chrome that hovered briefly. McAdams grunted and heaved and the refrigerator shot from his hands, seeming to pause for a brief moment before accelerating down towards a face that was now open to emit a scream that never had time to erupt. Instead, there was a crunch of bone and tissue as the missile hit the man squarely in the face. The force of heavy, moving object meeting flexible, wobbly man was such that both flew backwards down the stairs faster than McAdams could follow, lamp in hand.

By the time he reached the bottom of the stairs, the redneck lay sprawled on his back, his head twisted awkwardly to one direction, the refrigerator off to one side in the other direction, its contents strewn over the concrete garage floor. McAdams' hand with the lamp dropped to his side. He was done. There was no need for additional defensive measures. The youth's face was a bright red pulp, his top row of teeth taken by the brunt of the blow and simply swept from his jaw leaving bloody stumps. Shards of teeth lay scattered over the floor. The baseball cap was nowhere to be seen and the skin on the man's forehead had been peeled back to reveal a bare snatch of skull. Blood was gathering in a glimmering pool under the man's head. As the adrenaline pulsed through his body, McAdams briefly worried that he might have killed the punk, but then a hand twitched feebly and a soft groan escaped through the bubbling blood and he knew that, this time, there would be no awkward coroner's questions to answer.

He turned away to look up the stairs for Linda and that small movement saved his life. The blade of a skinning knife flashed past his cheek, close enough for him to feel the movement of air. The steel flashed, it looked enormous and McAdams knew that one well-aimed cut and he would bleed to death in a few heartbeats. He had been there before, with Anne that night long ago. He had felt the searing slice of a deep cut through soft flesh and the harsh thud when it hit bone. He had felt the flapping skin, remembered trying to slap it back in place, the blood coursing down his face.

Instinctively his right forearm came up to drive the knife arm away from his face and he turned under the arm and into the man who was still moving towards him. McAdams spotted a cap with a Confederate flag atop a ponytailed man, the passenger from the pick-up with the thick arms and thick tattoos. McAdams' left fist followed the movement of his body and drove forward into the beefy stomach of his attacker. He felt the jar of pain straight up to his shoulder and he realized he was in desperate trouble. He was badly outmatched.

He fell to the floor from the collision and crabbed away backwards, trying desperately to get some space between himself and the second thug. His assailant was huge, standing over him now, and bigger than he imagined, more massive, with the arms of a lumberjack or a home run leader. He felt the bile of raw fear force its way up his throat, threatening to spill into his mouth and onto the floor. He would soon be dead or maimed. He suddenly noticed the book from the loft, with Tidback's notes and the diary pages, was on the floor, open, next to the redneck's feet, dislodged during their initial violent encounter.

The man read the fear in his eyes and his mouth opened into a gap-toothed grin. He looked down and spotted the book and smiled. He began to move slowly forward towards McAdams, breathing heavily, the hunting knife making lazy circles through the air as he searched for the opening that would begin to slice Mac apart. Already, the investigator could feel the slither of blade through flesh, could smell his own fear and could taste the acrid flavor of blood he knew would rise into his lungs to choke out his life. There was a lunge and McAdams felt fire shoot up his left arm.

"I'm gonna do you, boy," the knifeman growled, smirking at his first strike. "Cut you long and deep for what you just did to my kid brother. I'm gonna make you hurt. And I'm gonna like hearing your ass scream real loud while I'm cutting you up."

McAdams picked up a flurry of movement down the stairs. He risked a quick glance. It was Linda.

"Get out!" he screamed, blood now coming from his left arm. "For Christ's sake, get away!"

Linda just stood there, carefully eyeing the man with the knife. He looked over and his eyes widened. He took in every inch of her long body.

"Perfect," he laughed. "Just perfect. I'll just finish him off and then I'll get you for dessert. You just stay right there, muffin, don't you go nowheres."

McAdams prepared to run at the man in what he knew would be a suicidal act that might just buy Linda enough time to get away. But, before he could move, she rose on to her toes, did a little hypnotic dance, spinning once, twice, three times before lashing out with her right foot. It connected with a loud smack against the knifeman's nose. There was a crack of breaking bone, a fountain of blood and he reeled back with a squeal of surprise and pain. But Linda was moving again, poised on one foot now, the other flicking out in a series of balletic probes, each looking elegant and effortless, but each snapping against the neck and the face of the man. There was power in every probe and his face became a bloody mess. With the growl of a wounded bear, dazed, he stretched out both arms and ran towards Linda, his arms ready to contain her, to engulf her slim frame and squeeze out her life. But she danced to one side and as he charged past connected with a long kick that cracked into the back of his neck. The force combined with his own momentum drove the man headfirst into the cinderblock wall. He paused there for a moment before sliding to the ground, leaving behind a trail of blood and mucous on the whitewash.

Linda moved quickly across to McAdams and tenderly lifted his arm.

"Are you alright?" she asked gently, eyeing the cut wound and the blood on the ground. "I saw he made contact with the knife." A thin film of sweat glistened on her smooth forehead.

"Am I alright?" Mac replied. "Yeah. Sure. I'm fine. But what the hell was that?" he added, gesturing feebly at the crumpled body of the man.

"Oh, that," Linda said dismissively. "I kick box. Second team All American."

"I'll keep that in mind." He bent over to retrieve the book and the freezer bag. They left quickly, closing the garage door behind them.

Chapter Twenty

"Ready to go?" Crockett was up from his chair with his bag in his hand as McAdams entered his office, breathing a little heavy. He was late for their 6:30 rendezvous, delayed by a quick visit to the student medical clinic for antiseptic and bandages and then to Linda's dorm to drop her off. But Crockett seemed oblivious to the passage of time. Although the arm of McAdams' sport coat jacket bulged slightly from the medical wrapping, he knew Crockett wouldn't notice it and wonder what might have transpired during the long afternoon.

McAdams drove to the airport in silence, his arm throbbing, and his chest still tight from the encounter at Tidback's hideaway, worrying about Linda Walker back there, alone. Why he worried, after seeing that display of controlled violence, he wasn't sure. But still he worried. Crockett, eager for company, made amiable conversation. He was a fountain of information about the terrain, the College, airports and air travel, the states of Virginia and Mississippi, and more. McAdams had only to nod and steer.

It was a little after 7:00 when they pulled into the parking lot. As they gathered up their belongings from McAdams' car, Crockett offered to carry his overnight bag.

"Gracious, with those books and papers, you look like the professor here, not me." Crockett smiled as he picked up McAdams' bag from the trunk of the Mustang. McAdams' serious, tanned face, his wavy brown hair and sunglasses stuffed in his blazer chest pocket shouted this was some serious academic, probably offering courses like Radical Political Philosophy or Early American Utopianism. That gash under his eye gave him a hint of danger and mystery, to boot. The coeds would have lined up at course registration time.

"Let's see ...," said McAdams after they walked into the Richmond terminal. He glanced down at his tickets and scanned the airline desks assembled like lemonade stands around the walls of the concourse of the small air terminal.

"US Air," he intoned as he found the airline counter he

wanted and nodded his head for Crockett to go with him.

A man followed them. He wore sunglasses and moved jerkily into line behind them as they waited for the airline representative to beckon them forward. The man glanced down at McAdams' bag that Crockett had placed momentarily on the floor as he was shifting his own bag between hands.

The man leaned down to read the ID tag on McAdams' bag. He straightened up and stared into Crockett's back.

Crockett bought a ticket after McAdams offered his for inspection and insertion into a boarding pass. They asked for seats together, and got the fifth row with Crockett closest to the aisle and McAdams against the window.

"I need the leg room..." smiled Crockett.

They stepped back to find the departure gate. They didn't think twice about the man behind them who rushed passed to the ticket counter. The ticket agent did. She didn't like the way he kept his sunglasses on and the way sweat gathered on his face. She called security on her phone right after the man purchased his ticket to Memphis with cash.

Alerted, security asked the sweating man to step aside as the passengers filed through the metal detector. A pat-down and inch-by-inch coverage with a hand-held wand detected nothing. The two guards shrugged at each other as the man headed for his gate.

The DC-10 with its 40 passengers bound for Memphis lofted gracefully into the pale blue sky dotted with puffy white clouds. McAdams watched the Appalachian mountains come up, grateful for a break in Crockett's stream of chatter.

He thought about his call last week to the University of Mississippi's history department chairman. Tidback was a sterling, twice-a-week lecturer, fully prepared for all classes. No one had a clue what research he was conducting. His office contained course syllabi and other class-related material. No one could say where he stayed at night. Maybe Linda could dig up more from her perch at Randolph-Macon.

The sudden silence startled McAdams. He glanced over at Crockett who was dozing with his head back and his mouth still wide open. McAdams smiled, turned back to the window and watched the gathering darkness begin to ooze over the horizon. His smile faded as he thought about the discoveries in Tidback's loft and about Linda, alone back there.

Ten rows behind Crockett and McAdams the man with the sunglasses got up from his seat. The woman next to him breathed a deep sigh of relief and uncrossed her legs, relaxing for the first time since she sat down. The guy gave her the creeps - big time. And he smelled terribly.

The man walked back to the rest room and closed the door. He reached into the small compartment labeled "Sanitary Napkins" and pulled out the .38 caliber handgun that had been secreted there before the flight. He held the gun up and looked at it, and himself holding it, in the mirror.

He smiled. It was going so easily. He took off his sunglasses and basked in his image in the mirror. Geoffrey Larcher was in his glory, some 3 months away from his last dose of medicine. In the mirror was a man who would be famous. A man with a heavy burden. Not as heavy as those who went before him perhaps, but a burden nonetheless. He was a man handpicked to carry on the job of eliminating those standing in the way. He smiled because he looked good and he felt good. He would not remove the copperhead medallion around his neck like they wanted. He was proud of it, of what it meant he was and what it would say to those who found him. This was to be his grand and glorious day.

A knock on the door shattered his homage. Larcher put the gun in the pocket of his varsity jacket. He opened the door and left hurriedly. The old, distinguished-looking Southern gentleman with red suspenders and bow tie, waiting outside, winced as Larcher passed, his nostrils assaulted by the rank smell of an unwashed, sick man.

Larcher walked easily up the aisle, as if gracious in accepting an award. He came silently to the fifth aisle, stopped and turned to face the man he had been sent to eliminate. The man was asleep. That was a shame. The noble thing would be to look him in the eye. He pulled the gun out of his pocket, brought it within an inch of Crockett's left eye socket and fired two quick shots.

McAdams' head spun around even as his body involuntarily pulled away from the deafening sound of the explosions. He caught the assassin's eyes as the man turned the gun quickly into his own mouth. McAdams' face, tense with terror, nonetheless betrayed a clenched smile and he was sure the killer realized his mistake just as he pulled the trigger again. By the time the bullet had left the back of his head in a shower of bone, gristle and blood, the shrill, piercing screams of the passengers had converted the plane into an echoing horror chamber. It lurched left and then right, bags dropping from the overhead containers, as the pilots reacted to the sounds of the bullets.

Chapter Twenty-one

The next day -- Harpers' Ferry, West Virginia

Jackson, already awake, shot a glance at the alarm clock next to the bed when the phone rang. 5:30 a.m.

He could always tell what kind of call it would be by the sound of its ring. This one was cutting, insistent. It was a wake up call, a call to arms. He leaned over to pick up the receiver and smiled at the familiar voice.

It was Duncan Williams, the Richmond chief of police. They had known each other since the days they served together in the Korean War.

"I'm calling ya, Chuck, 'cause you and I know that the damned Virginia State Police will take their sweetass time to get to you on this. ... We got your man Larcher. But he's no use to you now. He's dead. It went like this ..."

Jackson sat up in bed and twisted his legs and feet onto the floor as he listened to Williams's report. The Richmond cop was familiar with Jackson's "Mystery of the Woods" as his friend took to calling it. Jackson had put out an all-points on Larcher for the past week, reaching into Maryland, Tennessee, Ohio, Virginia, West Virginia, and the District of Columbia. He had called Williams, too, to talk the case over.

"We don't know yet," Williams concluded, "how he got the gun on board. Larcher was thoroughly searched at the gate. The weapon had to be waitin' for him on board the plane. The victim's companion, the Congressional investigator John McAdams, says Larcher was going after him, not Crockett."

"Did you tell McAdams we found copies of Tidback's articles in Larcher's closet?"

"No. I gave him some of the lowdown on your Mystery of the Woods but I didn't get into that."

"All right ... I believe Larcher had to be goin' after McAdams' too. My deputy's been telling me to call McAdams and now here he pops up in your jurisdiction."

Williams grunted as he rustled through papers on his desk.

"Larcher was wearing a medallion," Williams began. Jackson waited.

"A copper medallion on a gold chain. The medallion had Lady Liberty's head on it. Same as the one you found in the trailer. I'm telling ya, my man, you've got a damned cult on your hands."

"Mebbe, Dunc, mebbe. Larcher's medallion matches the one we found next to Ted Samuel's body and the ones the rest of the boys had. OK - I'll grant you that. They were members of the same group. There's no doubt about it. But ... a cult? No ..., I don't know that's what I'd call it." Jackson reminded Williams about the penal codes and the yellowed journal pages with etchings and names.

"Maybe it's just a different kind of cult, that's all. ... Listen, I got work to do. I'll send you Larcher's autopsy results in three or four days, by Friday for sure. And I'll send McAdams' statement and a picture of the medallion."

Williams spoke McAdams' phone number over the phone as Jackson wrote it down. "Call him, Chuck. Pronto, this time."

"What's he like?" asked Jackson before Williams hung up.

"He's been around. A real pro. A cop with a strange beat, no uniform, and better pay. He asked me as many tough questions as I asked him. He's just out tryin' to solve his own case. He's true-blue, Chuck. ... Call him."

Jackson hung up and walked in his undershirt and boxer shorts through his one bedroom rambler to the screened porch that overlooked a round pond in the woods. He looked beyond the pond into the dense trees just becoming distinguishable from one another in the rosy light of sunrise. A deer with big black eyes, a familiar friend who came to check up on him now and then, stared back at him from a distance. It sensed no threat and went back to grazing at the base of a pine.

Things were starting to fit. The dead "boys," had gone to the trailer in the woods often, the last time for a meeting that never happened, or never finished. Larcher had been there with them that snowy night; his prints were everywhere, as were those of the other boys. The forensic team he had borrowed from a neighboring town had found other, unknown prints as well. And the nub marks of chiseled-down fingertips. Not chewed, like Samuel's, but chiseled - as in professional elimination of fingerprints. Jackson remembered the Washington papers said that David Tidback's killer had his fingerprints chiseled away.

Larcher must have left the trailer sometime during or after the first night they got up there, promising his friends that he would come back for them. But he never went back. The ones left behind went outside at some point, and wandered about - confused or exhilarated in the heavy snows that had fallen for two days and kept falling on and off during that next week. They got disoriented, lost. They froze. They died.

He sat and rocked, savoring the quiet of the chilly, dew-soaked morning. He fiddled with two ropes he kept near the chair, making and unmaking nautical knots as he always did, in preparation for that far off day when he would retire near the sea, a little boat at his beck and call. His thoughts, as they did every new day, turned to his son, Charles Jr. Every day he'd look skyward through the trees and talk right to the clouds like they were messengers appointed to carry his words to his son's ears.

He would've been 49 today. Would've been a grown man, with a family and a life. Jackson shook his head. He missed the boy so much. It felt like only last week that he and his wife Mary had seen him off proudly from the port at Newport News. Only yesterday that the Army Major somehow found his way up the road to deliver the news on an early spring morning exactly like this one. Tet Offensive, he began. Your son's dead. Jumped on a grenade and saved a bunch of other boys. A hero the major called him, a man. My boy, Jackson sighed, dead and long gone from this earth.

There would be a big, bright smile on Chuckie's face today. The boy liked his birthdays. He liked the partying and the celebration. He'd be elbowing his father, talking loud and laughing, as he cut the cake and opened the presents.

He wrapped his arms around his large stomach and heaved a deep sigh. "I love you, boy," he whispered. He looked up through the trees and breathed a short prayer to Mary, seeing her standing next to their boy up beyond those big, puffy clouds. He mouthed a brief kiss and came back to earth, studying the motion of the silent ripples of the pond. His deer moved to the base of another tree and paused, its eyes wide in expectation.

Chapter Twenty-two

Tuesday, April 14 -- Washington, DC

In the early morning hours of the next day McAdams stood at last before the door to his suite. He looked up and down the hallway and then quietly let himself in.

He exhaled loudly when he got to the other side of the door, feeling for the first time a deep, throbbing ache in his body. It wasn't the lack of sleep or the Richmond cop's two-hour grilling that bothered him. It really wasn't the interminable time it took for the plane to turn around and land and then wait on the tarmac with its grisly cargo next to him the whole time. What drained him was the proximity to another awful death, and having Crockett's final slumber take place under a blanket next to him, gurgling and sighing as the body's gases escaped. Death's smell still clung inside his nostrils. He tasted it still on his tongue and felt its warm, moist fingers on his face.

He silently locked the door behind him. After listening to the darkness for a few moments, he flicked on all the lights room by room and searched in the closets, under the bed, behind the furniture. He was alone. Home.

He stopped before his bedroom mirror and winced. Crockett's blood, and the spray from his exploded head, still spotted McAdams' clothes. Specks of dark, dried blood and ooze and flecks of bone were in his hair and on his arms and face despite the furious cleansing he applied in the airport bathroom.

He shuddered as he suddenly saw the badly mauled image that had appeared in another mirror, another time - only two years ago. He knew it was his face back then because it hurt so much, even with all the morphine they had given him. Deep bruises and red welts rose on his skin like craters and seas on the moon. There were two or three patches of stitches. Under his left eye, swollen shut, was a huge patch. The hunting knife, the cops said it had to be serrated, had missed his eyeball by an inch. They were going to carve out that eye no doubt, the cops told him. They must have missed when he pulled away.

Annie was worse off, ending up in intensive critical care, recovering from a severe beating with seven broken ribs and a punctured lung. She had lost the baby. It was a girl, they had told him. A little, baby girl they would have called Shannon. She would have been beautiful, a girl he would've loved forever.

McAdams shook himself and came back to the present. He rubbed the chicken wishbone of a scar left by the hunters' knife. Within the tracks of dead skin there still resonated a slight but throbbing and almost unbearably maddening itch. It never went away.

He spooked the memories away for another time, wiped his eyes with his sleeve and turned away from the mirror. He flung off his clothes and threw them on the floor. He showered and jumped into a pair of shorts.

A tall tumbler filled with scotch and ice in one hand, he returned to his bedroom and grabbed the TV remote control. He moved into his walk-in closet and aimed the remote precisely at a spot at the intersection of the back and side walls and the ceiling. A door in the back closet wall swung silently away from him. A light came on in a room beyond the door. It was a jail cell-sized room lined with shelves.

Inside on the shelves were a few dust-covered documents from prior investigations and the only hard copy of his first draft of the Report of the King Assassination Committee. On a shelf below the draft he placed Booth's letter to "Secretary Nathaniel Brock and the Committee," the threatening creed of something called "OAK" and Tidback's checklist on an index card.

The hidden room was getting busy again. He had it built a few years ago when he and Senator Mossingame were going after Mafia involvement in labor unions. There were deaths among potential witnesses and all manner of threats back then, too. During that time he trusted no one - not the FBI, not the special Labor Department investigators, not even fellow Congressional staff. So he had one of his buddies from the bars come up and put in a hidden room lined with shelves. It worked like a charm. The IRS investigators couldn't find it when they came with a subpoena for documents that should've been in his office. The Mafia hoods that twice ransacked his dwelling also missed the secret room.

From the inside, when the door was closed, no light appeared through any cracks. Inside he had only to flick a switch to activate the fast and silent battery-powered motor that closed and opened the door.

McAdams sneezed as he let himself out. The dust was bad. He fell backward on the bed, thinking about Geoffrey Larcher. Williams had told him in Richmond that Larcher was linked to the deaths of four men in West Virginia. Williams had told him about the Lady Liberty medallion around Larcher's neck. It was the same fine lady McAdams found at the bottom of the Booth diary page from Tidback's loft.

McAdams wondered behind closed eyes if the entire affair - from Washington, to Harpers Ferry, to Richmond - could be chalked up to nothing more than a bunch of mindless, overactive neo-Nazis or Ku Klux Klan. Was this Tidback's conspiracy? Were Booth's progeny Klansmen and mountain "boot boys" bound for glory?

In less than a minute he fell into a restless sleep.

Chapter Twenty-three

The first call came at 6:30, maybe an hour after he had passed out on the bed. He stared at the phone, not knowing for an instant where he was. Then he knew and scrambled to fish a fresh pack of cigarettes out of his dresser drawer. He lit one and inhaled deeply as he picked up the receiver.

"McAdams." The smoke in his mouth muffled his greeting.

He grabbed last night's unfinished, watered-down scotch from his nightstand and gulped a mouthful down. A rhythmic pulsation came over the phone. A cleared throat and then the click of the phone being replaced in a far-off cradle followed it.

"Just checking to see if I made it home, I guess." He fell back on the bed and rubbed his painfully dry eyes.

The next call rolled in. McAdams sighed as he picked up. He didn't have time to say anything.

"John? This is Senator Brock."

He took a drink from the tumbler. "Yes?"

"We must talk. Quietly. It's 'bout last night and what's going on." Brock was breathless.

"Why don't we meet now?" He sucked on his cigarette.

"My God! No! ... Tomorrow night. Somewhere where we can't be seen."

"Here?"

"That would never do!" It was a dumb idea, McAdams agreed, but it was early. It had been a tough night.

"I'll meet you at the bandstand outside the Museum of Natural History," Brock continued. "Around midnight tomorrow night."

"I know where it is." McAdams put the phone down and twisted his cigarette into the ashtray. He turned around on the bed and looked out the window to view the dome of the Capitol Building four blocks away. Many days its inspiration got him up and going.

A week ago Tidback was getting ready to testify and the King Assassination Committee was rolling to a suitable close. Now David Tidback and Rufus Crockett were dead, as were their two assassins, and there were four dead boys in West Virginia. The FBI was all over his case like Grant took Richmond. And in his secret room were materials implicating Lincoln's murderer, John Wilkes Booth, in a conspiracy with a "Secretary Nathaniel Brock" whose illustrious descendent now was Vice-Chair of the Senate Select Committee on the Assassination of Reverend Martin Luther King.

The same Senator Taylor Brock he was going to meet in the dark of midnight.

He sipped from his tumbler of warm, watery scotch, wondering why the normally glowing Capitol dome looked so gray in the early morning sun.

Chapter Twenty-four

The same morning -- Dirksen Senate Office Building

Lewis Shephard sat at his office desk staring at a note he had found slipped under the door. He ripped it into little pieces, threw them into his empty coffee cup and tossed a lit match in after them. The sudden flames grasped the rim of the cup and then quickly fell back and expired. He took the cup to his office sink and rinsed it out. The black, soggy ashes twirled slowly down the drain.

The two goons had followed McAdams and a young woman and come up with nothing, the note said. They were now in the hospital. And Geoffrey Larcher had failed. He was dead and John McAdams was alive. Next steps had to be planned and executed. Shephard was to wait, here in his office, for a call.

He returned from the sink and sat down with a sigh. He put his head back on his chair and looked at the ceiling. It was almost three years ago that he got the first call. He was on the staff of the House Committee on Postal Operations, in the dead zone of an obscure, Congressional career. The call came during the terrible times right after Congressman Robert Boreman's arrest for soliciting boys in the park. Bob Boreman - the conservative wordsmith with the golden tongue who had instilled in him and many others a new appreciation of how this country was losing its way. Bob Boreman - his lover of several years. He still hurt, he still ached from the betrayal and now the loneliness.

No one should have known about him and the powerful Congressman. Theirs had been one of the best keep secrets in Washington, one limited to the midnight hours and the private gay bars of the city, and the alcoves of the Longworth House Office Building. But they knew Bob Boreman, he must have been one of them at one point in time - and they threatened whispers of Shephard's involvement with Boreman's little boys if he did not do as they said.

The voice on that first call told him to show up at Senator

Brock's office, just like that. He was to meet the Senator and discuss the open chief-of-staff position. And Brock offered it to him, just like that. Probably had to. Shephard endured the petty jealousies of Brock's staff. He rose above the condescension and the whispers of the Senatorial chiefs-of-staff club.

They called again six months later, just when he was beginning to wonder if he had been abandoned. He was told to monitor Brock's comings and goings and provide a report when called upon, especially in connection with the upcoming King Committee proceedings. And there would be other jobs to do. Lewis Shephard was working for them full time now.

They knew he would succeed. They knew he was persistent, and inspired. They knew he wanted to get back at the freeloaders and sycophants. They even helped him realize his anger. Yes, he would join them. He would watch Brock. Yes, he would help organize the campsites. Yes, he would get the campsites ready to take on any task, even those that inflicted a little pain and suffering. It was only right, after all. A lot of people needed a little pain and suffering. It was justice, after all. And only fair. Everyone had to pay now and then. Everyone SHOULD have to pay, now and then, for what they got. It was the American way, at least it used to be.

The ring of the phone pierced the heavy silence of the room. He stared at it. They will be angry with him, angry about Larcher. The phone rang again. He considered not answering it. The ringing sliced into him. He should ignore it and just walk out the door. Another ring lashed out. He could run away and hide. But they knew he was there, watching the phone, listening. He fumbled for the receiver on the fifth ring and pressed it against his ear.

"Yes?" came his hoarse whisper.

"He was wearing the medallion when he shot the professor last night." Shephard listened as the harsh words spat across the line. His heart bounced off his chest.

"The medallion! Around his neck for all to see. Didn't you tell him to remove it? And, Lewis, he shot the wrong man! Didn't you have a picture? Didn't you describe McAdams?"

"Larcher became unreliable. He couldn't function in the end."

"It's inexcusable that the medallion has fallen into the hands of the police. That alone can point our adversaries in directions we want them to ignore."

"I ..."

"We've had to take serious steps, Lewis. The Richmond mayor will keep tabs on the investigation for us. And eventually the medallion will disappear from the police files. But this kind of lapse cannot happen again. We have enough problems with Harpers Ferry."

"No. I ..."

"The execution of Tidback was flawless. You have shown us what you can do. We have rewarded you. But, listen to me - no more mistakes. No more nights like last night."

"No, no more ..."

"Not one ..."

"Right ..." Shephard shifted nervously in his chair.

"Are you any closer to the missing diary pages?"

Shephard gripped the desk with his free hand. "We're doing what we can. We've searched Brock's office, his home, and the bank deposit box where he had them. You said there were 18 missing pages. My God, he could have put them anywhere, in 18 different places if he wished! I ..., I don't know where else to look. This is not easy. I ..."

"If those pages," came the tense interruption, "see the light of day, things will change dramatically - for many, many people. Some will pay huge sums of money for the documents. Some, as you know, will kill for them. You, too, will be ... vulnerable."

"Brock was responsible for safeguarding the diary pages," the voice continued. "We think he leaked them to Tidback. How else could Tidback know enough to file those FOIA requests? ... Focus on Tidback's travels. Somehow he and Brock linked up, or had a drop-off arrangement, so that Tidback could collect the diary pages. Check whatever travel logs you can. Investigate Tidback's colleagues, peers, students, his dry cleaners, whatever. And follow Brock himself. He may lead you to what we seek."

"Yes ..."

"I'll let you in on a little secret, Lewis. Your Senator is

desperate. He has lost control of the most important thing left in his life - our organization. Those lost pages will allow him to regain power - if only to tear us down and rebuild our organization in his own image."

"But what am I looking for? What's in the diary? Whose diary is it? Who are you? I've never even seen you! It's time I knew these things. I've proven I can be trusted. Why won't you let me into your full confidence?"

"In time, Lewis, in time. Secrets are buried in the dark, cool tombs of our forefathers. They have taken with them their dreams ... and their vision, their secrets ... and their sins. We carry on what they started and what has been entrusted to us through the many generations. It's a noble heritage, Lewis, one you will come to know. But today we must deal with our enemies who surround us. We rely on you. Don't let us down. ... I must go now. You'll hear from us again. ... Get the diary pages, Lewis."

Chapter Twenty-five

Tuesday afternoon - April 14 - Washington, DC

McAdams hurried down the marbled hallway to his office. Word of his assault last night had spread rapidly in the small community of Capitol Hill. A few colleagues shook his hand, worry in their eyes. Others, knowing him better, wondered if he managed to get his frequent flyer miles anyway.

He ducked into the suite of offices that housed his Committee's staff and entered a large central room filled with a dozen cubicles. Administrative staff occupied some and researchers while the others overflowed with boxes, three-ring binders and manila folders stuffed with papers. At the front of the room was a formidable reception desk behind which reigned Jasmine Speed, Committee secretary. Two offices shared by his three investigators sat off a corridor to the left of Jasmine's desk. His was to the right.

He absent-mindedly scooped up his pile of message slips and headed into his office without saying hello. He stopped, frozen by his enormous sin. He turned slowly, and winced. Her eyes blasted like the coals of a locomotive.

"You jes walkin' by?" Her face collapsed into a dark, nettled frown. "You tellin' me that you almost get shot last night and now you jes walkin' right on by?" She looked like she was going to swoon with the horror and keel over.

"Jazz ..."

"I've been workin' for you for way over 10 years, doin' this and doin' that, and now you doin' this to me. You gonna tell me what's what or you gonna treat me like this piece of furniture I'm sitting behind? Cuz, Mister, if all I am to you is a piece a furniture then I'm goin' to get up and ..."

"Jazz! I haven't slept. I'm not responsible for my actions! I ..." He was losing ground so he ran around behind the desk, kneeled, took her hand and kissed it twice and held it to his cheek. "Forgive me," he pleaded.

She held his hand between hers. He felt her bright hazel

eyes scanning his face for evidence of damage or pain. She smiled, finally, in relief. All was well for the time being. The stormy weather had passed.

He stood and marveled. Jasmine Speed. She was pushing 55 by all accounts, but her dyed and teased auburn hair against her soft brown skin, her repertoire of skin-tight pantsuits and her pouty lips kept her looking lively. That plus her stable of young men.

She waved him on. "Go on with you! Get back to work! I don't want this standing around, doing nuthin'. I mean what would I do if you got let go? Where would I get a damn job in this damn Republican economy?"

He started backpedaling into his office. She caught him before he disappeared. "Hold on! ... There's a Chief Charles Jackson from West Virginia that called you a bit ago. Says he's been lookin' for the nut that tried to check you out last night. And then there was this Linda Walker girl calling, saying the word is 'all over campus' about what happened to you and that Professor Crockett, saying she wanted to be sure you was all right." Jazz spoke with arched eyebrows as she recounted Linda Walker's call. "Now tell me, what have you got goin' with a college girl?"

He snapped the note from her raised hand. "Thanks. She 's not a college girl, Jazz, she's a P.H.*D*.!"

"Well," Jazz sniffed in reply, "I want to *hear* 'bout it then. And soon!"

He nodded and retreated at last into the office. She shook her head and exhaled with relief after he closed the door. He was back where she could keep an eye on him. No one would get past her today, and to him, without some kind of real good reason.

He headed for the phone and punched the numbers on his dial pad. Linda picked up after several rings.

"Linda ..."

"Mac! Are you alright?"

"Not half as bad as that sucker you left on the floor in the garage!"

She laughed then grew silent as McAdams assured her he

was untouched and gave her a brief recounting of what happened on the plane.

"Now it's Professor Crockett ..." she began.

"They were after me, Linda ..."

"I don't want to hear it, Mac."

"It's too much. Tidback. Now Crockett."

"It's like a funeral on campus. There are black armbands and banners everywhere you look. All classes are cancelled for the entire week. Tonight there's a memorial service for both Crockett and Tidback."

"You going?"

"Yes. And tomorrow I'm going to search Tidback's office, start talking to his colleagues, start doing what we talked about."

"Don't say anything more on this phone. Remember how we agreed to communicate."

"You called me. Remember?"

"It's good to hear your voice…"

"Mac?"

"Yeah?"

"Take care up there, OK?"

"I will. You too?"

"Yeah. I'll talk to you soon." She hesitated and then hung up. McAdams sat with the receiver to his ear for a while, listening to the buzz she left behind. He leaned over and dialed again. This time the phone rang once on the other end.

"Jackson," came the greeting.

"Chief, this is John McAdams."

"Chief Williams in Richmond says we should talk."

"I'm listening."

"The Chief says you're good people so I'll get straight to it. OK?"

"Shoot."

"There's a connection between our cases, son. Geoffrey Larcher - the man who shot Crockett - had copies of some of Tidback's articles in his room, under his dirty picture books."

"Williams didn't mention that."

"He wasn't s'posed to."

"But tell me how our cases are connected, Chief. What's the

link between Geoffrey Larcher and your Mystery of the Woods, and Professor Tidback and the King Assassination Committee? Are we talking about a resurrected Confederacy? Is Old Dixie rising again?"

"Well, isn't that what Tidback was tryin' to say?"

"He called it a Lincoln conspiracy - made up of the Confederate Secret Service, maybe others."

"One that threatens a Second Civil War," finished Jackson. "I read about it in the newspapers. Listen, I want to come up there and trade notes face-to-face. Not with the FBI or anyone else. Just you and me."

"Sounds good. When?"

"I got so much goin' on here this week with the trailer site. … How 'bout Saturday?"

"You're on." McAdams gave him directions to a meeting place and a time. "Chuck, watch yourself. There's no reason to think Larcher and the guy who offed Tidback are all the hit men they have. Whoever 'they' are."

"I'll keep my head low and my ass behind me."

McAdams chuckled as he hung up. Jackson was all right. But he had a whole lot more to say than he was letting on. And there was a whole lot more work to do, he sighed as he looked at the piles of papers and reports on his desk.

The final session of the Committee was a little over a week away. The Committee would meet in executive session. That meant only the Senators on the Committee would be permitted to attend, joined by McAdams and his investigators. No other staff could be there. Notes could not be taken nor documents removed from the Committee hearing room.

He would brief the Senators on the Committee on the conclusions that the evidence allowed them to reach. Then he would summarize the physical evidence, the witnesses' testimony, and the written submissions to the Committee that led him to those conclusions. The Committee would then vote.

The formal vote adopting the entire Report and its 26 volumes of accompanying documentary support would come later. If all went well, that later vote would be routine and automatic given the vote on the Report's major findings and conclusions at the executive session.

The Senators' staffs wouldn't be at the executive session. They wouldn't get to read the detailed written text of the many volumes of the Report until the last moment. To have any impact they'd have to find something buried in the huge, multi-volume Report that was important enough to force the Committee to reverse its vote during the executive session. Fat chance of that happening.

He thought about Lewis Shephard. The son-of-a-bitch could be trouble. Shephard doggedly followed things and wouldn't let him and Mossingame get off easy. McAdams paged through his copy of the Senate Rules trying to anticipate Shephard's, and Brock's, moves.

A quick rap on the door was followed by Jazz's worried, intense eyes peering through the crack she had opened. "Ed O'Connell called and said you better get yo' ass over there before his mark-up at two or you were, and I quote the pasty white boy, 'shit outta luck.'"

He nodded and closed the folder in front of him, locking it in his desk drawer. He bolted up out of the chair and shot out of the room. "I'll be back ...," he called over his shoulder.

She smoothed her hair in place as a new handsome, young messenger wheeled a cart of mail into the office. "Well, well ...," she murmured, leaning over to catch a view of his tight, round ass.

"Yo, honey, you forgot something over here ...," she called after him.

Chapter Twenty-six

The Senate bells rang five times in the Dirksen hallways. That meant there was a vote on the floor of the Congress and five minutes left for Senators to cast an aye or a nay. The subway would be jammed with Senators, staff, and lobbyists talking on the run and squeezing through the underground tunnel to the Capitol building.

McAdams decided to walk. It would take about 10 minutes to cross the Capitol grounds over to the Rayburn House Office Building and O'Connell's office.

He passed the gauntlet of security at the Rayburn "Members and Staff" entrance, found the staircase to the basement level, and headed into the Committee offices for the House Judiciary Committee. Five staff members were squeezed into a not-so-large room, with bookcases and file cabinets creating a virtual cubicle per staffer. Each of these so-called working spaces was stuffed with a desk, a terminal, and piles of paper and reports. A raft of cartoons and memorabilia were stuck here and there by the staffers in a noble attempt to personalize the cramped quarters. On the right was the secretary's desk. She smiled at his familiar face as he blew past and opened the door behind her into O'Connell's office.

He was on the phone, arguing with someone about his upcoming mark-up. He motioned McAdams to come in. O'Connell, once upon a time, was a lean, tanned athlete with blond hair and seriously freckled skin. He now sported a gut, and the gray, sallow complexion of someone who didn't get out much. His thin, dirty blond hair wouldn't stay put anymore, the thinner it got, and he constantly pushed a swatch off his forehead. He was dressed in his usual wrinkled khakis, blue shirt, red and blue striped tie that was frayed at the top of the knot, and tired penny loafers that hadn't seen a coin in years.

O'Connell hung up. "Can you believe this?" He stood wide-eyed and pointed to the phone. "Senator Dumb Shit expects to unload three entirely new amendments exactly ... ," he looked at his watch, "two minutes and 28 seconds before the

Committee's final mark-up of the bill." He shrugged. "Too bad, I hope he didn't put too much time and effort into 'em. I've already got 14 amendments on the table, and Jesse Helms has threatened to put a hold on the bill, and that's without seeing our amendments - which, of course, he will hate. And, to top it all off, the NRA lobbyists want a shot at me now to give me religion on several provisions of the bill."

O'Connell grew quiet as he reached over his desk to shake McAdams' hand, his washed-out blue eyes finding a twinkle. "Mac, I'm glad to see you. But you gotta get outta this business, my man. I mean, last night…. The attack on you and Annie a while back. That's twice in recent memory that things have gotten real ugly. Does Anne have any idea …?"

McAdams' memory jogged. "Oh Christ, we're getting together tonight!"

"Her idea or yours?"

"Uh, mine. I kinda promised Mossingame I'd make another try. I thought, maybe, maybe it deserved one more shot."

"Really?" O'Connell's eyebrows almost touched his receding hairline. "Why are you bothering?"

"I guess I need to."

"Well, do yourself a favor. Tell her what happened. Bring it up yourself, before she does. God knows, it's on the news so she'll know. Tell her that whoever did your ex-witness is now after you. Give her the option to pull out of the dinner or whatever. You don't want deja vu all over again."

O'Connell was right. The ruthless attack on them had been the final warning from the Las Vegas Mob that he ought to steer an investigation away from some family captains and union pensions he had targeted. At least that was what the note said on the red orchids that somehow appeared against hospital rules in Anne's room in the intensive care unit.

He had never told her of the gangland threats over the weeks leading up to their vicious beatings. When the Mob carried out its threats, and Anne learned why they had been attacked, her grief over losing their baby - a deep and searing grief - festered into a raw and bitter rage that stoked the betrayal she felt at his hands. She ended things with him right there in the hospital and they didn't speak to each other until months after that. They never talked about what happened. Never got a chance to mourn together over what they both had lost - except for the hot, angry tears they both cried during the final, wrenching argument.

"Yeah, I know," McAdams said in a low voice. "I'll give her a chance to run …."

"Mac, Mac," O'Connell shook his head, surprise and pity warring on his face. "Don't be hoping some cherub is gonna shoot an arrow into her and she's gonna get all romantic on you. She's gone, off in her own wild blue yonder. Maybe you should take some lessons."

"Yeah," McAdams mumbled. "Maybe I will. Maybe it's time." He felt lectured, embarrassed. He sat down, dejected.

"Now tell me, how did the hit man last night mistake your butt-ugly face for a wise old professor's?" O'Connell's features lit up as he let out a bellow of laugh.

McAdams had to smile back. "Beats the shit outta me."

"Why were you in Richmond?"

McAdams gave him a lowdown on his trip to Randolph-Macon and the aborted flight to the University of Mississippi.

"Damn, I'd stay at home from now on, son." O'Connell looked at his watch and sat down behind his desk. "Look, I'm runnin' late. I'll give you the small conference room across the hall from the Committee's office. It's B-202. You can go over the Lincoln materials there."

"Good ... " McAdams started to rise from his chair.

"Mac, sit for a minute."

He sat. "What?"

"The FBI called yesterday."

McAdams grabbed O'Connell's cigarette pack from the desk, pulled one out and lit it. "Go on," he said as he exhaled, peering at his friend through a bank of smoke.

"They want me to return all materials in my possession relating to the FBI investigation into the Booth diary. Everything you're gonna look at, they want, badly."

"After all this time, suddenly they want this shit?"

O'Connell nodded.

"Do they know I'm nosing around?"

"I can't say. The call came in yesterday. Last week, I got some heavy-handed calls from the Department of Justice. They wanted to know if our two Committees were sharing files, if there was anything going on they should know about. Maybe they were reacting to this Tidback murder, I don't know. Knowing you, you probably have your nose way up their collective ass. And someone is getting very uptight about this Lincoln conspiracy nonsense."

O'Connell's face grew somber as he mapped out a game plan to call off the Department of Justice dogs. "I'll get the Committee Chairman to jot down a hand-written note to the Congressional Affairs Offices of the FBI and Justice complaining about the bad precedent and claiming separation of powers. The usual bullshit. I'll get him to call the Chairman of the House Operations Committee, which happens to be handling the FBI's annual appropriations at this very minute. That should give you a couple of weeks."

"Can you find out who in Justice and the FBI wants the Lincoln material? It's important. I think the Justice Department knew what Tidback was gettin into, what he might say at the hearing." McAdams explained Tidback's FOIA requests and the Department's subsequent inquiries to Crockett at Randolph-Macon. "I bet there's someone in Justice who can tell us why Tidback's testimony was relevant to the King Assassination Committee."

"You're making some big claims. And your witness is dead - you've got nothin' to back you up."

McAdams ground out his cigarette in the filled ashtray on O'Connell's desk. "Ed, can you get copies of the FOIA requests? And find out what happened to them? There's got to be a paper trail ..."

"Yeah! ... Sure! ... Hey, thanks, Mac! ... The last guy who pushed those buttons got shot in your hearing room. Remember? Bullets to the brain? Thank you very much. Any other requests? ... Jesus! Come on, let's go." O'Connell and McAdams left the office.

"I put all the Lincoln shit you want in the room myself. No one knows I'm showing you this stuff. No one knows we have even talked about it. Let's keep it that way."

O'Connell pushed the same swath of hair back from his forehead, trying to arrange it. "I have a present for you. In light of your near-death experience, I'm gonna let you see everything the Committee has."

O'Connell clapped him on the shoulder and walked away in the opposite direction down the hallway. McAdams watched as he slapped high fives with two staffers and looked around at a group of young women he passed.

Chapter Twenty-seven

McAdams looked up and down the hall before putting the key into the door of B-202. He slipped inside and closed and locked the door behind him. He flicked on the light and found a long conference table surrounded by chairs in a windowless room.

On the table was a large box. He looked inside and took out three large envelopes, placing them on the table. The first, dated August 23, 1967, was labeled "Report of the FBI Laboratory Upon its Examination of the Diary of John Wilkes Booth" The second said "FBI Photos". The third held the transcript of a September 5, 1967 executive session of the House Judiciary Subcommittee on Crime and Criminal Justice.

He sat down and scanned the photos. There were identifying labels at the bottom center of each of the glossy prints. The photos were of the pages currently intact and residing in Booth's diary in Ford's Museum. There were obvious similarities between the documents from Tidback's loft now locked away in his bedroom and what appeared in the photographs in front of him.

There was no question that the Booth letter and the OAK creed from Tidback's loft had been written by Booth, if it was Booth who authored the documents from the box in front of him. There was no question that the photographed pages arrayed on the table matched the actual pages he had in his possession. They came from the same journal or notebook. The explosive documents he and Linda had stumbled across were missing pages from the diary of John Wilkes Booth. Lafayette Baker had been right. Someone had been playing around back then.

He bent over the table to study the photographed pages. They had printed dates from June 11 through July 1, 1864. Booth had crossed these out and penned entries in his own handwriting for April 13, April 14 and April 21, 1865. Lincoln had been assassinated on April 14, 1865; Lafayette Baker's boys had shot Booth on April 26, 1865.

He read the two journal entries from the Ford Museum. The

first was dated April 13 and 14 and set out a short statement of Booth's self-serving belief that he was acting as he did in order to save the country. The second passage was a rather romantic and lengthy account of Booth's escape from Washington into Virginia. Other pages from the diary had random scribbles, some in Latin, as well as doodles and hand-drawn calendar months for the year 1865. The FBI photos of the journal revealed stubs of missing pages that had been torn out as well as the smoothly sliced remnant edges of pages that had been cut out.

He reached for the FBI report. The introductory pages answered his questions about how and why the FBI got involved in looking at the diary in the first place. The Interior Department, custodian of the diary in the Ford Theater Museum, had requested the FBI to examine the diary after repeated inquiries from historians about whether the diary was genuine and whether it contained, as some maintained, invisible writing. The FBI then subjected the diary to writing comparisons, chemical composition and carbon dating tests, and infrared and ultra-violet photo examinations.

The next hour sped by as he paged through the 1-inch thick report. Much of it discussed the FBI's tests, how they were conducted, and what they revealed. There was no evidence that the writing had been altered, there was no writing in invisible ink. The exam confirmed the diary was Booth's, a fact further validated by FBI review of interview notes of Booth contemporaries made by House investigators during the post-Civil War inquiry into the Lincoln murder conspiracies.

The FBI report stated that twenty-seven pages were missing from the front of the diary -- the pages for January 1 through June 10, 1864, with three days to a page. An additional eighteen pages were missing from the back of the diary. The report noted that FBI Laboratory analysis of the page stubs and edges still lodged in both the beginning and end of the diary suggested that the first section of 27 missing pages had been removed one page or several at a time. They were probably torn out by hand according to the FBI report, for occasional notes and other random uses.

The 18 missing pages at the end of the small book had been sliced out, according to the FBI, probably with a knife or similarly sharp instrument. The Lab could not pinpoint the date of excision, but the physical evidence suggested a time contemporary with the handwriting in the diary. There was definitely writing on the missing pages, the report concluded, because there were traces of writing and parts of words on the remaining stubs and edges. That was it.

He read the short transcript. There were three Members present from the Subcommittee on Crime and Criminal Justice - just enough for a quorum to do business. One of the House Members was now dead, one was currently Chair of the House Foreign Relations Committee, and the last was a nondescript member still rattling around in anonymity on the Hill. The FBI staff was identified by title and function.

The transcript of the September 5, 1967 executive session revealed the practiced art of manipulation. An old hand at it, McAdams knew it when he saw it. The meeting had one purpose: to put under lock and key the FBI records examining the Booth diary as well as the 1860s records of the two House Committees caught up in the FBI diary examination.

Under the House rules, unless the Subcommittee affirmatively voted to publish the records it produced during its inquiry, they and the investigation they revealed would be sealed from view for thirty years. Minutes of the Subcommittee's executive session meetings would be sealed for fifty years unless there was a vote to publish them. A nice, neat attempt at a slam-dunk into some dusty file cabinet in some government archives building in the woods in Suitland, Maryland.

The FBI staffers had come from the Director's Office, the Bureau's Legal Counsel Division and the office responsible for FBI Congressional Affairs. They arrived en masse to present their stripped-down version of the conclusions of the Laboratory Division of the Investigations Branch. That the Congressmen present did not comment on the incongruity of having such senior FBI staff present at such a mundane session was a testament to the trust and naiveté of the times. It would be some years, McAdams remembered, before Congress got the lessons in inter-branch warfare learned during Vietnam and Watergate.

One Congressman, now dead, asked tough-sounding questions. But it was clear that all present thought the FBI request for secrecy was natural. It was the late sixties, right before the assassination of Martin Luther King. The three Members said more than once that they wanted to get this "Booth business" done with, they did not want to get caught up in what they viewed as "hysterical" Lincoln conspiracy theories of the kind surfacing then in connection with the JFK assassination.

The FBI lawyers and lobbyists started off by setting out the Laboratory Division's conclusions. The Lab, they said, found that someone had used a knife or similar instrument to slice out the set of 18 missing pages in the last half of the Booth diary. It could have been the desperate work of Booth, the FBI opined, trying to hide lists of conspirators, or instructions or notes, written during his planning of the assassination of Lincoln or his escape from Washington, DC afterward. The Bureau could not say when the 18 pages were removed, but they were sure it was long, long ago.

McAdams mentally reviewed the Booth diary pages in his possession. One of the pages from Tidback's loft, the letter to Secretary Brock and the Committee, had a ragged edge along the left-hand border, as if it were ripped out. That meant it came from the first half of the diary. It probably was torn out by Booth himself, and mailed, or sent by courier, even handed to Secretary Nathaniel Brock or someone on the "Committee." Another page, the one with the OAK creed, had straight edges on both sides of the pages. It had to be one of the missing 18 pages that had been sliced out of the diary. Removed, if you believed Lafayette Baker, by someone in authority sometime after Lincoln was assassinated and Booth captured.

He leaned back over the transcript spread out on the table before him. The FBI representative from "F-DO," the Director's Office, made an aside in a dialogue with one of the Members. Yes, there was something new discovered during the FBI Lab's examination. Something not known before.

McAdams' eyes darted over the text. The discovery came at

the hands of an exuberant FBI technician. He had performed an analysis of the existing diary page that came immediately after the remnants of the missing 18 pages. The test he performed on this page was the infra-red equivalent of running a pencil over it to see if any impressions had been left from someone pressing down when writing or drawing on previous pages. The FBI representative explained that when one ran the side of a pencil tip over a page with depressions from writing made on a previous page, the pencil would color all but the depressed sections of the page. What you would see, he explained, would, in effect, be an image of writing in white on a background of lead-pencil black.

This test indicated that the first page following the excised section had depressions from writing on previous pages. The writing leaving the deepest indentation, probably writing from the last of the sliced-out pages, was a list of names. According to the technician, he saw the numbers one through 11 run down the page one after the other, with one through six in a left-hand column arranged under the letter "C" and the remaining five numbers in a column that appeared on the right-hand side. The technician could not make out the names.

There was also a small circular impression at the bottom of the page, made by a coin or stamp. The impression was of the head of Liberty, according to the FBI.

The Congressman who launched the line of questioning guessed that the impression was left by a Lady Liberty head cut out from the copper penny that was in circulation in the North during the Civil War. He explained that northerners that opposed Lincoln, sometimes violently, banded together and wore this Lady Liberty medallion around their neck as a symbol of their unity and their cause. These disloyal Northerners became known as Copperheads because of the necklace. Copperheads were also poisonous snakes that struck without warning. The double meaning, at least for the loyal Unionists, was intentional, said the Congressman.

McAdams' fingers tightened as he held the transcript. "Copperheads ...," he whispered.

He skimmed the rest of the transcript. There were questions

about the technical steps used in raising the impressions on the last page. The Congressman asking the tough questions wanted to know what the FBI thought of the list of names. The FBI responded it had no interpretation.

The FBI Director's man interjected to suggest that the report and the transcript of the Subcommittee session should be held confidential pursuant to the House Rules. This had the effect of re-sealing for another thirty years the materials, records and transcripts of the 1860s House Committees. All that could come of releasing the information, the FBI suggested, was idle gossip and futile speculation about who was on the list and whether they were involved in the Lincoln assassination. The FBI noted that there was no way to raise the names on the list and thus no further examination was necessary. In all likelihood, they said, all that would come from release of the report and transcript would be endless and fruitless testing with further damage to the already crumbling pages left in the historic Booth diary. It was too late now, in the eyes of the FBI, to do anything anyway about the Lincoln assassination.

The FBI suggested returning the diary to the Ford Theater Museum, "where it belonged," and recommended there be no publication of the House subcommittee record and executive session transcript. The tough Congressman insisted on a public letter to the Department of the Interior and the Curator of the Museum providing answers to the questions raised about the genuineness of the diary and the absence of invisible writing. Suitably chastened, the FBI agreed.

McAdams could see the bored faces of the Members of Congress. They had done their job. He could see the FBI reps. Had it been a practice then, they would have done high and low fives just outside the Subcommittee's door.

He looked at the photos. The request from the Curator was probably genuine and innocent enough. Odd, but odd enough to have happened exactly the way it was portrayed. It probably caught someone by surprise, someone who could pull strings real fast and limit an FBI and Congressional inquiry. But someone who could not prevent transcription of a Congressman's rambling about Lady Liberty and Copperheads.

He could see why the FBI and the Justice Department now wanted the photos and documents on the desk in front of him - they linked the murder of Abraham Lincoln to eight contemporary deaths involving Lady Liberty medallions. They might somehow point to other assassinations if Tidback's checklist could be proved. David Tidback - a man pursued by the Justice Department for research he was conducting on the Lincoln assassination, a man murdered trying to get in front of the King Assassination Committee. A man whose murder investigation now was being controlled by the FBI.

"A continuing conspiracy...," McAdams breathed as he looked around the small room.

Chapter Twenty-eight

Tuesday night, April 14 -- 8:45 p.m.

McAdams sipped from a glass of ice water and sat, waiting, in the far-left corner of the open porch of the twelfth floor restaurant, only the cover of an awning above him. He had dressed up for the occasion, wearing a blue suit with a lightly starched blue pin-striped shirt and a new tie the kid salesman had said was cool and coordinated. He rebuffed the several waiters wanting to ply with him liquor. No booze tonight, he swore. He jostled the ice in his glass back and forth in front of his eyes. Tricky waters ahead.

He put down the glass and breathed deeply. It was a classic Washington spring evening - crisp and clean. The stars were out and shining and there was a soft breeze. Twelve stories directly beneath him was the busy corner of Pennsylvania Avenue and 15th Street.

This had been his and Anne's favorite table in their favorite restaurant, atop the Hotel Washington. Every once in a while he would come here to this place, most times alone, always at this table. The maitre d' always knew exactly where to seat him.

He looked out into the restaurant. It was packed with the wheelers and dealers of Washington and a few families of brave tourists trying to rub elbows with the native movers and shakers. Not a few executive branch officials were holding court, many from Treasury across the street. Seated this way McAdams knew he would catch her grand entrance, when the hotel elevator emptied its occupants out into the restaurant. Behind him the Washington Monument, not even a quarter mile away, glistened like a pure white stone splitting the night sky. The ground lights illuminating the grand obelisk gave it a sharp clarity that was magnified by the blackness behind it. Shadows played over the side of the Monument as the circle of flags around its base fluttered in the glow of the ground lights shining upward.

He looked down below and to his left to the long, gray building that housed the United States Department of the

Treasury. Just beyond that was the back of the White House. Peering intently, he saw figures moving behind the translucent curtains in the West Wing. He wondered why it was no one had yet taken the opportunity presented to lob a bazooka shell or a sniper's bullet from here. And he knew, with that single thought, that the Assassination Committee and the rednecks had gotten to him. Death now was to be anticipated.

He shook it off and watched a table load of children loudly buffeting their father and mother with tall tales of their day touring the town. A smile came to his face as one of the children, a little girl with clear blue eyes behind festive, red glasses and long, flowing yellow hair, starting bouncing a rubber ball on the table. The ball had the Presidential seal on it. The mother reached for it, hit it with her outstretched hand and knocked it in McAdams' direction. Embarrassment and alarm covered her features as she watched the ball bounce across the open space in McAdams' direction.

He caught it with one hand and held it out for the little girl. She bolted from her table and ran over to him.

"Thanks, mister."

"No problem." A mischievous grin crossed his face. "Don't you know this is the property of the President?" He pointed to the seal. "You can't just let it bounce all over or the White House police will come and get you, put you in the big jail they have over there." He nodded in the direction of the White House and laughed.

The little girl caught on quick. "Oh yeah? Well then, you gotta go, too, 'cause you're holding it!" She grinned back at him.

His eyes grew big as he looked at the ball. "Really? In that case, then, ..." He flipped her the ball and she skipped happily back to her family.

He looked up and saw Anne at the entrance to the restaurant. She had gotten off the elevator and had seen him bantering with the little girl. Her face was a stiff mask, her arms were wrapped tightly around her torso. She crossed the room preceded by a huge cold front.

She wore a black suit that matched her dark, furiously thick black hair. Her blue eyes gleamed with captured candlelight from the tables. She was slim, much thinner than the last time she had been here, in this place, before the attack, when she had been almost seven months pregnant and they had even dared to start talking marriage. He realized, with a sinking stomach, that they had their done their talking about marriage right at this very table.

He closed his eyes for a moment. "Jesus!" he whispered half aloud. "What am I doing here?" He heard in response only the muffled conversations around him.

She leaned over the table when she arrived, and pumped his hand. He lamely tried to get up from the table to greet her. "Oh, please, don't get up," she joked. He clumsily plopped back down in the chair and glared at his glass of water.

"Sorry I'm late, Mac. Had something due tomorrow."

"No problem." He waved the offense away. "I'm just glad to see you, especially after last night." It was a blatant sympathy move, but he had to warm her up somehow.

"Right ... You look intact, though."

"It was no accident," he blurted. "Someone wants me dead, Anne. Listen, you're free to walk away. You ..."

She looked at him, puzzled, and then her mouth shriveled. "Oh, I get it. Don't worry about it, Mac. Things are different now. Now I have nothing to lose."

She waited for him to say something, anything. He drew a breath and saw the waiter begin a swing in their direction. It took four seconds to undo his resolve and order a double Dewars when the waiter came within shouting distance. "The usual for you?" McAdams offered.

"Ummm, no. How 'bout a white wine." She turned her face up to address the waiter. "A glass of good California Chardonnay if you have it." He nodded and spun away. She looked back over the table at him and their eyes met.

"Anne, it's been over two years since we lost the baby ...."

"I'm not interested in this ...."

"Let me finish!"

She glared at him. "OK. ... Finish."

"I'm just so sorry - about everything. I can't explain why I didn't tell you about the threats I had received. I ... I thought we were immune, I never thought those hoods would actually come after me ...."

"After us. They came after us, if you remember."

"You've got to forgive me sometime. Maybe we ...."

"I don't have to fucking do anything."

"Then let's just talk about what we lost, let's feel sorry for each other. Then we can move on."

"Why? Why go over all this now? Why start talking about it now, now, when it doesn't make a difference? ... I've moved on, Mac. Work it out so you can move on, too."

"But there's a part we have to work on together. We never consoled each other, never grieved together over Shannon ...."

"DON'T ... mention ... that ... NAME!" Anne's eyes flashed and her jaw jutted in defiant rage. "She never got the chance to HAVE that name!"

People sitting around them stopped what they were doing and looked over at the two of them, a flash of worry in their eyes that things might get louder, uglier, during chow time. McAdams sat back, overwhelmed by the venom, the anger coming from Anne. He didn't understand her, didn't know what she had become. He began to hate himself for helping her become this person he did not know, this person he didn't even like anymore.

"Why can't I use her name?" he responded slowly, controlling his volume. "I was going to be her father! Can't you see what I lost? ... I've lost two families now!" He looked at her, his lower lip quivering a moment before he brought it back under control.

She stared at him, daring him to say more, her face red, defiant spittle dotting her lower lip. She dabbed a cloth napkin to her mouth and threw it back on the table. She folded her hands in front of her. She ached to get up and leave, but she had to stay. There was information to be obtained. There was the President's Commission on Women. That was worth the skin-crawling exercise of staying here at this table, and having this painful little talk.

The waiter saw the cleavage in conversation and inserted

menus between them. McAdams handed one to Anne and buried his face in another, grateful for the buffer, wondering when she was going to bolt. She watched him sink below the top of the oversized sheet of entrees.

She sighed quietly and looked out at the Jefferson Memorial behind McAdams. Lit up, it stood on the other side of the Washington Monument and to the left of it. Beyond that and across the river in Virginia was the illuminated mansion of Robert E. Lee. Arlington Cemetery would be stretched out in the darkness in front of the mansion.

She remembered that Arlington Cemetery was begun during the Civil War. Whoever started the national cemetery made sure that the first Union bodies from that war were buried on Robert E. Lee's front lawn. Death and more death, she thought. It never stops.

The night was so crystal clear she could see the flickering eternal flame beckoning from the grave of John F. Kennedy in the Cemetery. A loneliness came over her as it always did when she saw that solitary flame reaching out. She turned back to McAdams playing with his drink straw. She looked at her empty glass of wine in her intertwined fingers, and pulled one hand free to signal the waiter. They each realized they were going to stay and they ordered another round and dinner.

She gulped a mouthful down as the next goblet hit the table. "Mac, I don't want to think any more about what we lost, or the grief we had, or what could have been, what might've been, blah, blah, blah. Let's end it - everything - right here, right now."

She looked at him. "Agreed?"

McAdams nodded, his eyes feeling moist, his chest and heart fluttering from a wrenching apart, or a soaring liberation. He couldn't tell which. Maybe he was just tired.

She flung her hair back with one hand as she picked up and sipped from the wine glass. She needed to get past this discussion and into the information Mark Fisher needed, before Mac decided to pack it in and leave, or down thirty drinks in one sitting. "Mac ...," she began.

"Yeah?" He already had swallowed half of his second

double Dewars and was looking for the waiter again.

"Nelson Wilkins called me today. Said he heard about your plane ride."

"Really? That's strange. He didn't call me, the victim. Nice of him to think of you though." He got the waiter's attention and another round was coming to the rescue. "Come to think of it," he continued with heavy sarcasm lacing his words, "he never calls anymore. I'm hurt."

"It was a strange call." She sniffed. "You know he can be a real shit. He spent more time talking his power trip than anything else anyway."

McAdams nodded. He knew. Give Wilkins a couple of drinks, a round of applause, or a crowd around him larger than one and he was ready to pontificate on any subject, take on the world or exercise complete dominion over major parts thereof.

"That's twice in one week he's 'reached' out to you. Why the sudden interest?" The calvary came and now they each had two drinks working. A great night. A wonderful fucking night. A man and a woman so happy to be together they needed two drinks at a time to relate.

"Maybe Wilkins wants me again, Mac, I don't know. He asked if we saw each other anymore. I said no, not at all, like where had he been, and all that rot. And then the asshole said that you were probably too BUSY for me - because you were trying to prove that your dead witness was right, that Booth was part of a conspiracy of copperheads that snakebit King. That's exactly what he said, word for word. And then something came over him. He got agitated. He asked me again if I ever saw you anymore. He came at the same question several ways. He was odd from then on."

"Odd is a good way to put it." McAdams was suddenly engaged in the conversation. Tidback had said nothing about copperheads - with or without a capital C - in his brief statement and nothing, nothing at all, about King. He only talked about the Confederate Secret Service. And there was no way Wilkins could've gotten access to O'Connell's transcript dealing with the FBI examination of Booth's diary. No way O'Connell would have let Wilkins get his mitts on those valuable records. No, no, he thought. The Deputy Secretary of Defense came up with that profound insight about Booth and Copperheads all by himself.

She looked at McAdams, noticing the lights had come suddenly back on. Had she misplayed her segueway? Had she said too much? What was going through his mind? She pressed on anyway. "What did Wilkins mean, Mac?"

"About what?" He looked away, trying to avoid her gaze.

"About Booth."

"I ..., I really don't know." Their salads landed on the table.

She put her hand on his. "Come on, Mac. What was Tidback talking about with that conspiracy stuff? Have you found anything about King's assassination we don't already know?"

"Anne, you know I can't tell you what I've found."

"Well, who am I gonna tell?" She squirmed in her seat.

He wanted to answer "who's paying you?" but didn't. Instead he shrugged and watched her mind cranking through some process. Wilkins' remarks were strange enough. Anne's sudden interest in his Committee's work was getting there.

"Was James Earl Ray involved with others? Maybe someone in government? Is that why Wilkins was so weird? Was he fishing around to see if you told me anything?" She pushed away her $10.00 salad.

McAdams noticed she had put on her lawyer's face. She was going for the facts and the gold. The Wilkins' story was true, it had to be. But it was a set up, a springboard to dive into a topic she wanted to pursue. She had no idea just how much she had revealed, however. He decide to play a hand.

"Let me put it this way, Anne. James Earl Ray was connected with some poisonous snakes - inside and outside of government." He smiled. "That's all I'm gonna say, lady. Tell that to your friend, Wilkins."

She sighed, hating his self- satisfied look, and took her hand from his. "Have it your way, asshole." She turned in her chair and looked for the waiter.

"Where the fuck's our dinner?"

Chapter Twenty-nine

Wednesday morning, April 16 -- Washington, DC

The cab squealed to a halt at the 36th and O Streets entrance to Georgetown University. McAdams got out and ran through the rain to the library at the river end of the campus. Dorothy Browning, chair of the History Department, was waiting for him in a top floor conference room.

She shot from her chair at the large circular table that dominated the room to greet her old student. Somewhere in her late sixties, she exuded the contagious energy of one enchanted with ideas and discoveries.

"Mac! Welcome!"

"Your eminence, Madame Professor," he said in mock seriousness as he gave her an exaggerated bow.

"Ohhh ..." She waved him off like a frisky student.

He pulled from his folder and laid on the oak-veneer table photocopies of the Booth diary pages from Tidback's hideaway and copies of select sections of the Committee files that O'Connell had shown him. He closed the curtains across the floor-to-ceiling window that overlooked student carrels and bookshelves and then locked the door to the conference room.

He faced Browning. "Thanks for making the time. Let's get down to business," he said.

She nodded as she pulled from her briefcase her own photocopies that McAdams had faxed to her earlier in the week. Her scribbled notes on the documents covered all available free space. "I've been hard at work since you faxed these to me on Monday."

She ran her fingers over the copies of the Booth diary pages and looked up at McAdams. The nervous tic that haunted her left eye came to life and started her winking as she spoke.

"If you have the originals of these, Mac, and if they're genuine, you've come across a truly precious find. Historic! And if there are more of these missing Booth diary pages lying around somewhere, I'm a shoo-in for the history Pulitzer for the book I'm going to write!"

She shook her head and sat down, clapping her hands together hard in excitement. Her helmet of efficiently short, white hair wafted upward in the resulting slight breeze. On the other side of the huge plate glass window behind her, below them by a quarter of a mile at the base of a hill that fell away from the library, the brown Potomac river rippled solemnly in the rain toward the Chesapeake Bay under the Francis Scott Key Bridge connecting Washington and Virginia.

"Where do you want to start? I'm ready to go ..."

"Tell me about 'OAK.'" McAdams tapped one of the pages before him. "Tell me what this 'manifesto,' is all about."

"No free mason," she read aloud from a page she had taken from the table top and held in front of her face, "minuteman, federalist, republican, judge or any false patriot shall be allowed to interfere with the enjoyment and pursuit of property -- either by constitution, law, plebiscite, referendum, military rule, imprisonment or taxation -- without answering to our

punishment. And so, by such work, shall We the People secure the promise of our Revolution and our Nation." She put the page down and looked at McAdams.

He nodded. "What the hell does it mean?"

Her fingers pressed to her lips as if in prayer. "This is very, very similar to something called the Vigilante Creed that first appeared, oh, I guess it would be in the early 1840's. The 'Vigilantes' were just that. They set themselves up as local police forces to protect and defend farms, homes and what they selectively perceived as 'decent' citizens, from the wild lawlessness of pre-Civil War America. The Vigilantes could be rough -- they extorted, they entrapped, they planted false evidence and intimidated witness -- all in the name of their own peculiar sense of justice. But this creed you have come across is, in a word, unique. It differs from the Vigilantes' because it is purely mercantile, purely economic. It enshrines a way of life that is above the law and, at the same time a law unto itself. It isn't focused on ridding the world of common law-breakers like the Vigilantes' Creed. It's very bitter and insidious. Scary ..."

"What is 'OAK'?"

"The only 'OAK' I have come across in all my years is the Order of American Knights ... O-A-K. It was organized in 1862, maybe earlier, in St. Louis. Its leader, Phineas Wright, was picked up and detained the day after Lincoln was shot and interrogated by the authorities for possible complicity in the assassination. He was released the same day."

"The OAK creed I found in the loft is in Booth's handwriting, Professor. So is the note to 'Secretary Nathaniel Brock and the Committee.' There's no doubt of that. If they were in Booth's diary and cut out by someone, as this Subcommittee transcript states ..."

"... then that would have enormous implications for history," Browning finished. "And for the very legitimacy of the government that held Booth's diary after it was taken from him and then went on to prosecute him. And that's just for starters, Mac. Who knows what is being revealed to us here? Who knows what else is in that diary?"

McAdams ran his fingers through his hair. "What WAS the Order of American Knights? What did it do?"

"Let me put OAK in perspective. The two decades before the Civil War were rife with conspiracies, hate groups, separatist movements - all that rot. Most of these were centered on slavery. These groups hit their glory days during the War itself. Some of them were made up of no more than out-of-work ruffians, thugs. Some were sophisticated, composed of politicians, industrialists, military officers, journalists - the best and the brightest of the North."

"Sophisticated? How?"

"Well, take the Knights of the Golden Circle. The Knights were very wealthy, very establishment, very conservative Northerners. They had elaborate membership rituals focused on a mythical circle of entry to what was to be a vast slave empire in the New World. The 'golden circle' was said to be located somewhere in Havana, Cuba. Only the privileged Knights were able to enter the Circle and thus assume their leadership mantle in the slave empire.

"The Knights of the Golden Circle started to come apart in the late 1850's but the group was resuscitated by Jefferson Davis and the Confederates just before the Civil War. The Knights railed against Lincoln's Republicans in the newspapers and through pamphleteering, but what else they did during the Civil War has never been nailed down.

"That brings me to the Order of the American Knights. Some historians, including me, think OAK was a violent successor to the Knights of the Golden Circle. OAK burned brilliantly and briefly and then simply disappeared from history after 1865 or so. After OAK came the Sons of Liberty and the Copperheads. Both were made up of Northerners disaffected enough with Lincoln and the war to act as an arm of the Confederacy during the fighting."

"I've always believed," she smiled, "that the Sons and the Copperheads were a bunch of big talkers who walked away from the real nasty stuff of violence, murder, guerrilla warfare and mayhem. These guys liked to dress up in paramilitary garb. They'd meet in secret meeting houses, talk big, act conspiratorially, get drunk and wake up in the morning feeling self-important and headachy."

McAdams chuckled. "Like the Knights of Columbus."

"Or the DAR," laughed Browning.

"How violent was OAK? You just mentioned murder, guerrilla warfare, mayhem ..."

"We have no records, Mac, no autobiographies. Nevertheless, we have newspaper reports, letters, interviews, government reports, trial transcripts, oral history, etcetera, that lead me to think OAK orchestrated the worst of the guerrilla warfare that erupted from time to time during the darkest days of the Civil War. And, then, when the bright lights of notoriety came upon it, OAK simply vanished. Poof! Maybe to emerge later."

She looked at the papers on the table before her. "Maybe, God forbid, to emerge in the here and now."

"There was guerrilla warfare during the Civil War?"

"Oh, yes, some very vicious stuff. And Professor Tidback published some of the seminal research in this area."

She stopped and her face darkened at the thought of her fallen colleague. "There were," came her raspy voice, "massive draft riots in New York City in 1863. These, ostensibly, were in protest of the Union's effort to begin draft conscription. Blacks were hunted down and assaulted during the riots, lynched! -- in the heart of the North! -- during the War to free the slaves! Over 100 people were killed in what was the worst civil disturbance in this country until the LA riots in '93."

"I, and others, including David, think the riots were instigated by the Confederacy, perhaps in allegiance with OAK, which was unusually visible and active in the north at the time. Anyway, the disturbance eventually spread from New York City to New Hampshire and to Newark, New Jersey. Lafayette Baker, the brave soul you recently learned first went public about the missing Booth diary pages, he helped quell the outbreak through his detective work."

"There's more. Northern soldiers were exposed to yellow fever bacteria lodged in new uniforms. There was an attempt to expose old Abe Lincoln himself to yellow fever. There were plots to kill the President in Baltimore in 1860, to blow up the Capitol building in 1861, and to kill the Governors of Indiana, Ohio and Illinois in one fell swoop as a prelude to armed insurrection in those states. There was another plan at the war's end to mine the Executive mansion."

"Many of us, including David, blame these plots on OAK, sometimes acting with the Confederacy and its Secret Service, sometimes operating on its own. Others pin the guerrilla warfare on the Copperheads. Maybe we're all right. What you had at this time, really, was a very confusing situation, perhaps deliberately so, where the true culprits behind the violence and the mayhem never exposed themselves, never claimed credit as terrorists do today. During the Civil War, you had a hard core of trained individuals in the North who supported the South and slavery and moved in and out of the many partisan groups that sprang up. In this way they were able to maintain cover, sow confusion and inflate perceptions of their numbers."

"Was Booth a member of OAK?"

"Don't know for sure. There is evidence, though, to suggest that Booth was a member of the Copperheads."

She tapped an outstretched finger on one of the photocopies.

"As the Congressman noted in this hearing, Lady Liberty's head, cut from the Civil War-era penny and worn on a necklace, was the Copperhead symbol. You came across an impression of Liberty on one of Booth's diary pages and that discovery is an absolutely important historical find of the first order. That it was stifled by the FBI and a Subcommittee of the US House of Representatives is unconscionable."

"So, what about OAK?" he prodded. "Was Booth part of OAK?"

"Oh, there've been articles in journals over the years associating Booth with OAK. Now, thanks to you, we know he carried in his diary a hand-written copy of OAK's creed. But it's of little practical consequence, Mac. As I said, the members of these various pro-South groups flowed into and out of them all the time - to fit their needs and their targets, to propagandize - as the War progressed. Look, the diary page with the OAK creed carries at the same time a Copperhead impression at the bottom, almost like a seal!"

"So," McAdams pondered, "Booth worked for the Confederacy. He worked for OAK and he worked for the Copperheads. And he's reporting in to Secretary Nathaniel Brock and a 'Committee' of some sort."

He looked intently at Browning, his deep, brown eyes searching for answers in her face. "Who pulled Booth's strings, Professor? Jeff Davis? The Confederate Secret Service? The economic vigilantes of OAK? The Copperheads?"

"Maybe," she shrugged, "maybe the Confederacy used John Wilkes Booth, a creed-carrying OAK member. Maybe OAK and John Wilkes Booth used the Confederacy. Maybe getting rid of Lincoln was something OAK wanted, too."

"I see how OAK might be pro-South, pro-slavery, maybe even prone to strong-arm tactics and aiding the enemy," McAdams replied, "but these were establishment, conservative, old line citizens we're talkin' about. Hell, even John Wilkes Booth was a famous actor. Why take on the terrible crime of murdering a President. Were they all that far gone?"

"Not gone, but desperate, angry. Their world was collapsing. Perhaps OAK - like Jefferson Davis - saw it was still possible for the Confederacy to snatch victory from the jaws of defeat by bringing down the whole US government in one swift stroke - Lincoln's murder."

"OK. But what would Lincoln's execution do for OAK?"

"Read OAK's creed carefully, Mac - no one is to interfere with enjoyment of their property without OAK's 'punishment.' Remember, the slavery issue then was an economic one, first, and a moral issue, second. One in three people in the South were held in slavery and considered property. Slavery was an enormous, low cost engine of the Southern economy. In turn it supported Southern trade with the North and, of course, Northern profits. When Lincoln freed the slaves it was the single greatest uncompensated liberation of 'property' this country ever saw or will see - bigger than Truman's nationalization of the steel mills. Perhaps OAK saw the Southern cause as more aligned with its economic goals. Perhaps OAK saw a Lincoln victory, a Northern conquest, as a real threat to its own commercial, propertied interests. In sponsoring the killing of Lincoln, OAK might have figured it would be the primary beneficiary of a change in government."

McAdams sat quietly, rubbing his chin.

"That's it, Mac. That's all I got so far."

McAdams began to slowly pack up his papers. "One last thing," he said. "What happened to Lafayette Baker?"

"Oh, yes, you asked me about that. President Andrew Johnson kicked him out of the National Detective Bureau. Baker died about a year after he made his allegations concerning the Booth diary before the House Assassinations Committee - at the grand old age of 43. Some claim he died from arsenic poisoning. Baker's wife claimed that several gunshot attempts on his life had been made just prior to his death."

"Perfect ...," he mumbled as they left the room.

Chapter Thirty

Wednesday night, 11:45 p.m.

The red eyes of the Washington Monument winked at him in the dark. Sometimes they would wink at the same time, sometimes they would alternate.

The red eyes were lights set just below the triangle at the top of the Monument, blinking to alert the planes bound for nearby National Airport. McAdams considered them the jaded, bloodshots of a lonely sentry watching Washington play out its many scenes. Or the eyes of the myopic monster that came to eat Washington. It all depended on his mood. Tonight the Monument looked hungry.

He sat in the Victorian bandstand located outside the National Museum of American History and across Constitution Avenue from the Department of Commerce. The bandstand was in the middle of a sunken bowl carved out of the ground. Elevated almost twenty feet, he could see everything around him. Anyone joining him would have to come to the base of the earthen bowl and then up the steps to where he sat.

Downtown Washington was eerily still. Washington's workers had headed for the suburbs, leaving the bars and the late-night scenes in Georgetown, Capitol Hill, the K Street corridor and Adams Morgan to the college students, the young professionals and the diehards like him. Some 20 blocks directly north was where the trouble usually was. Last night there were three homicides among crack dealers. One was twelve years old.

The rich, mostly whites, lived in Northwest Washington. The native Washingtonians, mostly blacks, lived in the northeast and, like Jazz, southeast parts of town. Here in the core part of town where government buildings stood impassively, he was alone except for the occasional steam heat grate full of street people basking in the lamp light.

He caught a moving shadow emerge from a line of pine trees behind the Museum to his left. It slowly made its way to his perch. It was Brock. The erect posture and hesitating gait gave him away. The old man peered up into the bandstand.

"Ah sure hope that's you, John. Ah'm comin' up." He puffed up the stairs and sat down about six feet away from McAdams.

"Ah'm not used to this skulking around like a chicken thief."

McAdams watched Brock fumble for a handkerchief from his suit jacket pocket and wipe a sheen of perspiration from his wrinkled brow. Brock was over seventy and the exertion was testing him. That or the nature of his late night call. The old man shifted uncomfortably on the hard bench seat.

"Well, it's late and we should begin. But Ah hope your, uh, run-in on the plane has not left you harmed."

McAdams shook his head. Ground lights reflecting off the wall of the Museum fell on Brock's face, illuminating the lines in his forehead and accentuating the deep crevices in his cheeks and the overhang of his heavy eyebrows. His gray hair glimmered in the dim light.

"John, Ah know who was behind the attempt on yo' life the other night."

"What?" McAdams croaked. "How, how do you know?"

"Lewis Shephard works for me."

"Lewis Shephard tried to have me killed?" McAdams cracking voice rose above the hoarse whisper of their conversation.

"Let me lay it out fo' ya. Ah've known for a while that Lewis Shephard has been involved in some kind of an effort to bring together right wingers and anarchists carrying guns. He was workin' to pull together groups like the KKK, the Posse Comitatus, the Order and others of their ilk." He peered into McAdams' face. "You familiar with these folks?"

McAdams, numb, nodded.

"I think Shephard is all caught up in the full load of chickenshit these twisted dime-store terrorists parlay."

But Shephard's bosses, admitted Brock to himself, the new boys, wanted something more practical from these bands of outlaws. They desired a ready supply of brainless, hate-filled, money-hungry thugs to take care of their dirty business, to maim and intimidate, even kill, upon command. In the end, he knew, this senseless anarchy was risky. It would expose, and ruin, all that he and his ancestors had worked to establish over the generations. In the end this nightmare possibility forced him to come to McAdams in the middle of the godforsaken night, in the great wide open, where he could be seen. Forced him to reach out to McAdams in the hope something he might say might bring them together.

Brock sat back, infinitely tired. He wondered how much he could do to save the new boys, Shephard's mentors, from themselves.

"But surely others are calling the shots," McAdams pleaded. "Lewis Shephard can't be organizing fanatical groups!"

Brock waved his right hand and emitted a little laugh. McAdams had been reading his thoughts. "He works for others, all right. They give him money and resources and point him in the right direction. Some of 'em are at the top levels of our government, which is why I am meetin' with you, here, in the dark." He glanced around and was wiping his brow again when a city Metro bus screeched to a painful halt in front of a red traffic light glowing at the corner of 14th Street and Constitution Avenue. They both watched a man get off the bus, hesitate and then walk away from them.

Brock turned back to McAdams. "Ah'm takin' a great risk coming to you like this. My life is in jeopardy if Ah am discovered." He gathered his breath before continuing, looking around him at the same time into the night.

"Listen to me. Lewis Shephard was instructed to have you killed a few nights ago 'cause his people was worried. You got them all riled up with your pokin' around into what the Professor was gonna say befo' our Committee. They got worried you'd find somethin' and head straight fo' them, or fo' Lewis Shephard's group of nuts that he's got scattered 'round the country, and then eventually you'd stumble on the people pullin' Shephard's strings. You see, the Professor found out somehow that Shephard's group had come together under a grand design over the last few years. Tidback believed that this crowd, and its masters, had their origin, at least spiritually, in the Civil War and all the Confederate and pro-slavery groups that grew up in that war between the states. The good Professuh just didn't understand that Shephard's boys, and his bossmen, have gotten lost in the woods, they've moved way beyond the noble sentiments that gave rise to the Confederacy. ... He found that out the day he was shot."

"Why would Tidback come to our Committee about punks and rabble rousers? We're looking at Martin Luther King's assassination"

Brock shifted back and forth on the seat. "Ah don't have an answer fo' ya, John. Ah came here to get you to help me - to help root out Shephard and his crowd before they get carried away, like they did with Tidback, and go and ruin this country of ours."

"How do you know all this? I mean about Shephard, his 'bossmen,' his gang of hoodlums ..."

"Ah know. Lewis works for me. Jes' leave it at that."

"I can't. By failing to go to the FBI or police on this you could be seen as feloniously assisting in the commission of a crime. And if the man who killed Tidback and the man who came after me come from the groups Shephard is organizing, then you're talking complicity in murder, and attempted murder."

Brock hissed laughter. "Big stuff, John. But Ah'm not worried!" He raised his large hands and waved them back and forth. "Ah have much bigguh worries." Looking at the shadows and crevices in his face, McAdams believed him.

"Tell me who in the government knows of this, and tell me who else is involved."

Brock shook his head.

"I'm not walking away from this. Tell me what you know ..."

"John, what you have to do is sweep all of this under the rug. That's why Ah am here, why Ah'm telling you all this. Ah want you to close down your investigation into Tidback's murder. You have to let the Committee go away May 1, and then you have to seal the record - as a matter of national security or something. Ah know you, you'll find something good we can hang our hat on. And then, John, you and Ah will work together to remove Shephard and the others involved with him. Ah promise you that. We'll make sure they leave the government, retire and such, and move on to somethin' else. We'll expose the ones that need to be run out 'a town."

"Then I'll be guilty of a conspiracy to obstruct justice - at best. Like you. And whatever link exists between Shephard's group, and his hoodlums, and the King Assassination, will be left unexplored."

"There are worse things. Look at it this way. You'll be savin' the people from finding out things 'bout our history, our government, that they jes' shouldn't know. You're talkin' 'bout a century of conspiracy and death here ..."

"What ...?"

" ... the true criminals, Shephard and the rest, will disappear or escape conviction. They'll walk away if I let you do it your way. Scott free."

McAdams leaned forward. "What do you mean by 'a century of conspiracy and death'?"

Brock's head lowered to his chest. "Work with me, John," he said with what seemed to be ages of fatigue.

"What do you mean by a century of conspiracy and death? Is Shepherd's group, its leadership, linked to King's murder? Are they tied to the Lincoln assassination?"

Brock stood. "This has been going on for some time, Mac. Tidback was on to it and he died for it. Ah just wish Ah ... took the chance to get him into the fold like Ah'm doin' with you." Brock slowly shook his head. "But it's too late for Tidback now. It's not too late for you."

McAdams jumped to his feet and grabbed the old man as he was turning away to walk down the stairs. "This isn't just a bunch of nuts 'spiritually linked' to the Confederacy like you want me to think. There's more! What was Tidback going to say?"

He flung Brock back onto the bench with a heavy thud. "Talk!"

The old man grimaced and then a bemused look blossomed. "Well, that was some display. Now what you gonna do? You gonna rough me up and have the police come and think we're doin' some kinky things up here all alone in the dark? ... There's only so much Ah can or will tell you 'bout all this, so listen hard! ... Close up the show, and help me. It's very important. It's what's right for our country. And, listen to me John. It's the only way you're gonna be able to put some of this to an end ... That's it. That's all Ah'm gonna say."

McAdams stared at the shrunken man beneath him on the bench. Brock looked small and frail. But, somehow - in that vulnerable position, with his incessant grace and courtesy - he gave off an air of invincibility, an aura of haughtiness and detachment accentuated by the darkness of the night that shrouded his grim features. It was the strength of a man who had lived through some kind of hell and now walked only in purgatory.

"You're part of this hundred years of death and conspiracy," McAdams rasped. His breath came in short bursts. His wishbone scar glistened in the moonlight. "I found a note from John Wilkes Booth to Nathaniel Brock written on one of Booth's diary pages. He was apologizing about failing to kidnap Lincoln and said he was going to go on and kill him. ... Now tell me, isn't Nate a relative of yours? Wasn't Booth one of the 'hoodlums' back then, reporting in to his sponsors? Just like Lewis Shephard and his boys do today?"

Brock's head shot backward. McAdams fell to one knee and put his face in the old man's. The sweet smell of bourbon hit him.

"You, and Shephard, are carrying on Booth's and Nathaniel's dirty work. And maybe Shephard has gotten a little too crazy for you. Maybe you've just lost control of it all. Or maybe there's been a little falling out among the conspirators, and you're just gonna use me to rat 'em out and pick up the pieces all for yourself afterwards."

Brock's chest rose and fell with his breath. He sat, silent.

"I think I'm close," McAdams continued. "I also think you knew Tidback. Did you know he had stumbled across missing pages from Booth's diary?"

Brock watched McAdams' face, trying to pick up what the younger man knew.

"It's all there, isn't it?" McAdams spat. "In the missing pages from Booth' diary."

"Fo'get about that diary," said a suddenly agitated Brock. "You see where it got Tidback! Don't you let all this get into yo' Committee Report. Don't let Shephard's crowd even think it's gonna get in there."

"What's Booth diary got to do with King's assassination? Why the fuck would I want to put it in my Report?"

"Now, John, get calm." Brock pulled his jacket together. "A couple a' ma men are right behind you on the lawn. They probably have you in their cross hairs. Ah am going to leave now. Ah would advise you do as Ah've asked, befo' you can't go back. You have no idea of the dimensions of what you are chipping away at. No idea at all."

He walked to the stairs, stopped and turned, exhaling loudly. He had failed. McAdams hadn't responded. The lines were drawn in the dirt. "Think 'bout it. Think it over, and join me. Ah'm beggin' ya. Together we'll clean up this mess. But if we wind up on either side of the battlefield, well ..." He shrugged. "It'll be brotha against brotha again, won't it? Just like it was long ago."

Brock, paused, looked down at his feet and then turned his face up again. His eyes gleamed with purpose. "Good night to ya, suh." He nodded and turned away.

McAdams watched Brock step down the stairs and across the lawn. He walked away into the darkness of the pine trees behind the Museum. Two other shadows followed him a few heartbeats later. The dark boughs of the tall trees began waving slightly in the first stirrings of a growing breeze.

McAdams looked at the government buildings with their black windows against the white shaft of the Washington Monument. A gust of cold wind rushed through the bandstand. He shivered and got up to leave.

Chapter Thirty-one

Thursday morning, 2:53 a.m., April 16 -- Ashland, Virginia

Linda Walker stood in her darkened dormitory room, peering intently between slats of the venetian blind covering her window. Three stories below sat the empty pick-up truck. The two rednecks that had parked it on the street a couple of hours ago had not yet come back.

Where were those two? Most of the night they sat in the cabin of the pick-up, leering at anything young and female, guzzling from beer cans, but now they were gone. They were ugly things, with thick arms littered with incomprehensible tattoos and sprouts of course hair that protruded nastily from under their T-shirts and baseball caps. They were cut from the same cloth as the two who had followed Mac and her just a few days ago. Indistinguishable thugs wearing a common uniform of T-shirts, flannel shirts, jeans and boots.

She shook it off. She was spooked. This part of Virginia was loaded with guys like this and the two outside in their pick-up were just part of the normal scene. Had she and Mac not been attacked, she wouldn't have even noticed it now. It was just a coincidence.

Just a coincidence. Sure. She took a deep breath.

A sudden slam of the hall door to the stairwell pushed her up against the blind, crushing some of the slats. A young woman's laughter, followed by the mumbled conversation of her boyfriend, echoed before a room door opened and then shut.

She walked over to her door and leaned against it, listening. Silence. She opened it a crack and peered into the hall. Seeing nothing, she widened the gap and stuck her head out, looking both ways. The hallway was empty.

She closed the door and locked it and then sat on her bed. Her father looked down at her from an old Polaroid that she had slipped into the frame of her wall mirror. The camera had been a gift to her from him one Christmas, long ago, the photograph taken by a little girl excited to see her dad at the end of one of his long days on the military base. His eyes looked tired, there were dark circles around them, but his wide smile, the smile everyone said she inherited, revealed how happy he was to pose for his little girl. He was twisting his chiseled Polynesian features into some comic attitude, making the funny face she remembered demanding from him before she would snap the picture.

Her mother was dead by then. She had been attacked – raped - and then shot by an enlisted man that had broken into their small housing quarters on the base. He was hopped up on drugs, her father would explain later; he didn't know what he was doing.

She was the first to discover her mother the day it happened, when she came home after school. Her mother's body was stretched across her own little, child's bed, a bed neatly made as it always was every morning but now made rumpled and horribly bloody red by a man with a gun hopped up on drugs. She remembered her mother's light brown skin, the color of coffee ice cream, laying flat against her favorite bedspread of white daisies. She remembered the dollops of blood that stained the bed covers and the enormous dark red wound in her mother's naked chest that oozed blood onto the pure white daisies they both loved so much. She saw the black gun next to the bed, on the floor, cold, quiet, dead. In the corner of the room, giddy and dazed by what he had done, by his dementia, was the enlisted man sitting by himself, his eyes blank, his mouth mumbling words and gibberish. It was she who called the MPs from the list of important numbers her mother had painstakingly taped near the phone. It was she who waited in that house with that gun on the floor, she who waited in that house, alone, with that man whispering and burbling and laughing in the corner until they came and took him away. They took her mother away too.

She pulled up her legs in the dark of her room and sat gazing at the photo in the mirror, hugging her knees, something she often did. Her father was the one who taught her to go on, how to be tough, how to defend herself, teaching her karate and other martial arts when she was a kid. She refused to touch a gun, any gun, after that day she had come home from school and found her mother. Her father, the military man, understood.

She thought of him the day she tried out for kick-boxing her freshman year in college over 10 years ago. She thought of him at every match, every victory. He had made her strong and resilient and free. He helped her surpass the tragedy that ruined him. But he was gone now, five years gone.

Suicide.

He killed himself with the gun that had shot her mother. It was a psychotic act, according to her father's psychiatrist in the Veterans' Hospital, a sickly romantic or desperate act, by which her sad, sorrowful father tried to link up with his wife, her mother, somehow. Whatever, she thought. It was an act by which he left me behind and all alone.

She missed him and his smile. His warm hugs and his soothing words. And she had kept up the kick-boxing all these years, kept up the self-defense, as he would have wanted. But she had never met a man who might replace her father. Never met a man who could make the worst all go away like he could.

She sighed and thought about McAdams. She slipped on her sneakers and went to the door again. Checking to make sure she had her key in her pocket, she closed the door behind her and locked it. She jogged down the empty hallway and down three flights of echoing stairs to the dormitory lobby where there were several phone booths.

Looking around the lobby she looked for the security guard. He was gone, absent from his normal post behind the front desk. Probably making rounds, she hoped. She shrugged, stepping into one of the phone booths. She closed the door, picked up the phone and dialed McAdams' phone number.

"Mac," she whispered hoarsely when she got his voice mail. "I'm sorry I'm leaving a message like this, so late, but … but I wanted to talk to you. And I was supposed to call you every week and so, well, this is my first official call …" She looked over her shoulder into the lobby when the door to the campus opened and several students entered. They waved at her and she waved back before turning to face the phone again.

"Anyway, Mac…." she continued, "I've gone through everything the Professor left here at RM. … I've come across some notes in his office. Remember the name Nathaniel Brock on Booth's letter? Well, it's for sure Senator Taylor Brock's ancestor. Booth called him "Secretary" because he was a member of Jefferson Davis' cabinet in the Confederacy. It proves that Booth was working for the Confederates! And there's more. The Professor was sure that Lincoln's assassination was a part of a coup attempt by OAK, in league with the Confederacy, with Booth as a cover - you know, the nutty lone gunman that always seems to show up in all our assassinations. If you remember your history, Booth's accomplices tried to take out, on the night Lincoln was shot, the Vice President, the Secretaries of State and War and Ulysses Grant, the leader of the Army. And, finally, about Booth's diary …. It's incredible, Mac. No one even SAW it for two years after it was turned over by Lafayette Baker to the government. It was the only thing NOT turned over!. The lawyer of one of Booth's accomplices, threatening mistrial, forced it into the light of day by demanding its production at trial in 1867. … OK? I'll call again. And, Mac? I've been reading everything I can get my hands on in connection with the King assassination. There has to be a link, something we can find, that Professor Tidback discovered. Something that made him conclude that the Lincoln conspiracy continues …."

She ran a hand through her hair. "I want to … talk to you, Mac. OK? … All right, that's it for now. I'll see ya. … Soon I hope. … Maybe I'll catch a train to DC." The voice machine beeped twice, cutting her off.

Chapter Thirty-two

Friday evening, April 17 -- A Maine Island

Governor Morrison Narkle of Wisconsin looked out the open window toward the bay. The nearly full moon above in a cloudless sky cast a bright sheen upon the waters. He shuddered slightly as a gust of wind blew off the waters below him. There would be a chilling frost before morning. At points along the shore, the cold night settled in under a blanket of fog.

There was no heat inside the building where he stood. The windows before him were merely openings in the walls, with no shutters or barriers to the elements. The two story stone-and-mortar edifice was built just before the Civil War. During the war it served as an armed observation point, but never saw a minute of combat.

The building was hacked into the western side of a small island overlooking the mainland. About a half of a mile away was the coast of Cape Elizabeth, Maine. The back two walls of the pentagon-shaped structure were cut out of the rocky island, with the other walls facing the bay that emptied eventually into the frigid Atlantic Ocean. Each of the two floors had a row of windows, each window spaced about six feet apart and offering excellent vantage points for cannon and musketry.

He stood on the second floor and watched the lights of Cape Elizabeth and South Portland to the right flicker like candles in a soft breeze. Behind him, in the room dimly revealed by the soft blue light of the moon, there was a huge, collapsible table surrounded by folding chairs.

The table was prepared for the meeting. Green blotters in brown leather holders were arranged with note pads and pens in front of each of the 12 chairs now huddled around the table. A half-dozen kerosene lamps formed a circle in the middle of the table. None of the lamps would be lit until the windows were covered with the heavy black leather tarps now rolled up tightly and lying underneath each open space.

The two attendants dressed in black and waiting behind him

along one of the dark walls would see to the sealing of the windows and the lighting of the lamps. They would then serve the selection of wines and Maine cuisine that accompanied each meeting. Everything was arranged for, and was secretly brought to the island that afternoon. Everything followed the protocols of long tradition.

The formal setting, the stone walls and earthen floor, and the huge cavernous room with its flickering lamps had sometimes amused him in the past. Often he would feel he was attending a rite of some devil-worshipping coven from the Middle Ages. But tonight's meeting held no humor for him.

Things had changed. He had changed.

He listened to the mournful foghorns in the distance as they called home those who could hear. The ocean-going ferry that shuttled to Nova Scotia came into his view as it slowly slipped from Portland to the ocean. It was the nightly run. The ferry would be back in the morning. With lights on its mast lines and its port side, it looked like a floating jack-o-lantern grinning obscenely. Music softly floated on the wind from the boat to his ears.

He turned to face the attendants. "Is everything in order?"

"Yes, Governor," said the tallest of the two attendants, the one they called Sable.

"Cover the windows, then, and light the lamps. The rest will be arriving soon."

"Yes, sir," Sable replied.

Over the next half-hour, they came. Narkle bowed to each man as he arrived. Deputy Defense Secretary Nelson Wilkins was first, followed closely by Ameribanc chairman Reid Johnson and billionaire G.B. "Manny" Palau. Next came the dashing White House aide Mark Fisher. He immediately backed Wilkins into a corner with a flurry of hand gestures and animated remarks.

Congressman Nick Tomovitch came through the entry with Senator Brock behind him. Brock was elegantly dressed but was bent and distracted. He walked quickly over to Fisher, interrupting his conversation with Wilkins. Tomovitch had a long, easy stride and the usual remnants of a recent meal, a late lunch probably, on his tie.

Vice Commandant Lloyd Johansen, erect with his military hair cut, marched in while Deputy Attorney General Mankins, wearing half-glasses for reading, and shouldering a tired, conscientious load, followed. The old men of the room, Brock's contemporaries, sat slowly in the chairs - the patrician Mason Allen and the folksy Barry Ingram.

Ingram shuffled these days. He had long, wild wisps of red hair that spilled all over his pudgy face. Allen walked the stiff walk of the privileged. As usual, the peacock, Timothy Lillicut, brought up the rear. No doubt he wanted everyone to know he had struggled to put the Wall Street Chronicle, the largest business newspaper in the country, to bed.

Twelve strong, they were now fully assembled and seated. Narkle waited as wine glasses were refilled. He scanned the room. The shadows cast on the walls and ceiling swayed back and forth to the low, rhythmic murmur of conversations.

Narkle nodded to Brock who extended his hand and motioned for Narkle to proceed. The aging Senator slowly and deeply bowed as he did so. The others watched this exchange, silently marking the changing of the guard.

Barry Ingram ran one of his hands through what remained of his thinning hair as he watched Brock and Narkle go through their little dance. His mind went back to the night almost thirty-five years ago when Brock took over the reins of power from Josh Wellinger, the eventful night when Wellinger had failed in urging them to take the lead in assassinating John F. Kennedy. Others would do the job, Brock had argued. There was no need for their involvement. Brock had won, and taken control of the group. Just like Narkle had won out over Brock at their last meeting.

Ingram was startled back to the present with a loud banging. Narkle was calling for order, pounding his clenched fist on the tabletop. The group grew silent.

"Thank you, gentlemen," smiled Narkle. "Now, the creed ...,"

Brock reached into his suit jacket pocket and turned on his sensitive, voice activated tape recorder. The new boys, the 'professionals', were getting a little sloppy. In his day, when there were difficult meetings to be had, no one got in without a good body search. He leaned back and at last smiled, basking in the warmth and comfort of the familiar words of OAK's creed.

When it concluded, Narkle's face grew dark. He looked around the table. "Jackson is heading for Washington …."

Brock straightened, alarmed. "He has been in touch with McAdams?"

"Yes."

Palau's voice snapped out like a cracking whip. "Then we got some work to do, don't we, gentlemen?"

Heads nodded around the table as Palau craned his neck to lock eyes with Sable standing in the shadows against one of the walls. "Don't we?"

Sable shook his head up and down once. Cigarette smoke curled from the stick in his hand and lingered like the fog around his pale, puffy face. Behind him stood the second attendant, a squat, powerful Vietnamese man with thick legs and arms.

Brock squinted to see Sable in the dark. The man was frightening to behold. He was pure violence compressed into a bulging body, pure cunning pent up in a head that was too small. His face was riddled with pockmarks and his eyelids were reddened. The black orbs of his small irises floated in a murky, runny pus and bore down on the table of men like gun barrels. A greasy chunk of Sable's jet-black hair hung above his right eye. His bulbous nose reared up naturally, like he was about to blow snot across the room, and bulged out over an upper lip that curled naturally into the early stages of a sneer, telling you to get lost.

Sable represented what OAK had become, how much it had strayed from its careful, deliberate ways. Sable's whole bearing, his verocious, violent bearing, presaged where they would all go before all was said and done.

Brock felt a shudder trickle down his spine as he realized Sable was staring back at him. He shifted his eyes back to the table, to the discussions that had broken out. He let his eyes dart back once more to the menacing Sable. Sable's arms were crossed over his powerful chest. His eyes still were locked on Brock.

"Alright," Palau said above the conversations, "let's get down to business. Governor Narkle, you're the control now. Take it away."

Chapter Thirty-three

Saturday morning, April 18 -- Washington, DC

The National Botanical Gardens squatted at the corner of 1st Street and Independence Avenue, southwest of the Capitol building. Jackson hauled himself out of the cab he had taken from the train station as McAdams approached the car.
"Welcome, Chief."
Jackson wore a down-home look of light brown corduroy pants, a beige work shirt and a tan barn jacket fresh from a catalog. He had a folder under his arm. He gripped McAdams outstretched hand and pumped it as he peered into the clouded brown eyes taking his own measure.
"Well, you're younger looking than I thought." He stood on the sidewalk with his hands on his hips and sized up McAdams like a busybody uncle that came to visit once a year.
The younger man had an earnest, probing look. Jackson liked the firm handshake and the way he looked him straight in the eye. McAdams was dressed casually and looked just like Chief Williams described him - a college professor bidding a grudging farewell to most legitimate claims to youth.
"No wonder Larcher mistook you and Crockett on the plane," he observed as McAdams put a hand on his shoulder and led him back across the sidewalk toward the elaborate greenhouse of the Gardens. "Williams said you looked more at home on the campus of Randolph-Macon than the Professor did. He also said you was 'OK.' Good people to him is good people to me, even if you are a lawyer from D.C."
Jackson laughed easily. "You're hilarious," chuckled McAdams. He feigned a right-handed punch in Jackson's direction. "But don't worry, I haven't practiced real law in years. Now I've broken a few now and then - both professionally and personally ... Now let's get out of sight, quick."
McAdams clapped Jackson on the back as they entered the Gardens. They were hitting it off instantly, sharing a common

mystery, and common devils. Slowly they made their way through the front entrance hall into the main garden. It was filled with ferns and vegetation hanging from the domed ceiling high overhead. Trees, undergrowth and flowering plants spewed from the walls and the ground. The air was snug, warm and humid.

"I like this place," McAdams said as he guided Jackson along the walkways. "It's real hard for someone to follow you in here, unless they are planted among the bushes. Listening devices just don't last too long in this humidity either."

"I guess you Washington guys are used to all this cloak and dagger stuff," Jackson shrugged. He studied McAdams' cheek.

"Where you get that slash of yours? Nam? I lost a son over there ..."

"I got this a few blocks from here," McAdams answered as he rubbed the scar. "In the line of duty, you might say." Jackson nodded he understood.

"Sorry about your boy," offered McAdams.

"Oh yeah. Well, you just never get over it, Mac. Never. ... Your dad would know. Is he alive?"

McAdams felt a wave of discomfort come over him. Dad, such a strange word to call the man. "Uh, no, no he ... uh, died, when I was young. I didn't really know him too well."

Jackson put a hand on McAdams shoulder. "Well, he knew you, believe me. By the time he passed on he knew what you liked, what you didn't like, and what you were going to do about it. And you probably knew by then all there was to know about him, at least all he was ever going to show you anyway."

McAdams nodded as they sat down on a concrete bench in the main room. Behind them loomed a ten-foot bank of ferns. Jackson slapped his knee as they settled in. "So where do we begin, young man?" he said. "I got to get back to Harpers Ferry before the criminals know I'm gone."

McAdams, relieved the attention was shifting to another topic, began quickly, in a low voice. He started the morning Tidback was shot and went on from there, including Brock's midnight stories about Shephard's unseen bosses and a century of death and conspiracy. Stopping again to size up Jackson before proceeding, McAdams decided he had to trust him.

"Chief, the key to all this, to your case and Williams' in Richmond, is what's in those missing Booth diary pages. ... I found some of them. In a loft over a garage that Tidback used near the college while he was there. He used it until he got killed. No one seems to know about it, except the person who led me to it, me, ... and now you."

"Go on."

McAdams described Booth's letter and the OAK creed, right down to the Lady Liberty images. He stopped when Jackson's features froze.

"Damnation! I came across something myself," Jackson muttered. "If you're right about what those diary pages looked like, I think I have some!" Jackson explained his discoveries in the carved-out book he plucked from the trailer in the woods outside Harpers Ferry. McAdams listened intently as Jackson related how his hands shook when he found the handwritten list of names above a Lady Liberty impression, and two etchings of buildings, one a fort labeled "Maine" and the other a wide, multi-storied building.

"Chuck, the pages you found ... Were they old?"

Jackson nodded.

"Yellow? Crumbling?"

He nodded again.

"Were the edges ragged with stubs from a notebook, or were they cut clean?"

"Clean, I believe, but no matter, I brought 'em with me. We can both take a guess."

"You didn't make copies and store the originals in a safe place somewhere?"

"I've kept 'em in this folder when they're not in my safe. And I ain't going chance having them fall apart trying to make no damn copies. They're too valuable – as evidence, I mean."

"All right, all right!" McAdams held his hands up, apologizing. "My originals are safely tucked away, but I typed up what they said on a sheet of paper. I brought it with me." He tapped his sports jacket pocket as he began to explain the FBI photos he had scrutinized and the photos of the remnants of

Booth's dairy. He gave Jackson the gist of the FBI lab examination, the theory of the sliced and removed diary pages versus those torn out, and the manipulation of the Judiciary subcommittee executive session.

Jackson let out a low whistle. "The FBI? Looking at Booth's diary? And then sealing all the records. In 1967?"

"Right. And, between us, we got four of the missing 18 pages sliced out from the diary. The one page I have that is addressed to Brock and the Committee, with its ragged stubs and all, probably was torn out by someone, probably Booth himself, and probably delivered as addressed - to Nate Brock."

Jackson looked down at his shoes. "Mac, if it was the US government back then that sliced out those missing pages, well, ... maybe I don't want to know nuthin' about it. Maybe I just want to leave buried and unknown why bad seed in my government wanted to hide evidence dealing with the murder of Lincoln."

"Tell me about your case," McAdams nudged.

Jackson told McAdams the story of the Mystery of the Woods, filling in Chief Williams' summary version. "I think those young men were going up there regularly," he concluded. "And someone took advantage of their natural slowness and openness, and their strong, sad desire to 'belong' to something, and taught them - with all that Aryan toilet paper in the trailer - that it was legit to hate and to hurt."

"You know," said McAdams, "last night, Brock said that Lewis Shephard was traveling the country. He was trying to connect hate groups, white separatists and other aimless thugs, converting them into convenient mercenaries for those who were calling Shephard's shots. With all the other connections between our cases, could it be that your young men were waiting for Lewis Shephard the night they got stranded in the woods?"

"Get me his prints, and Brock's, too, and I'll get you an answer. I've had a special print job taken of every inch of that trailer, the books inside, and the sheds outside. If they even floated their hands over something, I got 'em."

"Larcher was one of their successful conversions," continued McAdams. "He became the hit man of their dreams, executing as commanded and then taking his own life."

"He did everything right but identify his target."

McAdams nodded. "Larcher's MO was the same as the killer that executed Tidback. Do you have any missing and unaccounted for boys connected with the trailer?"

"Only Larcher. And now he's accounted for."

"My experience with the rednecks down at Randolph-Macon, and now all this, means there are other trailer sites, other products of Shephard's work out there, filled with more Geoffrey Larchers. That means there are, or will be, other victims, too."

Jackson started shaking his head. "I have to tell you, Mac, I just don't feature those poor young men of mine as the kind that would take up with white separatists or the KKK." He paused again. "'Course Larcher was the leader of the pack and he was as bad as they come. Troubled, really, rather than bad."

"Well, I can't see Shephard as a messianic, David Koresh type either. But he's out collecting human cannon fodder. And I'm sure he secreted the gun used to kill David Tidback; it's the only way the weapon could have been brought in and taped to the underside of the reporters' table. But others are pulling Shephard's strings. Others are giving the orders to kill. There's more to all of this that we just can't see yet. ... I'll get you those prints, ASAP."

"While you're at it, check and see if Shephard - or this Senator Brock - wears any gold necklaces with a copper medallion."

"A Copperhead medallion," McAdams corrected. An uneasy feeling passed between them. The silence rose up thick as the humidity in the room.

"Maybe that's it," said Jackson at last. "We got a group of nuts organized by Shephard, or by someone Shephard works for, that traces its roots to John Wilkes Booth. That would explain the Copperhead medallions. But, if that's the case, why would they come after you on the plane? Why execute Tidback? Were you gettin' into Lincoln's assassination?

"No. But there are disturbing parallels." McAdams looked around them into the dense foliage. "Lincoln undid slavery and Lincoln gets shot. Martin Luther King mobilizes black freedom and King is killed. Booth was a part of the Copperheads, a pro-slavery group that historians say was active in guerrilla warfare. Shephard travels across the country starting hate groups anxious to terrorize and sometimes kill."

Jackson leaned back, placing his hands under his legs. He visualized Martin Luther King's familiar face. Jackson's life, surely that lonely part of him that felt a desperate need for parents or religion or something lofty and noble to show him the way, still felt an emptiness where King had been ripped out the day he was gunned down in Memphis. If it came to be that those behind Martin's death were ... tied ... to Lincoln's murder ..., well, he shook his head, it would be too damned much to consider.

And others would feel the same way. Some would explode in violent outrage. Frustration and betrayal would spill out into the streets, aggravated by all the revolutionaries, separatists and gangs. The nation would be divided. At best it would be a country filled with people who considered it irretrievably soiled.

Where would you, where could you, start over? Maybe Tidback WAS right. There just might be a second Civil War.

McAdams reached into his jacket and pulled out typed versions of his two pages from Booth's diary, handing them to Jackson. Jackson silently read the OAK creed and Booth's report to Secretary Brock and the Committee. He put them down, looked at McAdams soberly and then opened his folder. He showed McAdams the original pages he had brought -- two pages with drawings and one with a list of names and an image of Lady Liberty pressed underneath in black ink. They were inserted carefully into clear plastic sleeves.

McAdams tapped one of the etchings with an index finger. "Lafayette Baker, during his Congressional testimony about Booth's diary, said he thought that there were missing pages with etchings of forts and buildings. He testified that one of them looked like the house of Mary Surratt in Washington, DC. Surratt was one of the reputed Booth conspirators. She kept a boarding house in Washington that the government claimed was used as a gathering spot for Booth and other Confederate agents. And this building here sure looks like a boarding house." He picked up the list of names.

"The writing is identical!" said a triumphant McAdams after he had placed the pages side-by-side. Jackson's copies showed straight edges on the left-hand side. Like his OAK creed, they had been sliced out of Booth's diary.

McAdams studied the list. The first name on it was "N. Brock." He didn't recognize the others. "What's the 'C' stand for?" he asked.

"Maybe it's the 'Committee' Booth was writin' to."

McAdams shrugged and re-read the pages in his hands. Jackson was pondering the handwritten OAK oath.

He looked up at last. "Mac, this OAK group doesn't sound like a Ku Klux Klan to me. It sounds like a Chamber of Commerce, one that won't stand for anyone cutting into profits. They don't want no one messin' with business."

"The Professor over at Georgetown I told you about who helped me analyze the diary pages, Professor Dorothy Browning, she said OAK may have gotten behind Lincoln's assassination because he threatened them and their cause. His freeing of slave property without compensation sounded like very bad precedent to them, very bad for business and their profits."

"You got it. And don't forget something. Dr. King scared a bunch of comfortably middle class and wealthy folk. He was moving from civil rights to economic rights, and would have been a powerful force for organizin' labor and the poor - not just black folk - on a massive scale in this country. Don't forget that about Dr. King. He was in Memphis in the first place 'cuz he wanted to help out a sanitation union on strike. You got to remember that about Dr. Martin Luther King, Mac. He was scaring a whole lot of comfortable folk with a whole lot of money and power. He was becoming dangerous to the big boys."

Jackson stopped when he felt McAdams' hand on his arm. He looked over and followed McAdams gaze behind them. McAdams removed his hand and put a finger to his lips while parting the ferns with his free hand. Through openings among the ferns Jackson saw what it was all about. A thick man with black hair was standing with his back to them. It was clear he was listening. At the prolonged halt in the conversation the man darted out of sight.

"Should we follow him?" Jackson looked ready to charge.

"He's gone. Let him go."

"How'd you know he…?"

"I saw him when we came here," McAdams explained. "He followed us in here, and then disappeared. It suddenly occurred to me where he might be. I was right."

"Maybe he was just passing through."

"Right," McAdams cracked. "Anyone that ugly can't find comfort in the beauty of nature. He was bad news. Our bad news."

They got up and left, checking behind them every now and then as they made their way to the cafeteria for lunch.

Chapter Thirty-four

Anne Gardiner sat in front of her computer terminal, its blue screen vibrating warmly in her dimly lit office. The light cast on her yellow outfit gave her a green aura. She would type a few seconds, watch the result on the screen, curse, and then unload another barrage on the keyboard.

Her expansive office overlooked Pennsylvania Avenue, her building occupying the block next to the White House. Lafayette Park, directly across Pennsylvania Avenue from the White House, was just visible to the right if you leaned out and craned your neck from her fifth story window. Twenty blocks away was Capitol Hill. Her desk, credenza and walls were jammed with photos and mementos of trips, special projects and visits with two Presidents, foreign dignitaries, and a score of overweight Congressmen.

She had broken into computer systems before, she consoled herself as she stared, frustrated, into her unyielding screen, her fingers perched on the keyboard. Her friends at DOD and NSC had taught her well during her years staffing military intelligence for Foreign Affairs. And McAdams' Congressional system was not supposed to be that difficult; the Pentagon boys routinely cracked in to see how their budgets and favorite programs were doing.

"Wrong!" she sighed out loud as she sat back. It was easy enough to get into the Hill's local area network dedicated to staffers, Members and Committees handling national security matters and other classified material. She had the network's access code and password from friends who worked in the Senate. Everyone trusted ol' Annie. She had been around for years. She was as familiar as the unpainted halls of Congressional office buildings, as reliable as the Tidal Basin cherry blossoms in April. Her lips tightened into a smile - Old Reliable.

The LAN was cake - but getting into McAdams' personal computer files was another matter. The files were stored by the LAN in a minicomputer in a controlled access room in the basement of the Dirksen Office Building. She was almost there, just fiddling with the electronic doorknob. All she needed now was to reconstruct another access code and password combination, unique to McAdam's personal computer-stored database. The screen blinked as she tried another combination of codes.

Her mind flashed back to her champagne brunch with Mark Fisher leaning over the table, his moist lips inches from her own. Asking her for help. Promising the Women's Commission.

"He'd fuckin' better deliver," she mumbled to the computer.

Mark had called again this morning. He had sounded dead tired. She wondered where he had been last night, if he'd been out with some young, compliant thing starry-eyed about a poke from someone so close to the President. He complained he was fatigued because he'd been traveling in Maine and had only just returned this morning. She grew pensive as she keyed in more password/access code guesses.

She banged at the keyboard again. After three unsuccessful tries, the network would disconnect her. She had one more try this time around. What was the secret code?

She straightened up. It suddenly occurred to her. Mac's secret room. He had it built during the three years they had lived together in his apartment in the cooperative. His little hideaway.

She picked up the phone. "Mark?" she said when he picked up on the other end. "I've got an idea about where McAdams might have hidden the Committee's Report. But we'll have to move - right now ..."

Chapter Thirty-five

Late Saturday afternoon – Union Station

McAdams and Jackson spent the afternoon in McAdams' office, trading notes, reviewing the materials from the FBI's examination of Lincoln's diary and plotting strategy. Despite his best efforts, Jackson found his eyes wandering back to catch glimpses of Jazz Speed, his junior by about a decade, when she stopped by to finish up some work. Her sashay as she moved around the office was more pronounced than usual this afternoon, McAdams noticed, as she tried her best to tease poor old Charles Jackson. She was wearing the tightest leopard skin leotard outfit McAdams had ever seen and her hair color, freshly tinted since he had seen her at work only yesterday, matched the leopard's orange accents. The auburn scarf around her neck reached to her knees and the bush jacket that topped it all off looked downright predatory. She did not, however, give the Chief a tumble, just a couple of winks and a big, teasing kiss good-bye.

They left and McAdams dropped Jackson off at the entrance to Union Station. His train back to Harpers Ferry was scheduled to leave in an hour and a half but he could grab an early dinner this way, and let McAdams get back to work.

"Where can I get a bite, Mac?"

"Try inside, there's a ton of 'em. You got eateries, you got a wine bar, you got bistros, you got …."

"No, thanks. I got a hankering for a good ol' burger and onion rings. And a beer if you don't mind."

"Listen, I'm sorry that …. "

"Oh don't worry about Jazz. I can tell she likes the young stuff. And you can tell she's getting' it. But I'll show her what I got someday and she'll be dumping them dudes like they was spoiled meat." He smiled broadly and hefted his pants up. "Yessir."

"Actually I was going to apologize for dumping you here and taking off."

"You got work, young man. Get it done. No apologies needed."

"You have your gun?"

"Right here." Jackson bent over and patted his lower leg. An ankle holster, perfect for the larger man whose gut hung over his belly and might get impaled by the implements of destruction normally toted around on a waist holster. "Why, do I need a gun to get something to eat? I didn't think Washington was getting that bad."

McAdams smiled. "I was worrying about the re-appearance of the man who was listening to us at the Botanical Gardens."

"Don't worry 'bout me."

"You sure?"

"You'll be a lot more helpful to me if you showed me where I can chow down before I waste away or the train leaves the station."

"I ain't worried about the former," cracked McAdams. He pointed across the traffic circle in front of Union Station and down a broad street that led away toward northwest Washington. "Right at the corner there is a place called the Dubliners. Good cold beer, of course, it's an Irish joint. And it's got good burgers and *mean* plates of onion rings …."

"Now you're talking …." Jackson got out of the car, closed the door and leaned inside the open passenger window. "I'll be in touch."

"I'll get you Brock's and Shephard's fingerprints through Capitol Hill police and have them sent off to you …."

"And I'll see if I find a match in the trailer."

"And see who else is wearing Copperhead medallions …."

"Right. You too. It's a secret society we're dealin' with, Mac, I'm telling ya. Look for the Copperheads in the weeds."

"You sure you don't want a ride to Dubliners?"

"Nah. Looks like a short walk to me and I got the time. Besides, I could use the fresh air. Maybe it'll clear my head out." Jackson saluted good bye and McAdams drove off, heading back to the Dirksen Building a few blocks south.

Jackson ambled over to the restaurant and found a stool at the bar. McAdams was right. Good beer, good burgers. He had two of each, plus a plateful of spicy onion rings. He relaxed a little, taking in the laughter and vitality of the place. He paid and climbed off the barstool. As he did so a woman watched him out of the corner of her eye.

She had followed him after he and McAdams split up at the train station. She had arrived earlier herself, from Richmond, and hadn't been able to get McAdams on the phone. Waiting around, deciding what to do next, she spotted McAdams pull up in his car. He missed her wave as he pulled away from the curb and she had no idea where he was heading. That's when she spied two nasty looking men following the man Mac had dropped off. She figured she had no choice but to follow this man, so she did. She thought about sitting at the empty stool next to him, introducing herself, but what if she was wrong? What if this old guy wasn't a friend? What if was with ... the other side? Mac had warned her about being seen with him, about being connected at all with him. He had said people were watching. And now the two who *were* watching, the two men she had trailed here, were nowhere to be seen. She wondered what she would do next.

She waited for twenty seconds and then followed the black man out of the tavern. It was dark now. Up ahead she watched him make his way in the dim light coming from the headlights of the traffic heading toward traffic circle in front of Union Station. He was passing in front of a group of trees on the Union Station side of the garbage bin next to Dubliners when suddenly someone emerged out of the dark and shoved him with tremendous strength. She stopped, trying to take in what was happening. Looking around for a police car, anybody, she saw empty streets and sidewalks. She thought about going back into the bar to get help but it might be too late by then. She ran.

Jackson felt his arms pinned to his side as he was pushed behind the traffic bin out of sight of any passers-by. He managed to twist his head. His eyes widened when he saw the face of a Vietnamese man grimacing at his shoulder. The man was powerful but Jackson started to wiggle free. It was hard to hold a man his size at bay for too long, once he got up a head of steam. Suddenly he was wrenched to a stop. He looked up.

There was someone in front of him. A tall, thick man with black clothes, broad chest and muscular arms. A man with black hair, horrible pockmarks and runny eyes. The man from the Botanical Gardens. He had never seen such a hate-filled face.

Jackson saw a flash of a fist and he felt a steel wrecking ball of knuckle and flesh blast into his stomach and nearly out his back. Jackson doubled over into the rising knee of the man who punched him. He felt his nose crack and thick, warm blood spurt down his throat. He gasped, choking, and straightened up long enough to catch two more iron fists as they burst into his solar plexus. Warm sludge from his stomach shot up his throat and he vomited violently just in time to land face first into his own steaming pile of burgers, beer, onion rings and blood. The two assailants began kicking him with steel-toed boots straight off the shelves of an Army-Navy store.

"Hold it!" Linda stood next to the trash bin, her eyes flashing in the dim light from the street, her pulse racing, her arms stretched out in fighting position. The two men stopped their assault on Jackson's unmoving bulk. A loud groan went up as Jackson tried to turn his body to breathe. The two men separated and squared off, facing her. They moved silently toward her. Sable recognized the kick-box stance. He had mastered the art long ago, one of the many martial arts under his command.

"Whatcha want, girlie?" sneered Sable. "Looking for some action, huh?"

Linda said nothing. If she screamed God knows what they'd do to her and to the man on the ground, before anyone heard her and decided to do something about it. No, she would summon her own rescue. She waited as they approached, looking for openings.

Sable spun into a preliminary kick-box mode, lashing out with his right foot. The movement was so quick it was like a knife blade flitting through the air, making the same sound. Linda straightened for a moment, surprised at the agility and power the large man possessed, surprised at what she saw. She had seen the best in college competition but this man was a master. Fear rose in her throat.

The Vietnamese man saw the distraction. With the speed of a tiger, close to the ground, he covered the distance between him and the girl in the flash of an eye.

Linda caught the movement but it was too late. A hand sliced to the side of her neck. A punishing blow crashed into her throat, sending spasms of excruciating pain through her head and down her chest. She had to cry out but no voice came. She gasped but there was no air. It didn't matter. She felt herself collapse into a heap as darkness overwhelmed her.

Sable relaxed his stance and bowed to the other man. "Nice work, Mr. Thu." The other man returned the gesture. Sable returned to Jackson's side. The old man was still conscious. Sable grabbed him by the ear and picked his head off the ground.

Jackson felt his head elevate off the ground, felt the hand at his ear. It would have hurt had any feeling been left. Bent over Jackson, Sable winced in disgust at the blood and chunks of puke on Jackson's' face. He spoke in a low, urgent voice that meant more business a'coming as he shoved his prominent nose alongside Jackson's.

"Look, nigger boy, we want you away from McAdams. Stay outta Washington. Forget any promises you made here. Forget what you learned. Niggers oughta stay home cuz they get killed off the plantation." The man spat a mouthful of warm, sudsy spit into Jackson's ear to make some kind of point, but its meaning was escaping Jackson at the moment.

"And tonight some nigger is gonna get killed." He looked behind him at the woman's limp body. "Some bitch gonna get killed too. Consider it my contribution to society." He let go and Jackson felt his head drop back into the former contents of his stomach. The last thing Jackson remembered was that they were kicking him again but that he couldn't feel it. He wondered what girl had shouted out. He was numb and floating up, up, to the black sky.

Chapter Thirty-six

Dirksen Senate Office Building

McAdams entered his darkened office after seeing Jackson down to Union Station. The hairs rose on the back of his head as he closed the door. He checked around to be sure that the place was empty. It was, but it didn't feel that way.

He sat down at his desk and saw his voice mail light blinking. 19 messages were waiting for him. Running through the opening lines of each message, he listened for the name and voice of the caller. His heart jumped when he recognized Linda Walker. He missed her. He hadn't seen her since Monday.

He listened to the message. She sounded like she was leaving an update in case she couldn't at a later time, in case something happened. She wanted to talk ….

He quickly dialed her number. His breath stopped as he waited for her to pick up. The phone rang and rang and rang in what he could feel was a darkened, empty dorm room. He dropped the phone into its cradle and sat back. He should have checked in with her before this, to see how she was doing, to see if she was safe.

He spotted a new note from Jazz taped to his computer screen. It was coded in script only they understood. The Committee was in its last lap and he needed to produce, she reminded him. This afternoon, while he and Jackson were talking away, she had loaded his entire draft of the Final Report into his computer's memory for the last round of changes and additions. Jazz told him to get working. The Committee's Final Report was due in 11 days, May 1, and she was damned if she was going to put in much overtime to make up for his laziness. She signed her love.

She was right, it was time to get going. What she forgot to mention was that this Wednesday the Senators on the Committee would meet in executive session to hear his proposed Findings and Conclusions. They would vote then and there on his recommendations. So the timeframes were shorter. He felt panic well up in his stomach.

Five days to tie OAK and Shephard, maybe even Taylor Brock himself, to King's assassination. Five days to figure out what and who killed David Tidback. After that all the funding, all the investigators, and all the staff would be gone with the wind. He stared at the dark video monitor, wondering if the computer would ever boot up.

He sat forward with alarm when the welcome screen and introductory banners finally materialized before him. There had been 21 attempted but unsuccessful log-ins since Jazz had entered the data last night. No times were given for the aborted efforts. They could have happened this morning - or three minutes ago.

He entered his passwords and headed for the notes taken throughout the two year Committee investigation. They were stored on the LAN server under "Correspondence, May 1988." He figured that label a good enough cover in case anyone wandered through his files. He breathed a prayer he was right.

He scrolled slowly through his notes of interviews, his various listings of leads and facts, the drafts of his tentative assessments and minutes of free-form brain-storming sessions he would hold with his investigators over beers after a day in the field. The evidence he and his staff had gathered formed tantalizing leads suggesting an organized effort supporting James Earl Ray. Were the footprints of OAK there? Had he overlooked them in the days before Tidback had come on the scene? If his work was decent and detailed enough, he now might be able to detect OAK among the cast of suspicious groups and characters who walked into and out of Ray's complex, curious life before and after King was killed.

He came to his notes on the Committee's Miami and St. Louis investigations. He recalled how frightened he had been at the time. Frightened - and confused - at the whirl of hate for Martin Luther King and all the right-wing groups and militants that had surrounded James Earl Ray.

St. Louis ... Professor Browning said OAK was founded over 130 years ago - in that city. Coincidence? He scanned the St. Louis section. As he came to his concluding notes he was slapped by the sharp ringing of the phone. His heart jumped a second time.

"Yeah" he snarled, looking at his watch. It was almost seven o'clock.

"Mac, where've you been?" It was O'Connell.

"Uh, well, it's been busy. I ..."

"Hey, relax, my man! It's a rhetorical question, ckay? Listen, I've got something for you. Let's meet in the cafeteria for an early dinner." He meant the staff cafeteria in the basement three stories below where McAdams sat. At certain hours it was closed to the public and open only to Senate and House staff. Sometimes even a real Congressman would show up.

"Give me a half-hour," McAdams replied.

Chapter Thirty-seven

McAdams gnawed on the tough brisket of beef. He thought he might well be at it all evening long. He spat the gristle into his napkin and eyed the lumpy potatoes and wilted salad lying in wait on the plate before him.

O'Connell smiled at his friend's plight. "I've been digging around like you asked."

McAdams wiped his mouth. "What d'you find?"

"The Justice Department is very anxious about Tidback's case. They yanked it away from the DC Police and the Capitol Hill Police in the early stages, when they had no business getting involved. Justice pressured the DC Appropriations Committee Chairman who controls the DC cops' paycheck. And they pressured the House Speaker who yanks the chain of the Capitol Hill Police."

"Funny concept," mused McAdams, 'The Department of Justice'. Shouldn't all government be 'just', not just one department thereof?" He went back optimistically to another clump of meat, thinking.

O'Connell gave him a puzzled look. "While you philosophize about such matters, I got something real world for you. About Tidback's FOIA requests on the Lincoln diary ..."

McAdams stopped chewing and cogitating. "Requests? As in more than one?"

"Oh yeah. Tidback filed a bunch over the past six months, some with the Justice Department and others with the Interior Department. He wanted to examine the diary and was looking for missing pages or summaries of missing pages that might be in the agencies' possession. His requests were handed over to the White House - not the FOIA offices for each of the departments - but the White House."

McAdams put down his fork, still loaded with meat. "That violates a few laws."

"Yup."

"And I didn't know Tidback sent FOIAs to Interior."

"Now clue me in. What was Tidback up to?"

"He came across missing pages from the diary of John Wilkes Booth that suggested a conspiracy behind Lincoln's assassination, one that's still active, maybe even implicated in ... other ... political assassinations."

"King's?"

McAdams nodded. "Possibly."

O'Connell was struck dumb. He looked blankly at McAdams.

"Tidback was getting close to something, Ed. Someone, some ones, decided he had gotten close enough and took him out."

O'Connell began to show movement, stroking his chin. "The White House is all over this, Mac. They want what I let you see about the Booth diary examination - bad. Not the copies, the originals. And they're messing with Tidback's FOIA requests."

"Will any of your sources talk?"

"I don't know. Maybe ... I'll work 'em over."

"How high in the White House does this go?"

"Unclear right now."

McAdams stared at their plates littered with rejected food and inedible chunks of beef brisket. The bad taste coated his tongue like wax. He looked over at an unfamiliar man who was sitting down at their table. He had a hearing aid and was trying hard to ignore them.

"Let's go ..." McAdams began to rise.

"Wait ..." O'Connell grabbed his arm. "I've got more."

"No." McAdams nodded over at the man with the hearing aid.

O'Connell caught the signal. "Wait up."

He continued as soon as they got in the hallway outside the cafeteria. "Nelson Wilkins is very interested in the work of the Assassination Committee. Why would the number 2 guy at Defense care about what you're doing?"

McAdams shook his head. "Wilkins again!"

"He talks about Tidback's shooting and the King Committee with White House staff. He's been reported getting, how you say, 'exercised' about recent developments."

"Anne mentioned the same thing, about Wilkin's sudden interest. Suddenly every damned body is interested - the White House, the Justice Department, the FBI, the Defense Department."

O'Connell shrugged. "Speaking of Annie ..."

"What?" McAdams stopped in the middle of the hall. O'Connell pushed him gently back against the wall.

"She and Mark Fisher over at the White House are an 'item.'"

McAdams tightened. "Who the hell is Mark Fisher?"

"Mark 'Rooster' Fisher. He's one of the President's policy guys handling domestic stuff. Gets hot over national security, law enforcement, money laundering, BCCI, serious policy babes like Annie. He's been orchestrating White House input to federal agencies required to respond to your Committee's subpoenas."

"I've never dealt with him," said McAdams incredulously. "I have no idea who he is."

"He's the guy that Wilkins talks to in the White House about the Tidback affair and the King Committee. He's the guy at the White House handling Tidback's FOIA requests."

McAdams felt his skin becoming red and hot. Anne had been pumping him for information about the Committee. She was working with Fisher or Wilkins, or both, or just using them. She knew about his hidden room. He had shown her how to get into it. The Booth documents, and a hard copy of the Committee's Findings and Conclusions were there - for her, for anyone to see. McAdams let loose a cry as he turned and sprinted down the hall.

Chapter Thirty-eight

He smelled and tasted smoke, thick, choking smoke that swirled around his face. His cheek lay on a carpet, a rosy Oriental of some sort. Jackson rolled back as far as he could and started coughing uncontrollably. The wracking and heaving made him cry out with pain. He remembered the mugging he got.

He breathed a prayer. The pain, the short breath, made him realize he was alive. The ugly man and the Vietnamese had left him alive. He swore they'd regret that one day.

And they brought him here to this place where he would die. They'd regret that too, maybe more, he swore. Mary up above, he whispered half aloud, help me now. Chuckie, old boy, show me the way or I'll be coming upstairs to join you, son, and it ain't time. This ain't no way for a man to die, not in a fire, burning like a screaming, helpless animal locked up in a barn. Help me out of here, sweet Lord. Help me find a way out of this hell on earth.

A sharp cracking sound from some room behind him fractured the air, the sound of a raging fire snapping a door. Fresh, dark smoke billowed across the ceiling, setting off another painful coughing fit. The smoke was followed by something else, something he had never felt. A surge of pure heat, so hot it was physical, so tangible it rocked him backward. The fire was living, breathing, growing and soon it would come and consume him.

He struggled to get to his feet but couldn't right himself. His hands were useless. They were tied together behind his back with a rope that looped down and bound his feet.

Jackson started rocking back and forth until he managed to roll onto his knees, his bound feet sticking up in the air, his forehead hard against the floor. A sharp pain sliced through his chest and his breathing grew short. A broken rib, maybe several, from the boots of his assailants.

He began to shift his weight back and forth from his head to his knees until he got some momentum going. With a great cry he righted himself onto his knees, tottering one way and then the other before he came to rest upright. He took quick, shallow breaths, craning his neck as much as he could to take in where he was. He kneeled in the center of a living room, in an apartment of some sort, gasping for breath. There was a couch, a coffee table and a few chairs. He squinted into the gloom around him and saw the place was a mess. There were newspapers scattered everywhere. Lamps were pushed over, drawers left open. Cushions were split down the middle, with stuffing like geysers pushing up from the middle. Bright orange fire, reflecting off the walls, danced somewhere down the hallway that led away from the living room. He didn't have much time. It was coming for him.

He moved his fingers and felt the knots at his wrists. Amateur knots. Not the kind that would tighten with pressure or pulling, or constrict his blood supply with movement or stretching. If he never made it onto that boat of his at the end of this life, at least all his knot tying and untying in his rocker would come in handy right now. His fingers went to work and in a minute his hands were free. He rolled over on his rump and took care of the rope around his feet.

He grabbed onto a couch and pulled himself to his feet. An angry, rolling punch of fire roared out of the hallway entrance, like a fire breathing circus man belches out a long plume of flame. The fireball paused and pulled back as suddenly as it had appeared, spreading out across the ceiling in its retreat, licking it before devouring it.

Jackson felt dizzy. His hands went to his face and hair. It was singed, his face stung. Suddenly his throat was parched and his mouth hung open as he gasped for air. The ceiling over his head started popping open with fissures.

A new blast of flame burst into the room. In the explosion of light Jackson spied a body on the couch below him. He lunged over the coffee table and it collapsed under his bulk. He felt his way to the couch in the smoke and reached out to turn the head atop the body, feeling thick hair, peering into the face. It had to be the woman who called out, the one who tried to come to his aid. Linda's eyes blinked open. She squinted through the smoke at the man over her and started coughing.

"Let's go, little lady," Jackson gasped as he untied her. "It's getting a little hot in here."

Linda nodded her head and pulled herself into a sitting position. Her hand shot to the spasm of pain in her neck. Jackson grabbed the hand and led her over to the wall on the other side of the couch. Smoke billowed into the room, filling it. They were completely fogged in and could not see. The fire from the hallway flowed across onto the floor. The carpet snapped and popped as it caught fire. Jackson found the door and threw his weight against it. It collapsed into the hallway and with a loud smack slapped onto the floor.

The stairwell was inches away. Jackson reached for the railing and looked around for his companion. Her hand to her mouth she was close behind. Holding hands they stumbled down the stairs. Three flights of stairs. By the time they reached the front door to the building they heard fire engine sirens outside.

Chapter Thirty-nine

The fireman wouldn't let him inside. In the evening sky the flames soared above his townhouse like crazy neon-yellow, spiked hair. Dark smoke billowed out of his broken windows.

"That your place up top?" The fireman peered at him.

"Yeah."

"Well, forget about it. Everything's gone"

"Anyone hurt?" McAdams watched the fireman atop a hook and ladder pointing a hard stream of water at the building.

"That guy over there. And the woman." He pointed to two ambulances with their lights flashing. On a gurney, getting oxygen, was a heavy black man. Next to him McAdams saw another gurney and the top of full head of wavy, dark hair. McAdams squinted to see who it was.

"I don't recognize them. You sure they live in the building?"

"They came running out when we were pulling up. Damn near died in there. Looks like the guy got beat up, too. Bad. The woman took a shot to the neck." Another fireman shouted for him and he walked briskly away.

"Woman?" McAdams mumbled to himself as he spotted a group of his building's tenants huddled around the ambulance. They were kept at a respectful distance by a couple of DC cops. The housemates were chatting amiably, some with drinks in their hands, like they were watching a bonfire before the big game. It was his stuff going up in smoke, some guy on a gurney was getting damn near his last rights and they were all having a grand old time.

He joined the group and looked over shoulders at the gurneys. "Who's that?" he asked one of the women who lived on the first floor. He pointed his chin in the direction of the ambulances.

"Beats me...." She turned back to her earnest conversation.

The EMS squad suddenly scattered, pulling away from the gurneys to close up shop before heading off to DC General. McAdams squinted. "Jesus ...."

He pushed his way through the crowd. "Chuck! Chuck!" He got five feet away from the rear of the ambulance before one of the cops grabbed him roughly by the arm and twisted him around for a tete-a-tete.

"Look, my man, I ...."

"Wait!" The senior EMS medic walked over to the commotion and butt in. "Wait, officer. The patient says he knows this man. Says he wants him to come with him to the hospital."

The cop reluctantly released his grip. "Get over there," he snapped, but not with one last shot. "Let's keep things calm, OK?"

"Yeah, calm," McAdams muttered as he pushed past. "It's real calm around here."

The medic stopped him with a palm of his hand against McAdams' chest. "Look, he's in pretty bad shape but he'll make it. Someone beat the shit out of him before the fire. They left him there, tied up, to die in the flames. He was with the woman next to him. I'll give you a couple of minutes. That's all."

McAdams nodded and kneeled down at Jackson's side, examining his face. The eyebrows were singed and his face was smudged, but underneath the grime you could see the blistering from the heat he took and Jackson's nose was flattened. Broken.

"Chuck, you gonna make it?"

"Oh yeah, I'm too ornery not too. And I got too much to do."

"How you'd get here? Who beat you up? The fire, how ...?"

Jackson closed his eyes. "Not now, later."

"Mac..."

McAdams turned at the call of his name. It came from the other gurney. He squinted at the face.

"Linda!" He lunged and squatted next to her, wanting to touch her, daring not to for fear of what injuries she may have suffered. Leaning over her face, he kissed her eyes and her lips. "I'm so sorry..."

"I'm OK, Mac, I'm OK." She coughed and moved her hand, indicating she wanted it held. McAdams reached out and gently put his hand in hers.

"What happened?" he prodded

Linda started telling McAdams about following the man on the other gurney from Union Station.

"That's Chief Jackson from West Virginia. I'll tell you about him. We're working on this together."

"Mac...." It was Jackson.

McAdams patted Linda's hand as an irked medic came over. "OK, enough talking for now, Miss..."

McAdams leaned over Jackson's gurney. "What?"

"I just remembered. I lost my documents from the trailer.... They took 'em..."

"Booth's list of names above the Lady Liberty stamp?"

"Yeah, and the etchings. The fort in Maine and the other one, the boarding house. And something I didn't show you, Tidback's article that I found in Geoffrey Larcher's place ...." Jackson started coughing.

"Oh, man ...." McAdams looked up at the burning building. He had lost something, too, something tucked away in his secret room. The originals of what he found in Tidback's loft were long gone. The checklist of assassins and assassinations, the OAK creed with the Lady Liberty image, Booth's letter to Nathaniel Brock. Unless Anne and her friend "Rooster" got there first.

"Mac, your place was all torn up," Jackson confirmed. "Someone was looking for something. And they must have gotten it before they torched the place, they had to. Everything is gone, everything we had, all the evidence, linking Tidback and the trailer, and those boys ...." Jackson started coughing again, his face grimacing in pain.

"OK, Mr. Jackson," interrupted the medic attending to Linda, "you need to stop now. You boys can talk all you want later. No more chatter, hear? We got to get you two to the emergency room." He signaled for some help to lift the gurneys into the back of the ambulances.

McAdams stood back as they worked and watched the black smoke of his life filling the dark sky. Things were slipping away from him, bit by bit. He imagined one last glimpse of Anne smiling in front of that tree in the park in the photo next to his bed, one last sparkle caught in his mother's eye, memories from snapshots of worlds long gone. He looked up to see the shell of his apartment on the top floor, the windows burned out, and the outer brick blackened from the now extinguished flames.

"You coming, sir? He wants you to come."

McAdams started to object, pointing at Linda.

"No way," the medic replied, "the ambulance for her is too small. You two can catch up at the hospital. You go with him." He pointed at Jackson.

McAdams nodded and got in the back of Jackson's ambulance and they closed the doors. He looked through one of the back door windows at the building again in the moment before they took off. The report. The only hard copy of the Assassination Committee's Findings and Conclusions had been in his secret room in his apartment, along with the documents from Tidback's loft.

Whoever had dumped Jackson and Linda in there to die, whoever set the fire, was connected to what he was investigating. And right now they had in their hands the basic guts of what the King Committee would say in its Final Report. The sirens pierced the night as the ambulances accelerated away from the curb. Jackson peppered McAdams with questions about Linda, who she was, what was up with them and more, until the medic riding in the back threatened to knock out with an injection of a fearful-sounding substance. Jackson shut up and McAdams answered all the questions, talking all the way to the emergency room.

Chapter Forty

The White House

Anne Gardiner sat impatiently in Mark Fisher's office in the West Wing, waiting for him to get off the phone. It was the third call he had taken during their conversation which began only minutes ago. Each was cryptic, filled with coded messages she could not understand. A crisis was at hand and Fisher was doing his best to manage it without clueing her in.

She drummed her half inch-long, crimson-painted fingernails on the glass on top of his impressive mahogany desk. She spread and crossed her long legs, slowly, with exaggeration.

Fisher had enough presence of mind to catch the show but said nothing, his face a taut mask of mission and intensity. He said a few words, listened, grimaced and finally hung up.

"OK," he said absently, "where were we? What's up?"

"What's UP? Remember the tip I gave you this morning? I want you to tell me what you found."

"Yes, yes, I'm sorry. Of course. Well ..., Anne, you were dead right. We found a hard copy of the Committee's Findings and Conclusions in the room. 600 plus pages."

"What does he find and conclude?"

"Well ..., he fingers Guy Flaherty, our current Secretary of State, back when he was CIA Deputy Director and Jerry Cosenza, our Attorney General, when he was number 3 at the FBI."

"'Fingers'? What do you mean?"

"The Assassination Committee." replied Fisher in exasperation. "If it listens to McAdams, the Committee will ask Justice to investigate and seek criminal indictments against Flaherty and Cozensa for destruction of King investigation documents during the late sixties and early seventies. He thinks they permitted the removal and destruction of these records. And in the case of the FBI section under Cosenza at the time, McAdams wants the Committee to say that the FBI was sloppy, even negligent, about protecting King. Worse - that the FBI increased the threat of harm to him by stirring up dissidents, disrupting King rallies, generating fake hate mail, and planting provocative letters and stories in the papers."

"Mark, you were right! McAdams was going to tar and feather the Administration!"

Fisher's mind was a million miles away. "There's more, Anne. Something very troubling. God!" He rubbed his forehead.

"What's more troubling than indictments against senior members of the Administration that employs you?"

"McAdams says the feds mishandled evidence during the investigation of the King crime scene."

She couldn't hide her look of incredulity. Fisher was not making any sense. "OK, so ...?"

"He claims they ignored evidence of possible conspiracies behind the assassination. And that a presently unknown conspiracy assisted James Earl Ray. Thank God, it doesn't look like he names any names, but who knows? We only have the Findings and Conclusions, not the full Report!"

She sat back, stunned. Fisher showed zero concern about the Flaherty and Cosenza news, even though indictments loomed and despite the chance there would be press inquiries if the Committee's requests for indictment were leaked. There would be cries from civil rights groups, maybe hearings. And huge potential for political embarrassment. Maybe more, and more damaging, revelations.

"What ... why ...," she stammered, "why are you so worried about this conspiracy shit? It's nothing. It ..."

Fisher looked up at her and flashed impossibly white teeth in an automatic smile that looked like the tilting grin of a mad circus clown. "You won't - you can't - possibly understand."

Blood rushed to her face. "You're right, I DON'T understand, you condescending son-of-a-bitch. But I do know I delivered for you. Now do what you're supposed to do - protect your fucking President! And get me my fucking appointment!"

Fisher's lips flattened against his teeth. "My, my, how lady-like."

"Fuck you!" She moved to the edge of her chair. "Listen to

me, Mark. You'll look real good if you get the White House press office to prepare a reaction from the President. Something like ... 'the Committee Report is a 'valuable contribution' which will help the FBI and federal law enforcement improve procedures and cooperative efforts to be sure this doesn't happen again, blah, blah blah.' You can be prepared to go with a statement saying that Flaherty and Cosenza were acting well within established procedures back then, that they ..."

"Anne!" He looked disgusted. "Stop it, right now! Don't tell me what to do! I ..." He caught himself, noticing the look of dismay on her face. He blew it. He had let their familiarity lower his defenses and had admitted to her his concern about the Committee's conspiracy allegations. To her, he was reacting very oddly. She knew something was very wrong.

"Anne, Anne ...," he breathed deeply. "All right ..."

He got up and walked around the desk. He sat in the chair next to her. "Look, ... its Saturday night. It's late. I'm tired. Let's have some dinner, and some exquisite wine, and pursue this in a more pleasant environment. You did very well. And I thank you. Of course I'm worried about Cosenza and Flaherty. And there's nothing to any of the unknown conspiracy nonsense that McAdams will spout. ... I ... I'm sorry for my outburst." Another flash of teeth said he was done apologizing and all was right with the world.

She rose stiffly from her chair. She had to get out of this room. "I'd rather not, Mark. I'd like to go home."

He stood, too, glaring at her.

"I'll see myself out." She backed out of the room and through the door. Her footsteps echoed as she walked quickly down the empty hall.

Fisher stood, staring hollowly at the closed door. Anne Gardiner might be a problem, a problem he knew he would be asked to handle. That's how they worked it. The muscles in his cheeks pulsated. He locked his desk drawers and closed his wall safe, spinning the tumbler to lock it. He walked out of the office.

Chapter Forty-one

A block away, across Lafayette Park, was the Hay-Adams Hotel. On the bottom floor was the Grill Room. Outside that were pillowed chairs to sink into with a stiff drink. Next to each chair was a private phone on a side table.

"Hullo, Mistuh Fisher," said the aged hotel doorman, bowing.

Mark Fisher nodded brusquely as he flew through the held door. He walked through the small lobby to the back stairs to the Grill Room. There he ordered a double Chivas on the rocks from the waiter who also welcomed him warmly by name.

He sat deeply in one of the high-backed, thickly cushioned chairs. He picked up the phone and called Manny Palau's private number at his pharmaceutical headquarters in Texas. The billionaire picked it up on the first ring.

"Yup," came the pronounced twang, "Palau here."

"Manny. It's Mark Fisher."

"What's up, boy?"

"We found the Assassination Committee Report."

"Good news! Now tell me what I wanna hear ..."

Fisher summarized the Findings and Conclusions. He finished by saying that OAK had not surfaced in the Report.

"You sure of that? You've seen the Report itself?"

"I've seen the Findings and Conclusions, but not the entire multi-volume Report."

"Tha's not good enough. There could be all sorts of evidence and talk about OAK in the full Report. Right?"

"Right."

"What about the diary pages? And Richmond? What about McAdams and that nigger Jackson? What else is going on?"

"The diary pages, and Richmond, are Narkle's problems. He's got Shephard working on the diary, and he has the mayor handling Richmond. In fact the mayor's called in our friends at Coast Guard and the FAA, and Vice Commandant Johansen has delivered. The federal authorities have taken over the entire investigation now..."

"Good!" snapped Palau. "And Jackson? McAdams?"

Fisher paused and then continued. "As for Jackson, he's alive. McAdams too. But I'm sure they've gotten the message"

"The message ... They've gotten the message. Let me tell you somethin', that's not enough. We need to do more!"

"Careful, this phone is not secure."

"I don't give a good God damn. I want Jackson out. I want McAdams out. That's it. I'm getting' Narkle on the phone."

Narkle picked up the phone on the first ring in the Governor's office. "Yes," he answered in a low voice. He breathed deeply, bracing himself. Only OAK used this line.

"Narkle, we need to put some plans into action. But tell me what's going on with Shephard."

Narkle had gotten used to Palau's caustic, abrupt style. He lived with the abusive calls, the insulting language. What he found most difficult was making the transition from Governor to supplicant, and making it quickly and in the right tone of voice so no one noticed.

"He's found nothing. I've sent him to West Virginia ..."

"... to search the sites he and Brock used when they were recruiting out there," finished Palau with an edge in his voice. "It's about time. Tha's where he left those diary pages. Tha's where Tidback picked 'em up. I'll bet a month of Fisher's salary on it."

Palau snorted. Narkle registered an obligatory chuckle. Fisher was silent. He resented being the butt of a joke.

"So," mumbled Palau, "the Declaration is still out there and so is..."

"So is the Lincoln material and ... Booth's accusation...," concluded Narkle.

Fisher choked on his next words, fearing the outburst. "We found some of the original Booth diary pages in McAdams' townhouse and got some off of Jackson. We've recovered the OAK creed, and Booth's letter to Secretary Brock and the Committee, the drawings, the Committee list. And we came across another list in McAdams' secret room ..."

"Another list ...?" began Palau.

"By Tidback. Of hits, assassinations and attempts - since Lincoln ..."

A heavy silence filled the phone line. "McAdams knows ...," snarled Palau. "Who else knows?"

"He knows just a part of the story, Manny," Narkle replied. "He may not know everything. He may be unable to piece it together at all, much less in a way that can hurt us. And there may not be any one else who knows."

"Mebbe this, mebbe that, mebbe yes, mebbe no," spat Palau. "McAdams must be put to sleep, like a damn dog gone bad. Then we got to find the rest of the diary and handle those who know or may know or can know. Then we destroy the damned pages this time. I don't know what Brock was up to lettin' them out."

"You will recall he claims they were stolen from a safe deposit box where he kept them" said Narkle.

"And you know and I know," replied Palau, "tha's absolute chickenshit." He snorted loudly. "Look, they can't produce anything on us and King. But they could use those damned diary pages against us and it would be plenty easy to use the Assassination Report to do it. That means Brock's got to be handled, too."

"Manny," Narkle's deep voice cracked, "we aren't secure!" Narkle looked around as if someone might have crawled in to his office. "Jesus Christ!"

"To hell with it! Let's get our big city banker on the phone. I want Fisher and Sable to have money for some real talent."

Fisher's drained his glass and motioned for another from a passing waiter. Sweat glistened over Narkle's top lip half a country away in Wisconsin. "What about consulting the others?" he asked.

Palau erupted. "There's no time! We're losing opportunity and control! If they don't like it, what they gonna do? Resign? Call the cops?" His raucous laugh scraped like sandpaper over skin. "Fisher, McAdams and Brock are your job? You'll get Sable to work? Get him the money for more talent?"

"Yes. But, allow me …. We are at a delicate time. Taking … drastic steps now, with them and Jackson, might send up some red flags. Make people, more importantly, make the *Committee members*, think there is something going on that they need to further investigate. I think we should wait on Brock until after the Committee meets on Wednesday. McAdams and Jackson have been warned. They can be taken care at a later time, in a week or two, when the Committee's work is over."

"Hmmm," Palau purred as he mulled over the suggestion. Fisher took a long drink from his fresh glass. Narkle leaned back in his chair, staring at the ceiling.

"I'm with you," said Palau at last. "We may need Brock's help as the Committee gets down to the short strokes. But we should work on a replacement for Brock now, someone from the Senate if we can. And quickly. I'll get Tomovitch to make the initial contacts. Now, then, it's time for our banker." Palau conferenced in Reid Johnson.

They heard two rings and then a voice. "Johnson."

"Reid, it's Palau. Narkle and Fisher are here too."

"Yes?"

"We're moving against McAdams and Brock."

"And Jackson?"

"Unsuccessful. We need to work on that, too. I want untraceable money down to Washington, by Monday morning. Can you do it?"

"Of course," he sighed. "How much?"

"$300,000 for Brock? He's a Senator, after all. And maybe another $300 thou for all the rest of 'em."

Johnson's end of the phone turned quiet for a moment before he spoke again. "We'll do this with an electronic funds transfer to First Virginia Bank; we'll do it through the New York Fed's discount window."

"I don't give bull balls how you do it," barked Palau. "You deal with Fisher. Narkle and I are hanging up. We don't need to know any more than we have to. And by the way, *Rooster*, don't forget your sweetheart. Take care of her. Get Sable to help if you need to. And tell him he's got a few more clean-ups to do. Tell him time's running out."

Narkle and Palau disconnected. Fisher listened to his instructions as he studied the color of the amber liquid in his glass in the glow of the table lamp beside him.

Chapter Forty-two

O'Connell sat back at his desk and glanced at his clock. Eleven on a Saturday night and he was working. Pitiful. He shook his head, got up and left, locking the door behind him.

He came out the South Capitol Street side of the Rayburn Building. South Capitol was a narrow, two-lane road between the Rayburn and the tall Cannon House Office Buildings. Even in daylight it was dark and threatening.

He passed a few parked cars tightly lining the curb and then squeezed through two to get to the street. He began crossing to the other side, lost in bleak contemplation of his miserable state. What had looked like an empty car came to life. Tires squealed as the sedan pulled into the street. Brilliant high beams came on, freezing him like a deer.

Something, his dead mother maybe, shouted at him to move. He dove into a truck on the other side of the street. The car just missed him. It took a screeching hard left at the red light at the corner and was gone.

O'Connell sat up and spat into his hand a mouthful of blood and the bottom half of one of his two front teeth.

"S'umbags!" he shouted after the car.

Chapter Forty-three

Sunday morning, April 19

Scattered around the labyrinth hallways leading to and away from the Capitol rotunda were dozens of hidden rooms. The members of Congress were assigned these rooms on the basis of seniority. Some were no better than dusty closets or oddly shaped cubbyholes tucked into the recesses of the Senate and House wings, or the domed rotunda itself. Others were large and elaborate, such as the one Daniel Webster used over a century ago to serve whiskey to his constituents and fellow members while regaling them with eloquent tales and strong-arming them for support.

The old Webster Room was on the ground floor of the Senate wing, less than 30 yards from the rotunda. It was located inconspicuously behind an unmarked door in a dead-end corridor that branched off the main hallway leading to the Senators' dining room. The highly coveted room was assigned to Senator Mossingame for his personal use because of his seniority and his Committee chairmanships.

It was perfect, McAdams knew. It was fully equipped with a fax, a phone with a speaker set-up, a copier, a fold-away bed and a huge couch, kitchen appliances and a large eating table, a bathroom with a shower, a large desk and coffee table and bookcases. And, because it was in the rotunda, it had 24-hour security. It also had an icemaker and a cabinet stocked with plenty of booze.

McAdams sat at the large wooden desk in the Webster hideaway, a cup of brown coffee steaming in front of him. The rising steam looked too much like the smoke above his building last night. It was 7:00 a.m., the next morning, and he hadn't slept much.

An explosive snort rocked the room. McAdams' took in O'Connell spread-eagled on his back on the pull-out sofa bed. One of his sickeningly white, hairy legs poked out like a dead man's appendage from under wrinkled sheets. His mouth was wide open, emitting snores that seemed to erupt from the very bowels of earth's volcanic core.

McAdams shook his head as he examined the spectacle. One of the first things he had done when he had entered the safety of Daniel Webster's hideaway was warn O'Connell about the fire and Jackson's attack. O'Connell told him about his own, late night near hit-and-run. O'Connell took a heartbeat to take McAdams' up on his offer to join him in the hideaway for a while, bringing with him copies of the FBI Booth diary examination materials he had let McAdams see. It didn't take him much longer after he arrived to down four fingers of scotch and fall into a heavy sleep.

McAdams leaned over and picked up one of his sneakers and fired it at O'Connell's stomach. It caught him in mid-snore and he turned over, grumbling at the unseen assailant.

A burst of laughter erupted. Linda Walker smiled at him from the couch, a huge Afghan blanket over her. "Nice shot. Is he going to be our alarm clock until we get out of here?" She stretched and rubbed her eyes, a huge welt on her neck.

McAdams stood and walked over to her. She had on extra-large T-shirt that looked good against her copper skin. Except for the deep bruise and the need for physical therapy for her neck, she was OK.

"Coffee?" he asked.

"Love some." She ran her hands through her brown frizzy hair, stretching again until her legs threw off the blanket. She put her feet on the ground and watched McAdams pour her a cup.

"Is Chief Jackson going to be all right?"

"Yeah. I called this morning. A little smoke inhalation, like you. Four broken ribs. A bruised kidney. A ton of bruises and lacerations on the outside, too. He'll be sore but he'll heal, he'll live. He already wants to head back to Harpers Ferry."

Linda shook her head, wincing at the pain in her neck. "We were lucky."

McAdams returned with the cup and gave it to Linda. She put her hands over his and they held the cup together, feeling the warmth. He smiled. She rubbed her hands up and down against his. He leaned in and she closed her eyes while they kissed. They pulled away, smiling.

"Yow!" O'Connell was awake. "Did an angel appear while I was in slumberland?" He swung his legs out of bed, a big grin on his gray face. He was wearing a T-shirt just like Linda. The effect was not quite the same.

"Looks like I got the couch tonight!" O'Connell let out a laugh and came over to shake Linda's hand. "But, believe me, sister, with the state of the world around us today, you and Mac got me as a roommate for a little while, so don't get too excited about playing house." They all laughed while McAdams made introductions. More coffee all around and then McAdams made egg and bacon sandwiches for everyone. They sat at the eating table and downed the food hungrily.

Linda eyed the pile of material on the wooden desk that McAdams had been going through. Her dark brown eyes had sparks. She was awake and engaged, and looked intently at McAdams as she spoke. "Have you found something?" She tilted her head at the desk.

"Those are computer printouts of the files from my investigators' field work in St. Louis. I was going through them last night before all the extracurricular events happened." "St. Louis? What's St. Louis got to do with the King assassination?"

"Right after the King Assassination Committee was created a couple years ago, I got a tip. A muffled voice said that long ago, in 1966 or 1967, someone had offered a financial reward to anyone who would kill Martin Luther King. Well, to make a long story short, I dispatched some investigators, they worked for months, the tip panned out and they found gold. It seems a local criminal named Gus Ryant acknowledged he had been offered a $50,000 bounty to kill King. Ryant claimed the offer came from a "hot shot" St. Louis lawyer and businessman, Winston Summerland. According to the investigators, Summerland was a descendent of early Virginian colonists. He was 'one who never let the Civil War die,' one who considered John Wilkes Booth to be a 'real American hero.' He belonged to several rabid segregationist societies, was a leader in an organization of businessmen and industrial leaders opposed to the 'dilution' of America by 'Negroes,' communists, homosexuals, foreigners, and 'Jewish interests.'"

"That's interesting," replied Linda, lost in thought.

"What?"

"Professor Tidback was from St. Louis."

"That's right! It was mentioned in the very first Washington Post articles about Tidback. I forgot!"

"In fact he taught there during the time King was shot. During the sixties he first became known as one of the country's pre-eminent experts on the Civil War and the use of guerilla warfare by the Confederacy. He held very famous conferences during that time, at St. Louis University, that were open to academia from all across the country and, interestingly enough, they were open to the public. He complained once about all the right wing nuts who used to attend, ranting and raving about one thing or another, but mostly about blacks, integration ...."

"And, I'm sure, Martin Luther King," finished McAdams. "Huh. I wonder if Tidback ever ran across Summerland."

"If this guy was as obsessed as you say, Mac, he had to."

"Check it out, if you can, in Tidback's files. The St. Louis work provides strong circumstantial evidence of a conspiracy behind King's murder. And David Tidback came to Washington saying he had proof of some sort that the conspiracy responsible for killing Lincoln was alive and well."

"A continuing conspiracy," said O'Connell.

McAdams nodded his head. "Three months ago when I wrote the first draft of the Report, Summerland and his cohorts like a racist group of nuts dressed in Civil War garb but largely unorganized, ineffective. They seemed certainly incapable of implementing a sophisticated plan to execute a nationally known figure like King."

"But, now, after Tidback and OAK, the Copperhead medallions, Brock's midnight visit and what he called Lewis Shephard's 'confederation of misfits' I mean, everything looks different, everything *is* different. OAK, David Tidback's continuing conspiracy, may be lurking in the shadowy background of what my investigators found in St. Louis."

Linda got up and walked over to the desk and was examining

a list of names. "What's this?"

"Chief Jackson found a list of 11 names from Booth's diary in the trailer outside Harpers' Ferry, plus some etchings Booth had done. Last night, Jackson tossed and turned in pain and couldn't sleep. He also was distraught about losing the originals of those diary pages. He lay there all night trying to reconstruct the list of names from memory. When I spoke to him this morning he made me write down those he remembered."

Linda looked at the list. The names glowed on the page. "Nathaniel Brock," she read. There's a Senator Brock on your Committee, right?"

"Yep."

"Mac, there's a Thomas *Summerland* on this list."

McAdams got up and took the list she offered. He read it. "Thomas Summerland ...," he began. "Jesus! I didn't catch it. I hadn't really registered anything after Brock's name. Or maybe these names meant nothing, until now." He scanned the list. There was a Bartholomew Wilkins, too. Members of Booth's cabal from a hundred years ago. This was the "Committee" that Booth wrote to, apologizing for failing to eliminate Lincoln on the grounds of the Old Soldiers Home.

Summerland. Brock. Wilkins. Senator Taylor Brock was not the only one who had an ancestor among OAK's membership when Lincoln was assassinated. So did Winston Summerland - the man fingered by an informant as posting a bounty for the head of Martin Luther King. And so did Nelson Wilkins, the Deputy Secretary of Defense so interested in the King Assassination Committee, Anne Gardiner and the White House special assistant, Mark Fisher, who was handling Tidback's FOIA requests. The descendants were carrying on the horrible trade - and legacy - of their forefathers.

"Linda," asked McAdams with a distant look in his eyes, "remember the checklist from Tidback's loft?"

"How can I forget it?"

"Lincoln, Presidential candidate Teddy Roosevelt, and Senator Huey Long were checked off. Next to these names were those of the successful and wannabe assassins. There were hand-scrawled question marks beside President James Garfield's name. And Martin Luther King's."

"Lincoln, Garfield and Long were assassinated. Roosevelt survived an assassination attempt only to lose in a presidential election. According to the evidence I have, Winston Summerland, descendent of an OAK member, put a contract out on Martin Luther King."

McAdams clutched a cigarette from the pack on the desk, lit it and inhaled with a long, trembling breath. He moved over to the couch and sat back in a smoky haze.

"Mac," interrupted O'Connell, "you're gonna have to verify their ancestry, tie Summerland, Brock and Wilkins back, I mean, to the three guys on Booth's list."

"We know a lot already. We've confirmed that Nathaniel Brock is Taylor's ancestor. And my investigators have established that Winston Summerland was a descendent of some of the original colonists who had come to Virginia. For that matter, Senator Taylor Brock had the same colonial pedigree, his ancestors had some of the original land grants in Virginia. And, don't you remember, Ed? Our buddy, good ol' Nelson Wilkins, used to brag to you, me, Anne, to anyone who'd listen when we all started out in Washington, how his ancestors were among the first settlers of America."

"'I'm a son of the American Revolution,' he would shout out when he was really drunk," O'Connell remembered.

"And you would answer him back, Ed. 'You're a sonuvabitch,' you'd say. We would all laugh. Then."

"Right."

"David Tidback," McAdams finished, "died talking about a conspiracy that began in the Civil War. ... But maybe he had it only half right. Maybe OAK has been around ... before that - since the nation's earliest days. I wondered if John Wilkes Booth had written anything down in his diary on that subject."

The three of them sat without moving, lost in thought. The missing pages from the Booth diary held the answers.

Linda sat next to McAdams. "Maybe this 'Committee' that Booth was writing to about his failed attempt to kidnap Lincoln on the Old Soldiers' grounds in Washington, maybe this Committee and OAK, were connected, and maybe they had been around for a while, a long while."

"You know," McAdams replied, "Professor Browning over at Georgetown told me something. She said the OAK creed that we found in Tidback's loft was similar to something called a Vigilante Creed, which dated from 1840 or so. So, there's a possibility …. You and I have to talk to her. Maybe you and she can work together and help us figure this out."

"OK, but …."

"Wait a minute!" McAdams grounded out his cigarette in an ashtray. "I just remember I faxed copies of what we found in the loft to Professor Browning so she could give me some idea what I was dealing with."

O'Connell punched the air in triumph. "That means she has copies of what you thought burned up in your apartment!"

"Unless OAK found 'em first."

Linda held up her hand. "I just thought of something. … I came across a connection between Booth's 'Committee' and OAK, in Tidback's files at Randolph-Macon."

"Go on," McAdams prodded.

"It was a note in the Professor's handwriting asking whether the Second National Bank was a bridge between the Secret Committee and OAK."

"What's the 'Secret Committee'"?

"I don't know. But it's a '*Committee.*'" She put up her fingers to indicate quotation marks. "But here me out. I thought the note was unimportant. I mean I know OAK is key to all this, but I didn't see what help the note was. But listen, there *is* a connection."

"What's the Second National Bank?" asked O'Connell.

"The Second National Bank was the second attempt by this country to set up a national banking institution to counter the influence of all the state banks. Well, Andrew Jackson wanted to bring down the Second National Bank. That effort led to an attempt on his life."

"You mean someone tried to kill Andrew Jackson?" O'Connell asked.

"Yes," answered McAdams. A man named Richard Lawrence tried to assassinate him in late January of 1835, but his two pistols misfired. Jackson responded by going after his assailant with his cane, shouting, to those who tried to restrain him, "Let me alone. Let me alone. I know where this came from!"

O'Connell stared at McAdams incredulously. "How …."

"Listen, I know this stuff. Remember I've studied every investigation the Congress has ever done when it comes to assassinations. And, it turns out, the US Senate back then set up a Special Investigating Committee to look into the attempt on Jackson's life. The Committee's lead suspect was a businessman - George Poindexter."

"George Poindexter was a prominent businessman. There were allegations that he hired Richard Lawrence to shoot Jackson. It must have been an easy sell. According to reports back then, Lawrence felt he was owed money by the Second National Bank and since Jackson was trying to destroy the Bank, that meant Jackson was taking money out of his pocket. The Senate Committee was not so dedicated or diligent. It disbanded without finding any evidence to nail Poindexter to the wall, to determine his motivations, his *own* sponsors if there were any. Nothing. No report, nothing."

"A lot of big money hated Jackson," continued Linda. "Jackson's enemies were big banks, big national merchants and the wealthy elite. He devoted his second inaugural speech to attack what he thought was the country's tilt toward the accumulation of money and power in the hands of the privileged few. Can you imagine that? He said the country's national bank - the Second National Bank - was controlled by the rich and powerful who were bending the acts of government to suit their own selfish purposes."

"Andrew Jackson had offended the same kind of people Abraham Lincoln did when he freed the slaves."

"Professor Browning told me Lincoln pulled off the biggest nationalization or liberation of private property in the country's history with that one act."

"She was right," Linda replied.

McAdams thought about Tidback's list of assassinations. "Andrew Jackson and Abraham Lincoln offended the big money people. The same people that Teddy Roosevelt and Huey Long - and Martin Luther King - antagonized. They all were good at pissing off the big boys." Except for Andrew Jackson, all those names appeared on Tidback's list with its checkmarks and question marks.

McAdams looked at Linda. "Tidback was doing a visiting professorship down at the University of Mississippi, right?"

"Right."

"This George Poindexter was a businessman from Mississippi."

"Tidback went to Mississippi to research where Poindexter came from, his roots ….," began Linda.

"His connections to OAK, and maybe OAK itself! And this thing called the Secret Committee," McAdams replied.

"He must have found something down there that drove him to Washington. Something he had to tell your Committee, Mac. … I have to go to Mississippi, Mac! All his stuff is still down there!"

"You can't, it's too dangerous to go alone."

"I have to. We have to find the animals that killed Professor Tidback and Professor Crockett. We have to…"

"You cannot go alone, Linda."

"You come with me, then."

"I have the Executive Session of the King Committee this week. I can't. We'll have to wait…."

"You know we can't wait. What if Tidback was working on something that's important to the investigation of the King assassination? What if you can't solve King's murder without knowing what Professor Tidback knew? What if OAK gets there first, Mac, and does what it did to your apartment?"

McAdams knew she was right. They hesitated and then both turned to O'Connell.

"Where's Mississippi?" he replied weakly. "Do I need a passport or something?"

McAdams walked over to the phone. "I'll get you guys tickets for later today." He rang Jazz at home. She was getting ready for early morning Sunday service. She had fever in her voice when she picked up, practicing and vocalizing as she got ready to lead choir.

McAdams told her where he was staying, in code in case anyone was listening. Jazz knew where the "Tank" was - it was Daniel Webster's hideaway. McAdams had spent quite a few nights there for one reason or another over the years - late work, some young thing, a heavy drinking binge every now and then. He told her Linda was with him.

"Oh?" My, my, my, she mused, that boy works fast.

"And Ed's staying here, too." He told her about the fire, Chief Jackson and the near hit-and-run.

"Oh, Lord," she prayed. "I'm going to visit Chuck right after church. We'll be praying fo' him, too."

"Good. Because he tells me he's checking out first thing Monday morning." He asked her to get the plane tickets. She told him there were all sorts of calls on the office voicemail. Lewis Shephard had called several times, wanting to see the entire Committee Report before Wednesday, including the Findings and Conclusions. Senator Brock wanted to talk to him, too. And so did some pushy asshole from the Department of Justice.

The sharks were circling.

Chapter Forty-four

Late Sunday morning, April 19 -- Alexandria, Virginia

Lewis Shephard winced in pain as he caught in the rear view mirror the first blinding daggers of sunrise slashing over the horizon. His eyes fled to the speedometer. He was going 70 on an empty Route 50. He had left Washington an hour ago, heading due west for the campgrounds and parks used to set up the West Virginia campsite. He'd be at the first in about 30 minutes.

He had been told to search for Brock's missing papers. Brock had joined him on some of his trips into the woods, and may have hidden the old diary pages at one of the sites. Perhaps Tidback was told to find them there, under cover of night when no would know better.

Shephard remembered how surprised he had been at Brock's interest in joining him on the recruitment trips. But Brock wanted to witness the "herald to arms" as he called it.

They stayed at the trailer site where Larcher's group died. And once they had spent the night at another remote campsite in the woods. Shephard shook his head as the empty highway rolled under him in the early sun. Larcher ….

That cold, winter night blasted into his mind again, the night he was to meet Larcher and the West Virginian campsite at the trailer in the woods. It was to be their formal initiation into the confederation. They had met maybe a number of times before - for lessons, weapons and offensive drills, and background on ways to avoid the harshest provisions of the criminal code.

He taught them the purpose of the West Virginia campsite. They were to be shock troops, the front line, ready to carry out the instructions of the Leaders as relayed to them by Shephard. He saw blossoming in their dull faces the thrill they felt in joining a nationwide confederation, one that fought for the integrity of the true America and the true Americans.

There were other campsites for sure. On the West Coast, in the Northwest and the South and Appalachian areas. He was ordered where and when he was to go and recruit and train. Travel vouchers were quickly approved by Brock. And then at some abandoned building, some forgotten campground or overgrown park in the woods, he would find cells of men. And there, as instructed, he would teach.

He, Lewis Shephard, could assemble a growing band of hard-core followers that now numbered close to 100. They were skinheads from Baltimore, aimless members of the Ku Klux Klan from Mississippi, white power mongers from Idaho, and disaffected members of other, loosely organized Christian power movements and white separatist groups from across the country. They came from the wide west, the bayou, the decaying towns of the plains and from the mountains -- all across America -- to him. More and more, the audience included bands of men like those in West Virginia. Lost, nowhere men of limited means, hope and intelligence that trudged out of the small, forsaken towns that were seemingly everywhere in America.

"Shephard's Confederation," he whispered aloud, a little crooked smile on his lips.

Campsite members felt important. There were so many jobs to do, things to learn, missions to run! And on the night that was to be their grand initiation ritual, the West Virginian campsite would belong at long last to John Wilkes Booth's legacy of campsites. At the culmination of the ceremony they would have the historic Copperhead medallion placed formally around their necks. They would then hold hands in a circle and recite, for the first time, the confederation's creed. The medallion was theirs to admire - even wear when permitted. They would be American Knights!

Shephard grew pensive. Larcher had been a promising candidate. The West Virginia camp showed promise. The Leaders were pleased and gave him a $25,000 cash bonus. On one of his phone calls with his unknown contact, he was actually told that the West Virginians would rise to the top of the national campsites because they were primed and poised, and close to the nation's capital where so many enemies lurked.

But the formal initiation did not come to pass. And Larcher took it into his own hands that night, giving the camp members their medallions. Since then nothing had gone right.

He barely saw the road in front of him as freakish images of what had happened inside that trailer flashed just outside his vision. Larcher had taken them to the campsite without a stitch of extra clothing. In some kind of dementia or meanness Shephard could not begin to understand, Larcher somehow convinced the others to not touch the plentiful supplies of food, heat, water. Not one of them, even Larcher, tried to work the ham radio. Instead, that night, Larcher used the battery-powered cellular phone his stepfather had given him, the space age toy that had so impressed Larcher's minions. One of them had gushed to Shephard one day that the cellular phone was a modern warrior's communicator, like on Star Trek. They each wanted a communicator and they were pooling their money to get some.

Star Trek! Shephard shook his head. Little boys ... And while they waited that night for him to arrive for the initiation, the terrible snow came. He had spoken to Larcher at the trailer from a payphone and begged him to wait, that he'd get there one way or the other.

God knows, he tried. He tried to make it up that hillside. But the car got stuck on the snow-clogged road that led to the trailer site. He had to turn around, or he would have frozen to death himself! It had snowed almost a foot by then and it was still coming down. Almost 24 inches fell that night.

The second time he called, at 1 or 2 in the morning, someone began to answer and then there was silence. Did the phone battery die? Was Larcher, or someone, pulled away from the phone? Where WERE they at that moment?

He remembered, in the driving snow in his high beams, a dark mound some distance up the road in front of him before he turned around. It must have been their car, but how was he to know then - in the snow, in the dark? It looked like a snowdrift! He remembered shapes wandering among the trees that stood so close together they seemed like the log walls of the old west forts. But when he called out into the driving snow, the shadows stopped moving. Had he seen a flashlight's beam dancing as if in a running man's hand? Had the light gone out, or fallen in the snow? A moan escaped his lips.

He had pleaded with Larcher to wait for him in the trailer. He had told him he would call again. Did they leave anyway in panic or fear, trying to make it back by foot? Why didn't they stay and make do with all the provisions he had left stored for them? How could Larcher just leave them in the cold, in the woods?

"Why didn't they know better?" he screamed into the dashboard as he pounded the steering wheel. "They didn't have to die!"

Tears streamed down his face. Samuels with the doe eyes, Hughlette with the wide smile, the soft skin. He wiped his face with his sleeve. His foot hit the accelerator hard. The car began swerving down the highway, moving inexorably closer to the darkened foothills that haunted his nightmares. Tears filled his eyes, blinding him.

Shephard pulled on the steering wheel and over to the side of the road, stones and rocks spitting into the sky and cracking against the windows. The car lurched and heaved to a stop on the soft shoulder. Angry blasts of a truck's air horn screamed past him.

He punched his balled-up fists into his eyes as tears streamed down his face. He pounded the dashboard and cried until he could cry no more. They had been such good boys.

His sobs finally broke down into wracking laughter as he heaved himself again and again against the seat back, his fingers clutching the steering wheel, his head viciously whipping back and forth.

Chapter Forty-five

Sunday – Cleveland Park, Washington, DC

"Yes, Mac," replied Dorothy Browning. "I've still got the pages you faxed me, the ones we've spoken about. I have them right here. I'll fax them to you." She wrote down the number to the fax in the Tank that McAdams had given her.

McAdams let out a huge sigh. "You're a life saver!" It wasn't direct evidence, it was a copy without the original, but it would do if push came to shove. He activated the speakerphone and introduced Linda, now showered and changed into black jeans and a T-shirt.

"I'm sorry to bother you at home about all this…."

"Not a bother, Mac, you know that. And Linda, I know you must feel awful about what has happened. David was a wonderful teacher, a wonderful man. I'm terribly sorry about what has happened."

"Thank you," she replied, her eyes filling up.

"Professor, Linda came across a reference to something called 'the Secret Committee." Tidback was theorizing that the Second National Bank was a bridge between the Secret Committee and OAK."

"Well, you remember what you and I discussed about OAK morphing as the kids say today into one group or another, having one name or another, in order to cloak themselves …."

"… to disguise and maybe inflate their numbers and strength," concluded Linda.

"Very good! You know I have an opening for a grad assistant up here, Linda. Maybe I can talk you into coming north sometime soon."

"I think I'd like that," she replied.

"OK, we'll talk. Anyway, Mac, back to you. Even with all this morphing talk, you have to understand the Secret Committee, at least the one I am familiar with, was real. It was an important part of the birthing of this country. If David Tidback was right about this, that the Second National Bank served as a way to allow the Secret Committee to evolve into this OAK, well, then he had achieved another remarkable discovery that changes the entire perception of this country, its origins, the framers, and all that."

"What *was* the Secret Committee?"

"The Secret Committee was set up in late 1775 by the Second Continental Congress. It was our soon-to-be-nation's first official body for buying supplies, ammunition and weaponry for wartime and dispersing it all among the colonies. Robert Allen, a legendary merchant, a member of the Congress and a signer of the Declaration of Independence from Pennsylvania, was asked by George Washington to head it up. The Secret Committee was "secret" for a reason. The colonies had to buy guns, powder and ammo to fight the British, but British law made it illegal for them to trade with any country other than Britain! So they had to do it in on the sly. The Secret Committee covertly made arrangements around the globe to fortify the warrior colonists."

"The Secret Committee was made up of the commercial giants of the day -- the maritime merchants. These guys had the great naval fleets of the time, and the greatest experience in foreign trade. The Committee could enter into contracts on behalf of the Continental Congress for arms, ammunition and foodstuff. They could draw on the Treasury of the Continental Congress for funds. They bought or traded for weapons, gunpowder, salt for preserving food, and food itself in Europe and elsewhere, bringing them to America through the Caribbean. Only the Secret Committee was empowered to trade for and distribute all this stuff to the colonies, and to the new American army and navy. It was our first government-sanctioned monopoly."

"It was the great commercial engine of its time and, as it turned out, it was used and abused by those entrusted to keep it primed and running for the benefit of the emerging country. The Secret Committee became an unchecked source of war profiteering and secret self-dealing. Many of America's great family dynasties were built upon the wealth and power they grabbed through the corrupt money machine known as the Secret

Committee. Allen's was one of those families."

"The excesses were so great that, in a short time, the Secret Committee no longer was quite so secret. Thomas Jefferson, John Adams, the Lees of Virginia, and some of the other liberals of the time began to protest. Some of Robert Allen's supporters became shocked, disaffected. The government ordered an audit of the Secret Committee, right at the beginning of the Revolutionary war for heaven's sake. That's how serious the abuses were. There could have been major prosecutions at the time. But it was all hushed up. The country didn't need the diversion. After all, there was a people's war for democracy and independence going on. That's when the Committee ended."

"And maybe that's when OAK started?" McAdams waited for his answer.

"Remember OAK's creed, Mac? I'll read it, omitting some words. But listen: 'no free mason, minuteman, ... or any false patriot shall be allowed to interfere with the enjoyment and pursuit of property – without answering to our punishment.' It has been reported in the history books that Robert Allen and the Secret Committee were bitter about how they were handled by the patriots Jefferson, Adams and the rest. They felt they had engaged in great sacrifice to help arm and supply the struggling new country, at great risk to themselves and even loss of profits, and they believed they deserved a little skim off the top, a little piece of the action. Maybe they felt they knew no other way of supplying the country other than through self-dealing. Who knows, Mac? I can easily find the seeds of OAK as we know it in the Secret Committee, or in what it had become."

"But wait," McAdams protested. "Robert Allen goes from seafaring merchant and business leader, to signing the Declaration of Independence, to serving in the Continental Congresses, to chairing a special Committee that mobilizes the colonies to fight a grand War of Independence, to starting a ... a vigilante hit squad? From patriot to terrorist in two years?"

"It's not that hard to understand, Mac," answered Linda.

"The great merchant families of the colonies, mostly seafaring, made all their wealth by breaking the law - English law! From the 1760's on, they burned competing British ships and shot cannon over their bows trying to intimidate them from engaging in trade. But they themselves would trade illegally with nations other than Great Britain and they'd avoid British custom agents and taxes like the plague. And when it suited them, they would trade with the Brits during the war, violating the American non-importation bans directed against British goods. They'd hoard, they'd price gouge, and they'd take and accept bribes.

"During the war they had these things called Committees of Safety and Inspection which terrorized and punished other merchants, property holders and ship owners they suspected of being sympathetic with the British. Or who maybe made too much money or took away too many customers. One Committee in New York published something called a 'Declaration of High Treason' which was followed by a bloody ocean of property confiscations, hangings and terror in the region. There was a group called the Regulators during this time that was a vicious "law-and-order" league, operating like a true vigilante squad. Executions, missing landowners, ... accidents ... were not uncommon things."

"Well," concluded McAdams. "I think we found the beginnings of OAK."

They bade farewell and Browning hung up. She stepped immediately over to her packed bookshelves that filled one wall of her office from floor to ceiling. She pulled down an early American history volume and thumbed to a discussion of the Second National Bank. "A link between the Secret Committee and OAK," she mused. She stopped when she came to a chart taking up a page of the book. It showed the men, again they were all men, who founded and ran the Second National Bank. Her breath caught as she scanned the names.

Suddenly the front door bell rang downstairs. She stepped over to her office window and looked down. There was a solitary man with broad shoulders and dark black hair standing in front of her door, a briefcase at his feet. He was matching the number over her door to a piece of paper he held in his hand. She looked at her watch. It was a little after one in the afternoon. Odd time for solicitors.

The doorbell rang again, followed by urgent knocking. She hesitated. She should answer it. Something might be wrong. Someone might need her help. She dropped the open volume on her desk and began to move through the room, heading for the stairs.

She passed the fax machine and stopped, knowing she'd forget the fax she promised if she didn't get it done now. She punched in the numbers McAdams gave her and lined up the pages. "Oh, go away!" she muttered as the room echoed with the commotion at her door. "Go away!"

The first two pages went on their way and she waited until the last one started crawling through. As it went she cursed the knocking on the door that was now pounding through the house. She ran down the stairs, peeked through the spyhole and saw nothing.

They're gone, she reasoned. And good riddance. She opened the door to be sure.

Sable burst in. The door flying toward her caught her chin and its impact knocked her over onto the carpeted floor. She lay at the foot of the stairs, holding her face with one hand, stunned, a slicing pain shooting down her neck.

"You're Professor Browning, from Georgetown." It wasn't a question. It was the name he had overheard at the Botanical Gardens.

There was no emotion in the clipped, plain voice. It was all business. He was nothing but killing business. She lowered her head and nodded slowly in response, knowing her fate, her eyes darting around her looking for some escape, some weapon.

Sable closed the door behind him. His eyes on her as she sat on the floor, he opened the brief case and removed a black handgun with an extended barrel. It looked fake to Dorothy Browning but Sable knew it was a well-kept 9 mm Glock 17 handgun. She could not move. There was no use, she knew that. But she struggled to get to her feet anyway. The end would not come this way, not on her derriere, not waiting for it to come. She would stand proudly, looking him in the eyes.

She was on her haunches, trying to rise, when he brought his hand up and emptied two silenced rounds into her chest, the killing zone. With blood barely beginning to pump out of her breast, he planted the final round in the middle of her forehead as she lay thrown back against the stairs. The slug lodged into the carpeted step under her head with a single thumping sound and a deep red stain appeared from under her gray hair.

History lessons are over, Sable chuckled to himself. Class is dismissed.

His head cocked when he heard a beep upstairs. It had to be a fax machine. He deliberated about leaving. No one had seen him enter the walkway to her modest townhouse. The front door was not visible to anyone from the outside. No one had seen him. To stay longer risked discovery.

She had faxed something to somebody. It might be important to know. She hadn't answered the door for some time after he began knocking, time enough to fax off an SOS, even his description. Maybe something about OAK.

He put the gun back in the briefcase and bounded up the stairs, his powerful legs taking three at a time. He found her office and the fax machine. He picked up the three pages that had been faxed successfully according to the blinking LCD. He punched several buttons until he saw the destination fax number. He didn't recognize it. He committed it to memory, folded the faxed pages and tucked them in the chest pocket of his black denim shirt.

He methodically walked through each room searching for anything of interest in plain view. Seeing nothing, he went down the stairs, stepped over her dead body avoiding the growing blood stains, and left.

Chapter Forty-six

Sunday - The woods outside Harpers Ferry, West Virginia

The trail to the abandoned Army campgrounds that unfolded begrudgingly before him was congested with tall grass and weeds. The car bottomed out repeatedly on deeply pitted stretches of what used to be a well-used dirt path. The trail turned sharply and ended abruptly at a wide, overgrown field. The gray concrete bunkers waited at the far end.

Shephard sat in his car, his eyes blank, and his skin cold, pale and damp. Crumbs from a stale, unbuttered roll covered his lap. He took the last bite, then brushed himself off as he scanned the last site he would inspect.

The abandoned Army campgrounds sat deep in the woods outside Harpers Ferry. He and Brock had stayed there once. Brock insisted on going with him to the back room of a bar in downtown Harpers Ferry where recruits could be found. The bar had no name, no beckoning neon lights. It consisted of a large room with a few hanging lights and wide, green-painted tables surrounded by ancient wooden chairs. It was a place where two-bit robberies were planned, drugs bought, women bought and grabbed, and where the local favorite drug - crank, amphetamines laced with cocaine - was snorted loudly and repeatedly by men with runny noses and dead eyes.

Next door to the bar was a vacant lot covered with high grass, broken glass and racing vermin. Down the hill, on the other side of the bar, was the oil-stained Potomac slithering like a glistening serpent to Washington.

He shuddered at the memory of Brock sitting at one of those tables, his hair wild, his eyes aglow, his spirit charged. Thank God he had said nothing that night. One word and everyone would have known him, or at least known the man was far from home. Shephard dispelled the image with a shake of his head. At some point Brock had gotten sick of it all, claiming that the campsites had gotten out of control, that the "new boys" - the Leaders - threatened all that he, Brock, had worked for. He never joined Shephard, never talked about the campsites, again. And it was good riddance, too. Shephard opened the car door.

He walked to the one-story building. The grass was as high as his knees, as high as his waist in some places. As he approached he noticed the door was slightly ajar. He breathed and pushed it open. The two sets of bed springs where they had placed their sleeping bags and foam mattresses were still rusting out in the open. The wooden furniture had crumbled even more. A thicker coat of dust, pollen and grime lay on the kitchen counters.

The interior walls were plaster layered over cement blocks. Nowhere was there an opening or a niche into which documents could be stuffed. The floor was cement. The only other hiding places were the kitchen cabinets and the wooden rafters that spanned the width of the building and the canopy above the rafters. After searching the cabinets, he examined the rafters through squinted eyes and peered beyond to the underside of the roof ceiling. Nothing.

Outside a cluster of birds flew overhead screeching their warnings to some unseen intruder. His heart thumped loudly in his chest as he moved over to the window and peered outward. The high grasses between him and his waiting car bent in a stiff breeze suddenly rising before a spring storm.

He eased out of the building and moved to search the other two, which looked identical from the outside. The first was just to the right, the other was directly opposite the one he had already been through.

A rapid search of the first revealed nothing. He stepped outside and saw the sky had gotten darker. Above him dark, sullen clouds had gathered, pregnant with heavy rain. He hurried over to the last building.

He stopped short. The door was wedged shut. He threw his shoulder against it several times without success. The windows, too, were closed and covered with dust and grime. Inside were the dim outlines of the layout in the other buildings.

Around back he found a rock the size of a basketball. He scooped it up with his hands and carried it to the front, heaving it through a window. The rotted frame gave way, leaving jagged shoots of wood and glass protruding menacingly from the sides. He listened to the silence of the dark woods and the throb of his own pounding blood and then pushed through the remnants of the window.

Once inside, he took in the room. Beer cans, cigarette butts and snack wrappers were scattered about. Someone had been here recently, perhaps some of the same men he had recruited in this very building, before the trailer was set up.

The one-room building was darker than the others were because it was settled deeper into the woods. He wished for a flashlight as he peered into the recesses overhead. Shaking his head with disgust at his forgetfulness, he pulled over a chair and climbed on top. Gingerly his hands ran along the tops of the crossbeams and the parts he could reach of the undersides of the sloping roof. His eyes moved over every bulge and dark spot in the cobwebbed, black corners he could not reach. He repeated the search at several other spots in the room.

He stepped over to the kitchen area, noting there were more cabinets in this building than in the others. He opened each of the cabinet doors and felt around inside. Spider webs and rodent droppings met his fingertips. In the cabinet in the far corner of the kitchen, right next to the empty space where a refrigerator probably had been, he felt something.

A large manila envelope had been stapled securely, with a staple gun perhaps, to the underside of the bottom shelf. Anyone looking in, especially in the dim light, would notice nothing unusual, even if they sprawled prostrate on their backs on the floor and looked up into the cabinet itself. But a hand slipping along the side and top of the cabinet interiors could not miss the package.

He carefully pried the staples loose with a rusted knife from one of the drawers. The folder fell to the bottom of the cabinet. He picked it up, hurriedly searched the remaining cabinets, finding nothing, and then left the way he came.

He made it to the car and sighed deeply after the doors were locked and windows tightly shut. Now, in the security of glass and metal, he could catch his breath and examine his find. Heavy raindrops startled him as they suddenly exploded against the windshield and roof.

There was a note from Brock to David Tidback on top of a number of clear plastic folders in the envelope, each holding a yellowed page about 4" wide and 6" long. The note looked to be the continuation of instructions to Tidback on areas of research into something called the "Secret Committee." The note said the yellowed pages had been sliced out of the diary of John Wilkes Booth.

Shephard swallowed and realized his heart was pounding. Thunder rolled into the field and the rain grew heavier. He peered into the shadowy woods and searched the rear view mirror before settling again on the pages on his lap.

The first three were old, hand-drawn maps of Washington, Maryland and Virginia. They were neatly penned and marked precisely with legends, scales, compass directions, and distances. The pages had many hand-written notes and marks.

There was a route marked from Washington to Richmond. Landmarks and strange references, in code of some sort, were jotted periodically along the southern route as if to indicate way stations or sources of information and help. There was nothing on the backs of these three pages.

The fourth page took the form of a ledger showing the receipt of dollar amounts and corresponding dates stretching from November 1864 to April 1865. The entries showed that someone got paid a total of $50,000 over six months in 8 periodic installments. The recipient was the J. W. Booth whose name was signed at the bottom of the page. Below the name was a smudged circular stamp bearing a blurred image of a head.

A Copperhead medallion. "Booth's medallion!" Shephard found himself whispering half-aloud. The badge of his confederation!

The last three pages composed one long letter. It was dated July 19, 1776. Along the top of the first page of the manifesto ran a title - "A Declaration of Order and Commerce." Shephard's brow creased as he read the document.

The Declaration, although dated 100 years earlier than the journal pages and the ledger entries, was in the same handwriting as the ledger and the maps. Same handwriting but 100 years difference in date. Booth's handwriting. Booth had copied the Declaration into his journal. Maybe he found the original, or had stolen it, and wanted a record of it. Maybe he thought it would be handy, or valuable, someday.

He stopped reading when he came across the familiar words of an oath. It was his creed, the Knight's creed, the one recited time and again by the eager members of his campsites, at their initiation and then at every meeting thereafter.

He turned to the last of the three pages that Booth had copied into his journal. The Declaration of Order and Commerce was signed, albeit in Booth's hand, by Robert Allen. Of Philadelphia. Under his name were those of 10 more men. The first was that of Alexander Brock.

Allen's Declaration sounded like something out of the National Archives. Allen and his colleagues were unhappy. They had long served the country, fighting the British even before the Declaration of Independence was signed. Robert Allen had signed the Declaration of Independence, for God's sake, but the Declaration of Order and Commerce said he regretted that act. He and his group felt betrayed. They felt the country had turned from its true destiny. The rich and the powerful, the families and generations destined to lead, them!, were not in charge anymore. The people were to be feared and too much democracy was a danger.

The eloquent document bled Allen's worries over where the country was going, and his own hurt and frustration over the betrayal he had suffered. Betrayal at the hands of the Congress and ... Benjamin Franklin, George Washington, John Adams, Thomas Jefferson and Alexander Hamilton!

Allen had been involved in something called the "Secret Committee," a group the Continental Congress and the founders of the country had asked him to head up. The Secret Committee helped keep the country fed and armed as it moved toward freedom and into the Revolutionary War. But now the Continental Congress was auditing it. Claims of misdeeds were being leveled by Washington and Jefferson and the rest ....

That was the last straw and, like the "Regulators," Allen and the other signers of the Declaration of Order and Commerce agreed to form the Order of American Knights. To set things straight. Right all the wrongs. To defend and protect ... "Order and Commerce and Progress."

"The Order of American Knights ...," he said aloud. OAK. Suddenly his own confederation of campsites, and the men in the shadows behind the voice that called him time and again, the Leaders, looked differently. He was only the latest in a long, long line.

He breathed deeply. He had only found 7 of the missing 18. Where had the other pages gone? What was on THEM? He prayed the Leaders would believe he had found no more.

Shephard slipped the plastic folders with their contents under the passenger seat. He started the car and began to back up. The wheels spun on the wet, tall grass, churning up a heavy, dark dread within his chest. The tires finally took hold and he sped to the trail. It led away before him into endless, gray woods that waited for him in the dismal mist and rain.

Chapter Forty-seven

Sunday, midnight - Madison, Wisconsin

Governor Narkle locked his office door and picked up his OAK phone. He activated the encryptor before dialing and ensured that each of his called parties switched on his own.

"Gentlemen," Narkle began, "Lewis Shephard has recovered some of the diary pages."

"How many?" asked the quiet voice of Reid Johnson.

"Seven."

"Jesus Christ ..." Manny Palau snarled.

"That means," calculated Nelson Wilkins, "if you include the one that McAdams had, the one with the OAK creed, and the three pages that Sable took off Jackson – OAK's membership list and the 2 etchings - then we've recovered 11 of the 18 missing pages that were sliced out of the diary by one of Stanton's men so long ago"

"And," Narkle continued, "we recovered from McAdams one diary page that Booth probably tore from the diary himself, his letter about his failure at kidnapping Lincoln."

"All we need is ..." Palau replied.

"... Booth's 'finger of accusation," concluded Mark Fisher. The conversation stopped as each man considered the implications of this last document falling into the wrong hands.

"What did Shephard find out in West Virginia?" said Congressman Tomovitch at last. .

"Booth's maps," replied Narkle, "his record of reimbursements and, Mason ..., are you now on?"

"Yes." replied Mason Allen. "I've heard everything."

"Good," continued Narkle. "Lewis also recovered Booth's copy of Robert Allen's Declaration of Order and Commerce."

"Excellent!"

"And a note from Brock to Tidback about researching the Secret Committee."

"Can someone," blurted Coast Guard Vice Commandant Lloyd Johansen, "tell me what Brock was up to? I cannot for the life of me fathom it."

Mason Allen took the question. "He was using the Booth diary pages to entice Professor Tidback to unearth the beginnings of OAK. I'm sure of it. Tidback would have wanted to see the originals."

"Why the hell would Brock want to do this?"

"He spoke to me over the last few months of his interest in how the Secret Committee evolved, what happened after it was prematurely, shall we say, 'terminated.' Brock had high regard for David Tidback. I believe Winston Summerland introduced them, if I'm not mistaken, after Summerland attended several of Tidback's conferences in St. Louis. Brock's library holds all of Tidback's works. And Brock knew the Booth diary pages would whet Tidback's appetite and give him a start."

"I vote," barked Palau, "to destroy the diary pages that Shephard found, before ..."

"NO!" Barry Ingram interrupted. "They're our record of origin, our Magna Carta. They set out our identity, our validity. If we destroy them, we lose something of ourselves."

Palau snorted. "That's weepy, God-damned sentiment. What you're doin' is puttin' your usual personal loyalty to Taylor Brock over OAK. You know that is unacceptable."

"May I speak, gentlemen?" Mason Allen cleared his throat. "Long ago I destroyed the Allen family records documenting the creation of the Secret Committee and OAK. Likewise, almost two hundred years ago, the Continental Congress and the first US Congress destroyed their Secret Committee records. Those bodies knew that keeping this material would expose the nation's new government to highly damaging criticism and protest."

"We destroyed recently the only original record of the Secret Committee - its handwritten journal of proceedings. The journal was passed down from Alexander Brock to one generation after another in the Brock family. When we discovered that it yet existed we took the matter up as OAK. You recall that Senator Brock argued against the destruction of the journal. I thank God he was unsuccessful in that effort. We destroyed it - something that should have been done two centuries ago."

"Are you sure we burned the real thing?" asked Johansen. "I

have to wonder now that I see what Brock was up to."

"It doesn't matter now," sniffed Allen. "But I am sure that we shall destroy the Booth diary pages. In them John Wilkes Booth copied down everything OAK showed him as it tried to win his loyalty. He transcribed OAK's original documents. He did this - for nefarious reasons."

Allen's voice rose. "We were fortunate that OAK was able to have these troublesome pages removed by its allies in the government, before they made their way into the courtroom during the trials of Booth's accomplices, before they were revealed during the Congressional inquiries into Lincoln's assassination. But Nathaniel Brock convinced OAK back then to keep the diary pages even if that meant preserving the only evidence connecting Booth - and a President's murder - to OAK. He argued that because fire had destroyed OAK's original founding documentation, including the original Declaration of Order and Commerce, Booth's handwritten transcriptions were all that were left. Much like you argue today, Barry. And Nathaniel passed the diary pages down through the Brock family, for safekeeping, to Taylor."

"It was a mistake then to keep the diary pages. It is a mistake now. Had the Secret Committee records gotten into the hands of the Federalists, their secrets would have threatened our early government, some of our nation's founding merchant families, and OAK itself. They would have threatened those that breathed life, strength and genius into this young, fragile country. A hundred years later, had Booth's records gotten into the public's hands, OAK would have been destroyed. This country is still young, gentlemen. OAK must not be exposed. We know what we must do."

"We'll meet," said Narkle, "... in Maine. And there we will destroy the pages from Booth's diary, in front of everyone, for everyone to see. And with that last step, if all goes well with the King Committee, all this will be behind us gentlemen. We may even be able to plan for the future."

"When do we meet?" snapped Johnson.

"This weekend. Saturday night. The night of a full moon, the grass moon."

Chapter Forty-eight

Monday afternoon, April 20 – Washington, DC

"Hosea Kenwood is here, Senator."

"Thank you, uh, what's your name again?" She was a temporary secretary and Mossingame was damned if he could remember her name.

"Elisa," she smiled. She had only repeated it about a hundred times today.

"Elisa, Elisa," Mossingame responded vacantly from behind the massive desk that filled his office. His eyes were flat. He looked pale. The man who had come to visit him, that Congressman, had said something, done something to shake him. Elisa could feel it in the charged air. Whatever conversation they had, whatever deal it was, was painful and raw. She felt badly for the old man. He suddenly looked years older, resigned to some dismal fate.

"Show him in," Mossingame sighed.

Hosea Kenwood walked through the doorway followed in his wake by an entourage of four black men with briefcases and three women clutching papers to their breasts. Kenwood held himself erect, his chin up, and his back straight. He was unburdened with any load, paper or otherwise. He was head of the NAACP and came from a long line of black leaders. Some said he was descended from the proud and noble blood of Fredric Douglass, the great black abolitionist. With his thick neck and his receding gray hair, if you put Kenwood into his fabled denim overalls, he would look like a steelworker or a farmer, appearing for all the world like he was ready for a day's labor for an honest wage. Mossingame sniffed.

"Senator."

"Mr. Kenwood."

"May I sit?"

"If you wish." Elisa managed to find enough chairs for the rest of the assemblage.

"So, what do you want from me, Hosea?"

"Yes, let's get right to it, Senator. Let's do that. I hear reports that the King Assassination Committee will find that there are members of this Administration who long ago mishandled the investigation into the murder of the Reverend Dr. Martin Luther King."

"I cannot …."

"I hear that all you intend to do is send this information over to the Justice Department for further criminal investigation. That you intend to do nothing to publicize these facts."

"Hosea, that's about all I have the authority to do. I …."

"I also hear that there are others responsible for the death of Dr. King. Others besides James Earl Ray. And that you do not intend to publicize this conspiracy. That once again you will lob the ball to Justice."

"Hosea, I resent the implications of what you're saying. That I am covering up. Not doing my job. I resent …."

One of the men sitting in the back jumped to his feet. "You *are* covering up if you do not lay it all out for the world to *see*. You *are* covering up if you are unable to bring to *justice* the most heinous of murderers."

"You, sit down!" shouted Mossingame. The room echoed with his command. Hosea Kenwood grew stiff at the volume and the tone of the Senator's voice.

Mossingame became silent, distant, and then he came back, his face set in grim resolve. "I will not be lectured to by *you*. And, Hosea, I will *not* listen to you telling me how to do my job. I have responsibilities to seek evidence and to make referrals. That's all. I have no responsibility to conduct a lynching in the public square."

The words stung. Kenwood bristled. He had never heard such a thing from this man, Walter Mossingame. They had been through some battles together, but never had he seen Mossingame so worked up, so belligerent. Never had Mossingame insulted or offended with his actions or his speech.

"I'm telling you something, Hosea. Back off. I don't need you, or your…."

"….*kind*?" Kenwood asked incredulously.

"You or your swaggering entourage barging into my office

like this, throwing the weight of your organization around and haranguing me over how I conduct the people's business."

"Then these facts are true. You have found men in the Administration perhaps responsible for the death of Dr. King. You have found conspirators, trigger pullers, and you will shrink from your responsibilities to the people who elected you as you claim to conduct the people's business."

Mossingame stood, the veins in his forehead pulsating. "This is what is true. Hosea Kenwood has gotten more from me, from this Adminstration, from this *country*, than he could possibly deserve. Despite that, he comes back for more. Always more. More, more, more."

Elisa stuck her head in the office, the faces of several anxious staffers hovering over her shoulder. "Senator, I heard shouts. Uh, is, is everything ...."

Mossingame dismissed her with a sweep of his hand. "Shut the door! I'm not finished here."

Elisa closed the door gently, not daring to make a noise. Mossingame walked around his desk. Kenwood stood quickly, as did the men behind him. Mossingame brought his face several inches away from Kenwood's. "If I may continue," Mossingame hissed, "Hosea Kenwood has done little for this country other than promote his own ... *people*, his own self-interest, his own cause. What had he done for *America*?"

There was pulsating silence in the room until one of the younger men erupted and had to be held back. "Don't you talk like that to the Reverend Hosea Kenwood!" Hosea Kenwood said nothing as he stood there stoically, his hands clasped in front of him, his jaw pulsating as he painfully swallowed his words. Something was terribly amiss here and he did not want it to get out of hand. Mossingame was different. Something had happened to him.

"Well, young man," Mossingame countered. "I *will* talk like that. Now, *get* out of my office. All of you."

"There will be riots in the streets if I leak what I know, Senator Mossingame."

"If you leak anything, I'll have you arrested and prosecuted."

"And there will be more riots..."

"And more arrests, even bloodshed…"

"Senator…! Walter, what has happened? Who is putting pressure on you? Why are you acting this way? Let us talk and …."

"My people have been hurt. Professors have been killed. Innocent people have been harmed. There is a war going on around this Committee and you dare come in here and tell me how I should conduct myself. What I should do. This country is being undermined, *attacked*, and you come to me with these petty grievances of yours."

"I'm sorry, Walter, perhaps you and I can meet another time. Perhaps …."

"There will be no other time. I don't have the time for … *this* anymore!" Mossingame turned and walked briskly over to the door. He left the room without bothering to close it behind him, leaving a stunned audience in his wake.

Chapter Forty-nine

Tuesday night, April 21 -- The Fairfax Diner, Virginia

Chief Charles Jackson limped into the brightly-lit diner halfway between Washington, DC, and Harpers Ferry, West Virginia, and saw McAdams sitting at a front window booth. He had a cup of coffee in front of him and the remnants of blackberry pie on his plate. Over his head was an unnecessary red swag lamp suspended from the ceiling.

"They make a good pie here at the Porcelain Room," Jackson cracked as he stuffed himself into the bench seat. He tossed his police cap onto the seat beside him. He had a bandage over the bridge of his nose and another one over his forehead. There was a thin layer of greasy medication on his face, probably for the burning he got. But, except for his slow motion and the occasional wince when he turned too suddenly, Jackson looked pretty good, considering what he had gone through.

"Well," laughed McAdams as he surveyed the crumbs on his plate, "it WAS good! Jackson looked around. Two couples in the booths. A few loners at the counter.

The waitress came over and eyed up Jackson. An eyebrow arched she glanced at the bandage on McAdams' arm. She had a pencil behind each ear, Clairol's latest attempt at blond in her tired hair, and painful looking crowsfeet. McAdams stared at the gum. She was able to chew while talking, with the gum dangling out like a gray chunk of lung or something. She ended each sentence with a pop of gum.

"You look like cow manure, Chief." POP. "Or maybe, like a cow manure truck ran over ya!"

"Why, thanks, Wendy. Thanks for noticing. Now, can I get some of that pie - and a cup of black?"

"You bet." POP. She looked McAdams up and down, as if he were the one who had wounded her man Jackson, and sniffed before she turned and walked away.

McAdams sniffed back at her. "They put cow manure in trucks around here?"

Jackson shrugged and promptly grimaced in pain. "Damn!"

"This is all your fault," McAdams began, "us being out here. ... Are you OK?"

"I'm fine. I'm fine. You?"

"Yeah, ducky."

"Good, I'm glad to hear it." Jackson looked for his coffee, fatigue loaded up in the heavy bags under his dark eyes.

"I have to tell you something, Chuck."

"What?"

They found the Georgetown Professor I told you about, Dorothy Browning, the one who was helping me. They found her dead in her townhouse, two bullets to the chest, one to the head. She had to die within minutes of faxing me copies of the documents I found in Tidback's loft."

"Good God almighty." Jackson crossed himself and looked around the diner.

"Thought you'd like to know."

"Too many bodies, Mac."

"I know, Chief. I know." They paused while Wendy delivered the pie and coffee and refilled McAdams' empty cup. Jackson watched her walk away.

"So, why'd you call me out here in the middle of the night? I've got the final, executive session of the King Committee tomorrow. I got a lot to do." They were both tired, cranky, and neither apologized for it.

"A few things - things that need a face-to-face. First off, I spoke to Duncan Williams from the Richmond department. He tells me that a few hours before your flight two federal agents from DC showed up to inspect the plane."

"Which agency?"

"One was from the FAA's Aircraft Certification Service. The other was from the Security and Investigation division of the Coast Guard. They were on board the plane a grand total of fifteen minutes according to airport security."

Jackson leaned over the table for emphasis. "The FAA office based at the Richmond Airport got no advance notice of the agents' visit. When the Richmond FAA boys called up to Washington, they couldn't find a trip report by any agent and there was no specific request for travel allowance. The agents had come and gone, without gettin' their travel fare reimbursed and without filin', within the required three day period, the trip report that would get them paid. What do you think?"

"It's an unheard of event in civil servant history."

"That's how the gun got aboard. No doubt about it."

"If so, there's a bright audit trail waiting for us. I'll see what I can find out when I get back to Washington. Those are both Department of Transportation agencies"

"You do that."

"Next?"

"We matched the prints you sent. Shephard was in that trailer, alright. His prints are everywhere."

McAdams silently shook his head. "That's good."

"And Brock's were scattered 'round the trailer. There was a fresh set on that carved-out book where I found the pages from Booth's diary. Brock musta put the diary pages there for safekeepin' or somethin'. Shephard's prints, and those of Samuels', Larcher and all the boys, were all over the trailer and the magazines and criminal codes I found."

"And, finally," he continued before McAdams could say anything, "we got a hold of Larcher's cellular telephone toll records. We tracked his outgoing calls for the past six months. He called Shephard - at home and at work - a whole lot. About 10, 15 times all told.

"No shit ..."

Jackson explained the calling patterns. The phone activity between Larcher and Shephard had three spikes. One spike occurred the week before and on the day Larcher and the boys disappeared to stay overnight at the trailer. Another came around the time of Tidback's execution, with several calls to Shephard on the early morning of the day Tidback was shot. The last call to Shephard occurred right before Professor Crockett was killed. In fact it was the only call Larcher had made during the entire three-day period prior to the assault on the plane.

McAdams listened as he sipped his steaming coffee. He found himself looking out the window a few times to size up the parking lot and the traffic passing by on Route 50. There were a whole lot of pickup trucks in this neighborhood. Too many were passing slowly in front of the diner, looking in the window. Probably just sizing up how crowded the place was, he reasoned, probably just going slow to find a place to park. He looked away.

"And listen to this, Mac. We did a special run on calls from local public phone booths to Larcher's cellular number for the entire period from the time the boys went up into the woods until Larcher shot Crockett and himself. Larcher got two local calls the night of the big snowstorm in January. One was at 10:00 pm.; the other was nearly 2:00 a.m. These calls were from two phone booths - one along the highway and one on a side road leading to the trailer site. I put my deputy, George Landry, out to find anyone who'll say they saw Shephard on the phone, using the photograph you sent me."

"And ...?"

"He nabbed ol' man Tom Coonce up at the local gas station. He says he saw Larcher toolin' by in his car and jabberin' with some 'candy ass' sittin' next to him. The passenger had a sweety lookin', plump face and greasy hair, and wasn't a local, according to ol' Tom. Says he didn't like it at all."

"'Candy Ass' sounds a whole like Shephard."

"Coonce says 'Candy Ass' LOOKS like him too. *And* he says he saw Shephard in a phone booth the night the boys disappeared, the night of the big snow fall."

"Damn, Chuck, this is good news ..."

"Mac, there's a reason I had to see you tonight. ... I want to arrest Brock and Shephard. I want to charge 'em as accessories in the negligent homicide of those boys. I want their asses in my station house. I'll break 'em, give you what you need and get justice for my boys."

McAdams put his coffee cup down and looked hard at Jackson. "Are you nuts? We got more to gain by waiting them out! You bring them in now, they will stonewall you ..."

"No, no, son. I'll break 'em ..."

"You'll get nothing out of 'em!" McAdams interrupted. "Brock will raise all sorts of constitutional problems with some of the most expensive lawyers these parts have ever seen. Even if you won extradition of a US Senator, OAK would eliminate him before you got him to say anything. Same for Shephard."

"I want them - in my station house."

"It's not Brock and Shephard that's important. It's OAK, damn it. OAK!" McAdams' hand hit the tabletop in emphasis. The cups and plates rattled. Silverware flew onto the tile floor with a clatter. Heads turned this time. Wendy gave them the evil eye from the counter.

"If you move too early, you'll cut off all contact with OAK. We'll lose the trail. You can't do this, Chuck, not now. We got to take advantage of a grand jury..."

Jackson shook his head. "Now you listen to me, boy! You've got a week, no more. You tie them to OAK or show me evidence of worse crimes than what I got against 'em -- and you call the shots. If you can't, if you don't, they're mine. One week, deal?"

"Deal," said McAdams, nodding his head.

They sat back as Wendy gave them refills of their coffee, popping her gum like crazy. She gave both of them a look this time before she walked away. "Look," Mac began when she was out of earshot, "I'm sorry I went off, banging the table and all."

The old man smiled and held up his hands. "Forget about it. No harm done. No offense taken. We're just doing our work. But don't let them slip away, brother."

"I won't. ..."

"And if you are thinking of a grand jury, I want you to go to my home state. Morgantown, West Virginia has a jury sitting. And there's a crackerjack US Attorney there who will get you an indictment."

"Are you sure about this US Attorney?"

"Oh yeah."

"'Cuz if we don't get what I need out of the Assassination Committee, then the grand jury may be all we have."

"What are you thinking?'

"I'm thinking we have one shot with a grand jury," began McAdams. "And an indictment may be all we need to expose OAK."

Jackson's face creased in puzzlement. "You tryin' to get

them on the murders of Professors Tidback, Crockett and Browning?"

"No."

"Obstruction of justice in connection with the King Assassination Committee?"

"Bigger. We need something that will shake OAK to its foundation. Maybe topple the whole damn thing."

"What's going do that for you? You ain't gonna get an indictment in connection with the King murder, Mac." Jackson shook his head. "You may get a Congressional Committee to make some sort of findings, maybe make the right criminal referrals, but you ain't never gonna get a grand jury to indict. Everyone's dead or disappeared. The evidence is too old."

"I don't want to waste all our effort and risk on an indictment that goes nowhere. We got one chance to let every one know what OAK is and what it's done to this country. Now listen. Let me tell you what I have in mind..."

A scream pierced the diner followed quickly by the sound of a china plate breaking into a thousand pieces on a cold, tiled floor. McAdams and Jackson twisted their heads in the direction of the sound. Three flannel-shirted longhairs with baseball caps jumped up from the counter and spun to face them.

McAdams blanched, waiting for the longhairs to pull up some guns. Jackson squinted at them, his right hand going for the revolver at his ankle.

The longhairs were looking out into the parking lot. Their mouths dropped to their stomachs before they fell to the floor.

"CHUCK, get down! CHUCK! DOWN!!" It was Wendy staring over them into the parking lot, and screaming from behind the counter, her hands to her cheeks, her eyes wide in fear.

The window over their heads exploded and showered the diner with glass as they both lunged to the side and dived beneath the table. Two more shotgun blasts erupted before the squeal of spinning tires rang out in the cool night air pouring into the diner. They jumped to their feet in time to see the back of a pick-up truck fishtail out of the parking lot, straighten and then disappear down Route 50 to the foothills of the Shenandoah.

Jackson grabbed his cap from the seat and shook it free of glass. He was about to head out the door into his squad car when another high pitch screamed stopped him cold. This scream sounded different. It had a higher pitch than Wendy's and echoed painfully off porcelain. It came at them again and again, a wave of breathless screams each one getting higher than the last.

It was the cook, Wendy's sister, standing behind the counter, standing where Wendy had stood. They rushed over and looked over the countertop. Wendy face, what was left of it, her mouth open in one long, silent scream, looked back. She had taken the second and third shots in the face and chest and lay sprawled, awkwardly, in a pool of thick, crimson blood.

Chapter Fifty

Dirksen Office Building, Washington DC -- Wednesday, 6:00 a.m.

McAdams sat in his office, his script before him on the desk, the executive session of the King Assassination Committee only three hours away. He gingerly touched the bandage above his right eyebrow. He had taken ten stitches about five hours ago from the shower of Fairfax Diner window glass that had cut him. Jackson had taken some too, to lace up a gash under his right ear. They managed a joke about being the "Slash" Brothers until Wendy's corpse wheeled out of surgery past them.

Another body. OAK was racking up the count. He noticed he was sipping stone cold coffee when the phone rang.

"Mac? It's Senatuh Charlton. I found something in my mail yestiddy. I've been trying to reach ya since."

"What is it?"

"It's a package. From our Professuh Tidback ..."

Chapter Fifty-one

Wednesday, April 21 -- Senate Judiciary Committee Hearing Room

He squeezed through the crush in the hallway leading to the hearing room of the Senate Judiciary Committee. Reporters beckoned with tape recorders. The broadcast media tempted with microphones and false smiles. Shouted questions assaulted him.

"There's word on the street you're gonna drop a bombshell, Mac. What is it?"

"Who killed King? Was it just Ray?"

"Sir, are you ready to implicate anyone currently in government?"

"Why a closed Committee session, Mac? Why won't you let the press in?"

"Hey Mac, what's with the bandage?"

The crowd pressed forward, narrowing his passage to a perspiring body width. Ahead of him loomed the armed guards in front of the Committee room doors. He plunged ahead, and they opened the doors just in time to let him fall inside.

He breathed deeply, alone under the gold leaf decorations, the arched ceiling and the shimmering crystal chandeliers of the ornately gilded hearing room. It was only a half-hour until the final session of the Assassination Committee. The ballroom-like beauty around him clashed with the dirty work ahead.

Mossingame, as planned, only last night had notified the Committee members by phone that the session would be in secret. It was strictly a party line decision. The Democrats thanked their Chairman for calling. The Republicans mumbled their objections. There would have to be a perfunctory vote this morning, as required by Senate Rule 26, on Mossingame's motion to go into executive session, but majority ruled, so there was no doubt as to the result.

McAdams took a seat. Today his job was to lay out for the Committee members those findings and conclusions that he felt the Committee was entitled to adopt based on its two-year investigation. Then the Committee would vote them up or down. The Report of the Committee's Findings and Conclusions had to be issued in printed form within ten days, by May 1. He was hoping for an earlier date - late Friday if possible - to limit opportunity for the staff and the Members to tinker with his work.

Over the next thirty minutes, McAdams watched Senators straggle in alone or in groups of two or three. There were 11 on the Select Committee -- six Democrats including the Committee Chairman Mossingame, and five Republicans including Brock, the most senior Republican. Most were grateful as he was to be exhaled, like Jonah, from the jammed hallway.

The Senators sat around a collection of four conference tables that were joined in the center of the room to form one large rectangular table. McAdams stayed put in the middle of one of the long sides of the table, facing the door leading from the hallway. His staff of senior investigators sat behind him, ready to provide background and detail on portions of the Committee's Report, and ready to answer questions.

He looked up at the clock over the door. It was a little after 10, about the same time of the morning when he sat watching Tidback's brains spew almost directly over the spot where he now sat. Behind him was the Senators' dais. For a moment he saw Tidback in slow motion - sitting, speaking, dying in a hail of bone and blood. It still made him cringe.

Mossingame walked briskly into the room. He eyed the bandage on McAdams' forehead. "What happened to you?"

"You don't want to know. ... I'm here though."

"If you say so. ... Look, it's your show, Mac. I want a unanimous vote in support of your findings and conclusions, nothing less. No majority, partisan-driven votes on a matter of this importance. Either we all think like you or you go down in flames. That's how we'll proceed."

"But I thought, if we had to, we'd settle for majority on some of the close calls. I thought…"

Mossingame held up a hand and leaned over to put his mouth near McAdams' ear. "I've told the Democrats on the

Committee to give you some leeway so you can create a record, draw out some answers to your questions. They'll be ready to back you up. If I know you, you'll be very persuasive." He straightened up. "Now, let's get going."

McAdams looked up at the man who had been so much to him over the years. If he were wrong today, if he misplayed his cards, he would bring Mossingame ridicule, even ruin. If he were right, he might bring him death. In any event, nothing would be the same.

"I'm ready, Walt," he replied in a thick voice. "I won't let you down."

Mossingame stood erect and nodded. "You never have, Mac." He took his seat several down from his chief investigator and gaveled the Committee to order.

As the gavel fell silent, tension reigned. The harsh light from the chandeliers overhead exposed every facial gesture in the room, every sideways glance.

"Gentlemen, we will wrap up the work of this Committee today," said the Chairman. He slowly scanned the table, catching the attention of those standing and talking, those who dared ignore the first gavel.

"If we approve the Report that Mr. McAdams will summarize for you this morning, then the written text - with the additional views of those of you who don't have enough to do - will be available for signature on Friday. That means we will have our Final Report ready a week earlier than required. Any problem with this expedited schedule?"

Surprised murmuring ran around the table. Mossingame was driving the Committee report home, tolerating no dissent, no last minute changes of heart. Everyone kept his powder dry, saving it for later.

"Proceed, Mac. By the way, Senators, I take it we have voted to go into executive session and that the vote is unanimous."

"Senators," McAdams said at last to the expectant audience, "good morning." He shot a glance in the direction of a tired Taylor Brock. Brock caught the look and squinted back, trying to decipher what McAdams was up to. McAdams continued his introduction.

"We have had enormous difficulties in this investigation into the killing of Dr. Martin Luther King. The events themselves are almost thirty years old. Leads, memories and clues are beyond stale; they have crumbled into dust. The original King investigation was so bungled that we have no reliable set of documents, interviews or physical evidence that could help us. We started from scratch, more than a quarter century after the man's death."

There was a rustling at McAdams' first pause, as if the Senators were settling in for a long haul. Some leaned back, bringing their hands to their chins, foreheads, and eyes. Others waited for McAdams' first finding.

"And scratch we did." McAdams paused for effect. "We have done much over the past year in particular. I want particularly to thank the investigators behind me who have worked 15 and 18 hour days - seemingly forever." The three bobbed their heads in response to a smattering of applause.

"Now ..., we're here today to put the finishing touches on our Report. We're going to present the findings and conclusions we recommend you adopt today. These are fully supported and substantiated in the volumes of material that are, and always have been, available to you and your staff for review."

McAdams took a sip of water and gulped some fresh air. He scanned the table while doing so. Each Senator, to a man, wanted to avoid hearing the ugly facts, wanted to say "yes, yes, thank you" and leave the room. But they couldn't. They had to pass on what he presented.

"First, the Committee should find that James Earl Ray fired one shot at Dr. King. That shot killed him. It was fired from the bathroom window at the rear of a rooming house at 422 1/2 South Main Street, Memphis, Tennessee. James Earl Ray fled the scene immediately after the assassination, depositing the crime weapon at 424 South Main Street."

"Ray bought the rifle that was used to kill Dr. King, with the help of his brothers, and transported it from Birmingham, Alabama, to Memphis, Tennessee. Ray stalked King for a period immediately preceding the assassination, as King traveled from city to city in the south. Ray's financial transactions and his travels both before and after the murder indicate substantial planning and funding, and sophisticated coordination requiring the cooperation of others."

"Next, the Committee should state its belief, based on affidavits from several informants from St. Louis which I have circulated and other circumstantial evidence, that there is a likelihood that James Earl Ray assassinated Dr. King as a result of a conspiracy."

Brock pounced. "Whoa there, John! Whooaa!!! The Virginian cast a belittling smile, trying to enlist the others in a campaign of derision that might have an intimidating effect. "What kind of conspiracy you talkin' 'bout?"

McAdams fixed Brock with a steady look. "The conspiracy of John and Jerry Ray, the brothers of James Ray, and the 'St. Louis conspiracy' made up of Gus Ryant - and James Korman and Winston Summerland."

Brock stiffened.

"You know Winston Summerland, don't you, Senator Brock? You and he ran in the same clubs and circles back in the 1960s. Your families settled Virginia in the early 1600's. The Summerland and Brock names are side by side on some of the original land grants, aren't they? And weren't the families colleagues and allies during the Civil War?"

Brock fell silent, the black circles around his eyes darkening. Senators at the table eyed McAdams. It wasn't often that an investigator took that kind of a tone with a Senator; it wasn't often that a Senator let it go so placidly.

"I'll continue," McAdams said to the silence in the room. "Gus Ryant was approached by James Korman, in late 1966 or early 1967. Ryant had known Korman almost 5 years. Korman asked if Ryant wanted to make $50,000 in cash. Ryant, saying yes, was brought to the home of Winston Summerland. The three men met in Summerland's den -- a room filled with Confederate flags and insignia, and Civil War memorabilia. Ryant told my investigators that Summerland wore a Confederate colonel's hat during the entire meeting."

"Summerland repeated Korman's offer. When he asked what he had to do to earn it, Ryant was told either to kill Dr.

Martin Luther King himself, or arrange to have him killed." McAdams looked up from his papers. Somber, pale faces hovered over the conference table.

"Ryant," he persisted, "asked where the money would come from. Summerland told him it came from, and I quote, a 'secret organization with plenty of money.'"

"Where..." Brock sputtered, "where you goin' with this ... 'secret organization,' Mistuh McAdams?" The most junior Republican made supportive grunts, but tread lightly. Something odd was brewing. Something between Brock and McAdams, something that stunk. Something he wanted no part of, not if it concerned King's murder.

"Korman and Summerland were active members of George Wallace's American Party. Summerland had been a member of the White Citizens Council of St. Louis, the Southern States Industrial Council, the National States Rights Party, and the Order of the Veiled Prophet -- all virulently racist, segregationist and militant organizations of business and industrial leaders. As some of you may know, Ray was represented by a lawyer for the National States Rights Party for a short period of time right after the assassination."

"And," exhaled Brock, "are these the secret groups you say are behind the financin' of King's murderer, James Earl Ray? 'Cause if that's what you is sayin', I object, Mr. Chairman. There's been no evidence introduced to support this charge. And I was once a member of a few of these fine groups, before I realized of course how bad some of them had gotten ..."

"Not these organizations, Senator. Another one..."

"A ... another one...?"

"Senator, I am recommending that the Committee state its belief, based on circumstantial evidence before it, that the Korman-Summerland conspiracy to execute Dr. Martin Luther King was orchestrated by an organization known as the Order of American Knights, or OAK."

Comments and conversations erupted around the table. McAdams had to shout to be heard above the tumult.

"OAK, gentlemen, is a secret and long-lived organization that counts leaders in government, the press, business and banking among its membership."

The cacophony eased and then died down.

"OAK arranged for the execution of Professor David Tidback, in this very room, to silence his testimony which would have linked OAK with the Korman-Summerland conspiracy to kill Martin Luther King and would have tied OAK to the murderer of Abraham Lincoln, John Wilkes Booth."

"What ...?" came a cry in the room.

"Mr. McAdams!"

McAdams raised his voice above the resurgent din, ignoring the outcry. "Professor Tidback had evidence in his possession, Senators, which he says supported his assertions, including missing pages from the diary of John Wilkes Booth."

McAdams stopped, letting the haunting echoes of gunshots crawl back into the hearing room. Members shifted uncomfortably in their chairs as the cacophony of voices receded. Recall was working. Mossingame unconsciously brushed something unseen off his jacket lapel and then leaned forward.

"Mac," he began, his face reddening, "with all due respect, how the hell do you know what Tidback would testify to?"

"Becuz Ah have his written testimony, Daniel." Heads twisted at the sound of the thick voice of Mississippi Republican Senator Richard Charlton, Tidback's "sponsor" that awful day. McAdams couldn't take his eyes from the livid face of his surprised mentor, Walter Mossingame.

Chapter Fifty-two

"Ya all remember," said Charlton to the Committee members, "we never did find the Professuh's written statement and we never got copies. Well, now Ah got a copy. It was sent ta me by certified US mail, postmarked in Washington the day of the Professor's testimony. He probably mailed it before he came up to the Hill. It was signed by him and duly notarized. We're checking out its genuineness, of course, but it sho' looks real."

Charlton took off his glasses and looked around the table before he continued. "My office received this package a few days after Professuh Tidback was gunned down. It got logged with all the othuh correspondence we've been gettin' on this King matter since that awful day. One of my staff came across it late yes'day when we wus preparin' for this session and opened it up. Ah called Mac 'bout it fust thing this mornin'."

Charlton started handing out copies of Tidback's written statement. "It's only a few pages, gentlemen, and it says what Mac told ya. It's dated April 6, the day befo' he got shot in this hearin' room." He watched his colleagues as they pored over the pages in their hands.

"The Professor," Charlton continued, "says that OAK sponsored Booth's assassination of Lincoln and he can prove it 'cuz he's got pages from Booth's diary that have been missing all these years. The diary pages show the complicity, according to Tidback, of others in government and industry, others whose ancestors have maintained OAK down through the generations, right until today. And Tidback, finally, says that OAK had somethin' to do with King's murder. That OAK had a member - this Winston Summerland that Mac has been talkin' 'bout – who paid Ray to kill King. Tidback says he knew the man, for Chris' sake, back in St. Louis in the '60's. And he says he'll prove everythin' before an impartial panel of some sort that he wants pulled together from the public, the media, academia, and so forth. He says it must be an impartial panel - he doesn't want it to be this Committee."

"There's no evidence here," sniffed Daniel Byers, the second ranking Democrat on the Committee after Mossingame. "Only a statement of understanding and belief. Where's the evidence to support all this, John?"

"If we had more time ..."

"We don't, Mr. McAdams! Isn't that right, gentlemen?" Byers looked around the room. Shrugs and silence greeted him.

A junior Democrat spoke. "If there's new evidence or the real possibility evidence will emerge with more spadework, then I for one feel we are duty-bound to go back to the Senate and seek more funds and more time ..."

"There's no new evidence," snapped Mossingame. "Only a flimsy statement from a dead history professor. Mac, I have to tell you, I'm a bit shocked about what you're asking this Committee to say and do, given the evidence you supply."

McAdams stunned, began to formulate a response. Doubt crashed through his brain. Perhaps he had gone to far out on a limb. Maybe he should have briefed Mossingame on how tenuous a case he was trying to make about OAK, so they could posture and politic together. But it was too late now, too late to go back.

Jason Hemnes, the Republican Senator from Wyoming, pointed a bony finger at McAdams. He was the third ranking Republican on the Committee, right after Brock and Charlton. He was a lifelong litigator with a string of successful prosecutions.

"Jes' hold on. I'm gettin' on in years, so le's go real slow, a step at a time. OK? Would ya do that for this ol' cowboy, Mac?"

"Of course ..."

"OK, then. Now, even if we presume the existence of a Korman-Summerland conspiracy - a reasonable presumption that's based from what I can see on the testimony of reliable informants as well as a believable Gus Ryant, what's the connection between that conspiracy to finance King's murder and James Earl Ray who pulled the trigger? Without that nexus, ya got nothin'.

"If Ray," he continued before McAdams could answer, "was in direct connection, as you suspect, with the St. Louis conspiracy through Gus Ryant, then this establishes a clear conspiracy between the two sets of parties. If, however, Ray operated independently of the Korman-Summerland conspirators, even if he had full knowledge that the Korman-Summerland cabal would reward him financially upon completion of the mission to kill Dr. King, then there's no conspiracy in the eyes of the law between Korman-Summerland and Ray."

"You're right, Senator Hemnes," McAdams rallied. "No quarrels with your summary of conspiracy law. We can show the existence of the Korman-Summerland conspiracy to finance the assassination. We can show the existence of a conspiracy to murder Dr. King between and among James Earl Ray and his brothers. You and your staffs have seen this information, and have developed it with us, over the past months. But we have more. We have gone back and looked at our files. We have found significant circumstantial evidence which ties these two conspiracies together." McAdams gestured in back of him. "Bob Gibbons will elaborate. He's been with us only a month, but we will use his considerable prosecutorial skills to help us lay out for you our evidence and our conclusions in the Final Report."

Gibbons, a US Attorney in Maine until 30 days ago, stood and launched right into his presentation without any hesitation. "The investigation established several connectives, Senators, between Ryant, Summerland and Korman on the one hand, and James Earl Ray and his brothers, on the other. First, Ryant's brother-in-law was one of James Earl Ray's temporary cellmates while Ray was incarcerated at the Missouri state penitentiary in the months prior to the King murder. Ray could have heard about the financial reward from Ryant's brother-in-law, and from Ryant himself when he was visiting the penitentiary. In fact, we have credible evidence that Ray and Ryant and the brother-in-law were close and were confidants. Ray could have stored the information away for later action. Unfortunately, we could not produce the brother-in-law for testimony before our investigators, Senators. He stepped into his trip-wired Cadillac one morning last year. His legs were ripped away. He died before the ambulance could even show up."

Gibbons had scored a point or two. The Senators were listening.

"The next linkage we found consisted of relationships shared between and among Ray, Ryant, Korman and Summerland." Gibbons looked down at his legal-sized note pad and rattled off over twenty names. "This includes linkages formed under the umbrella of the American Party Presidential campaign of George Wallace - in 1967 and 1968."

"Finally, James Earl Ray's brother, John - an avowed racist - owned a bar that was used as a small campaign headquarters for home-grown American Party activists dedicated to getting the vote out for George Wallace in St. Louis. Korman, Summerland, Ryant, James Ray and others flowed in and out of that bar for many, many months, presenting numerous opportunities to collude. In fact, they were all seen together on numerous occasions, sometimes heard discussing King and the need for his elimination. John Ray's Grapevine Tavern became a hotbed of hatred. Members of the John Birch Society, the Minutemen - a radical right wing group, the Ku Klux Klan, and the other, lesser known groups claiming Summerland as member, spun in and out of that bar for the six months preceding King's death."

"This is all circumstantial and inconclusive," snarled Byers.

"That's just what we been sayin' from the beginning!" McAdams replied. He heard Mossingame tried to interject, but McAdams pretended he heard nothing and kept talking.

"All the Report can say, Senators, is that the Committee believes that a conspiracy was likely involved in the assassination of Dr. Martin Luther King. That the conspiracy likely included Ray's brothers and the Korman-Summerland-Ryant crowd, maybe even this OAK crowd that Tidback refers to in his statement. The evidence supports these assertions and I think it is the responsibility of this Committee to make these assertions. That is what the Congress asked you to do. And to go further, if I may, I would recommend that you direct the Justice Department to investigate the Korman-Summerland conspiracy and its relationship with James Earl Ray, and OAK, and bring indictments if necessary."

McAdams watched the Democrats nod their heads along with Jason Hemnes. McAdams was absolutely right. While the Committee was not a court of law or even a prosecutor's office, it had wide authority from Congress - the responsibility - to find facts, come to conclusions, and issue recommendations and requests for criminal investigations based on evidence and data it collected. Mossingame grew quiet.

"Alright," came Jason Hemnes cracked voice. "But what connects the Ray boys, Korman-Summerland and this group called OAK? What connects these three groups of actors in one conspiracy to assassinate Dr. King, other than witness Tidback's statement and some unsupported allegations?"

Mossingame began to speak but Hemnes interrupted. "I believe," he explained, "I have the right to have the Committee's investigator answer my question, Mr. Chairman. "If I may..."

Mossingame paused in thought and then nodded.

"So what connects OAK and Ray and Korman-Summerland, Mr. McAdams?"

McAdams hesitated and looked down at his legal pad. "There's significant ... circumstantial ... evidence showing that the Korman-Summerland conspiracy was an instrument of OAK. We can develop additional evidence, perhaps direct evidence, and produce direct testimony of the connections between the two groups. But it will take time, beyond May 1."

Brock and Mossingame shook their heads vigorously. "No way ...," began Brock.

"Let me finish. We CAN show, right NOW, however, a number of the connections you're looking for, Senator Hemnes." continued McAdams. "Based on field research and the testimony of principals, AND my own direct testimony..."

"Your *own* direct?" asked Hemnes.

"Yes, and that of others - under oath. Based on this testimony we can put together the following linkages between James Earl Ray, Winston Summerland ... and OAK."

He stopped and threw a hard glance, loaded with meaning, at Brock. It was poker time. Brock absorbed the look while McAdams returned to his notes. Before him on the table was a list of what Chuck Jackson, Linda Walker and he had found and surmised over the last two weeks. It was either probative of the horrible OAK conspiracy, or wild speculation. Either way, he knew, it was time to let it go and let it flow. It was the last round in his chamber. The last hurrah. He looked and saw Brock leaning forward.

"Jason, if Ah may..." Hemnes frowned and then nodded.

Brock cleared his throat as he put his elbows on the table and his fingers to his lips. His mind raced. McAdams was a wild card. But who knew what he had uncovered so far? Maybe he found Tidback's collection from Booth's diary. Maybe he had stumbled across something more, something worse, maybe whatever it was that moved Tidback to come to Washington. He spoke at last.

"Ah'd like to say somethin befo' Mistuh McAdams continues. ..."

"There's really no need, Senator Brock," began Mossingame. "I ...."

"Ah insist on my right to speak, Mr. Chairman. And Ah will do so right now. ... Ah believe, gentlemen, that it would be perfectly acceptable for this Committee to choose the path laid out by Mr. McAdams. Ah recommend the Committee state its belief - not a finding mind you, but a *belief* - that there's some connection between Korman-Summerland and this thing called 'OAK.' Then the Committee should tell Justice to investigate and report back after the Committee's Report is issued, and seek indictments if necessary."

"But, Taylor," protested Hemnes, "let's first review what Mac has, before tossing this over to Justice and the FBI. It may be speculation, baseless rumor, lies, innuendo ..."

"Maybe, Jason, maybe, but sometimes that's all we need and you know all we ever really need is a strong personal opinion about the facts or the evidence and that's enough to send it on over to Justice. ... Look, we got to wrap this up. We promised the Minority Leader we'd bring this Committee to an end. We promised we'd do our best not to look for any more money or time. Le's end this. Le's ship this stinkin' mess over to Justice and let them finish our work."

Hemnes shrugged and sat back in his seat in the face of his

senior's wishes. McAdams felt uneasy, and then he put his finger on what was bothering him. It was Justice, and the FBI that were demanding the return of the FBI's examination of the Booth diary. It was Justice that had hounded Professor Crockett and Randolph-Macon College looking for Tidback. Now it was Justice that would surely squelch the OAK referral from the Committee.

Several Senators spoke at once, expressing favor or disfavor at Brock's compromise. Others huddled in impromptu groups, exchanging comments and waving hands. Mossingame stood up slowly and walked behind McAdams while Brock called his party members into a caucus. Byers sat back, his face blank.

"Mac," said Mossingame in a whisper as he leaned over to speak in McAdams' ear, "if Hemnes gets his way, he'll surely tear you, your logic and your paltry evidence to wee, tiny, little bits. Listen to the voice of experience here. Brock's scared to death you got more on that little, yellow pad than you do. He's scared to death you're gonna spill some big, ugly ol' beans onto the table and that it'll become part of the record. He's scared enough to back off. Let's take what he's given us. It's the best you'll ever get - you'll have OAK on the record, you'll have a referral to Justice, you'll have time to dig further. And, basically, you have no other choice because that's how I want to proceed."

"But Justice belongs to OAK. Brock knows that. If it goes to Justice, it's over."

"Brock is gamblin', Mac. He thinks he's winning something 'cause he's preventing you from reading your litany of tawdry hearsay and supposition. But, if it goes to Justice as a result of official Committee action, we win! I say it's the making of a compromise. You in, or out?"

McAdams looked up at Mossingame. The old man's eyes were clouded but his jaw was resolute, his demeanor defiant. McAdams nodded. "I'm in," he breathed.

Mossingame clapped McAdams on the back and returned to his seat. He banged the gavel loudly. "Gentlemen, let's continue. We got a long day ahead of us and this is only the first wave of findings, conclusions, beliefs and facts that we must vote on. ... Mac?"

McAdams was hunched over his note pad, writing feverishly. He stopped and looked up. "Sorry, Mr. Chairman ... On this issue, Senators, the Report will read along the following lines." McAdams looked at the pad before him.

"The Committee will state its belief, based on the evidence available to it, that James Earl Ray killed Dr. King as a result of a conspiracy among himself, his brothers, and Korman and Summerland, said conspiracy possibly involving an organization known as the Order of American Knights. The Committee will direct the Justice Department to review and further develop - if possible - these tentative findings, to investigate the murder of witness Professor David Tidback, and others, and, further, the possible role of OAK in the murders of Professor Tidback and Abraham Lincoln, and to assess whether additional action and indictments are necessary. The Department will be advised to report en camera to the full Senate Judiciary Committee as soon as practicable, since our Committee ceases to exist on May 1."

"Chairman Mossingame..." parried Brock.

"Go ahead, Taylor."

"Ah'd like to commend Mistuh McAdams for his facile wording and put his statement into the form of a motion. Ah want to amend it a bit, however..."

McAdams tried to protest but was silenced by Brock's raised palm. "As I was saying, Ah don't mind if we formally express these 'tentative findings' as John calls 'em, but the referrals to Justice should be sealed from public scrutiny until the Department responds and tells us whether the evidence presented warrants fu'thur investigation. If it does, the material will have to be held confidential as part of a criminal investigation. But, if the Department does not proceed, then whatever evidence or information the Committee and the Department produced should go to the full Senate Judiciary Committee for fu'ther vote on whether it is to be released or sealed from public view."

Touché. McAdams heard the sound of the second shoe falling, the second prong of Brock's gambit. Brock gets a bland reference to OAK in the Committee Report and no public record or newspaper reports of the Justice referrals until Justice did its dirty work.

Mossingame nodded. He cast a quick glance at McAdams and then called for a recorded vote. Brock's motion prevailed. An 8-3 majority in favor of the compromise was the final vote. Brock, and Hemnes, Republicans, voted "nay" along with Democrat Dan Byers. Even though the final wording was a victory for him, Brock would never support the ultimate compromise naming OAK. Charlton cast a difficult "aye" vote siding with the Democratic majority. He had to, what with Tidback's final delivery to him. He was joined by the most junior Republican who saw a tight election in an urban district, heavily minority, in the fall. Mossingame's vote came at the end.

McAdams watched Mossingame cast an aye, exhaling deeply at the last vote. He was stiff, as if he had been taking body blows in the ring for several hours.

Only after the vote did the enormity of its implications echo in the cavernous room along with Mossingame's gavel signaling consideration of the next set of findings and conclusions. It was an imperfect decision, one that might be upended or buried when all was said and done, particularly by the Justice Department. But it was a vote - by a Select Committee of the United States Senate - giving silent support to the notion of a murderous OAK conspiracy reaching back over 100 years into the nation's past to the assassination of Abraham Lincoln.

Just like Tidback said.

Chapter Fifty-three

Wednesday night, April 22 -- Key Bridge

Brock sat grimly behind the steering wheel of his black Eldorado Cadillac. His long, bony hands clutched the wheel as if the car were rampaging without breaks down a hill. The all-day executive session had just ended and OAK's midnight meeting was in a few hours. Time enough to head home and shower, and have a few bourbons, dinner and some pleasant talk with Mrs. Keating next door.

Time enough to think about what had happened.

He weaved the sedan back and forth from lane to lane, cutting in front of the other cars heading for home in Virginia from a spring evening in the bars of Georgetown. His campaign evinced sharp horn and vocal blasts that burst from the sludge of traffic oozing across Key Bridge into Rosslyn on the other side in Virginia.

It was beginning to unravel. He had managed today to contain most of McAdams' damaging information. But the bastard had tracked down Winston Summerland and put his name out there for all to see. And McAdams had succeeded in connecting OAK to Booth, King - even Lincoln. God knows what else McAdams had found. Maybe Booth's accusation.

He shook his head. All right, Mankins - the Deputy Attorney General - could stifle Justice's investigation, making sure it produced nothing after a great deal of time. And that peacock Lillicut, with his press contacts, could put the pimpers on an inappropriate story, even dictate what the reporting might look like. But there was still the risk that the full Judiciary Committee, stoked by rumors, McAdams or an eager reporter looking for his own Watergate, would want quicker action, more information, more hearings. Already Hosea Kenwood and the NAACP were throwing around claims that the Committee was suppressing evidence of a conspiracy behind King's assassination and of complicity at the highest levels of government. He was calling for a march on Washington, to the steps of Congress, until the Committee issued its Final Report. He threatened worse after that.

Maybe OAK would be lucky, he sighed. No one gave a good God- damn about who really killed King. It was not like the Kennedy murders. There, nothin' you could do dissuaded the conspiracy nuts. But with King, plain and simple, no one cared, and that just might work out to OAK's advantage. Mankins just might get away with months of no action on the Korman-Summerland and OAK referrals.

He exhaled heavily, his cheeks puffing out. OAK had been named before the Senate Select Committee on the Assassination of Martin Luther King! And so had Winston Summerland. The nightmare feared by Fisher, Johnson, Palau, Wilkins, Narkle and the rest had become real! Despite their efforts - despite David Tidback's murder and the bungled attempt on McAdams' life - OAK was to be named in the final Committee Report on the King assassination.

His hands quivered on the steering wheel. OAK's new breed, these desperate men without direction or a core of belief, would go to great extremes now. It would not be beyond them to find out who was in the Committee room today and then eliminate them one by one - 11 Senators, 12 if they included him, McAdams, the three investigators, the legislative reporter - all dead and gone. Maybe they'd take out the guards outside the Committee hearing room, too.

It was up to him. OAK could no longer take matters into its own bloody and vengeful hands and teeth. Sable and his thugs, the campsites, would have to go. To let them continue, to let OAK continue like this, would hasten OAK's demise. A country without OAK behind the curtains -- staging the play, feeding the dialogue, leading the actors -- would be unacceptable. Intolerable! But what to do? McAdams wouldn't join him before.

Maybe a different appeal would work, one more direct. McAdams might yet understand what OAK was meant to be and what it could be. He and McAdams were not so far apart - they each had spent their entire careers enforcing their own sense of right and wrong. Others had responded positively to the call to join OAK. Maybe there was still hope. He shook his head at his own desperation.

Brock entered one end of Rosslyn circle and headed to his right for the George Washington Parkway. A ten-minute ride and he would be at his grand house in McLean. He drove on automatically, lost in thought, and was surprised when his driveway materialized in his headlights.

The growing darkness had settled in among the tall trees looming above him. He grumbled yet again at the stingy, perfunctory light cast by the many lamps he had recently installed along both sides of the drive. He pulled his car into the circular loop that passed the front of his house and parked at the stairs that led to the front door.

Hidden in the dark shadows, a man dressed for combat in black fatigues with blackface smeared on his forehead and cheeks, waited. He watched the headlights pass him in the bushes and poised on his haunches as the car came to a stop. He moved low to the ground, passing the rear of the sedan, and crouched. He watched Brock's outstretched hand grasp the top of the opened car door as the old man slowly pulled his aging frame out of the front seat. The compact man from the Louisiana delta rose and raced to meet Brock as he turned. The man lunged forward with an eight inch hunting knife.

Brock's eyes reacted too slowly to the blurred movement in the blackness of night. He stumbled backward but it was too late. He felt the long blade slice through the skin of his stomach about six inches above his pubic hair. It entered with a harsh "shush." Then came a searing hot pain as the knife ripped diagonally up through his intestines and stopped where the ribcage resisted further movement. He felt another sharp pain as a rib snapped. Brock's last thought concerned the amazing strength of his small assailant as he felt himself lifted off the ground by the force of the thrust. He fell off the blade, against the open car door and onto the ground when the man brought him down.

The small man's nostrils flared with the sweet scent of fresh blood pumping into the open air. His face fell into a frown. The gathering, sticky wetness didn't pool fast enough. He had failed to sever the inferior vena cava, the blood vessel that collected blood from the lower half of the body before pumping it on to the heart.

He heard a door open on the other side of a line of trees and his head snapped up. Porch lights next door blazed. A voice called out in the night. "Taylor? Is that you? Taylor? What's the matter, dear? What's goin' on over there?"

He watched a slight figure on the front stoop crane her neck to see where Taylor Brock was. She had been waiting for him! She had seen his headlights come up the driveway. Now she saw the interior car light was still on. She knew something was wrong.

There was no time to be more surgical. She would surely make her way over. He lifted the blade above his head and brought it down with a heavy thud into Brock's back. He aimed for the heart but Brock's awkward position prevented him from being sure his aim was true.

He bent over the body, found the lump that was Brock's wallet, and sliced it away. The man took the wallet, not caring what it held for him. He wiped the blade on Brock's suit jacket and slipped it into a scabbard strapped inside his fatigues under his arm.

He squatted on powerful legs and eyed his surroundings. The woman was coming down her stairs. There was no reason to eliminate her. He had done his work for the evening and he hadn't been paid to do her. He looked at his watch glowing in the dark. A quarter of a million for ten minutes of action. He smiled.

Swiftly he rose, ran and reached the empty, darkened street. Soon he would be back with a glass of scotch in his motel room outside Rosslyn. His job was done, his cash would be waiting in an envelope held for him in a fictitious name at the private banking desk of the First Virginia Bank. After that he would return to New Orleans.

He heard a noise behind him, the sound of crunching gravel, and turned. Coming at him, her headlights off, was Mrs. Barbara Keating, behind the wheel of her 1998 Oldsmobile sedan, her hair wild, her eyes wilder. She was travelling over fifty miles an hour when she hit whoever it was she saw attack Taylor Brock. The EMS, when it arrived, speculated the assailant had suffered a broken pelvis and a broken skull, but that he would live. Mrs. Keating, comforted and consoled that it was not her fault, that no one should have been dressed in black and walking on the street, was congratulated by the police for felling a felon and escorted home. They even poured her a glass of sherry to calm her nerves.

Chapter Fifty-four

Dirksen Senate Office Building

McAdams' stared at his desk clock. It was almost 8:30 at night and he was replaying the Committee session in his mind as two Capitol Hill guards stood outside in the hallway. The guards were now fixtures after the torching of McAdams' place and the assault at the Fairfax Diner. McAdams didn't say no.

McAdams reviewed the scorecard one last time. All of his findings and conclusions had been accepted verbatim by the Committee after a lot of discussion and heat, and some good old horse-trading and arm twisting on the part of Mossingame. Three Senators wanted to file short "additional views," deviating only to a minor degree on some of the Committee's findings and conclusions and throwing around some lofty rhetoric about justice and equality for all, for the folks back home. The junior Democrat had to be convinced to tone down; the firebrand wanted to crucify the Committee for not going far enough.

But that was it. No one dared touch or revisit the findings about OAK, Korman-Summerland, Tidback or Lincoln. They didn't come up again after that painful, first vote.

A flat, tired Mossingame told the Committee members they had one day to submit their additional views if they wanted to see them in the final Report that was coming out Friday. The final vote approving the Report would be taken Friday after the Members reviewed the text. It would be a routine vote, accomplished by the Chairman's phone calls.

Barring last minute hitches, the Report was done and would be approved more than a week early. All he had left to do now was forward it to the right places, develop the investigation referrals for the Justice Department, including the sealed but controversial referrals to Justice's Office of Ethics regarding Secretary Flaherty and Attorney General Consenza, and then process a few communications to the CIA, the Senate and the House of Representatives. After that he would close down operations and seal for fifty years those files that needed sealing, sending them to the National Archives for storage.

He stretched his back and hoped it was the chair's deep creaks and cracks that resonated in the air. Outside he heard the gathering protesters brought on by Hosea Kenwood. He promised day and night gatherings in front of the Dirksen Building and on the Capitol steps until justice was done. Worry about Linda and O'Connell fell over him. He hadn't heard from them since Monday when they called to tell him they were checked in and ready to begin the rounds at the University of Mississippi. They said they would change motels every night, for safety's sake, and let him know where they were. But he'd heard nothing since.

There were eight days and nights left, eight left until May 1, the Committee's last day. While the Committee's votes today were significant, they weren't enough to bring OAK down. They may not even see the light of day or the inside of a courtroom. There were eight days to bring OAK to justice, before Jackson hauled in Shephard and Brock, scattering to the wind what hope they had of tracking the organization down. Eight days of funding, air plane tickets and staff time left to do something. After that, it would be the Justice Department's ostensible job to hunt down the dogs of OAK. Eight days of escalating protests outside his window.

The phone rang and he jumped for it. Linda....

"Mac?" It was Joyce Thompson, the Washington Post reporter.

"Joyce?" He sat back in his chair.

"My Metro desk tells me the police radio bands are crackling with a big one. Senator Brock was knifed outside his home. He's in surgery at Georgetown. What do you know?"

"It's news to me."

"A perpetrator has been arrested. All he'll say is that he belongs to the Phineas Priesthood and that they're 'God's executioners.' Have you heard of them?"

"No." McAdams fell back in his chair.

"They've been fingered as maybe behind the 1963 murder of Medger Evers and the 1996 Olympic bombing. You know who Medgar Evers is, don't you?"

"Of course. The civil rights leader gunned down in his driveway in the middle of the night in Mississippi, after a NAACP rally. The first of the political assassinations in the US during the '60s. I thought they got the guy who did it."

"Oh they did, all right." replied Thompson. "But it came out during the trial that he was part of this Phineas Priesthood. They say the Priesthood is ultra-right wing. That it's the group the others, like the Christian Identity Movement and The Order, go to when they want a job done."

"Look, I'll call you later, Joyce." He stopped, then made up his mind. "And maybe what you hear will be Pulitzer material."

"What?"

"Wait, I'll be in touch…"

"Mac …!"

He hung up and dialed 411. He got the number for Georgetown University Hospital and called it. "Housekeeping," he said when someone picked up.

"Yeah," came the unhappy answer on the fifth ring. It was the voice of a tired and hassled worker. Someone who had to deal with a senior United States Senator and wanted desperately to be somewhere else. Like in bed, between his woman's legs, or with his mouth around the rim of a bottle.

"This is hospital security," said McAdams. He was winging it, there was no time to waste. "We got a US Senator tonight and we need to get things going up here. When are you gonna have things squared away?"

"Squared away? What the fuck …? Don't shit with me, man. You know we're doing all we can. Fuck me! I got the FBI and God knows what other kind of law all over me. And now you. Shit, I got the nurses and the doctors bangin' my ass. They want me to tell you I ain't got no room. They want to stick him in the fuckin' open unit - seein' as how he's gonna die anyway. Now why am I in the middle of this?"

"What room is he in? I want my men up there - now."

"What? Don't you know? Damn …! He's just getting out of surgery. He's in recovery but they want him up in the VIP room on 7 and fast. That means I got precious little time to get it all ready. It ain't been used in two weeks. Now, you gonna let me do my work, or what?"

The flow of words melted into excruciating hesitation. "Wait a minute! The FBI told me they was handling protection. Who the fuck are you? You ain't hospital security ..."

McAdams hung up. He grabbed a denim jacket from the back of the door and slipped it on. He had changed out of his suit for today's Executive session into a blue shirt, khaki pants and hiking boots. He ran his hands several times through his long hair and decided to remove from his forehead the bandage, replacing it with a couple of Band-Aids from his desk drawer. It would have to do, he shrugged as he left.

Chapter Fifty-five

Georgetown University Hospital, Washington, DC

The cab screeched to a stop on soft tires. McAdams got out in the front circle where, just days ago, he had passed on his way to see Dorothy Browning. The library rose impassively to his left, its tall, rectangular windows flooded with light and students hunched over tables.

He moved to the shadows of the trees surrounding the circle and quickly set out for the rear of the Hospital less than a quarter-mile away. The old Hospital had plenty of entrances other than the main one. He knew that from his college days and, more recently, from visits to friends and colleagues over the years - the Hospital was a favorite for Washingtonians with alcohol and drug abuse problems. Sometimes it felt as if he knew most of the patients.

He approached the back of the Hospital and stood quietly in the shadows of the walkway to observe the staff parking lot. It suddenly flashed that he should have told O'Connell, or someone, where he was going. He was alone in the dark, entering a place where neither Brock - nor he for that matter - might ever leave. And he hadn't said goodbye to anyone.

He dashed the 15 yards across the parking lot until he reached the back wall of the Hospital. The closest door was locked. A second was propped open with a brick, letting in the cool, fresh air of the spring evening.

He slipped inside and found himself in a hallway. At the opposite end were signs for the cafeteria, a vending machine room and employee locker rooms. There was an exit sign above a door halfway down the hall. A staircase would be on the other side. The critical care ward was on the seventh floor. The trick was finding the VIP room without being noticed.

He made the door to the stairwell quickly, opened it and began taking the steps two at a time. There was a bulb hanging from the ceiling at each landing, covered with steal mesh to prevent someone from knocking it out. Some of the bulbs were intact; some actually gave off light.

By the fifth flight he was panting for air and his thighs ached. He rested with his back against the wall. The beat of his heart thundered against his eardrums as he moved again, to the seventh floor. By then he noticed that the door leading from each landing in the staircase to the corresponding floor had a small window with an embedded wire screen.

He stopped to breathe. He was going strictly on instinct now. There were no Congressional rules of order, no procedural niceties or protocols. He was desperate and running out of time. He had to get to Brock.

He peered through the window in the door to the hallway of the critical care floor. The dingy glass made it difficult to see. The hall lights were down for the night shift.

A group of people spilled abruptly into the hallway from a room five doors down. First came a large nurse with burly arms and a thick neck. Her ponderous mound of hair was tied up in a bun which protruded from under her cap. A few other nurses and orderlies followed in her wake into the hallway and dispersed in all directions. One pushed an empty gurney.

Next came Nelson Wilkins. McAdams stiffened. Wilkins pulled the door closed behind him and looked up and down the hall. His features were stretched into a grim mask.

The large nurse and Wilkins stood arguing in front of the room they had left. The nurse pointed to an open bay at the end of the hall where there were five beds separated from each other by curtains. Each bed save one was filled with what looked like a human science experiment. Machinery, monitors and hospital staff congested the area.

The bay was for patients needing acute critical care. It had the most sophisticated equipment and monitors. Wilkins and OAK had pulled strings and put Brock in the private VIP/security risk room - where Brock could be observed and ministered to, maybe by someone other than the medical staff.

McAdams watched Wilkins' mouth twist around angry words spat out in response to the nurse's latest blast. Unruffled by the assault, she smirked and shook her head. The two of them stormed away from the door hiding McAdams.

He heard a noise echoing faintly in the stairwell. He flattened himself against the wall. Above him a door had opened and closed. Someone light on their feet was approaching his position, fast.

He pulled open the door. Trying to walk on air, he headed for the room Wilkins and the nurse had exited. He passed patients huddled in the darkness of their rooms or strung up in various devices that looked like torture machines.

Ahead, only 100 feet away, the nurse and Wilkins were walking away, their backs to him. Lost in the heat of their angry words and gestures, they could, at any moment spin on their heels, twist their heads, and see him. The room they had just left was 717. Brock's last stand.

Chapter Fifty-six

He turned the handle and walked in. The hinges squeaked twice, when he went in and when he closed the door behind him. He did not see Wilkins and the nurse stop at the end of the hallway. He did not see the nurse look back at the sound of the second, painful squeak. She squinted down the dimly lit hall before sending Wilkins off with the parting salvos of an index finger thrust repeatedly at his chest.

In the dim light he could see Brock was alone. One large intravenous unit dripped through a line into his chest. Two hanging bottles entered the veins of his left arm. Lines taped to his chest and arms led to an electronic monitor with two digital read-outs and three screens showing heartbeats and other rhythms. An oxygen tube emptied into his nostrils.

As he stepped cautiously toward Brock, he noticed that the still man's skin took on a ghostly, green pallor from the faint lights of the five monitor screens crowded precariously on a shelf just above his head. Brock looked dead.

He had to act quickly. Either the nurses or Brock's doctors would be back soon. Or the FBI guards would set up shop. Or whatever guards OAK was using to protect its property would show up. Or Brock would just up and die.

He stepped through the cords and the lines to the top of Brock's bed. He put his mouth near Brock's right ear.

"Senator Brock ... It's John McAdams. You're dying. OAK attacked you. Tell me about OAK."

There was no movement. "Senator, it's McAdams. Can you hear me?"

The monitors showed something elevating. Numbers climbed. Lines edged upward. It must have been the heartbeat.

He reached his hand through the bed rail and squeezed Brock's arm. It was stone cold.

"Tell me about Summerland. And Tidback. About OAK and Mankins and Fisher. You're dying and OAK wants you to die. Don't die without helping me bring them down!"

Brock's eyes flickered. They fluttered open, and then fell

shut. McAdams began squeezing the icicle arm again, his hopes for a breakthrough fading.

"It's John McAdams," he said insistently. "You wanted me to help you before and now I'm ready. This is our last chance. Let me finish your job. I didn't know what you were after, didn't know you wanted to take OAK back to what it was. Tell me about OAK..."

Brock moved his head sideways in McAdams' direction and his eyes fell open. A glimmer of recognition fought through the dull eyes of sedation and gathering death. McAdams placed his ear near Brock's mouth but nothing came out.

He drew his head back and scanned the room for a water pitcher. There was one on a table in the corner of the room. Little paper cups stood inverted in a leaning tower next to the white plastic pitcher. He threaded through the equipment and the lines to get a cup of water.

He came back to the bed and, placing his hand under Brock's neck, lifted the dying man's head. The old man weakly sipped some water. McAdams softly brought him back to the pillow.

Brock nodded slightly and coughed. "Better," he gasped.

McAdams threw a glance at the door. No shadow interrupted the line of light under the door. He turned back to Brock, leaning in close to the old man's right ear. "Let's talk - quickly."

Brock nodded again. The effort forced him to close his eyes.

"Are Mankins, Wilkins and Fisher part of OAK?"

He hesitated and then moved his head up and down.

"And there are other government officials involved?"

Up and down again, but barely.

"Are there others in OAK? Others not in government?"

Some seconds passed as Brock worked his mouth around the words. "There are others. Not ... just ... government. 12 in all." He wheezed in pain. "It's not important."

"What's important, then?"

"OAK ... OAK is important. Cleanin' it up – tha's important."

"Is OAK a hit squad?"

Brock slowly rolled his head to the left and then halfway back. Did that mean "no?"

"Does OAK kill ... to get what it wants?"

Brock tried to open his eyes. His eye lids flickered open, stayed that way for several seconds, and then fell shut. "It must. Sometimes it must. Nuthin' comes easy ..."

"What does OAK want?"

"Once, only what America needed. Now ..." Brock's hands, resting on his stomach, open tentatively and then closed.

"Killing Martin Luther King was what America needed?"

"Ohhh yesss ..." The voice warbled in pleghmy liquid.

McAdams was momentarily stunned. He knew it had to be so, but didn't expect to hear it. "OAK issued the execution order? Summerland paid the tab? Ray did it?"

Brock nodded. "Yesss ..."

McAdams visualized Tidback's notecard checklist. "What about Huey Long, TR?"

Brock let out a dry and deep cough, so deep it could not surface. His face wrinkled with pain. "David's did his homework. Ah knew he was good ..."

"And Kennedy?"

"Not us," he coughed. "Others ... My study, my library. There's a tape, Mac. Get it. Listen to it. It's all there. The Committee's journal is there too. ... Get them."

"Wha ...? Get who? OAK? How do I do that?"

"The tape. The journal ..." Brock's lips were chapped and colorless. His thin, lifeless skin pulled against his skull.

"What journal are you talking about?" asked McAdams.

"Get them, stop them," Brock begged. The old man shivered. "OAK cannot be ... ruined by these men, by..."

"Lincoln? Was that OAK's work? Did Booth carry out OAK's execution order?"

Tears formed in Brock's haunted eyes. The pain came not from recent wounds but remembered ones. "It ... had to be done. There was so much to lose ..., back then."

"Summerland, and Wilkins, had ancestors on OAK when Lincoln was assassinated ..."

"Yesss ..."

"Nathaniel Brock, your ancestor, was head of OAK then?"

"Yesss ..."

"What about Vice President Andrew Johnson? And War Secretary Stanton?"

"Oh ... they were ... OAK's pawns ... back then. But ... not ... OAK." Brock coughed.

"The Booth diary pages. You leaked them to David Tidback?"

Brock nodded weakly. "I sent some to him in the beginning, to start him off. I hid some for him to find. Some I jes' never got to him. ... I did it all right under OAK's, and Shephard's nose.... It wasn't easy. They watched me ... like a hawk." He coughed again.

"What were you trying to accomplish?"

"To get Tidback to ... document our - OAK's - noble history. An official..., public record.... There'll be a day when ... it all can be told."

"How long has OAK been around?"

"Since the ... beginnin'." Brock's cracked, gray tongue ran over his lips. His long, white eyelashes fluttered.

"The beginning of what?"

Brock smiled slightly in response and then he shook his head. "Ya don't have all Booth's writings, then. Ya bluffed me at the Committee today, John. Ya bluffed me. You're good." His smile faded and nothing more came from the death mask. A peace began to settle into Brock's face.

"What is OAK?" McAdams whispered, his face close to Brock's. "What am I fighting?"

Brock's eyes were six inches from McAdams'. He stared deeply into the younger man. "Order. Commerce. Progress," Brock mumbled. "Tha's what OAK stands for. But, now ..." The hands on his stomach twitched again as his eyes rolled backed into their sockets.

Brock's pulse monitor showed the heart beat count rapidly accelerating and then dropping. An alarm would sound soon, somewhere. Nurses and doctors would burst in.

McAdams stood up. He felt dizzy with alarm and tension, from bending over too long. He had to get out. He placed his left hand on the brow of a man he had known for twenty years. A man who had ended up a monster, or maybe one who had been that way all along.

Brock lay motionless, his mouth wide open, his cheeks caved in. McAdams turned and navigated the maze of wires and equipment. Placing his ear against the door, he listened for conversation or movement in the hall.

"Get them, Mac. You're the only one now!"

McAdams stiffened as the voice scratched and scraped over to him with the sound of dry, dead leaves running over pavement before the wind on a brittle fall day. He turned to see Brock's head slightly elevated off the mattress.

"The tape, the journal. Get them! It's up to you. ... And listen, listen to me now. It's up to you. ... There's a meeting, an OAK meeting – next week, midnight, when the Committee expires. It's in Maine, it's called Fort Scammel. ... You get a boat. ... You must.... Get themmmm ... They're bringing all the diary pages, they're gonna destroy 'em all ... OAK. .... Get themmm .... Before they ... disappear."

Brock's head fell back on the bed. The monitors counted out the end of a life. A raucous alarm shrieked in the hall. McAdams opened the door. Above him a blue light blinked insistently. He ran to the staircase. Running footbeats echoed behind him. A rough female voice rose to a shout.

"Damn! Who are you? What are you doing? ... Security! Guards!"

The door to the staircase banged shut behind him. He swung on the handrails down the stairs, taking five or six at a time. It took maybe three minutes to make the ground floor hallway that led to the staff facilities. He slowly stepped out from the stairwell and looked both ways.

Several orderlies in white jackets congregated at the cafeteria entrance as they spoke to two men in dark suits. They stopped their conversation and peered down the hall at him. The men in the suits stood, poised. He nodded, looked at his watch, turned, and walked slowly in the opposite direction to the door to the parking lot. He fumbled for a cigarette from the crushed pack in his jacket pocket. Just a harried employee catching a moment out for a smoke. Sweat spilled down his forehead, stinging his eyes.

The suits watched his back until he left the building.

Chapter Fifty-seven

McAdams ran across campus and then down P. Street, hiding in the shadows of the Federal townhouses. When a car would pass, he would run under one of the many staircases that rose from the brick street to the front door almost a story above his head, shrinking into the shadows to wait. He hailed a cab on the Georgetown section's busiest street, Wisconsin Avenue, and climbed in back

"McLean," he gasped, short of breath. He heard sirens echo in the distance and wondered if they were heading for the hospital, or coming from there and after him. Twenty minutes later the cab pulled up to a corner address in McLean, Virginia.

He fished a twenty out of his wallet and threw it onto the front seat. He got out and began walking the several blocks to Brock's home. He knew his way, he had been a guest a handful of times.

There were a couple of lights on inside Brock's house, night lights to keep away the burglars. Mrs. Keating's house next door was ablaze with light.

Brock had a large and majestic white brick colonial set back from the road about 200 feet. He lived alone now. His wife, Judy, had died a horrible death from throat cancer some 10 years ago. His two children had long ago left, never to return. They were in their late thirties by now. They called once a year, McAdams remembered Brock telling him once, usually around Father's Day.

He moved down the long, dark driveway. The storm had become a drizzle and the pin oak trees towering overhead dripped from the downpour. Around back was a patch of grass you could call a yard if you had to. What yard was there quickly ended at a steep hill that led to a dense forest, which reached higher than the three-story home itself. He stood at the bottom of a pit, waiting for earth and wood and brick to tumble in on him.

He moved to one of the large living room windows at the back of the house. Inside a table lamp revealed expensive colonial furniture and paintings in dark, vibrant colors. There were no blinking red eyes of a newly installed alarm system, no wall-mounted light-interrupt system to alert the police department, no window wires that triggered alarms upon a hair's weight of pressure. McAdams knew Brock didn't believe in them. More trouble than they were worth, he would say. And, tonight, Brock was right.

The window ended at McAdams' knees. He wrapped his right hand in his jacket and lashed out at the window. The crashing sound flew out into the night. No dogs started barking, no lights suddenly appeared in bedrooms of nearby homes. Keating's house remain well lit, but still.

He breathed again and removed the glass jutting out from the window frame. He stepped through the window into the room and silently made his way to the front hall. On the other side of the foyer, as best he could recall from a holiday party, was Brock's office. All he could hear in the darkened house was the rhythm of his racing heart.

The office door was locked. It gave way on the fourth slam of his full weight. From inside came the heavy smell of rich leather. He made his way over to the large desk in the center of the office and turned on the solitary desk lamp made from an antique spittoon. It cast a soft light that brightened only the lower half of the room.

Books. There were books everywhere. They lined the shelves, which in turn climbed up every wall. They formed tall piles on the floor. History books, all of them.

They were, to the last, books of American history. There had to be a couple of thousand. Old books, new books. Some were falling apart. Many were first editions. There were original works by Benjamin Franklin, John Adams and James Madison, worth thousands of dollars. Some of the books amounted to no more than notes and correspondence on yellowed and brittle parchment bound miraculously into volumes tied together long ago with twine.

His fingers ran across the titles. Brock had one of the finest collections he had ever seen. It matched priceless private collections donated to the Library of Congress over the years and housed in huge private reading rooms bearing the donors' names.

Immediately behind the chair and desk were biographies and autobiographies of members of the Brock lineage. The Brocks evidently thought the world deserved learning about them. He was sure Taylor Brock, Virginia Senator, had an autobiography in the works somewhere.

He found two titles that beckoned him. One was a history of the Brock family, the other an autobiography of Nathanial Brock. He took the two volumes and put them on the desk.

The library, other than the shelves dedicated to the Brock family, was organized in chronological order. Brock had labeled the shelves with dates measured in decades.

McAdams found the Civil War period. There were over twenty volumes dealing with Booth and his famous acting family. There were seven dog-eared books by Tidback, including several about the Confederate Secret Service. Brock had been a fan of the Professor's.

McAdams' eyes were drawn to another shelf where a book was lying horizontally across the top of a row of books in the 1750 -1790 AD section. The book was particularly old. He carefully pulled it out and laid it on Brock's desk with the others. Inserted near the end of the book, as a bookmark, was an index card bearing a typed listing of Brock's appointments for Wednesday, April 22. Today. The day Brock died.

The worn cover was once dark green. The title, emblazoned long ago in gold leaf, was faded. Its pages were like the thinnest peanut brittle. He read aloud the title on an inside page. "The Official Journal and Accounts of the Secret Committee of the Second Continental Congress, September 18, 1775 to July 30, 1776." It had to be the "Committee's journal" that Brock had begged him to get.

He looked around the room for where Brock's tape could be hidden. He sat down behind the desk in a large swivel chair. The drawers in the antique piece of furniture protested loudly when he pulled them out. He rummaged through the folders, junk and papers and came upon a hand-held tape recorder in the center drawer of the desk. Inside it was a cassette. He put both in his jacket pocket. No other tapes surfaced on the sea of paper and office supplies.

The desktop, and the tops of the two small lamp tables in the study, were covered with knic-knacs. There were dozens of mementos from associations, foundations and corporations. Many of them were metal or wooden boxes of one sort or another, some had the giver's name on a gold plaque on top, and some had Brock's name or his initials.

He furiously opened the various boxes. They contained calculators, golf tees, ball markers, lighters, clocks and thermometers. One gold box on Brock's desk produced a purple felt interior and three more cassette tapes. He slipped them into his pocket. On a table a champion's cup welded to a wooden base yielded two additional tapes.

Seeing no other hiding places in the room, he turned off the desk lamp, and tucked the books he was taking under his arm. He left the room and bounded up the hall stairs taking two stairs at a time. He felt along the walls and made his way into the master bedroom. The bed was unmade and a slight odor greeted him. An old man's dirty laundry.

He entered Brock's room. On top of his nightstand next to the bed was a tape. There were several more in the pockets of suits hanging in the closet. There was nothing in the drawers and nothing else looked useful so he headed back downstairs in the darkness and returned to the library. He found an atlas in the bookcase behind Brock's desk and looked for a Fort Scammel on an island off the coast of Maine. That's what Brock had called it, Fort Scammel. His brow furrowed as he squinted at the page. Off Cape Elizabeth, south of Portland, was a dot of an island, circled. That had to be it. Closing the book, he left the library for the last time.

He froze at the foot of the stairs as the lights of a passing car briefly flooded the front hall with pale yellow light. A vehicle slowed down directly in front of Brock's home. He peered through one of the long, rectangular windows next to the front door and watched the car lights go off.

He picked up the hall phone. The local taxi company would pick him up in fifteen minutes at the High's convenience store about a mile away on Old Dominion Drive. The road led straight back to Washington.

Chapter Fifty-eight

Thursday morning, April 23 -- The Daniel Webster Room

When he got back, McAdams saw his phone was blinking. It was Linda and O'Connell, calling last night after hearing about Brock on the news. They were OK, but scared. They didn't want to call too much because there was nothing to tell him. They had uncovered nothing and they didn't want to expose themselves by making long distance phone calls that might get traced.

He listened to Brock's tapes. It took all night. Most of them whispered the random observations and recollected experiences of Senator Taylor Brock, Virginia statesman. It was just as McAdams thought - Brock, not to be outdone by his family, was putting together his life story to put on the shelf right alongside those of his ancestors.

One tape told a different story, however. It may have been the one he found in the voice-activated tape recorder in Brock's desk drawer. It now was clutched in his hand.

The cassette spewed the contents of an OAK meeting. Some of the voices could be identified. Brock could be heard. So could other, distinctive voices he swore he could recognize. The taped meeting was recent given the references to the Tidback and Crockett murders. There was a long debate about what OAK was becoming, about what it had done, and what it wanted to be. The taped meeting must have taken place in Maine given the reminders about waiting boats at the end of the meeting.

He had listened through the night without moving from the sofa, taking long gulps of scotch and smoking cigarettes. He ran the tape twice, replaying some portions multiple times.

McAdams knew he couldn't use the tape, without more, in any trial or Congressional investigation. Without the testimony and collaboration of Brock, without having Brock or a meeting attendee available for cross-examination, the tape was inadmissible. It could be portrayed as unreliable or a fabrication by a vindictive investigator. But in the correct context, upon comparison with the verified voice recordings of the OAK membership, and with corroboration and other evidence and testimony, the tape could lend credibility - particularly before a prosecutor's grand jury - to what otherwise might seem to be wild incriminations.

It was almost six in the morning. He flicked on the local TV news. First up was a report of Brocks' death "around midnight" the night before.

"In what may be simply a startling coincidence," droned the announcer, "local authorities in McLean, Virginia, have told us that the home of Senator Taylor Brock burned to the ground only several hours ago after an explosion in the house rocked the neighborhood. Fire officials believe the fire and explosions were related to a faulty natural gas furnace. The fire consumed the entire structure in less than an hour."

A picture flashed on the screen. It was Brock's brick home caught by a camera in a pleasant fall setting.

"A brick home that big burned to the ground in one hour?" McAdams was talking to himself out loud. "What'd they use, napalm?"

The reporter on assignment did not answer but continued breezily with the story. "Although authorities are continuing their investigation, there is no evidence of foul play. Police from McLean, from the Virginia state police and from the FBI are investigating to see if there is any connection between the fire, Brock's death earlier in the night, or his work in the US Congress." The anchor picked up the flow when the reporter handed back the airtime. There was no mention of a priesthood, much less the Phineas Priesthood. News management had kicked in quickly.

Chapter Fifty-nine

Thursday afternoon, April 23 -- University, Mississippi

Linda Walker looked at her watch. 4:30. She opened her motel room door. She looked up and down the unoccupied sidewalk that separated the barren rooms from the near-empty parking lot and ran to her rented car. She threw her backpack and some clothes onto the rear seat and got behind the wheel. O'Connell followed from his room.

She breathed easier with the doors locked and the engine on. This was their last day here. It had been a weird few days in this town, really nothing more than a bunch of fast food joints and stores serving the massive University of Mississippi.

The chairman of the University's History Department had been great. They showed them where Tidback worked and slept, ate and taught. Tidback's Mississippi colleagues and students really tried to help. But they didn't have a clue what Tidback was into. They knew nothing about any work on assassinations, the Confederacy, Lincoln, John Wilkes Booth or OAK.

There was one last stop before heading east - the University's library to see the staff guy responsible for assigning carrels. According to the formal records Tidback didn't have one. But the Dean had told her that it was University policy for every professor - tenured, full, assistant and temporary - to get one, one located on the upper floors of the library, where they could do research, writing and class preparation. It was one of academia's few fringe benefits. For Tidback not to have one was very odd.

O'Connell and Linda agreed in advance to let Linda work the library staff. She was better at getting information out of people. She was more their age, too, and a lot prettier than the pallid O'Connell. There was one other thing. He seemed to have a way of making people suspicious. Everyone clammed up when he was around. The vote was unanimous that he sit in the rental car in the parking lot, like he was waiting for someone.

She found the staff assistant in a cubbyhole of an office

behind the front desk on the first floor of the massive library. He was a geeky and frail man in his late forties. The poor soul's head hung forward from a bent back and, it seemed, the weight of his thick glasses. A ring of brown hair encircled a bald spot on top. When he spoke or thought, he'd tap his fingertips together in front of his concave chest. She tried to look directly at him when she had something to say, even though some kind of a nervous condition made his eyes shoot to the ceiling only to float lazily down again.

"Why ... why do y'all want to know if Professor Tidback kept a carrel?" The eyes blasted off and then returned to around the level of her navel.

"I, I - uh, I was his assistant at Randolph-Macon - his home base." Trying to look the part, she was wearing jeans, an RM T-shirt and running shoes. "I'm supposed to bring his materials home. He had a carrel didn't he? The Chairman said all professors did."

"I'm, I'm quite sure he did." The fingertips tapped a mile a minute. "Quite sure. But ..., maybe not. I will have to see. Can you come back later? It's the end of a very long week. I'm quite busy." He turned with a jerking movement and started back into his office, leaving her stranded in front of the checkout desk where he had steered her.

"No! Wait!" she exclaimed. He stopped and slowly turned to face her. "I can't come back," she continued. "I have to leave in a couple of hours. My stipend from the College is gone. I ..., I've been looking everywhere for his things. If I don't come back with all the Professor's stuff ..." She caught her voice, pretending to choke back a real good cry that would embarrass the shit out of him if it came out.

He grew flustered. His eyes started bouncing rapidly. "Just a minute, now, just a minute. Hold on ..." He peered at her, his upper lip curled in disgust, to see if she was going to start bawling right there in the sanctity of the library. Confident she was holding up, he spun on his heel. She watched his bent back disappear into the office.

He poked his head out several minutes later to see if she was still there. Linda applied a tissue from her pocket to the side of her nose. She even sniffled. Loudly.

His eyes squeezed tightly shut as he shook his head and then retreated again. He emerged several minutes later with a folder. His one empty hand beckoned rapidly to her, telling her to lean over the desk toward him.

"The Professor wanted me to keep quiet about this. He ..., yes, he has a carrel. Everyone does! It's my job to keep the entire bunch of these eccentric professors happy." He sniffed. Linda nodded sympathetically, showing with an exasperated sigh that she understood his plight.

"The Professor paid me good money to keep his carrel and its location secret. I never ask why in these situations. Never have. Never will. ... You won't tell anyone, will you?"

She looked sincerely into his dancing eyes. "Of course not!"

"OK, OK. Here you go ..." He looked over his glasses at pages inside the folder. "He's on the sixth floor, top floor. Carrel 667. It overlooks the campus. Very nice."

She nodded again.

"You're the only one I've told. Others have asked. But you're in ... different shoes ... than they." She wondered if he was trying to be charming or flirtatious. He flashed a secret, sweet smile in her general direction.

"Anyway, here's the key. Here. Bring it back after you clean it out. Hurry. I want this over and done with. Now, get along with you." The nervous little man was bobbing up and down on his toes, tapping his fingertips incessantly.

She smiled a "thank you."

"He was a nice man," he offered as she began to walk away. "He always had time to stop a while and talk to me. I'm awful sorry about what happened ..." With the folder under his arm and the hands coming together rapidly, with his gaunt frame bobbing up and down, he looked like an ecstatic monk in fervent prayer for the recently, dearly departed.

She smiled gratefully and headed quickly for the elevator. Her features locked in tension until the elevator arrived and the doors opened at last. She lunged inside. It took forever to get to the sixth floor.

Chapter Sixty

She found number 667. Tidback's carrel WAS big. It was not a room for a desk with shelves overhead and a chair. It was actually an expansive corner office overlooking the lush campus. She turned away from the view and got to work. There was no time to waste. And it was going to be dark soon.

She looked over the desk. The calendar was turned to Sunday, April 5, two days before Tidback got killed in Washington. To get to Washington by the 7th, he'd have to have left Mississippi by Monday night, the 6th, at the absolute latest.

From the chaos of books and papers scattered all over the desk and room, she could see Tidback had left in a hurry. Sitting back in his chair, taking in the room, she spotted an open magazine on an ottoman in front of an overstuffed chair in the corner. She walked over and sat down in the chair and picked up the magazine. It was the local newspaper's national Sunday supplement, open to an article on the Senate's investigation into the assassination of Martin Luther King. There were two big photographs of Mississippi's own Senator Richard Charlton who, according to the caption, sat on the Select Committee and was one of its leading lights. One of the photos was with Senator Taylor Brock, Charlton's party leader on the Committee. The lead paragraph indicated the Committee's last public hearing was on Wednesday, the 7th, in Washington, D.C.

She closed her eyes. putting one hand to her forehead. He saw this, she realized, and started a course of action that led to his death three days later. She was probably sitting right where he did when he hatched his final plans. She jumped to her feet, shaking off the creeps crawling up her back.

Making her way back to the desk, she sat again and skimmed the piles of paper and journal articles. She thumbed through the books that had protruding bookmarks. As was his custom, Tidback had scrawled or typed copious notes all over yellow "Post-Its," legal-sized note pads and index cards.

The entire desktop was covered with research devoted to one subject - the 1835 assassination attempt against President

Andrew Jackson. A rogue wind set the room's old, wooden windows clattering in their loose frames. She glanced quickly around and then fumbled urgently through another pile of paper. There was nothing she didn't already know, nothing she and McAdams hadn't already talked about. She noticed a Post-It repeating the question she had heard before: "Was the Second Bank a bridge between the Secret Committee and OAK?" It was stuck to the corner of the desk like it was used to keep him focussed, a reminder of why he came here.

She looked around the room. There had to be something else squirreled away. Something that had led Tidback here to Mississippi in the first place, instead of Canada where Tidback had told nearly everyone he had gone on sabbatical. She scanned the floor. Floorboards, like in the loft ....

She fell to her knees and pulled up the area rugs, looking for scratch marks where a board might have been pried up. There was nothing under the rugs, nothing under any of the furniture. The walls looked like solid plaster.

Where would the Professor hide more Booth diary pages?

Another burst of wind rattled the windows. The door to the hall rattled. Then came a sharp knock. And then another. She spun around. It wasn't the wind.

"Miss? ... Miss?"

Her heart quieted just enough for her to think. It was the assignor of carrels, the fingertip man with the wild eyes. She panicked. She didn't even know his name.

She walked over to the door. "Is that you?" she whispered.

"Yes ... It's me, uh, it's Bennie, Bennie Longley. I'm the staff assistant from downstairs who ..."

She opened the door. He stood there with a package in his hands. She knew he was trying to look her in the eye, but his eyes were locked on her neckline.

"The Professor left this when last he was here." Bennie looked at a paper stapled to the side of the envelope. "That was late Sunday - the 5th of the month. He asked my weekend assistant to keep it in the library safe until he returned for it or someone came to claim it. I wasn't sure I should give to you, but ..." He looked forlornly at the obligation occupying his hands.

"Here ...," he said at last. He thrust it at her and stood nervously in front of the door.

"Thanks, Bennie," she said at last. "I owe you one. Professor Tidback would think you did the right thing. AND, you've saved my life."

A smile lit up his face. She beamed back. He straightened a bit, turned and headed back to the elevator.

"Don't forget to drop off that key ...," he called.

The door was closed and locked by then. She fell to a cross-legged sitting position on the floor and fumbled with nervous hands to open the sealed package. She peeked inside before emptying the envelope of its contents.

Old, yellow pages in clear plastic folders. Seven in all -- from the diary of John Wilkes Booth.

Her breath came rapidly as she read the now familiar, ornate handwriting.

Chapter Sixty-one

Booth was going to Washington to clear his name - by naming his sponsors, the ones who gave him the $50,000 to kill the President. The sponsors were, in Booth's own words, the 'olde Secret Committee.' Secretary Nathaniel Brock headed up the Committee. Booth claims he can name all the members of the Committee, all of Lincoln's murderers.

He says the names are listed on the last page of his note. And that now they call themselves OAK. She ran her damp fingers across her mouth. There was no page at the end naming any names. Where was it? Who had it? She and Mac hadn't found it in the loft. But hadn't Mac said that Chuck Jackson had found a list of names in Booth's handwriting?

She read on. Booth felt abandoned by his sponsors in OAK, betrayed in the days and hours after the assassination. He wanted to turn them in since they have failed to come forth and assist him in his desperate hour of need. He singles out Thomas Summerland and Isaac Wilkins as the Brutus to his Caesar. Booth says he was once proud to be the one appointed by the Committee to execute Lincoln, and proud that he was successful, unlike ...

She stopped as her eyes took in the words.

" ... unlike the one chosen before me to rid this land of the scoundrel Jackson."

She finally exhaled. This is why Professor Tidback came to Mississippi. Why, in the end, Tidback died. Why they were coming after Mac, and following her.

There was an 8" by 11" envelope stuffed into the back of the last plastic folder. Inside was a copy of an article from a St. Louis newspaper dated November 17, 1967. It was an interview with someone named Winston Summerland, on the first page of the local section. She gripped the paper as her eyes flew across the print. Winston Summerland was boasting of his role in the National States Rights Party of St. Louis and the reporter tossed him numerous softball questions. One was about King. Summerland said that King was a "no good Commie" and "dangerous." He said he'd pay "50 grand" to anyone who would do the country a "favor" and "take the sumbitch out." That was it - sheer, unadulterated newspaper play for a vicious racist with not a hint of editorial disapproval or reporter outrage. She turned several pages and stopped at a full-page ad in the form of a "Wanted" poster with a picture of Martin Luther King over the words "Communist Traitor."

An index card slipped from the pages of the newspaper onto the floor. Like the card she and Mac found in the loft near Randolph-Macon, this one had a list in Tidback's handwriting. This list had only one line:

1968 - King - Summerland/Ray

She stared at the check mark. The question mark next to King's name on the list from the loft had moved to a check mark. On the back of the index card Tidback had written notes.

"Met Summerland in late '67 at Civil War history conference at St. Louis U. Was interested in my article on Confederate guerrilla warfare. Boasted of role of Phineas Wright's OAK in Lincoln's assassination. Boasted that Phineas Wright came from St. Louis - in case I didn't know. Hated King. Said 'OAK' just might have to get busy again. Winked at me when he said it. Couldn't keep his little 'secret' in. Seemed like just a nut. Back then."

She swallowed hard. Now she knew what so urgently pushed Professor Tidback to Washington. She returned the card and newspaper to the envelope and stuffed Tidback's package into her backpack. Time to get to Mac. Time to get out.

Her hand pulled at the door handle. It was locked. She unlocked it and fell into the hall leading to the elevator. She raced down the hall to see the elevator was on its way up. An exit sign glowed at the other end of the hall.

She ran down the stairs. Once she fell, plummeting half a flight to a dank, musty platform. On rubbery legs she pulled herself up and stumbled down the remaining two floors. She burst through a fire door into the reading room. Eyes, everywhere, rose to scold her. She caught sight of Bennie behind the checkout desk. She ran to him.

Bennie was distraught, his eyes all over the place. "T-t-two men in suits h-h-heard about the carrel. I don't know how. Th-th-they went up in the elevator. I didn't know what to do. I ..."

"Don't tell 'em about the package!"

"I ... I didn't. I won't!"

"Don't tell 'em about me! Or that I've gone."

"You ... you bet!"

"Bye, Bennie!"

He lifted a hand. "S-s-so, so long!"

She burst through the library's front door and ran with her head down to the car. Fumbling for her keys, she looked from side to side. Where was O'Connell? Was anyone out there? Waiting for her? Watching?

She peered into the back seat. It was only the mound of her clothes. Suddenly, O'Connell fell out of the bushes on the other side of the car.

She screamed. But he was all right. "I had to go ...," he shouted.

"Oh, God! I'll drive," she replied. She opened the door, got in and then opened O'Connell's. Inside, at last, she twisted the ignition key. The engine coughed and caught. Tires squealing, she fishtailed out of the parking lot and headed for the interstate.

She stopped a half-hour later at a convenience store. O'Connell hunkered down in the front seat to keep an eye out while Linda went inside.

Pumping in coins at the phone at the rear, she still could not catch her breath. The bald man behind the store's counter stroked his handlebar moustache with one hand as he watched her in his security mirror behind the counter. The mirror came in handy to catch the occasional shoplifter, but mostly it was for watching the women bend over to reach the milk, bread, and other products strategically arranged on the low shelves at the back of the store.

Linda caught him watching. She turned back to the phone. "Senator Mossingame's office, please," she said when Capitol Hill Information answered.

"Offices of Senator Walter Mossingame. How may I help ..."

"Mac ... I mean John McAdams. Is he there?"

Linda heard a flutter of paper. "No, ma'm. He doesn't work in this office."

"Oh shit! He told me ..."

"I'm sorry ma'm. But I don't have him on the staff list and, by the way, I don't appreciate the language."

"I'm sorry. I'm in terrible trouble. It has to do with the Assassination Committee that Senator Mossingame chairs ..."

"Oh, honey! Why didn't ya say so? That's one of the Senator's Committees. That must be where John McAdams works. This is the Senator's personal office. You see I'm just fillin' in here. My name's Elisa and..."

"Please!" she cried in a cracked whisper. "Give me that number. Please hurry!"

"I'll do better than that. I'll connect you, hon."

A deep, endless silence fell. Linda Walker put one hand to her chest as she breathed deeply, her eyes closed. Her other hand clutched the phone. She dared not turn around.

A phone extension started ringing. Once, twice, three times. She looked at her watch. Oh shit!, she thought, it's after five! No one's there! She felt hot tears fill her eyes.

A voice came on the line. "Assassination."

She hesitated when she heard the odd greeting.

"King Assassination Committee. ... Anybody out there?"

"John McAdams, please. Hurry, I must speak to him."

"Listen, girl," replied Jazz Speed. "You and about everyone else 'round her wants to speak to him and set him straight."

"Oh, please. I have to talk to him. I'm the one who works, worked, for that Professor Tidback ...."

Jazz, hearing the fear in the girl's voice, sat straight in her chair. She shushed the young man who had been talking her up, his leg thrown across her desk as he sat on the edge.

"Is this Linda?"

"You know who I am?" She was bursting now.

"Girl, better than you know. Now what do you want him for?" Jazz's eyes grew wide as she listened.

"All right, now. You just wait right there, Sweet Pea." She put Linda on hold as she buzzed the private extension in the Webster hideaway, praying that Mac was there. No answer. She called Senator Mossingame's office. He picked up.

"You've got to talk to this girl, Senator ..." Mossingame listened without saying a word.

"Oh God, hurry up!" Linda begged in a half-whisper. The bell over the entrance jingled the arrival of two beefy men in work denim. They talked loudly as they bought cigarettes and beer. The man behind the counter signaled them, with a nod of the head, to eye up the young babe in the corner at the phone. They nodded appreciatively and craned their necks. She turned and glared at them until they left laughing.

An old man's voice filled the phone. "Where are you, Miss?"

"Who are you?"

"I'm Senator Mossingame. The receptionist explained who you are. I'm Mac's boss. I chair the Committee ..."

"Yes, yes ... But how do I know who you are?"

"Because I know who YOU are. Mac told me what you two found in Tidback's loft. I ..."

"OK, OK," she interrupted. She explained her location, a little over an hour south of the Memphis airport once she got on the interstate. "I have more information that Mac and you should know about. It explains why everything is happening. It ..."

"Now, you listen to me, young lady. Take the next plane to Washington, D.C.'s National Airport. If there isn't one ready to go, I'll commandeer one and you'll have your own private jet. I'll have clearly marked US Marshals waiting for you at the United Airlines ticket counter in Memphis. I'll alert United that you're coming. They'll put you in a secure place until take-off. Do you understand? Can you get to the airport all right?"

Jazz picked up her extension, hearing Mossingame's last words and Linda Walker's barely audible "yes."

"All right, then. Now tell me precisely where you are."

She did her best but Mossingame was dissatisfied, nettled. "Well, how far are you from the airport?"

"Damn!" shouted Jazz. "Never mind that. Just go, girl," commanded Jazz. "You move. Don't wait for nuthin', don't talk to no one. Just run now, as quick as you can ..."

Linda slammed down the receiver. It bounced off the holder and swung dangling a foot above the floor. She rushed through the door where the two slobs had left, back into the parking lot darkened by nightfall.

"Hey! Bitch!" shouted the proprietor. "My fuckin' phone ..."

Chapter Sixty-two

The speedometer showed she was hitting 70. They were still there, the two men who had followed her as soon as she hit the highway. They came out of nowhere. They were directly behind her in a dark sedan. There were no other cars on the entire interstate highway. Two lanes going in either direction and there wasn't one other car or truck to flash with her lights or blast her horn at.

In the splashes of light coming from the pole lights whizzing by, Linda Walker caught snatches in her rear view mirror of two dark shapes in the front seat of the car behind her. Two sets of shirt, tie and suit jacket. Two closely cropped heads of hair. They had to be the pair that Bennie said had come looking for the Professor's carrel.

She breathed deeply as she brought it to 75. It was another 10 miles to the airport according to the map. She had to make it. O'Connell kept an eye on the car in his rear view. They said nothing.

Between them on the front seat was Booth's confession. His seven-page indictment of OAK, the "olde Secret Committee," as the sponsor of Lincoln's murder. His confirmation that OAK had attempted to assassinate President Andrew Jackson. And Professor Tidback's notes showing a connection between a modern-day OAK and the killing of Martin Luther King.

These documents had to see the light of day. She had to get them to Mac. She had to get to the airport and the Marshals waiting there for her. If something happened, all Mac's work, the mission that brought Professor Tidback to Washington, DC, only to get killed, the horrible truth of OAK, would disappear.

A billboard blew by along the right side of the road. Seven miles to the airport exit. She pressed down on the accelerator. Eighty miles an hour.

The car behind her kept pace. She pushed the pedal down a little more. Eighty-five. The steering wheel started to shake in her hands as she plunged down the highway.

"Do it, baby," encouraged O'Connell. "Just hold tight and

keep it floored." He looked back to the rear view mirror. The car was gone. Quickly he turned to look over his shoulder. The sedan was next to them, on the driver's side, in the other lane. Suddenly it swerved and crashed deliberately into Linda's left rear passenger door. The harsh sound of metal screeching against metal filled the air.

They were running them off the road. They'd kill them before they got to the airport exit.

Linda gasped as she wrenched the steering wheel back and forth, straightening the car. She floored it, thrusting the toes of her right foot into the floorboard, pushing her back as hard against the seat as she could. She approached 100 miles an hour. The wind whistled sharply through the air vents and around the sides of the windows, like there was an Arctic storm going on. The car wobbled and shimmied as they passed the next sign. Two miles to go.

The sedan smashed against her door, shattering the glass. The side air bag exploded into Linda's ribs, forcing the breath out of her, and then collapsed. She struggled to keep the car on the road but she couldn't. The sand and dirt on the shoulder shot up against the underside of the car, cracking and snapping against metal. Tall weeds whipped against the right windows. The sedan pushed and pushed, trying to force her into the weeds. They would finish her off right here, right now, she realized. They would come back, run through the weeds, find her, find O'Connell and smash her face and head against the car window and the dashboard until her face was crushed and her blood flowed. They would kick O'Connell and maul him, like they did Jackson, maybe even put both of them in the car and light it afire, incinerating them.

She pushed her foot down and pulled the steering wheel to the left. Up ahead the ramp to the airport forked off. She could see the halo of light that was the airport terminal. It wasn't that far away. She started screaming and jammed her two feet onto the gas pedal. O'Connell opened his mouth and started screaming too.

Chapter Sixty-three

Thursday, nightfall - Alexandria, Virginia

Jackson stood in the shadows of the bushes and watched McAdams' anxious face. The scar under his eye sometimes gleamed in the light from the street. George Landry, his deputy, was crouched in the bushes at the entrance to Lewis Shephard's cul-de-sac, ready to head off any effort by Shephard to retreat. Four Deputy US Marshals, acting on a federal warrant alleging Louis Shephard's unauthorized interstate flight to avoid prosecution, a so-called "UFAN" warrant, crouched in the bushes and alongside the several houses that surrounded the cul-de-sac. He and McAdams stood in the high bushes clustered on the right side of Shephard's front stoop.

"Alright," Jackson began. "Here's where I am. Remember I told you at the Diner that we had telephone toll records showing two calls from public phone booths to Larcher's cellular number?"

"Yeah ..."

"Well, now we have a reliable eyewitness who'll say that he saw Lewis Shephard at one of those phone booths around 10 o'clock, the time of one of those calls, on the night the boys got lost up in the woods."

"I like it ..."

"We got another witness who saw Shephard driving around the back roads with Larcher and some of the other boys. I got me a small town, Mac. People see things, sometimes they talk. Anyway, my witnesses have described Shephard and that shitty little VW he's got right down to the damned license plate."

McAdams smiled. "What else?"

Jackson's eyebrows shot up. "That's all we got in the forty eight damn hours since we last talked. I'm still hoping to scare up someone who overheard one of those cellular conversations they had. I'm combing all the trailers and the cabins up in those hills, trying to find how many of our low lifes listenin' to police radio transmissions and watchin' TV talk shows all day picked somethin' up. Someone had to."

"Small town, right?"

"You betcha, with a whole lotta nothin' goin' on." Jackson snapped an irritating branch that was sticking into his neck. "Listen," he continued, "what'd you get on the Coast Guard and FAA? Why'd they show up in Richmond out of the blue?"

"Nothing yet. But the Coast Guard and FAA are both in the Department of Transportation. So I'm betting that I'll find someone in OAK in one of those agencies pulling strings."

"You're saying maybe someone got them to do some dirty work for OAK down in Richmond?"

"That's right. I think that's how Larcher's gun got on board that plane. I bet we find a name from some OAK member or his or her designee of some sort all over the special passes that airport security said were flashed at them by the surprise inspectors."

"The ol' 'last minute inspection' routine," Jackson cracked.

They stared into the night. All the houses were dark as if everyone had gotten the hell out. The sound of barking dogs erupted in the distance and then faded away. A soft breeze rustled the bushes.

"I've been doin' a little history research myself, Mac."

"What kind?" McAdams wished for a cigarette but knew the glowing ashes would give them away in the dark.

"You know those names on the OAK list I found in the trailer? Remember, there were 11 names in all?"

"Yeah," replied McAdams. "OAK's Civil War membership. Six under the letter 'C.'"

"Well, I finally remembered them all and had my friend who runs the John Brown museum at Harpers Ferry track 'em down. The six listed under the "C" weren't Confederates. They were all members of Congress when the Civil War started. Of course, in the cases of Nathaniel Brock and Thomas Summerland, some of these Congressmen became Confederates during the war and went back to the Hill after the war. Anyway, the five names in the other column belonged to important merchants, financiers and industrial leaders 'round the Civil War. My friend says Winthrop Allen - his name was on Booth's list - was the great-,

great-something or other descendent of Robert Allen."

"Robert Allen ..."

"In fact," Jackson whispered, "during the Civil War, Winthrop was president of the same Philadelphia-based trading company that Robert Allen founded before the Revolutionary War. And that was an ancestor of Nelson Wilkins on Booth's list - Bartholomew Wilkins. He was one of the largest international cotton traders in the country during the late 1800's. The other three civilians were big time maritime merchants and industrial manufacturers."

"Congressmen and commerce men. ... Lincoln's murderers."

"Uh huh." Jackson looked for headlights.

"Chuck, did you get to the US Attorney? Has he a grand jury sitting?"

"Yep, they're waitin' for us in Morgantown."

"Can you produce that handwriting expert in Morgantown next week?"

"Sure ..."

"And the voice recognition expert - for Brock's tape?"

"The folks in Morgantown helped me find one."

"Let's meet in Morgantown at the courthouse on Tuesday, OK? Monday might be a big day." McAdams stopped when he felt the pressure of Jackson's grip on his arm. Lights had appeared at the end of the street that flowed into the cul-de-sac. Shephard's shitty little VW Cabriolet entered the trap and came to a stop 10 feet away from them.

Chapter Sixty-four

Shephard turned off the engine and opened the car door. He got out and looked up at his home. The fading sunlight enhanced the milky whiteness of his pale, pudgy face.

He's taking a last look, McAdams thought. He's on the run.

Shephard started moving to the house. Jackson parted the bushes and stepped onto the sidewalk three feet in front of him. Shephard stopped. He stared at the gun Jackson aimed at his face and took in Jackson's badge and his police cap.

Shephard stood with his arms dangling at his sides and studied Jackson. He recognized this black face. He had seen it before. In the papers, on TV. ... The nigger cop! The one who had found the boys in the woods!

He watched Jackson's mouth as it told him to raise his hands and drop to his knees. Shephard did what he was told as shouted commands came from others running up behind him. And then John McAdams' burst out of the bushes.

"Hi, Lewie," smiled McAdams. Shephard felt things spin.

"Lewis Shephard," boomed Jackson's voice as someone behind him twisted his wrists into handcuffs. "You are under arrest for trying to flee West Virginia's prosecution of you for the murders of Theodore Samuels, Robert Hughlette, John Murphy and William Sterling. I am taking you back to Harpers Ferry tomorrow for this state prosecution after you are arraigned on the unauthorized flight charge before the U.S. District Court for the Eastern District of Virginia. Tonight you will be staying in the federal jail at Lorton, Virginia, courtesy of these men. Gentlemen, would you read him his rights?"

Jackson put his gun away and his hands on his hips. Jackson smiled a tight one at Shephard. McAdams put a hand on Jackson's shoulder and they stood quietly as Shephard, on his knees, looked blankly up at them.

Shephard's face suddenly contorted. "Nigger!" he spat and he began to put up a struggle. The fleeting tough-guy routine ended as Shephard was hoisted roughly to his feet by the Marshals. Shephard cried out with pain and glared at a smirking

McAdams. "Fuck you, too," he said.

"Now, Lewie," Mac replied, "do go gentle into that good night."

"Enough, Mac. Let's move him into my car, officers," directed Jackson, "before we wake up the nice neighbors. Put 'im in the back seat next to one of you. Mac and I'll ride up front. Will you drive, Mac?"

McAdams nodded and jogged off to get Jackson's car parked on one of the side streets. Jackson stood in front of Shephard as two policemen held him. The others went to retrieve the rest of the cars.

"We'll talk when we get to the station, Mr. Shephard." Jackson's eyes narrowed as he got right in the prisoner's face. Shephard tried to elude his eyes by twisting his head back and forth. Jackson matched him move for move.

"We've got a lot to talk about. We got the deaths of those poor men in Harpers' Ferry. We got your campsite in West Virginia. We got them OAKies of yours. We got murders in hearing rooms in Washington and planes in Richmond. We even got John Wilkes Booth of all people. Oh yes, Mr. Shephard, we're gonna shake and bake all night long."

Shephard looked at last into the black eyes boring into him. Beads of sweat became visible on his forehead and upper lip.

Chapter Sixty-five

Charles Jackson sat at the long, black metal table and eyed the inventory of Shephard's possessions. The sap had almost $50,000 in cash on him. A pay-off, thought Jackson, maybe for finding those Booth diary pages.

He looked up as a local sergeant and Deputy Landry led a distraught looking Shephard into the interrogation room. A stenographer followed them with an unlit cigarette in her mouth, a pen behind her ear, and the haunted, gaunt look of emphysema etched severely into her gray face.

Shephard sat down as Jackson nodded it was all right for the sergeant to leave and close the door. Jackson smiled to the expressionless stenographer. She sat down in a metal chair about a foot from his right knee, facing him at an angle.

"George," said Jackson, "you got the name and number of that deputy from the next town over who's covering for us while we're here?"

"Sure do. It's Mike Schiffres tonight. From Lombard."

"Call him and tell him we'll be having a prisoner tomorrow. Tell him it's Mr. Lewis Shephard here. Ask him to call over to the federal penitentiary and reserve a cozy little cell for said Mr. Shephard. He'll be staying there a while, too. I want 'im where he'll be secure, not in my itty-bitty prison. Get Schiffres to get the paperwork going, would ya?"

Landry practically charged out of the room with his assignment. He left behind profound quiet, Lewis Shephard in handcuffs, and the stenographer at death's door.

Jackson sat quietly across the table from Shephard and stared at him. Shephard did not look up.

"Stenographer," asked Jackson as he turned to her, "what's your name?"

"You can call me Elaine if you got to."

She didn't like black folk, he could see. It was in her face, the way she held it away from him with her nostrils slightly flared, as if there were a bad odor in the room.

"Thank you, Elaine. Begin when I tell you, hear?"

She moved her mouth back and forth like she tasted something gone bad. Jackson leaned over the table to get his face closer to Shephard's.

"I want my lawyer," snarled the prisoner.

"You'll get one."

"Now."

"Just settle down, Lewis. I..."

"And I want to make my phone call. I know my rights."

"Who you goin' to call? Your friends in OAK?"

Shephard's face fell. The false bravado evaporated.

"I wouldn't call OAK. They'll kill you, Lewis. I wouldn't call any lawyer, either. He'll call OAK. And then they'll kill you. You're useless to them now. In fact, you're worse than useless. You're harmful, dangerous. They will exterminate you, like they did others we know. But, if you talk to me, freely and fully, we'll protect you. You'll be all right, son."

Jackson watched discomfort and conflict creep into the sweaty face. "You still want a lawyer?"

Shephard slowly shook his head, defeated.

"Good. You can start now, Elaine. And begin by noting that Mr. Shephard does not want a lawyer present."

Chapter Sixty-six

Lorton Prison

"Jazz, it's me ...."

"'Bout time you called. Did you get that Lewis Shephard?"

"Yeah. He's in jail."

"Where he belongs. I'd have put him there long ago. ... Now listen, Linda Walker called."

"Linda?"

"She called a little after 6 today."

"What she say? Is she hurt? What about O'Connell?"

"She's scared to death, poor thing, but they're OK. She's found something. Says it explains everything. She's headed for the Memphis airport. Walt's sent the US Marshals there to protect her ..."

"Have you heard anything since she called? It's ... it's almost midnight!"

A feeling of dread came on the line. "No," Jazz replied in a low voice.

"Nothing from the Marshals?"

"Nothing. ... She's OK, Mac. I can feel it in my bones. She's on her way."

They listened to each other breathing for a while and then McAdams spoke. "Listen, Jazz, there's things I need you to do as soon as the sun comes up tomorrow. The Report of the Committee's Findings and Conclusions is done. Tomorrow's the day it gets published. Contact the Committee Members first thing in the morning and tell 'em they can access it on the Committee's LAN. Tell 'em Mossingame will poll their vote by phone, by day's end."

"Hold on ...."

"And get a copy to the printers. We'll need 5000 bound copies by tomorrow evening if my budget is still there."

"Slow down, Mac. There's been a *development*. Senator Mossingame wants to hold up the publication until the official May 1 date. Says he not so sure of some of the Committee's recommendations. Says he wants to be *careful*."

McAdams caught his breath. Something smelled. "Ready to break the law, Jazz?"

"If you tell me how much you love me."

"I love you this much, baby."

"I knew it all along."

"Jazz, leak a copy of the Findings and Conclusions to Joyce Thompson at the Post. Now. Tell her I'll call her tonight. Make sure she takes a hard look at the parts about OAK. And include my notes about Lewis Shephard's little campsites."

"You got it."

"And Jazz?"

"Yes, Mac?"

"Say a prayer."

Chapter Sixty-seven

After the interrogation, Lewis Shephard sat in a special cell they had for prisoners they wanted to keep separated from the others. To his right was the tank for those facing an early morning court appearance and those sleeping off a bad drunk or a good high. There had to be ten men in there. The guard who had brought him to the cell had complained about how crowded it was tonight. The cell on his left, normally empty according to the guard, was jammed with three men going on to other prisons. They were sleeping. And snoring loudly.

The smells made his head reel. Urine. Sweat. Other smells, pungent and perverse, from an unkempt bathhouse filled with unclean men. He felt dizzy. The catcalls and grunts and groans from the holding tank cloyed at him.

Some blew loud, wet kisses at him, wondering why he got the special privileges of his own cell, away from all the rest, with a TV, a radio and sink. Some shoved their groins back and forth against the bars. "Come on over, here, pudgy." "Yo, do this." They called him "pussy". They told him he would like it. They grinned and enjoyed the only show they had.

Sometime during the night, a new one was thrown into the holding cell. He stood by himself, grasping the bars tightly with two hands as if he wanted to squeeze through. He wedged his mouth and nose between the metal rods as far as they could go into Shephard's space. He whispered, staring with black, vacant eyes surrounded by bumpy, gray skin.

Shephard paced as far away as he could from the intrusion. When he had to rest he would take a seat on his bed, facing away from the man who leered at him only a few feet away. Late in the night, sitting like that, he began actually to hear the man's insane, guttural whispers.

"You won't live long. Not in here, not with me. Ahhhh ..."

"You like gettin' butt-fucked, right? Well, they do it rough here, you fucking faggot. Then they'll bust through your teeth to get you to suck their pricks better."

"Why are you doing this to me?" Shephard screamed.

The loner kept it up. "After they do you here, you'll be brought to the federal penitentiary in Morgantown. They'll keep you as the house bitch. You'll do everyone. You'll be happy to die. And, if the niggers don't cut you up for what you did to their Martin, we will. Just for what you told the Fatman Nigger in there tonight. Remember what you taught me, Shephard - the vendetta code of silence."

The shock of hearing his name, the words 'vendetta code,' threw Shephard off the bed and onto his knees facing the man. "Oh my God!" he cried. "Oh my God! ... Who are you?"

"You taught me. In the woods ..."

"Leave me alone! Help me!!" Shephard ran to the front of his cell and pounded his fists against the bars. "HELP!!!!"

"Do it," the man hissed, "do it now!" Others edged closer to watch Shephard's face. To see the score.

"Go ahead. Do it. Kill yourself, now. I guarantee by Saturday night you'll have had it up your ass so many times you won't care what's being shoved up there anymore. They'll hunt you down. There's a lot of us in here, in Morgantown. We come and go. With pieces of glass, copper tubing, sharpened pencils, sheet metal. That's how you'll go. That's how you taught us. Remember? ... Make it real ugly, you said. Send a message, you said."

Shephard edged to the other side of the small cell. A hand shot through the bars behind him, then came a second. They landed on his shoulders and yanked him fiercely back. His head clanged violently against the bars, once, twice, a third time. Grasping hands choked him.

He squirmed and struggled. Sweating, he slithered through like a greased pig and fell to the cold concrete floor.

"Help! Help! Help!" It was a high-pitched chant, a faint and breathless yell. "Where are the guards?" wheezed Shephard as he lay collapsed on the floor. "Help me!" He crawled into the middle of the cell. Curling up into a fetal position, Shephard hugged his legs and rocked back and forth.

"Ain't gonna help, screaming like that," someone shouted. Even the guards don't wanna be in here this time of night.

"Uh, unh. They don't want to see what goes down in here."

Shephard saw the glint of the whispering man's long, sharp knife in the low lights. "Here," he offered, "for your faggot wrists." Then he tightened a piano wire between his fists. "For your pussy neck." The words poured, wave upon wave of insult, panic and lewd suggestion. On and on and on.

The guards would find Lewis Shephard during the next inspection, the smell of burnt hair and something worse than that hanging in the air. They would find that the prisoner had electrocuted himself while sitting naked on the metal seat of the commode. He had died biting into the electrical cord leading to the TV in his special cell.

The hunter in the holding cell wiped off his fingerprints and then threw the knife and piano wire onto Shephard's body, which was sprawled, across the floor. The man fell asleep soundly in the corner of the crowded cell, his buffer of space from the others assured. This was a sick one.

Chapter Sixty-eight

2 a.m. – Friday – The Tank

"There weren't any Marshals waiting for us at the airport," began O'Connell. "I think she broke too many speed limits and they didn't have a chance to get there before she did." He jerked his head in Linda's direction. "She went tear-assin' down the access road, mounted the sidewalk and crashed through the doors right into the terminal lobby. I do believe people actually relieved themselves then and there, all over official airport property, when they saw her coming through the plate glass. It was quite a moment."

McAdams held a cup of steaming, hot coffee in his hands, and smiled despite it all. "You're here. Right? What do you have to complain about?" He put his arm around Linda who leaned against him.

"He was a big help," Linda jousted. "He screamed the entire way."

"No louder than you." They all laughed with relief.

"The car that was after us," continued O'Connell, "barreled right on by. And exited the airport. They didn't make the plane."

McAdams squeezed Linda's hand and then picked up from the coffee table the last of the Booth diary pages from the University of Mississippi. "This," he waved the sheets of thin paper now enclosed in clear plastic folders, "is an incredible find, you guys."

"Professor Tidback must have seen Booth's reference in those pages to Andrew Jackson," Linda explained, "and headed for Mississippi. Scattered all over his desk at the University was research into the Andrew Jackson assassination attempt. He was trying to find evidence that would connect OAK to the Mississippi businessman that some thought was behind the attempt on Jackson's life."

McAdams held up Tidback's newspaper article on Winston Summerland and the scrawled notes of their long-ago encounter.

"Summerland approached Tidback at a conference in St. Louis. The guy was so full of himself, so brazen, he couldn't help but brag to Tidback that OAK was hunting down King. Maybe, in the end, it was Summerland who told Brock about Tidback and his work. Maybe he talked Brock into getting Tidback to look into the Secret Committee's origins in the first place."

A sharp knocking sounded on the door. McAdams got up and opened it. Chief Charles Jackson thanked the Marshals in the hallway and came in. He wrinkled his nose at the cigarette smoke. He leaned over and kissed Linda's proffered hand. "Compadre..." he smiled. "Good to see you well after our little bonfire."

Linda smiled. "You, too."

"Tell us about Shephard," McAdams invited in a low voice.

"Someone was in there with him," Jackson began with a sigh. "Someone was in there goadin' him into suicide. Shephard musta danced 'round that cell. A knife and a piano wire, to be used if Shephard didn't take himself out, no doubt, were thrown on top of his body like a final insult. There were no prints, of course. The cell next to Shephard was overflowing with an assortment of low-lifes and nuts, just the cannon fodder OAK uses. The cell on the other side had inmates ready for movement to other prisons. It coulda been any one of 'em who pushed him over the edge. No one talked. Nothin' could be pinned on nobody. The one, or ones, who talked Shephard into death will not be brought to justice. OAK can reach out and crush whatever and whenever it wants."

Jackson fell into an overstuffed chair. "I bet my Deputy's call to West Virginia triggered everythin'," he said in a low voice, as if confessing sins to a new priest. "Our back-up in Harpers Ferry called in Shephard's name to the federal penitentiary. Whoever was there then probably told Justice or the FBI or somebody that Shephard was here in Lorton."

Jackson read McAdams' sympathetic face and shook his head. "Don't feel sorry for me, Mac. I screwed up. I should've realized that any word to anyone at the federal penitentiary would be picked up."

"You did what you could, Chuck," offered McAdams.

"Not enough ... But I did get Shephard to talk with a stenographer - and no lawyer - present. Just before he died."

Jackson hushed the flurry of questions and filled them in on the interrogation. When he got to the part about hundreds of thousands of dollars in mysterious funds transfers from regional banks of the Federal Reserve System, waiting at various times for Shephard's confederation at various small banks, McAdams sat down again next to Linda. "Which banks?"

Jackson pulled a pile of index cards out of his rumpled, oversized sports-jacket. He pulled off the rubber band that held them together and squinted at them in the room's dim light. "One in Denver. One outside DC. One just outside Richmond." Jackson read off the banks' names.

"No-name state banks," said O'Connell, "with at least two near the scene of 'accidents.'"

"Accidents? " Linda wore a quizzical look. McAdams studied the smoke hovering at the ceiling. He nodded at something only he could see and lit another cigarette.

"One bank," Jackson replied, "for the hit men who got Tidback, I"ll bet. That's the one outside the District. One outside Richmond for those who got Crockett. And Shephard had records for a transfer to Denver, one a while back ..."

" ... for the hit on Alan Berg," finished McAdams.

Linda gave him the eye. "Who?"

"Alan Berg. The hard-hitting, and Jewish, radio talk show guy gunned down in Denver. He took on the hate groups with a passion and was gettin' famous for it. There's evidence he was shot down by The Order, the violent white power group. The Order fits OAK's campsite profile. And Berg's name came up on Brock's tape as one of OAK's hits."

"Well, now, maybe we do have something," breathed Jackson as he shifted position in the chair. "Shephard said a hundred plus thousand got paid to the Order out there." A glimmer of vindication crept into Jackson's face. Maybe there would be justice for his boys.

Jackson skimmed several index cards filled with notes jotted down during his review of Elaine's transcript. "Shephard admitted he and Brock went to West Virginia together. He got close to saying they went to the Harpers' Ferry trailer, but stopped. It doesn't matter, though. We got their prints." Jackson's eyes glazed over. "We got a bunch of dead men's prints right about now."

"I retrieved Brock's tape of an OAK meeting," continued McAdams, with a concerned glance at Jackson. "OAK believed Brock made the West Virginia runs with Shephard to squirrel away some of the diary pages from his safe deposit box, like the ones you found in the trailer site, Chuck. And, in the case of the pages Shephard found, to set up a drop site for Tidback where he could pick up diary pages in a remote location, where there wasn't the remotest chance he couldn't be seen or recognized. Brock knew he was dealing with OAK; he knew they were everywhere, watching."

"It makes sense," Linda agreed. "Only Brock didn't figure that Professor Tidback would be appalled at what he read. He didn't know that Summerland tipped off Tidback about OAK a long time ago, maybe even making the Professor a little guilty that he hadn't done something sooner."

"Taylor Brock," McAdams concluded, "just never figured that Tidback would try to expose OAK and seek justice before the King Assassinations Committee."

Jackson held up the leather folder that his wife had given him a lifetime ago. "I got something for you. Copies of what Shephard says he found in West Virginia, at a remote, abandoned campground near Harpers Ferry, and returned to OAK, probably to his contact, Governor Narkle. For 50 grand."

McAdams got to the envelope first. "You've been holding out," he cracked as he poured the copies into his right hand.

"Shephard had 'em hid," explained Jackson, "just in case he needed them one day. He 'fessed up about 'em during my interrogation. I got to 'em before OAK did, I guess."

McAdams scanned the papers. "Two, no, three maps of Virginia and Maryland -- from Civil War days I'd guess. They show routes into and out of the District of Columbia with way stations and landmarks noted along the way. All the way to Richmond, capital of the Confederacy. And here's a stop at Randolph-Macon where Crockett told me the Confederate Secret

Service used to train.

"I bet," McAdams continued excitedly, "that we'll be able to show this is a Confederate Secret Service map. And the handwriting here - it's Booth's, no doubt about it." He passed the copies to Linda to read. O'Connell leaned over her shoulder.

McAdams eyed the pages remaining in his hand. "It's a ledger, in Booth's handwriting, showing his receipt of payments totaling 50 thou over the six or so months preceding Lincoln's death. A lot of money back then." He handed the page to McAdams.

He studied the last few pages. "And these three ..." He stopped talking as his eyes widened. He looked up, blood draining from his face.

"These three pages are in Booth's handwriting, but they transcribe a 'Declaration of Order and Commerce' written in 1776 by Robert Allen - Mason Allen's ancestor. This is what an OAK member called OAK's Magna Carta. It's OAK's founding charter! The names listed at the end belong to those who founded OAK - at the dawn of America! Including Alexander Brock, and Abraham Summerland, and Isaac Wilkins!" The pages quivered as he handed them to O'Connell.

"This is where OAK began. And these three pages confirm it." McAdams waved some of the pages. "Look, right here in the second paragraph of Allen's Declaration. It's the OAK oath, the one recited on Brock's tape. The same one handwritten by Booth all by itself on one of the diary pages Linda and I found in Tidback's hideaway near Randolph-Macon."

Linda looked up from reading the Declaration. "I just figured it out. Booth calls OAK the 'old Secret Committee' in the pages I found in Mississippi," she began in a low voice."

"Allen's Declaration of Order and Commerce makes it all clear, but Professor Tidback never got a chance to pick up Brock's package at the abandoned campgrounds where Shephard found it. Tidback never got a chance to read the Declaration. And there you can see that OAK was formed in 1776, right after the Declaration of Independence. It grew out of the Secret Committee. That's why Booth addressed his note about the failed attempt to kill Lincoln to the 'Committee.' The Second

National Bank was used by OAK for all sorts of illegal payoffs and plots, it was an instrument of OAK but not part of its evolution."

McAdams jumped to his feet and briefed them on what Professor Browning had told him about the Secret Committee. He walked over to the desk and pulled open a drawer.

"I found this in Brock's home after he died."

He handed a thick binder of ancient documents to Jackson. Jackson read aloud the title that was printed in fading gold leaf on the binding of the book. "The Official Journal and Accounts of the Secret Committee of the Second Continental Congress, September 18, 1775 to July 30, 1776. ... What is it, Mac?"

"Alexander Brock, one of OAK's founders according to that Declaration," McAdams explained, "must have passed it down through the generations to Taylor Brock. OAK thought it had been destroyed but it looks like Brock saved it somehow."

"The journal," McAdams continued, "is a record of Secret Committee meetings, actions and votes. The journal has ledgers showing contracts, payments received, Congressional appropriations and authorizations, and goods and war materials obtained. If you look at the list of payees, you'll see that those who benefited most from the Secret Committee were the very same merchants who were members of the Committee, and their families and friends."

The phone rang and made them all jump. McAdams dived in the direction of the offending instrument and listened. He hung up and turned to the eager faces surrounding him. "The early edition of the Washington Post is out," he said. "Jazz is bringing it over."

Chapter Sixty-nine

Washington, DC

Lewis Shephard had killed himself. Mark Fisher couldn't believe it, couldn't believe he had been arrested even, but that's what Wilkins told him. He shook his head. It was time to act, now. They had no other choice.

He put the key in his right hand and slipped it into the lock. He turned it and the door opened. Anne had walked out on him, but she hadn't changed the locks. She had forgotten that they had exchanged keys during better days. It was a little thing, but something he knew she would forget.

He stepped inside and let his eyes get used to the darkness. It took a while. The rich, dark carpets, furniture and drapes that cluttered her apartment seemed to absorb the light.

He made sure the door to the hallway was unlocked to allow for a quick exit. He made his way to her bedroom. He knew where it was. Her door was ajar and he pushed it open. He flicked on a bureau light and watched her. She was asleep, her dark mane of hair spread provocatively against the pillow, her hands open and limp, her shape filling the sheets. As he watched, she shifted positions several times. Still the light sleeper.

She stirred and turned her face in his direction. He approached the bed and stood beside it. Her eyes fluttered open, and started blinking in the light. She looked up at him, putting up a hand to shield her face from the glaring lamp behind him.

"Mark?"

He reached into the pocket of his baggy suit jacket.

She watched his movements. "Mark, what the fuck are you doing here?"

He kneeled beside the bed, showing her the plane tickets he had removed from his pocket. "We are in danger. We need to leave. We're on the first plane leaving National this morning. Get your passport, we're leaving the country. Get packed."

She sat up, holding the sheets against her breasts, her mind groggily struggling to catch up. "What are you saying? Danger? From who, what?"

"Remember how oddly I acted the last time we saw each other? I was worried about McAdams and what he might have found out about King's killers? The conspiracy behind …."

Her eyes suddenly widened in horror, but she wasn't looking at him. She was looking over his head, to the doorway to her room. He turned.

It was Sable. Sable had followed him. Sable let his sneering mouth broaden into a wide, uneven smile showing yellowed teeth. He licked his lips and raised his arm. There was a gun in his hand.

Fisher turned to look at Anne. He began to say "I'm sorry," but it was drowned out by her one scream. The one scream she got out before two silenced rounds from Sable's Glock exploded her face. Fisher pulled his head in as he felt the blood and bone and brain rain down. He shivered, waiting for what he knew was coming. The next two rounds went into the back of his skull and the force of the blasts propelled Mark Fisher to fall forward crumpled over Anne's body.

Sable left. He had some more work to do before he had to leave for Maine. There were bank accounts to close. Sweeps of this apartment and Fisher's. And then there was Maine itself. Preparations had to be made.

He looked at his watch and grunted. So little time. He grabbed a green apple from a bowl on the dining room table on his way out, making sure the door was locked this time.

Chapter Seventy

The Tank

"Listen to this front-page headline," began Mac as he handed copies of the morning edition of the Post around. "'*Committee Ties King Conspiracy to Assassination of Abraham Lincoln.*'"

"Joyce Thompson calls OAK 'a shadowy, enduring and murderous conspiracy of business and government interests.' She links OAK to the murders of King, Tidback and Crockett, 'and maybe others,' and back to the assassination of Abraham Lincoln. And she ties OAK to recent reports of nationwide organization among violent, right wing extremist groups. Joyce says the Committee will ask the Justice Department to investigate OAK and its various acts over the years. Justice won't return her calls. Hosea Kenwood and the NAACP is crying out for more Congressional hearings into 'this sordid national tragedy.'"

"Where'd she get that bit about the hate groups?" asked Jackson. "How'd you work that into the King Report?"

"I didn't. I asked Jazz to leak the OAK story as well as my notes on Shephard's confederation of campsites - the aimless, the nutty and the desperate - and how they were OAK's front line. Maybe someday Joyce, or others, will unearth evidence that will tie the deaths of those four boys to OAK."

Jackson nodded. "I'd like to see that all right. Especially since you and I have been so spectacularly unsuccessful."

"Chuck, we're not done yet. Tomorrow we head to Maine tomorrow and Monday is Morgantown. We still have a few arrows in the quiver. I could have told Joyce Thompson everything. I could have given her something on the Booth diary pages and the Secret Committee - on all the assassinations and assassins. But how much could I unload at once?"

"How much could she believe at once?" responded O'Connell.

"And what about her readers?" asked Linda. "She couldn't

dump too much on them at the same time. It would be way too much."

"But, maybe," Jackson prayed, "maybe it's beginning to unravel for them. Maybe it's the beginning of the end for OAK and its campsites and hit men and followers."

"Maybe." McAdams thought about it as the others fell back to reading. He could picture, when morning dawned reluctantly, a father in worn pajamas sitting back at the breakfast table over an empty coffee cup and an open newspaper, looking out the window, wondering, with a knot of fear in his stomach. If the OAK story were true, what about all the American history he had learned? What about what he had told his own kids about this great country, its Founders and its leaders, its noble traditions? Was any of it left untainted?

What unseen hand was really at work here in America?

Chapter Seventy-one

Dawn, Saturday – Port Elizabeth, Maine

McAdams squinted into the early morning mist and spied Fort Scammel. The gray walls of the Civil War era fort were only fainted visible. He turned to face Ed O'Connell, still on the dock.

"You ready?" McAdams extended a hand to help O'Connell into the boat.

"You driving?" O'Connell eyed the craft bobbing in the water. It looked seaworthy. McAdams said it was a 22-foot bowrider that could handle the water between Port Elizabeth and the island with ease. But, still, it looked too small for the 3' waves already spitting at him. And the engine gave off a good roar, but nothing like it seemed you needed for waters so close to the frigid Atlantic.

"Ed, I've told you. I've been boating all my life. When you grow up on Long Island Sound like me, you know how to boat. We'll make it. Believe me."

"Get in the damn boat!" boomed Chuck Jackson. "We don't have all damn day!"

O'Connell shrugged his shoulders and got in. "I'm in. I'm in," he squawked. He put on a life jacket and found a seat, his hands grasping at anything steady and solid.

McAdams let loose the lines and soon they were plying the waters of Casco Bay. "And, Ed, you don't drive a boat, you navigate, you ride the waves. You lay out a course and follow it. You…."

"I get it. I get it." O'Connell sat in the seat next to McAdams. Jackson was in the stern seat next to the enclosed inboard/outboard engine, letting the spray from the water sprinkle his face as they made way. McAdams glanced at his watch.

"The funeral for Dorothy Browning will start in a few hours."

"Mac, it's OK we're not there," said O'Connell above the

engine. "Linda will represent us just fine."

"She'll be there for all of us. Tidback and Crockett, too." McAdams sat on the back of the pilot's seat, staring straight ahead over the windshield. They hadn't found Dorothy Browning's decaying body until Wednesday, almost three days after her murder according to the police. Today was her funeral at Georgetown University's Dahlgren Chapel. Academicians, students, friends from around the country would be there.

McAdams breathed in the salt air, steadying himself. When would the bloodshed end? Seagulls dive-bombing the boat cried out, laughing, screeching, back at him. Another human joke. He locked his eyes on Fort Scammel off the bow, less than a half-mile away, forcing his mind onto what lay ahead. "Tell me again what the South Portland police chief told you, Chuck."

"He's a good man, Mac. I trust him. I trust what his men have told him. They know these islands, these forts like the back of their hand. They have to."

"OK. So, there's an entrance into the fort...."

"Into all the these little batteries on these islands from the Civil War. An entrance into the structure itself through the ground on top of it. First you have to find the indentation in the ground that marks the entrance, then you gotta dig through the turf, you lift a wooden trap door of sorts that would have been exposed in the old days, and then you walk down a few stairs cut into the rock to a landing which, in the old days, had a ladder down to the second floor. It's how the soldiers got inside in the olden days."

"And you think it'll be a good place to watch the OAK meeting."

"It will be the only place unless you perch like a bird in one of the open window sills."

"And I'll know that OAK isn't using this roof-top entrance, that they're using some other way, because...."

"Because it will not be dug up. It will be covered by earth. And there'll be no evidence of digging anywhere."

"And the radio transmitter?"

"You hit the red button three times and we'll pick up the signal. Me, Ed and the finest from South Portland's Marine and

Sea Rescue Unit will be on the island in less than five minutes. We'll be on the eastern side of the small island, waiting in the dark, engines cut, anchors out, avoiding OAKs craft, waiting for your signal."

"Jesus, a lot of ifs …," began McAdams.

Jackson shook his head.

"And fives minutes is a long time."

"We got no other choice, Mac. You'll have a gun …."

"Which he's never shot," chimed in O'Connell, "since he's never even picked up a gun."

"It's simple, boy. Just point, take a breath and then squeeze your index finger against the damned trigger between breaths until there are no more bullets."

"There it is," interrupted McAdams, his voice far away.

Less than a quarter mile in front of them a thin green strip of land clung to the horizon against a sky of blue dotted with white clouds. The sun was hanging low in the sky now and its crisp, clean light magnified the detail of the island. They spotted the Civil War-era gunnery unit against a gently sloping hill that ended in a sharp 10-foot drop to boulders popping out of churning blue water. The battery was two-stories high and jutted out defiantly from the island. The back two walls of the pentagon-shaped structure were cut into the side of the hill with the other walls facing the bay that emptied eventually into the ocean. Each floor had a row of windows with each window spaced about six feet apart and offering excellent vantage points for cannon and musketry. On the flat roof grew the same low, dense brush that covered the island. Except for the fort and the undergrowth, the island looked empty from their vantage point.

It was Booth's building. The fort etched in charcoal and labeled "Maine" in the diary pages discovered by Jackson in a trailer in the hills of West Virginia. OAK's long-time gathering place. McAdams remembered that Browning said the etching looked like a bunker of some sort, one used during the Civil War, to protect harbors and waterways. The windows were large enough, she said to fit cannon or men with musketry.

She was right.

They studied the gunnery and the island as they slowly

approached. There seemed to be no one ashore or in the building. When they got less than 50 years away, McAdams shifted into neutral and held the wheel against the currents. "Look at all these rocks!" he exclaimed.

"Over there, Mac. Chief Gates tells me you can land over there somewhere." Jackson pointed to a spot where the line of rocks along the shore thinned and the drop-off to the water leveled long enough to become a shoreline of about 20 feet. "You pull up, I'll take over, and then you're gonna have to wade in, or swim in, whatever."

McAdams brought the boat in and put it in neutral again. While Jackson took the wheel, McAdams put on the wading overalls he had purchased at the marina. He gathered up into the plastic boat bag his flashlight, shovel, the gun with an extra clip, the transmitter, a thermos of coffee and a couple of sandwiches. He eased himself over the side and found his footing on rocky ground. The water came to his chest and he realized, with the 3' foot draft on the boat caused by the depth the propeller went into the water, that they could have dropped him off even closer to shore. He took the bag that O'Connell handed over the side and made his way to the island. The last 10 feet was sandy bottom under the water and McAdams realized this was where OAK would come ashore.

He made land, turned and waved. Jackson and O'Connell waved back as Jackson turned the boat back. McAdams removed the overalls and stuffed them deep into the underbrush. He made his way to the top of the battery.

He breathed with relief when he saw no evidence of digging. Finding the indentation, he pulled his shovel out of the boat bag and attacked the ground. Two feet down he hit wood. McAdams straightened up and looked out over the bay.

Chapter Seventy-two

Linda Walker stood in front of Professor Browning's brick colonial home and looked up at the faded green shutters and the black windows. A yellow ribbon marked "Police. No Admittance" crossed the front door and the garage door.

She turned when she heard footsteps behind her. Lieutenant Marty Welch of the Capitol Hill Police approached, his long legs eating up the walkway. He took off his cap and gave a quick bow to Linda, eyeing the shapely body packed into those blue jeans. She saw he was half-asleep and hadn't had a chance to shave.

"Thanks for coming, Lieutenant," she said.

"Well, I'm coming off the night shift and Mac said it was important for me to meet you here, before the funeral. I owe him one. I mean, I head up the Tidback shooting investigation on the Hill and I haven't come up with diddly. This is the least I can do. 'Specially if it turns up something." He turned at the sound of a car pulling up to the curb on the other side of the bushes.

"That's my buddy, now," said Welch.

A black man in the dark blue uniform of the Washington, DC police force emerged on the walkway. He saw Welch and burst into a big smile. "Damn, I'm impressed, Marty. You usually racked out by now." He turned to Linda and smiled again. "Course, meeting a pretty lady early in the a.m. is enough to keep anyone going."

"I'm Detective Bliley, ma'am," said the black man as he winked and extended a hand. Lieutenant Welch and I go way back. He says you need a little help here. 'Course any friend of John McAdams is a friend of mine, too. He's always lettin' us know how the appropriations for the DC Police is doin' up on the Hill and he's ...."

"Richy," interrupted Welch, spotting Linda's impatience, "let us in."

Wiley stopped. "Course. Now I'll let you in to look, but do not, I mean do NOT touch anything. This place is sealed off for further investigation. They's dusted the downstairs where the action occurred. But they haven't touched upstairs yet and I don't want you to do no touchin' either."

He pulled down the ribbon and stuck a key in the door. They stepped over the bloodstained carpet at the foot of the stairs. The acrid smell of stale death assaulted them. Linda put her hand to her mouth and nose as they gathered in the living room next to the stairs.

"Mac, wanted me to check the fax upstairs," she said in a muffled voice. "Professor Browning faxed us some important information the day she died. The fax wasn't too good," she continued looking over her shoulder as she mounted the stairs. "So we're hoping the copy she faxed is still there."

Welch and Bliley waved her on. "I don't want to hear about it. Just hurry up, Miss Walker," said Welch. "Just hurry up so we can get out of here."

She found Browning's office and spotted the fax machine. There were no pages in the collection bin. Mac had given Browning copies of what the two of them had found in Tidback's loft at Randolph-Macon and that was what she had faxed back to them in the Tank. But the copies were now gone.

Linda stepped over to Professor Browning's desk. The copied pages were not there either. She walked around the room. Nothing in the trash basket.

She walked into the other rooms on the second floor. The trash baskets were empty. Nowhere were there copies of the Booth diary pages from the loft or Tidback's assassination list. Whoever had come to kill the Professor must have taken them.

"OK, Linda, time's up. Find anything?" It was Welch shouting from the bottom of the stairs."

"Oh, here's the fax machine," said Linda in as sweet and little girlish a voice as she could muster as she stepped out into the hallway at the top of the stairs. "It's in *this* room!" She gave Welch a smile and he melted. "I'll be right down, Lieutenant!"

She gave Browning's office one more look. She moved to the desk and picked up an opened textbook. The volume was turned to a discussion of the Second National Bank, the institution that Tidback has said was the bridge between the Secret Committee ... and OAK. She looked at the name of the

President of the Second National Bank. James Marshall Mossingame of Vermont.

"Mossingame...." she breathed.

The realization crashed in on her. There weren't any US Marshals waiting for her and O'Connell at the United Airlines ticket counter at the Memphis airport. There wasn't any waiting plane. In fact, United knew squat about them when they rushed to the counter as Mossingame had instructed. And the promised safe room where they could wait never happened. Mossingame hadn't sent any Marshals, he hadn't arranged a thing. She remembered how he kept asking, again and again, where she was, how far from the airport they were when she called. And ten minutes later appeared the car on the highway to the airport, filling her rear view mirror, filled with the suits that tried to run them off the road.

And Mossingame wasn't going to be at the funeral today, she remembered. Jazz had said he was going back to Vermont, for personal reasons. Pamela, his wife, wouldn't be joining him. Personal reasons....

Maybe his personal reasons meant OAK and OAK's meeting. Maybe Vermont wasn't his destination at all. Maybe it was Maine!

She tried to control her breathing. Mossingame had access to the Committee travel records that showed Mac had flown to the Portland, Maine airport last night. Jazz had booked the flights for Mac, Ed and Chief Jackson and she must have used the Congressional travel service. What else would she have done? And Mossingame could have checked. Mossingame might know where Mac is, and he might have made some phone calls. Mac might be walking into a trap!

"Linda!"

She dropped the book to the floor and spun around as Marty Welch stepped into the room. "Marty..." she sighed.

"Yeah?"

"Can you get me to the airport?"

"When?"

"Now!"

"What about the funeral?"

"*NOW!*"

Chapter Seventy-three

Fort Scammel, Maine

McAdams reached up over his head and pulled the trap door down. He prayed it was too dark outside for anyone to see the hole he had dug. He felt around with his feet for the steps cut into the rock that he had discovered during the day and found the first one. Gingerly he stepped down and squatted in the landing that was cut into the back of the second floor of the gunnery some 20 feet above the earthen floor below him. If he leaned out and peeked around the crude stairway from above he could spot what was going on down below.

Men were standing around a large table. They had entered by some passage that he could not see from his position. He counted a dozen chairs. Six kerosene lamps in a circle in the center of the table provided harsh lighting. Shadows cavorted over the walls and the ceiling. His position was cloaked in darkness. He felt reasonably safe, if only no one came upon that hole above his head.

McAdams recognized Governor Morrison Narkle standing at the table. Only four years ago, Narkle had been a member of the House. He lost his seat some years back, but later became governor of Wisconsin. Next to Narkle stood a grim Nelson Wilkins.

He saw Reid Johnson, the prominent banker, pull out a chair and sit at the table with his back to the fire escape. Someone threw an arm over Narkle's shoulders as he spoke to him. It was G. Brent "Manny" Palau, the pharmaceutical billionaire who threw tons of money around the national political scene. Some said he was going to run for President one day and, if magazine covers were any barometer, he was already in the race.

He froze when he saw Congressman Nick Tomovitch - the number three Democrat in the House. Tomovitch stood talking in the corner to a bespectacled man with a rumpled white shirt and dark suit, the classic, high-ranking Washington bureaucrat, and to a granite block of a man wearing a bright white uniform.

A naval uniform, he guessed, but not quite. Maybe Coast Guard which, along with the FAA, was part of the Department of Transportation and probably involved in the last minute inspection of Rufus Crockett's plane. He heard someone call the uniformed man "Commandant."

A few well-heeled, horned-rimmed executives pulled out chairs and sat down. He couldn't place their faces but they looked like the icons that adorned the business magazines every week - strong, chiseled, cold men of commerce. Most were in their fifties, some their forties. They were pillars of capitalism, captains of industry, thick roots in rich soil.

Two were Senator Taylor Brock's age. One carried a regal air of superiority even in this setting, like he came from money and was bound to end up there after all was said and done. The other had a brilliant flash of thinning red hair and a down-home look. The old men sat down but they didn't speak or look at each other. Narkle started pounding the table with a clenched fist. "Gentlemen", he said wearily, "this is an emergency meeting. We must be quick. Let's begin with the creed."

"No free mason," began the chorus, "minuteman, federalist, republican, judge or any false patriot shall be allowed to interfere with the enjoyment and pursuit of property -- either by constitution, law, plebiscite, referendum, military rule, imprisonment or taxation -- without answering to our punishment. And so, by such work, shall We the People secure the promise of our Revolution and our Nation."

McAdams closed his eyes. It was the oath he and Linda Walker had found scrawled on a Booth diary page in Tidback's hideaway loft in Virginia. Hearing it from these powerful men, in an echoing chamber, this night, threw a chill down his sweat-soaked back.

"Now to the first item," Narkle began as he sat down, "Taylor Brock's replacement." The room grew quiet. "Senator?"

Walter Mossingame lumbered into McAdams' view, a somber look on his face. McAdams' head spun and he leaned back against the stone wall.

The others in the room below him stood and gathered, shoulder to shoulder, in a circle between the table and the windows overlooking the bay. McAdams returned to his position and saw that Mossingame had stopped outside the periphery as Narkle slowly turned within, momentarily meeting the gaze of each OAK member. The circle tightened, with each man's back to Mossingame. Mossingame shifted his weight from foot to foot, looking over his shoulder now and then and peering out the windows into the night. He was nervous, as if he expected someone he didn't want to see. McAdams swallowed and shrunk back into the shadows as much as he could.

"We have served since the beginning," Narkle began in a singsong lilt, "since the beginning of this noble land, anointed as we have been in a holy crusade. We seek order, commerce and progress. This is our mandate. This is our legacy. This is our privilege and this is our obligation - to serve as a beacon and a sword for a nation and people buffeted and beset. ... Order. Commerce. Progress. ... To these ends, and to each other, we pledge our lives and loyalties in this the Order of American Knights."

"So be it," replied all but Mossingame.

"Walter Mossingame, come into the circle. Pledge to us and to OAK your life and loyalty."

"I so pledge," came the quiet reply.

"Join us, then, Walter. Enter the Order of American Knights, like your ancestors have before you."

The circle opened broke as two men parted. Mossingame stepped forward to complete the circle, taking Palau's and Wilkin's hands on either side of him. Each man took another's hand and the circle of hands lifted to the ceiling as Narkle led the group again in the OAK creed. After they finished, Narkle picked up an old walking stick that was on the ground in the middle of the circle.

"This was Robert Allen's means of support in his last days - when he laid down the Declaration of Order and Commerce and founded OAK. So, too, as I lay it upon your shoulders, Walter, shall OAK be your support and so shall you support OAK, its members, and its destiny." Walters bowed his head and shoulders to receive the touching.

"You are one of us now."

"I am here," began Mossingame, " because I was informed by Mr. Tomovitch of the role my ancestors have played in OAK over the years...."

"Don't apologize, Walter," interrupted Tomovitch, waving Mossingame off. "Sometimes that's the only reason some of us join OAK. We get blackmailed into joining out of the fear that our ancestors' crimes, crimes that can't be traced to OAK, might be exposed. We ...."

"But, soon," said Manny Palau, "you get to see, you get to 'ppreciate, that maybe OAK's got a role, that maybe your ancestors had it right. That every society, every country needs a ruling force that will do the dirty work, handle the jobs that others cannot handle, to keep it in line. .... Don't worry, Senator Mossingame. You'll see the need one day for the kind of order and commerce and progress that we can produce. You'll see the need for us. Someday this will be the only Committee you care about."

"What I was going to say," said Mossingame, "is that that day may have already come. I am tired of the Hosea Kenwoods out there. I am tired of the many, many hands that have reached out to me for decades, hands that are eternally wide open and looking for a handout. There is no pretense anymore about work or effort. There is no recognition that this great country has blessed its people with abundance in addition to fairness and justice and equity and that these blessings are not free. They must be deserved, worked for, earned! I...."

Mossingame suddenly stopped and looked at the faces around him, his own slightly reddened from the emotions coursing through him, his eyes glazed. The room mumbled its approval and agreement. Mossingame grew quiet and sat at the table, taking stock of what he had said, how far he had come in so short a time. He looked around at the table of agreeable faces. McAdams thought he looked lost and bewildered. Something had snapped.

Palau banged the table with his hand and heads swiveled. "What about the Assassination Committee? Is what the Washington Post sayin' true?" Eyes turned back to Walter Mossingame.

"The Committee concluded," he replied, "that a conspiracy was behind King's murder, and that it probably involved OAK's Winston Summerland. The Committee...." Mossingame stopped and looked around him.

McAdams knew what he was thinking. His disclosures were illegal. The Committee's deliberations and its findings and conclusions were confidential by order of the Committee. Any violation of that confidentiality was punishable with hefty fines and lengthy prison sentences under federal law. Mossingame's revelations already went over the line. He was already compromised, already hooked to OAK. He could not go back.

"Senator?" Tomovitch glared at Mossingame.

"Yes. ... Yes... All right. ... The Committee will ask Mankins' Justice Department to see if the Summerland conspiracy resulted in King's death." Mossingame nodded in the direction of the bureaucrat hunched over the table.

"The Committee wants Mankins to see if OAK orchestrated Summerland's reward to James Earl Ray for King's death and if OAK, as David Tidback claimed, pulled John Wilkes Booth's strings. They also want Justice to see if OAK was behind the Tidback and Crockett murders."

Stunned concern cascaded from face to face. Mankins stared at his clenched hands.

"McAdams," Mossingame continued, "proposed the possible, and I stress 'possible', connection between Summerland, OAK, King, Lincoln, Tidback and Crockett. He had no proof. All he had was Tidback's written testimony flopped out onto the table by Senator Charlton. The statement, its last minute insertion, shocked us all. And that carried the day. There was a surprising consensus from both sides of the aisle that was at work. There was not much I could do at that point in time to head off the momentum that John McAdams created on his own and using David Tidback's testimony delivered dramatically right before the Executive Committee session."

Mumbling rose from the circle of men. Heads bowed as several conversations were struck up. It seemed to McAdams that they were second-guessing Mossingame, perhaps not sure of whether he was going to end up on the right side of things. Eyes darted back and forth between conversations and Walter Mossingame who sat stoically, awaiting the deliberations.

"Now before everyone goes off the deep end," commanded Tomovitch, "listen hard to what Senator Mossingame is saying. The Report only directs Justice to look into these matters. It doesn't say one damned thing about OAK except its name. There's nothing about who's in it, or what it is. Hell, given what little is said, OAK could be some damned low-life, state militia."

"Brock's referral to Justice actually saved OAK," blurted Mossingame. "It was a brilliant move. It pre-empted McAdams, heading him off before he talked on the record about any of Booth's diary pages he may have in his possession - or anything else. You need not worry about Mac, about John McAdams, that is, any more. I have put a stop on the Committee Report and I should be able to slow things down quite a bit. I may even be able to reconvene the Committee and further water down its referral to Justice. Maybe even ...."

"GENTLEMEN!" screeched Palau. The room grew quiet.

"OAK is NAMED? ... It is LINKED to Winston Summerland and King? LINKED to Lincoln's assassination, and to Tidback and Crockett? In an OFFICIAL document of Congress? And you're trying to tell us that all of this will just blow away?"

"Manny, everyone, listen to me," Mankins pleaded in an earnest voice. "I will see to it that the referral from the Assassination Committee gets the handling it deserves. It will sink into an abyss. If not, and if someone wants to find OAK and expose it, we will create one for them from one of Lewis Shephard's bands of merry men."

"This situation," replied Narkle, "can, and will be, managed. It is within our range of reaction and response. And don't forget that Senator Mossingame may be able to squelch the Committee report before it sees the light of day. It's been done before, you know ...."

"It's too damn late!" shouted Palau. "The damn Washington Post has got its hands on the Findings and Conclusions. And this Hosea Kenwood will not rest until the Assassination Committee spills someone's blood. I say we take out Hosea Kenwood, now. I say we finish up with McAdams and Jackson. Make it all look like some Goddamned tragic accident, only just do something, for Chris-sake!"

Palau turned around. "Sable! Get over here. You got some God-damned work to do."

Mossingame started to object until he spotted Sable. The effect of seeing that man stopped the Senator in his tracks. He sat back and waited. McAdams drew back into the shadows, sure Sable's piercing black eyes might see him, that something behind those black eyes might sense him skulking in his lofty perch.

"Hell," continued Palau, as he raised a hand to show off Sable, "if the Ayatollah, the CIA, the mob, the Medelin drug cartel, the god-damned Symbionese Liberation Army, the Michigan Militia, the Somalians, even a damned cheerleader's mother, can take out their opposition and shove their agendas up our asses, well, so we can do some shovin' ourselves. Am I right?"

Barry Ingram's puffy face grew red. The head of Central Plains Power, the nation's largest utility, had had enough of the cowboy billionaire from Texas. "I got somethin' to say." Ingram's mid- America twang and soft tone contrasted sharply with the harsh whine of the acerbic Palau.

"You say it's good OAK is asserting itself again. Good that it's flexing its muscles. Good for what? The country? Or your own sense of adventure? Tell me, just where are you, and your boys here, taking OAK?"

The men around the table, slighted at being called "Palau's boys," puffed themselves up. Narkle saw things were spinning out of control. Palau pointed a finger at Ingram, ready to let loose another stream of invective.

"I'm not finished," shouted Ingram. He looked at each man around the table. "OAK has been guardian and guide over the generations. We helped preserve a way of life that the country needed. Is the OAK creed nothing to you? Does the Declaration of Mason Allen's ancestor mean nothing to you?"

McAdams watched the man the red-haired man throw a

thumb in the direction of the old patrician next to him. Mason Allen was super rich, a descendent of the Mayflower. His relatives were among the country's founders. McAdams recognized him now. He was head of innumerable federal commissions of one sort or another and someone who was real busy on the Washington society pages, the heartthrob of every old grand dame in the city.

"What's your point, Barry?" spat the Commandant. "We really don't have time to replay this bullshit tonight."

"We've influenced politicians with good ideas, and money. We've bought elections when they couldn't be won. We eliminated problems when we had to, but we also were smart enough to play second fiddle when that was the right way to go. Like with Kennedy - some of you remember Wellington wanted us to take charge. Thanks to Taylor, we said no. We stood by, let others take the lead and take him out."

"Hold on!" interrupted Governor Narkle. "That's it! You make OAK sound like the Rotarians! OAK kills when it or its members are threatened. OAK kills when it has to send a message. OAK removes obstacles in the way of the economic and political controls this country needs. That's the way it always has been. Remember Martin Luther King? Remember the others? Come on, Barry, spare us the lecture, would you?"

"You can orate with the best, Governor," fumed Ingram, "when you get up the gumption. All right, let's look at King. He had to go. Period! He wanted to organize the minorities, the working class and the poor nationwide, even internationally. He could do it, too. We saw the impact he would have on the labor pool. We had a ton of studies showin' the effect on wages and profits if King got as far as we thought he would. Hoover couldn't get him to commit suicide, or compromise him, so we had to step up. We had to fix the problem. And we did. With one shot.

"King was just one more lesson about letting the unpropertied and the rabble take control - instead of bein' controlled. That's why OAK got started, if you remember. That's why OAK took action over the years. You will destroy this great tradition with your short-range, non-strategic, risky adventures and your killing sprees directed at nobodies with no real power, no real threat - to OAK. You are increasing the chance OAK will be exposed and destroyed."

"I disagree in these recent cases, Barry," said Allen. "Tidback had the Booth papers and he got them from Brock. Both men were clear and present dangers. McAdams and Jackson are immediate threats - perhaps the biggest we have faced. McAdams on his own may know more about us, have more on us, than any other single outsider - ever. If OAK is exposed, it will be compromised, perhaps neutralized. If that happens, then the way of life we seek to preserve and enhance will waste away on the vine. ... We have had to do what we have done. And what we have done is consistent with our history. We need to do what we need to do, especially in the case of McAdams now that the Assassination Committee is reaching its end and Senator Mossingame is with us.

"OAK has always acted when there was a threat to the established way of doing things, when some one person could have turned things topsy turvy. Take Huey Long. He would have defeated FDR in '36. My father, who sat in Governor Narkle's seat at the OAK table, who served on OAK along with Senator Mossingame's own father, knew this. Huey Long would have changed our way of life had he become President. He was a radical who would have fundamentally altered how things work. FDR wasn't a whole lot better, but he was not Huey. Franklin was not going to upend society and business like Huey. FDR was going to give a sop to the masses. The New Deal promised to keep the underclass placated and stable, and under our thumbs long enough for us to right the economic mess we got into. And that was the contribution of Walter Mossingame's father. He enlightened us. So we eliminated Huey Long, we took action of the killing kind when perhaps some vote buying and intimidation might have worked just as well and with less of a threat of exposure of OAK."

"And OAK responded decisively with Teddy Roosevelt. He wanted antitrust laws when we needed unfettered industry for the coming war. TR was a dangerous man in many ways. Thank God that OAK was populated by the monopolies then - the car companies, the phone company, the railroads and the steel mills! They knew what TR meant for commerce, they knew he had to be addressed suitably and rapidly. We failed, but Teddy got the message. He backed off, quickly."

"Barry," interjected Narkle, "do you want us to wait for McAdams and Congress to expose us? Do you want us to do nothing while they and others try to destroy OAK?"

"I simply want us to use restraint and judgment," said Ingram in a subdued voice. "Don't let these bully boys and hit men that you got in place with their hokey Copperhead medallions around their necks, don't let 'em get carried away." Ingram glared at Sable.

"Please! Please! Please!" begged the banker Johnson. His smooth, boyish face betrayed deep distress. "I don't care what or where OAK has been. Governor Narkle is the control now, OAK is on a new path, and the confederation of campsites is serving us well. We must move on now! McAdams is alive. He may have Booth's diary pages. And there's a Committee Report that implicates us in murder while Hosea Kenwood manipulates the politicians and the press in a way that only guarantees our exposure, maybe our prosecution. We are under siege! I want action and response!'"

"All right," agreed Palau. "Narkle, Wilkins - you got your orders. Let's do what we came here for. Let's burn those damn diary pages and get the hell off this island. After this crisis is fixed, I promise we'll move on to bigger, more 'strategic' things, like Barry wants!"

"After we burn these pages tonight," swore Johansen, "we will not meet for some time. We will return to our homes and to our offices and we will destroy anything that might link us together, or to OAK. We will not meet again until one of two things occurs: either we find the last seven pages from Booth's diary – the accusation – and burn them in each other's presence or Senator Mossingame does his good work and things blow over. Not until then, gentlemen!"

Nodding heads and mumbling indicated Johansen had spoken for the group. Narkle stood and removed yellowed, crumbling pages from an envelope. He put the documents one by one into a silver bowl in the center of the table as he ticked off the eleven pages cut out long ago from the diary of John Wilkes Booth, the eleven pages in OAK's possession. Booth's transcription of Robert Allen's Declaration of Order and Commerce. His record of payments from OAK and his maps from Washington to Richmond. The OAK creed, the Maine and Suratt boarding house drawings, the list of OAK members when Lincoln was assassinated. All that was missing were the 7 pages in which Booth had accused OAK of sponsoring his assassination of Abraham Lincoln, naming names, and of attempting to murder Andrew Jackson. Linda's discovery at the University of Mississippi.

Narkle threw in a match after the paper. McAdams winced. In an instant, after a brief flame peeked above the edge of the bowl, eleven brittle pages, eleven parts of history, had turned to dust.

"Could we move on, like to*night*, gentlemen?" interrupted Wilkins. "I want to hear one more thing. Those Booth diary materials held by McAdams' friends over at House Judiciary. ... Mr. Mankins?"

Mankins lifted his head. "We have obtained what we want from the House Judiciary subcommittee that had the materials. It was produced in my office last week, thanks to Mr. Fisher. The photos, the FBI lab results, the FBI report, have been destroyed. The subcommittee transcripts are thought to be back in the Archives' vaults. They, too, however, are gone."

"By the way, gentlemen ...." Sable stood over Narkle's shoulder and crossed his arms. His voice wormed its way into each man. "Shephard's been handled, as some as you know. And we've taken care of that woman Professor that McAdams was using. Anne Gardiner and Mark Fisher won't be a concern anymore either. It will look like murder-suicide which, in a way, it was. Gentlemen, we're slowly mopping up."

McAdams started pumping the red button on the radio transmitter. One. Two. Three. Three times. He kept pumping until he heard Sable's voice again.

"There's only a few left now," continued Sable. "Including this one."

McAdams craned his neck to see what Sable was talking about. He saw an Oriental man, Vietnamese probably, emerge from the shadows holding someone struggling in his thick arms. It was a slim figure, a woman …. Linda…!

Palau stood, as did several others. Mossingame looked up and his face drained of blood. "What the hell is this?" screamed Palau.

"One of my men found her on the docks on the mainland," Sable answered. "She was looking for a boat. She wanted to come here, to the fort. Tonight. Said she had to meet somebody …."

Palau turned on Mossingame, his eyes narrowing. "This is the woman working with McAdams. How could she know about this place? Mossingame, is this a trick?"

"No, no!" shouted Mossingame as he stood, his chair flopping backward onto the ground. "I have nothing to do with her!"

"Sable!" Narkle roared. McAdams couldn't tell if it was a command or a warning.

Sable's hand was already up. He pointed his silenced Glock at Senator Mossingame. Before anyone could move, before McAdams could cry out, the gun spat sparks and puffs of smoke, shell casings ricocheted against stone. Mossingame's body slammed against the wall and fell heavily to the earthen floor, three bullet holes in his chest leaking blood.

Linda screamed and Sable turned toward her. He nodded for the Vietnamese man to get out of the way and then he pointed his gun at her.

"No!" bellowed the old man with the red hair. "No *more*!" Barry Ingram, only steps away, lunged at Sable and jumped, landing with the full weight of his body on Sable's gun hand. The gun, dislodged, fell under Ingram's body as he hit the ground, the impact forcing all the air from his chest. Ingram lay on his stomach like a pale, beached fish, gasping for breath, immobile. Pain shot through his chest.

Sable looked around wildly in the flickering kerosene light for his automatic. The men around the table started shouting out orders, first to Ingram, then to Sable and Narkle. The din in the cavernous room thundered and resonated chaotically. Johansen grabbed Palau and shouted at the Texan. "Stop Sable! Tell him to stop!"

Johansen was pointing at Sable who had reached behind his back. Wasting no time, he was pulling out a small derringer to finish the job he had started. He held his arm out straight and pointed it at Linda, nodding once more for the Vietnamese to clear a path.

"No! No! No!" McAdams realized it was his own voice.

The Vietnamese, moving from Linda as Sable commanded, confused by the echoes, froze in his tracks and looked up in the direction from which the ghostly voice had come. The faces in the room followed his gaze. Sable, unsure, retreated into the shadows of a far wall. His eyes jumped around the room, looking for the unseen enemy's vantage points and his positions of attack.

The Vietnamese pulled a gun from his waist. McAdams stood, his own gun forgotten in the boat bag, shouting and waving his arms, drawing their attention, desperately buying time. Linda, released, fell and stabbed her feet repeatedly into the ground, pushing herself backwards.

Narkle spotted McAdams first. He pointed upwards toward the landing. "There! There!" The Vietnamese's gun, unsilenced, exploded in McAdams' direction and the painful roars careened against the stone walls. McAdams jumped sideways and back into the stairway. Bullets ricocheted off the walls and McAdams felt a searing burn in his leg. He had been hit. He screamed in pain.

Linda saw Mac go down out of sight and she stopped backing away. She saw Sable with his back against a far wall. He had another weapon in his left hand and was inching sideways, right to left, toward a position directly under Mac's perch. He beckoned to the Vietnamese man to get Mac's attention. They were the only two in the chamber who acted with purpose. The gunfire, the shouting and the screams that filled the cavernous room paralyzed the others.

The Vietnamese shouted to McAdams. "We got her!" he cried in his heavily accented English. "Come out or I will kill her. Now!"

McAdams gripped his wounded leg with two hands. Blood saturated his pants leg and seeped through his fingers. Hearing the call from below, he thrust his hand into the boat bag, fumbling for the automatic that Jackson had given him.

"*Now*, McAdams, NOW. You have 10 seconds and then I will shoot her! One.., two..." Ingram reached under his body and extracted Sable's gun, grimacing in pain. He had injured himself somehow and pain shot through his chest when he tried to raise his bulky body. He couldn't do it, he realized. He turned his head, spotting Linda against the wall. He slid his left hand holding the gun across the ground in her direction. She saw what he wanted her to do. She froze.

"Three.., four..."

She saw the gun on the floor next to her mother. Saw the cold, black, dead gun. Heard the man in the corner blubbering and laughing.

"Five..."

Saw the blood on the daisies, the gaping hole in her mother.

"Six .., seven..."

The Vietnamese man raised his gun, taking his aim, readying himself for the target that surely would emerge. Sable pulled back from the wall and held the derringer with two hands pointing directly over his head, bracing for his target.

"Eight..."

McAdams pulled the gun out. He couldn't remember how to release the safety or whatever it was Jackson told him to do. There wasn't time.

"Nine..."

Linda saw her father's face, his mouth worked into a shout, urging her to win. Suddenly she heard a noise. She looked up and McAdams was standing, his arms outstretched. He was shouting. "Take me! Take me instead!" he screamed.

Linda lunged for Ingram's hand and picked up the gun in one swoop. Prostrate, the dust rising into her nostrils, she raised the gun and pointed it at the Vietnamese taking his own aim.

"Ten!" The Vietnamese smiled and bore in on McAdams. "You lose, stupid sucker!"

Linda squeezed the trigger once, twice, three times, hitting the man in the neck and face, ripping away his jaw, which dangled by a dark, bloody red muscle crawling from his face as he collapsed without a sound to the ground.

Sable heard the muffled shots and saw McAdams still standing. He realized that wasn't Thu's gun. It was his own silenced Glock. He twisted in place, an ugly grimace across his face. Seeing his man down and Linda on the ground, her hand holding his gun, he screamed in rage. He coiled and began to run at her with his pistol extended.

Sable was stopped in mid-air by a powerful force that threw him backward and onto the ground into a sitting position. A great cloud of dust rose up around him. He looked down in surprise at the blood gushing from jagged wounds in his chest before he collapsed backwards.

The men in the room, OAK, turned as one and saw Chuck Jackson and a squad of men in uniforms pouring through the windows. Jackson's gun was drawn. He was the one who had taken down Sable. Someone from the assault force screamed at Linda to put her gun down. She dropped it.

Jackson put an arm on the man taking aim on Linda. "She's with us, Detective, she's with us!"

McAdams looked over the edge of his perch. "Chuck! Up here!"

Jackson walked over to the bottom of the wall under McAdams' ledge. "Told you it would be less than five minutes 'til we got here."

McAdams peered into room below and saw Linda on her back, crying and looking up at him. A smile managed to surface on her trembling lips and she wiped the tears from her cheeks with the sleeve of an arm.

"It seemed like forever," replied McAdams, looking at her.

Chapter Seventy-four

Wednesday, April 29 - Morgantown, West Virginia

Their testimony before the grand jury took two and a half days. There was another half day for the blood-pumping summary by Jackson's handpicked U.S. Attorney, C. T. Sunberg. And now the grand jury was deliberating. McAdams and the rest were packed and ready to leave.

"Who knows," said Sunberg in the court parking lot as they piled into an armored van for the return trip home, "we just might get that indictment. Maybe we'll even nail a few of the bastards at trial. In any event, we'll certainly dig up a lot of dirt."

"Like a grave digger," Jackson replied under his breath.

"What?"

"You'll be digging dirt like a grave digger. Question is, CT, are we digging up something putrid and ugly, or are we burying it?"

Sunberg shrugged and slapped the roof of the car before he walked away. "Drive safely. And try not to lose the Marshals in your haste to beat the scene. OK?"

The prosecutor stood on the steps and watched the convoy move out of the parking lot with squealing tires, sirens and rotating lights. They seared a trail across West Virginia and Virginia into Washington, DC.

The indictment came in late Thursday night. Sunberg shook his head when he read it. He picked up the phone to call them at Daniel Webster's hideaway.

Chapter Seventy-five

Thursday, April 30 - Train to Harpers Ferry.

The fresh sunlight of the new day danced across his lap as he rode the rails west to Harpers Ferry. He was going home at last, after a day or two with McAdams, Linda, Jazz and O'Connell in Washington, resting up, celebrating some, and counting the losses. His thoughts flew to his son.

What would he think today of this country, seen now in the dark and cursed shadow of OAK, the Secret Committee, and all the rest? He could almost hear the singsong curses.

He shook his head at an unwelcome thought. The boy didn't die in the swamps of Vietnam just so OAK, and its kind, could rule and prosper. His was a necessary, patriotic sacrifice.

Order, commerce and progress. Order, commerce and progress. A chill went through his spine at OAK's rallying cry. The clouds grew sullen and motionless overhead as the train whipped through the countryside. His eyes drooped and he found a fitful sleep.

Some time later the train slowly lumbered into the station in Harper's Ferry. The sunshine that brought brief pain when he opened his eyes then painted a blue sky and West Virginian hills that glowed bright green and yellow. Spring was finally taking hold in the foothills.

The train stumbled to a halt with a tumult of squeals and groans. Jackson anxiously gathered up his things and walked off the train and onto the platform. He stopped at the top of the stairs to survey his domain. From there he could see the main street of Harper's Ferry run straight through town. He breathed deeply and a small smile played over his lips.

The first bullet caught him between the eyes.

The second plunged into the side of his head as he was spun around by the first impact. His weight pulled him down backward, and he rolled head over heels down the stairs. His body crashed heavily into the street with a sickening thud at the bottom of the long flight. That was when the screaming around him began.

Jackson had landed face up, his unmoving eyes wide open. He looked upward to the skies with a slight smile inexplicably spread on his lips.

The assassin looked through his telescopic sight to make sure the target was dead. He smiled and folded his rifle and foot-long silencer into the special suit case and put it on the floor. He looked back through the window and into the street four stories below him. No one looked up at his location. There was no scuffle or scurry below. A quarter of a mile down the street, if he had looked in the sight again, he would have seen the small crowd gathering around their Chief Charles Jackson, a huge pool of blood spreading under his shattered head. But, by then, his footsteps echoed in the hallway as he rushed for the car.

Chapter Seventy-six

On Friday morning, the 1st day of May, the country awoke to an exclusive Washington Post news story with the largest banner headline since the day Nixon resigned.

"Defense Secretary Wilkins, Wisconsin Governor Narkle Indicted with Four Others in Cover-Up of Lincoln Assassination -- Conspiracy to Obstruct Justice Called the Longest in US History."

The paper named the criminally indicted: US Defense Secretary Nelson Wilkins, Governor Morrison Narkle of Wisconsin, US Coast Guard Vice Commandant Lloyd Johansen, US Deputy Attorney General Steven Mankins, Mason Allen, chairman of the US Appalachian Regional Commission, noted philanthropist and descendent of a signer of the Declaration of Independence, and Reid Johnson, CEO of Ameribanc, the nation's largest regional bank.

The grand jury found that each of the indicted had acted in concert as members of OAK, and with other unnamed OAK members, to obstruct justice. Each had taken an overt act furthering the century-old conspiracy, the OAK-inspired and -managed conspiracy, to prevent the identification, investigation and prosecution of those who had planned and funded the murder of President Abraham Lincoln. Documents had been burned, official government files destroyed, witnesses killed or silenced.

The conspiracy, according to the Post, was the longest-running conspiracy ever alleged in a federal criminal prosecution, longer than that cited in the successful federal indictment and prosecution in 1983 which alleged an 88 year conspiracy of Mafia family heads, called the 'Commission', to govern and run organized crime in the United States.

The OAK organization, according to the indictment, began in the 1770s. The OAK conspiracy to obstruct justice in the murder of Abraham Lincoln began in 1865. The crime for which the six were indicted began when they first saw and understood the Booth diary pages, and either failed to disclose the evidence contained therein or took steps leading to the withholding, cover up and destruction of the evidence.

The Post article named one unindicted co-conspirator, someone whom the grand jury believed was involved in the conspiracy but against whom the grand jury could find no probable cause - that is, not enough evidence - to bring an indictment charging the commission of an overt act furthering the conspiracy. This individual was G. Brent "Manny" Palau, the Texas pharmaceutical billionaire who had declared his intent to run for President of the United States only Monday.

There was a sidebar article on the work of the King Assassination Committee. The Post noted its earlier exclusive that the Committee had tied OAK to the murder of Martin Luther King, asking the Justice Department to investigate OAK and its involvement not only in King's assassination but also the murder of Abraham Lincoln and the deaths of Tidback, Crockett and others. Justice still wasn't returning the Post's phone calls.

The Post's lengthy and impassioned lead editorial was entitled "Something's Happening Here …."

Epilogue

Late August - The woods outside Harpers Ferry

Linda turned over in bed and reached for McAdams. He was gone. His smell, the faint impression of his head, lingered on his pillow.

She sat up and looked out the window. The pale light of dawn was spreading through the trees. He was out there on the porch that overlooked Jackson's round pond in the woods.

She walked through the one-bedroom rambler to the screened porch. McAdams was sitting in Jackson's rocker, looking into the dense trees just becoming distinguishable from one another in the sunrise. She walked up behind him and put her arms around his chest. She smelled his hair.

"Good morning," she said.

He reached up and stroked her arms. "Sit." He handed her his coffee cup. She took a sip. She sat in the new rocker that matched Jackson's old one.

"Is it over, Mac?" The trial started next week. Everyone told her that the convictions would come. Everyone said that, convictions or no, OAK was exposed, finished. Jackson's murder was a senseless act, probably carried out by one of OAK's vengeful campsites determined to keep the OAK flame alive but destined, in the end, to fade. The West Virginia State Police already had a suspect under arrest, a professional hit man connected with The Order.

"It's over," he said. Next week school would begin and Linda would be a graduate teaching assistant at Georgetown. A Dorothy Browning Scholar, no less. Tonight Pamela Mossingame and Ed O'Connell were coming out for Labor Day weekend, one last blast before the pressures of Congress kicked in. Pamela Mossingame had won, as expected, the special election to fill out her husband's term. Together they had conspired to make it seem that Walter Mossingame, like John McAdams and Linda Walker and Ed O'Connell and Chief Charles Jackson, had been a hero, but they both knew the truth about Walter Mossingame. They both knew he had caved in, collapsed under the weight of too much pain, too much pressure, and tortured logic that promised falsely to fix it all, to impose order in the world gone mad. Pamela Mossingame wore her hurt and her shame regally, and no one ever was the wiser.

McAdams pointed into the woods. Linda nodded and sipped her coffee. A deer with big black eyes had emerged from the woods and stared back at them from a distance. It sensed no threat and went back to grazing at the base of a tree. It came every morning and they both took comfort in its sentry. Linda continued watching it, rocking back and forth. McAdams returned to his fiddling with Jackson's knots.

-- The End --

Author's Note

This is a work of fiction. It weaves together facts, some of which are noted below.

1. There was a Secret Committee that was pivotal in arming and feeding the struggle for independence from Great Britain. It fell apart amid charges of favoritism and other abuses, and calls for audits and oversight. See The Secret War of Independence by Helen Augur (Duell, Sloan & Pearce, New York, 1955). The Committees of Safety, groups like the Regulators, and the tension between and among merchants, economic patriots, pure patriots, democracy and elitism existed throughout the first decades of the country. See, for example, Basic History of the United States, Charles A. & Mary R. Beard (New Home Library, New York, 1944).
2. The Senate did investigate the involvement of a George Poindexter in the assassination attempt on President Andrew Jackson. See "The Assassination Attempt on President Andrew Jackson," Carlton Jackson, *Tenn. Historical Quarterly* 26 (Summer 1967).
3. John Wilkes Booth did have a diary that was found on his near-dead body. It was placed in the hands of the US government by Lafayette Baker who put together the group that hunted down Booth and found the diary after one of its members shot him. The diary was mis-placed for several years until the impeachment hearings of President Andrew Johnson and the trial of one of Booth's accomplices.

   At least 18 and perhaps as many as 27 pages were cut out by someone. Who? We will probably never know. Lafayette Baker, accurately described in this book, did assert before Congress that he saw pages in the diary when he delivered it to the government which were missing when the diary resurrected some years later. Baker asserted that one of the missing pages contained a drawing of a building or structure. See "Booth's Diary" by William Hanchett, 72

Journal of the Illinois State Historical Society (Feb., 1979).
4. The FBI did examine the pages of the Booth diary - in 1977. See "FBI Probes Lincoln Assassination," Jack Anderson and Les Whitten, *Washington Post*, p. B15 (August 3, 1977) and the February-March and March-April, 1977 editions of *The Lincoln Log* (Seaford, New York).
5. There was a group known as the Order of American Knights or OAK which surfaced in 1862 and disappeared in 1863. It was known as an anti-Lincoln group and its founder, Phineas Wright, was detained and questioned, then released, the day after Lincoln was shot. See Copperheads in the Midwest, Frank L. Klement (Univ. of Chicago Press, 1960).
6. The dispute over who killed Huey Long, and why, continues to this day. See "Uncertainties in Huey Long Legend Lead Researchers to a Doctor's Grave", *New York Times*, p. A10 (October 21, 1991).
7. There was a House Select Committee on Assassinations which, in the mid-1970's, looked at the Kennedy and King assassinations. The Committee, which served as the model for the Assassination Committee in this book, issued the recommendations, findings and conclusions set out in this book (with the exception, of course, of those related to OAK). See US Congress, The Final Assassinations Report of the Select Committee on Assassinations (Bantam Books, New York, 1979).

The House Committee found "substantial evidence" that there existed a St. Louis-based conspiracy, perhaps a "secret southern organization", to fund the assassination of Dr. Martin Luther King. The Committee called this the John Sutherland-John Kaufmann conspiracy. The Committee stated its belief that James Earl Ray was made aware of the Sutherland-Kaufmann conspiracy and its $50,000 bounty for the head of Dr. King. The Committee also requested the Justice Department to investigate further some evidence that had been developed suggesting that a federal and state government agent or informant played a deliberate role in forwarding the news of the Sutherland-Kaufmann conspiracy to James Earl Ray or his brothers. Nothing has come of this request. There was, of course, no discussion in the House Committee Report of OAK or any relationship between OAK and the Sutherland-Kaufman conspiracy, or between OAK and James Earl Ray or any others actors in the assassination of Dr. Martin Luther King. The King family recently has sought a trial for James Earl Ray, whose early guilty plea prevented him ever going to trial; the King family has expressed its own belief in a conspiracy in the murder of Dr. King. See "King Family Seeks Trial for Ray Before He Dies with His Secrets," *New York Times*, p. A1 (February 4, 1997). Gerald Posner's Killing the Dream (Random House, 1998) concludes that Ray killed King and that there likely was a conspiracy involving Ray's family, acting in concert to secure the $50,000 Sutherland-Kaufmann bounty. Posner notes that J.B. Stoner, counsel for the National States Rights Party (NSRP), became one of Ray's lawyers; Sutherland was an active member of NSRP. Could NSRP been the "secret southern organization" that Sutherland boasted was behind the funding of the bounty? Posner also found that the individual most likely to have served as a go-between between the Sutherland-Kaufman conspiracy and James Earl Ray, John Paul Spica, was killed during the House Select Committee's investigation. This occurred in 1979, right before Spica was to testify before the Committee, when a trip-wired bomb in his car went off as Spica started it. The murder remains unsolved.

8. It was not until 1991 that the June 12, 1963 assassination of Medger Evers, the civil rights leader, was linked to a little known group called the Phineas Priesthood (see "Evers-Case Suspect Tied to Bias Unit," *New York Times*, p. A18 (October 30, 1991)). The Priesthood is being investigated in connection with the fatal bombing at the 1996 summer Olympic Games in Atlanta (see "Possible Lead in Bomb Blast at Olympics," *New York Times*, p. A13 (January 27, 1997). The Priesthood has been linked to the Christian Identity Movement or CIM, an anti-Semitic group formed in the US in the 1800s. It is not known whether the Phineas Priesthood takes its name from Phineas Wright of OAK.

The CIM, in turn, has been tied to The Order, a "white power/separatist" organization that has been blamed for a series of violent crimes over the last decade. The Order has been blamed for the bias murder of Denver talk show host Alan Berg, among other things. See "Skinhead Nation" by Jeff Coplon, *Rolling Stone Magazine* (December 1, 1988).

9. There are growing alliances found among groups like the Ku Klux Klan, The Order, the Church of the Aryan Nation, the White Patriots Party, the skinhead movement and other white supremacist, racist, and hate groups. See "New Report Warns of Alliance of Racist Groups," *New York Times*, p. A11 (February 6, 1989); "Armed and Dangerous" by Leonard Zeskind, *Rolling Stone Magazine* (November 2, 1995).

Here's an excerpt from P.M. Nugent's newest John McAdams' thriller

The Witness.

Coming in 2000.

One

Dawn, Washington, DC
January 2, 2001

"Mr. President, the strike force will enter Cuban air space within minutes. You should sign this now." The Chief-of-Staff arranged the signature page on the desktop.

Seven other men, in uniforms or dark suits, sat stiffly in front of the ample, dark mahogany desk in the Oval Office. Their faces were haggard. Their eyes gleamed in the low light. The tallest of them, a gaunt black man with sunken cheeks and a mane of bright white hair spoke. "Mr. President, if I may…."

"Please, Carl," replied the younger President with a slight nod. "This is the most difficult decision of my Administration. For twenty-five years you've given me good advice in tough situations like these. And this is one of the toughest."

Carl Crombie, Secretary of Defense, sat ramrod straight, his eyes locked on the President's. The other men, from the military and various intelligence agencies, watched him, some out of the corner of their eyes, others only with a glance, waiting for Crombie to speak.

His voice was gruff and painfully hoarse. "The Presidential Decision Directive that you're signing authorizes Operation Blue Sky, the air strike against the Juragua nuclear complex on the southern coast of Cuba. The Helms-Burton Act of 1996 stipulates that the completion of the nuclear reactor in Cuba will be treated by the US as an act of aggression and will be met with an appropriate response. Well, Castro and his gang have flipped us the finger, Mr. President. They've completed the reactor. And it's a ticking time bomb."

A gray-faced man on Crombie's far right interrupted in a high pitched, nervous voice. "Mr. President, if I may elaborate, the reactors are irretrievably flawed in construction and design. After 15 years of stop-and-go construction and with Cuba's lack of any kind of safety culture or operating expertise for these complex reactors…,"

" ... and given the certainty of defective materials and poor welding...," ventured another.

Crombie burst in, irritated by the interruptions, silencing them. "Net-net, Mr. President, 90 miles from our shores we have a Cuban Chernobyl, one just waitin' to happen."

The Defense Secretary let his words sink in. "Before they fire the bad boy up," he continued at last, "before any radioactive material is loaded up or generated, we will take it out, sir. The PDD you're signin' authorizes the air strike we need to do that."

"This is a risky action, Carl, a unilateral act with serious consequences" said the President somberly. "And technically, I'm a lame duck. I've completed my two terms in office. I have 20 days until the Vice-President is sworn in as the new President and I exit stage right. Must I undertake this action? Must I do so now?"

"If you don't, our Chernobyl down south might blow any time. There will be great risk to the health and safety of this country if you fail to act. Why, your Vice-President might be glowing by the time he puts his hand on that little ol' Bible. ... We have no choice, sir. We must act now, today, this hour. I daresay this minute."

"This might be considered an act of war. Are we sure other nations will not leap to Cuba's defense?"

"*Might* be considered an act of war?" A rough laugh whipped out of Crombie's throat. "Oh, it's war all right. It's a bloody war. And, so what? What if other nations decide to help 'em out? Who will it be?" Crombie looked to his left and right to the other men, stoking up the pep rally. "Who will come against us? Russia? Belarus? ... Grenada?"

The room erupted in a brief, obligatory burst of nervous hilarity. Crombie's own laughter spoiled into a coughing fit. His two hands flew to his mouth, his fingertips clutching at his cheeks, as his entire body heaved and retched for a few moments.

"You can relax, Mr. President," gasped Crombie as he recovered. "Your PR staff has put together a campaign that will be unfurled like the flag this evening, givin' us time to complete the mission, givin' us time to mop up if we have to. Your PR boys'll go on and on about our prior efforts to talk Cuba out of the reactors. They'll stress the safety factors at work here. This is an act of self-defense, after all. The National Oceanic and Atmospheric Administration in Commerce, the Department of Energy, the UN for Christ's sake, they'll all have their flip charts showing that a meltdown will produce a radioactive cloud that would contaminate a wide swath of the US from Texas," Crombie stopped and peered through the floor to ceiling windows behind the President to see if the sun had risen, "to our own backyard right here in good ol' Washington."

Silence filled the room as each man gazed out the window, sharing Crombie's apocalyptic vision. "There will be no casualties, Mr. President," he continued. "This is a surgical air strike. We won't lose one fly-boy. And since it's the day after the Cuban holiday celebrating Castro's liberation, no one's gonna be working at the reactor. Everyone's gonna be sleeping it off. So we won't lose any Cubans. Not that I'd mind takin' out a few of 'em while we're down there."

The accumulated expertise in the room nodded their collective heads. The President watched the bobbing faces and then stared at Crombie before he spoke. "We are going through with it then?"

Crombie looked back and nodded. He knew what was being asked of him. "We have no choice, Mr. President."

President Michael Taylor signed his name. He stood and handed the pen to his Chief-of-Staff. "Let's pray that our pilots will be as successful as they were in the Gulf War and the Balkans. Let's pray they haven't missed a beat." The room agreed and filed out of the Oval Office in single file. Crombie hung back.

"The other matter...," he began. The Chief-of-Staff paused in the alcove outside the Oval office, not following the other seven men who had left. He stopped and melted into the shadows, watching Crombie approach the President. This was strange, he thought. He watched as Crombie took something from the inside pocket of his suit jacket and handed it to Taylor.

"One more signature, Mr. President," Crombie said as he smoothed the paper out on the President's desk. "Operation Wooden Stake."

"Yes. Wooden Stake. … I was hoping there would be no need for it."

"The opportunity presents itself. Preemptive self-defense."

"Yes…, but I was hoping we could avoid it …." The President leaned over the desk, gave one last look at Crombie, and dashed out his signature. He handed the document to his Secretary of Defense. "Preemptive self-defense," he mused. "Exterminating the threat that is real, but before it become actual, before it comes ashore. It's a very neat, very tidy doctrine, Carl. A philosophical tour de force. By God, it avoids all the handcuffs that Congress has put on the Executive Branch, right?'

"By God, or by our lawyers. Our best legal minds have been at work, Michael."

"I trust it will hold up should all this see the light of day. Or should we be seen in the klieg lights of a courtroom or a Senate hearing room loaded with TV cameras."

"'Preemptive self-defense' will support us, sir. Count on it."

"You will keep that embargoed until when, and if, we need it." Michael Taylor watched the paper with his signature disappear back inside Crombie's jacket.

"I shall, sir."

"And you will brief the Vice President as soon as possible, I trust."

"You can count on me."

"I always have, Carl, always have. And now my Vice President must trust you as well." The hair on Taylor's neck rose in the cool air as he contemplated the Defense Secretary. Crombie's pale pink lips stretched into a slight, amused smile across his dark face.

"Good luck, Carl," said Taylor at last. "We've been through a lot. This might be our last great act."

"Yes, Michael, and good luck to you. We shall need it today, and in the future."

Chief-of-Staff Dennis Long took his cue and ducked out of the anteroom. Crombie's head twisted around at the noise behind him, his black eyes locked into a squint. All he could see were the shadows lingering outside the Oval Office in the anteroom.

Two

Dawn, Cuba

Fatima Bosong Barata sat up and pulled back the tent flap, covering her naked breasts with her husband Jose's jacket. It was the morning after the wild, night-long celebration of Liberation Day, commemorating Castro's deliverance of Cuba in 1959. The camp was quiet except for an occasional cry from a hungry, wet baby or a burst of laughter.

There was a score of women and children rousing themselves, beginning preparations for communal breakfast in the large clearing, leaning over fires and grills with pots and pans and ladles. The crisp, white sunlight was beginning to penetrate the morning mist. There were maybe 100 tents of various sizes scattered through the woods, under camouflage tarps and wooden lean-tos, sheltering over 400 people by Jose's count last night, most of whom this bright, shining morning were sleeping off the hangover of the Liberation Day celebration.

She spotted another couple of dozen men and women walking through the clearing, among the tents and on the periphery of the campground, their weapons in arm or slung over their backs, their dark eyes wide and alert as they scanned the tree line for intruders. A few hundred yards away in the distance roared the angry sound of the Caribbean crashing against the southern shore.

Beside her rustled her husband of 7 years, Jose Sorzano, and between them snuggled their daughter of 5 years, Joy, a petite image of her proud mother. While she, Fatima, long ago had taken Islam religion to her bosom, she would allow young Joy the freedom of mind a young girl needed, letting her take up the religion that rang true to her own soul as she grew to be a woman. And so she was, for now, Joy Jones-Sorzano, the fruit of a wonderful, passionate union.

Jose turned in his sleep, a little smile seeming to play out on his lips. He was younger than she by half a dozen years, dark and ruggedly handsome. His jet black eyes and matching hair emphasized the intensity within him, the intensity they shared for life and for living a meaningful life. He taught philosophy in the local school and was a devoted follower of Castro's Communism, even as it changed and softened over the years since the fall of the Soviet Union. He was a member of Cuba's Direccion General de Inteligencia, the DGI, the country's intelligence agency. Such as it was. The pay from DGI was so little that they had to live off what little money she raised from making clothing, blankets and crafts and selling her handiwork in the street markets. But that was fine.

She smiled as the breeze of the morning came to her. They had a good, simple, intimate life now, especially with little Joy. Their home on Isla de la Juventud was small and modest, with two bedrooms, a living room and a kitchen. Isla de la Juventud, a part of Cuba, inspiration for Robert Louis Stevenson's Treasure Island, was a sparsely populated, flat island burdened with swamp, tall trees and dense foliage. There wasn't much treasure except for what you carved out of existence every day, with your loved ones and your comrades. The four-cornered island lay south of the main, familiar island of Cuba by 10 miles and north of the hyper-capitalist Caymans by 30 miles. Isla de la Juventud was hard to get to, and Fatima liked it that way. They lived in the north, near the island capital of Nueva Gerona, where most of the island population settled.

Today, about 8 miles from her home, in the southern tip of the island, she lay with her precious family on a new morning, a new morning in so many ways. She could feel the excitement in the air.

She luxuriated in the moment, knowing she would need to wake Joy in a little while to join her in helping serve up the breakfast for the soon-to-waking freedom fighters. Last night, seeing all the different colored faces, the different eyes and hair, the babble of voices, the bouquet of so many different human smells and gestures, Joy looked out over the assemblage of men and women and called them the "planet people." They, indeed, were planet people, Fatima smiled, proud of her daughter's insight. And like the pirates that came to this island in the Caribbean for sanctuary over the years, Francis Drake, John

Hawkins, Thomas Baskerville and Henry Morgan, these modern-day soldiers laid claim to their destiny and freedom, took on the moneyed and the oppressors, using their own wits and skill. They were brothers and sisters united in revolution, united in their opposition to the American Satan and to the spread of western capitalism and culture. They came here to this island from around the world every few years, as they did for Sandanista brother Daniel Ortega almost two decades ago, and for Castro in the early '80s at Grenada and Carriacou, for three weeks of solidarity and training.

They came from Castro's DGI, of course, but also from the Sandanistas' National Liberation Front, the Lebanese Black September, the Spanish Basque separatist group ETA, the anti-US, anti-NATO Turkish Revolutionary Left, and the Italian Red Brigades. She drank with men and women from the Filipino Abu Sayyaf Group, the radical Japanese Red Army and the Egyptian al-Jihad which took the life of Anwar Sadat. She shared meals with fighters from the Iranian Hizballah, responsible for the suicide truck bombing of the Marine barracks in Beirut in 1983, and others from the Honduran Marazanist Patriotic Front and the militant Palestinian group Hamas. She embraced sisters and brothers from the Chilean Revolutionary Leftist Movement, the Puerto Rican FALN, the Salvadoran Farabundo Marti National Liberation Front and Che Guevara's Bolivian National Liberation Army. She toasted comrades in the Revolutionary Armed Forces and the Army of National Liberation, both from Columbia, and laughed with the reckless, young recruits bringing new life to Peru's Shining Path. And there were others, with watchful eyes and grim faces, others that were perhaps the roughest of them all - experienced agents from the governments of Libya, Iraq, Pakistan, North Korea, Sudan, and Syria. They kept to themselves when they could.

Brought together by four men – by Castro and the enigmatic North Korean - Kim Jong-nil, by Tomas Gorge - the Sandanista and al-Jihad's Dr. Ayman al-Zawahiri, and maybe by others, unseen others, the men and women of the revolution would train and gather strength here in Isla de la Juventud. Roughly three hundred armed revolutionaries, according to Jose, and over 125 family - husbands, wives, lovers, sons and daughters, cousins, uncles, aunts, grandparents - together, unified for this brief time in their crusade. Tucked away in some of the tents were sophisticated communications gear and new models of assault rifles, mortars, anti-aircraft cannon and new, sophisticated weapons easily hidden and those that could pass metal detectors, and protective, armored clothing. There were explosives of every variety, Semtex - the Czech-made plastic explosive - in a variety of new shapes and applications, and everywhere soldiers who were eager to share intelligence, techniques, escape routes, methods of disruption, ideas for the revolution, and eager to unite in a consistent, coordinated attack against common enemy. And, for the first time, there was a tent of slit-eyed men arguing, pushing for the revolutionaries to pick up biological arms to infect the American Satan.

It was necessary, she figured, all the violence, the struggle, the death. It was ... self-defense ... she shrugged. All of it but a natural response against the encroaching, and corrosive, destructive western ways of capitalism and Americanism. The beast cared only to feed itself and it was getting stronger every day, its potential to overrun the dwindling ranks of planet people only growing greater as time went on. If you did not reach out and strike the beast as it came to you, where it was most vulnerable, most weak, the beast would devour you. The beast would most certainly devour you. She knew that.

She could feel her time, their time, Joy's time, growing short. As the sun climbed in the sky their time diminished.

She wished it would stop some day, the killing and the fighting. She wished it could stop. She prayed her Joy might have a chance to grow up in a different world. And the men with the viruses, with their scientific terms and their darting, wild eyes, scared her to the core of her soul. There was no sunlight or dewy mornings, no laughing children, in their world.

A sudden pressure in her chest interrupted her thoughts. She gasped. The air was getting sucked out of her. Dust in the clearing rose straight up and the trees surrounding her began to rustle and wave wildly. She looked up, as did the rest of the waking revolutionaries. Overhead five, six, no, now it was seven black helicopters emerged silently from the mist. And then more. She suddenly couldn't count them all because they descended all at once and hovered, filling the sky like locusts, blackening the morning sun.

Three

Dawn, Moscow

In a smoky, dank and dark room in a building in downtown Moscow, Russian military officers stood crowded around a solitary computer screen displaying processed images transmitted from a satellite via a ground station thirty kilometers away. Two senior officials stared in silence at what they were seeing unfold in agonizingly slow motion on the screen in front of them. Not daring to breathe, one by one the officials leaned close to the screen and grunted now and then. Sometimes one of them pressed the screen with a dirty finger, pointing at things appearing before their eyes. The images would need further processing and detailed analysis, of course, but the officers knew they had something. It would take all night, maybe two, but they were sure they had something. Most definitely, they were sure.

Almost eighteen years ago, on October 28, 1983, during the United States invasion of Grenada, the Soviets had moved USSR satellite Cosmos 1504 to a position over the Caribbean, keeping an eye on the progress of the intervention. Since that day and even after the fall of the Soviet Union, they who were left – they who filled the rank and file of the Russian military - had been required to maintain satellites in this position, in recognition of the sensitivity of the area. The latest such satellite was Cosmos 3446, launched from the Baikonur launch pad in northern Kazakhstan in mid-December of 1998. The soldiers had been required to watch and wait. It was their duty. Day in and day out they would stare at the computer monitors waiting for the alarms to ring, waiting for glimmering pictures to float like ghosts across the screens.

Cosmos 3446 had an on-board camera technology known as KVR-2000. The KVR-2000's capabilities and operational aspects were not entirely known outside the Russian military and intelligence community. The soldiers knew that KVR-2000 images contained more spatial detail than any other satellite image on the commercial market, more detail, perhaps, than all but the most advanced American spycraft. Deployed in a low orbit below 200 kilometers in order to get as close a look at the ground as possible, Cosmos 3446 acquired photographic images covering areas from 2 x 2 kilometers up to 40 x 40 kilometers. Unknown to the US military or intelligence community, and impossible to deduce so far as the Russian soldiers were told, were KVR-2000's extended capability to capture raw data less than two feet in diameter, and Cosmos' capability to scan the film product on-board the satellite and download the image to a ground station electronically, almost instantly.

On January 2, 2001, Cosmos 3446's extended capabilities and the KVR-2000's rapid photography feature were triggered, for the first time in years, by an automatic radio command from the Cuban air defense system transmitted to Cosmos 3446 when Cuban air space was violated by the US Juragua strike force. And the computer monitor alarms had shrieked in the empty silence of the bunker. A beautiful, haunting, high-pitched scream to come, come and see.

After a while the two officers stood straight. Their eyes locked. They brought flaring matches to cigarettes squeezed between their tight lips. Slight smiles in gray, creased faces acknowledged the value of what they had recorded, and the accompanying shot in the arms to their stalled careers. They handed out cigarettes all around. Vodka bottles and glasses emerged from under desks. They smoked and drank to their future, the vodka taking their breath away. A cloud soon hovered over their heads as they spoke excitedly and continued to watch the computer screen.

Four

"Turn that up!" John McAdams suddenly sat erect on his stool and pointed at the TV hanging from the ceiling. He leaned over the dark, glistening bar that stretched away from him in twenty feet in either direction under a score of elbows, beer bottles, glasses and ash trays. EJ's was busy tonight, even though New Year's Eve was only 2 Happy Hours behind them. The bar was loud with the crash of a thousand resolutions nose-diving into the ground.

"Bones" Jones, his elbow on the bar, was trading jokes with a patron two stools away. He squinted death at McAdams' outburst and then turned his head to check out the TV screen. It was the local 11 p.m. news.

Jones reached over his head to pump the volume button, his shirt rising up and revealing a flash of pale, hairy gut. Satisfied, he leaned with his back against the bar alongside McAdams' perch and listened. He fondly stroked his long beard that now mercifully covered his stomach. McAdams frowned at the noise level around him and leaned closer to the TV. If he were king, he would have shouted for everyone to shut the fuck up. But he wasn't, so he strained to hear over the cacophony.

The local anchor, his blond hair immobile for the past half-hour despite the whirl of global events spinning around him, tried to return McAdams' frown as he got serious. He waited for the similarly blond woman speaking next to him to finish what was to be a concluding humorous segment, a story on feline monogamy. She finished. Blondy got his breath. "Special Report" ran across the top of the TV screen. Over Blondy's left shoulder popped a photo of Fidel Castro, his mouth open in an ugly grimace and his finger piercing the black air over his head as he spoke from a podium. "Strike Against Cuba" suddenly materialized in a bold red banner over Castro's picture, in effect – an effect obviously intended - crossing his ass out.

"From cat conniving to international intrigue, Sue, more on our late-breaking story." A few groans rose up from the stools around him. McAdams pumped his hands up and down to get quiet.

"World reaction to America's strike today against Cuba's nuclear reactors continues to pour in, almost all of it predictably positive. But Pentagon spokesmen refuse to give details beyond the President's short television appearance earlier tonight. What we know is this. Fidel Castro was about to start up a set of nuclear reactors that could have blown any time, threatening a Cuban Chernoble, a China syndrome, according to the President. US jets, launching a score of missiles, efficiently annihilated the nuclear complex, with no loss of American, or Cuban, life. And so far, Sue, so good. No fallout has been detected. The reactors are destroyed and the air is clear. The third millenium, which really starts today, Sue, starts with a bang. The Pentagon promises a full briefing tomorrow. We will air reports through the night as news comes in. Now back to you, Sue...." Sue nodded wisely and told everyone to stay tuned for Jay Leno, that there'd be special reports all night long, and the bar went back to business.

Bones turned down the volume and shot a glance at McAdams. "So?"

McAdams drained his short glass of Dewars on ice and nodded for another. "We should have heard about this beforehand. This is serious. This is *unbelievable!*"

Bones Jones plopped a generous refill on the counter top and eyed his friend and favorite customer. He was long familiar with McAdams' fevered outbursts at the TV or some poor soul trying to make a point at the bar. "*We?*" He began to roll a cigarette, squeezing tobacco from a pouch under the bar onto a wedge of paper cupped between the fingers of his left hand. Later, after hours, Bones Jones would do justice to his nickname and roll the cigarettes tight with aromatic marijuana and bid good night to all the troubles he had today.

McAdams watched the familiar routine. "*We.* As in the Senate Intelligence Committee. As in Pamela Mossingame, and me. As in the Administration's top go-to-guys and confidants on the Hill when it comes to stuff like this. As in Members of the fuckin' President's God-damned own party." He took an angry swig. "Jesus Christ, he's a lame duck! He should be lining up his book deals and his speeches, not bombers on a runway!"

"Why should they give you guys the head's up? Maybe it was supposed to be, like, top secret, ya know?" The barb came amidst puffs of smoke that poured out of his Bones' mouth. He plucked bits of tobacco from his tongue as he waited for McAdams to parry.

"Because she's the leading Democrat on the Intelligence Committee and I'm her chief investigator. And, Mr.-Savvy-Insider-still-hustling-drinks-behind-a-bar, they need her. She's the leading Democrat on military and intelligence matters. Republicans listen to her. Everyone listens to her. If the President needs support on the Hill, in the Senate especially, she gets it for him. If, no, *when*, the assholes need bucks to finance their little adventures like *this* one, she gets it. And sometimes we know things even they don't know, things they might *need* to know before they pull a stunt like this. You pick up all sorts of information when you control the budgets of all the spies and spooks in America."

McAdams lifted the glass again to his lips, wiping his mouth with a crumpled up napkin. "It's just smart. That's all. They should've checked in before starting the party. The Pres should've gotten Mossingame on board, as much as the leadership as possible for that matter, before launching an act of war as a lame duck. Damn! Congress is gonna go apeshit! I mean, the papers, the Republicans…. Oh, man! It's going to be nuts tomorrow! The Constitutional historians will call this an unprecedented, dangerous, reckless, unconstitutional act by a powerless President. They'll…"

"Whoa!" interrupted Bones. "The Constitutional historians! Watch out!" Bones laughed. "Look, Mac, I hate to disagree with you on a matter in which you clearly have superior expertise…."

"I'm sure," McAdams cracked in reply. "It's always stopped you before."

"… But, listen. All right? We took out a nasty thing belonging to scumbag Castro, a nasty thing that could pollute the world of our children, much less fry their brains with radioactive waves that make the energy waves from the power lines look puny. So, who the fuck cares? Relax! OK? It's late. Kick back, Mac! You get way too hot and bothered over things." He shook his head at McAdams' poor coping mechanisms and walked down the bar to fill an outstretched glass.

"Someone's got to get hot and bothered," McAdams brooded. He ran a hand through his thatch of wavy, brown hair streaked here and there with gray and sat back in his stool. His long mane hung below his collar now, he was going hippie in Bones' estimation, and it framed a ruddy face rugged from a youth that saw a lot of idle hours spent in the sun and on the water off the coast of Connecticut in Long Island Sound. The scotch and the passion of the moment gave him a little more floridity than usual and he could feel the heat in his skin. His brown eyes darted back and forth as he toyed with his feelings.

The President never failed to give Pamela Mossingame a head's up whenever there was something meaningful going on in the military, intelligence or world affairs. Between what the President told them and what they picked up themselves, they knew when North Korea was going to sneeze, and when the latest coup attempt against Hussein failed. They knew when a division was deployed or an aircraft carrier diverted to a new location, for Chris' sake. Sometimes they got the word even before the Joint Chiefs of Staff did. And they *always* got the word before C-SPAN and CNN did, much less the local news. Except for today's little foray against Fidel. Except for what had to be the most controversial act by a President only three weeks away from turning in his ID badge.

Bones strolled back into conversation range. "Feelin' any better?"

"No. But, one more drink, on you, and I'll have a whole new outlook on life."

Bones complied and plopped an overflowing glass on the bar. "So what's Mrs. Mossingame gonna say about it all?"

"She's gonna be pissed, royally," McAdams answered.

"And appropriately so, I guess. The 'royally' part, that is."

"Huh?" McAdams' arched an eyebrow at him.

"I read the Time magazine article. 'America's Maggie Thatcher'?"

McAdams finally nodded, his mind coming off the Cuban air

strikes. "Oh, yeah. Right."

"Is she really that big?"

"Pamela?" He nodded. "If Time says so …."

The weekly magazine had done a cover story on Senator Pamela Mossingame. If there was a negative word or implication in the entire feature article, McAdams couldn't remember it. They trotted out her glowing history in Time's typically breathless prose. She was serving out the term of her late husband, Walter, and so inherited the legacy and the prestige the old man had accumulated over the 30 years he had represented Vermont in the Senate. But Pamela Mossingame was no slouch. No sir. She earned her own way, even before she took office. Along with Walter Mossingame she had been a power center in Washington, a leading light on the political and social scene, for longer than anyone could remember. She carried it well too. She reeked of wisdom and had the bearing of a great stateswoman. For many, over her past four years in the Senate, she invoked the authority and leadership of Margaret Chase Smith, the famous Senator from Maine. Mossingame even got the recent nod on several occasions to address the nation on the Democratic Party's behalf. Her future was bright, never mind why her husband died, never mind his last days when frustration turned him against every good thing he stood for. Only she and McAdams and a few others knew her husband's final acts. *Her* future was bright before the issue of Time came out, and now she had been crowned as America's Maggie Thatcher. A sensational title for a fresh face, a woman in her late 60's, going places, fast. She might even be the President four years from now.

McAdams swirled the amber liquid in the glass, watching the diminishing ice in the whirlpool. The Cuban mission ticked inside his brain.

Bones sauntered back down the bar to tend to some new arrivals and then returned. He beckoned McAdams to come close as he held up his rolled cigarette "Wanna join me later in a special delivery I got this morning? Take your mind off all your global crises."

McAdams stood and sucked the last of his drink back. He

looked wistfully at the cigarette and then the empty glass in his hand and then checked his watch. "Nah…," he began and then stopped to put his glass on the bar. "With us taking on Castro, it'll be the crack of dawn for me."

"Suddenly you go stone cold sober on me?" Bones was crestfallen.

"Later, buddy." McAdams waved and turned away, pushing through the crowd at the bar until he hit the front door. The earlier mist had turned into a light, chilling rain. McAdams let loose a curse as he ventured from the snug, warm comfort of EJ's and took off down the sidewalk to his apartment three blocks away.

Five

January 3 - US Naval Base, Guantanamo Bay, Cuba

He heard the hoarse voice scratching over the already static-filled line. "I'm encrypted," it began. "Are we secure?"

"Encrypted at this end, too, sir." Captain Paul Ellroy squirmed in the leather swivel chair. Washington was on the horn. He preferred Washington where it was and out of his face. But today was not going to be his day. It had that feel.

In Washington, D.C., Carl Crombie peered at a device next to his phone that measured electrical impulses originating at the called destination and transiting the phone line, to see if he was being recorded and ensure end-to-end encryption. He waited for the screen to indicate he was OK to proceed.

"Sir? You still there?"

"Why didn't you *deal* with her," Crombie rasped at last, "when you first came upon her, in the tent? Clearly she was associated with the target. Unquestionably you were authorized to eliminate the target, and every person associated with the target."

"She took us by surprise. She claimed she was an American. We blinked. She won."

"Did she have proof she was an American citizen? Right there and then when you discovered her?"

"No, sir, but there was no question in my mind…."

"Mind? You are not *asked* to have a mind, Captain. You execute orders last time I checked. You led a highly successful, clandestine mission, but this one mistake, your one instance of creative thinking, jeopardizes the entire operation. It puts us *all* at risk." The brittle voice scratched its way out of Crombie's throat.

Ellroy fingered the manila envelope on his desk, swallowing his retort. He had heard rumors that Crombie had throat cancer, that this was the reason for the deterioration of what was once a rumbling, deep voice that shook trees into a harsh, grating whisper. He hoped the rumor was true. He hoped it was a long, lingering, painful, awful death.

"Who is this woman?"

"We searched her home near Nueva Gerona, sir. Cuban-government issued identification that we recovered there says she is Fatima Bosong Barata, an American citizen living as a guest of the Cuban government, since late 1977."

"Fatima ... Barata. The prisoner, this survivor who witnessed the operation, her name is Fatima Barata? She gave you that name?"

"No, she says nothing. We got her name from documents seized from her home. We know it's her home because of papers that were in her possession that led us there."

"Are you sure she is this Fatima Barata?"

"Yes, quite sure. We found photo IDs and...."

"Any aliases?"

"None we know of, sir. Unless you consider the name of her husband, Sorzano."

"Sorzano.... She' been in Cuba since 1977?"

"Again, according to what we found, yes."

Hearing deep, dark silence, Ellroy paused, waiting for some go-ahead.

"Go on." The reply was barely audible.

"All right.... Ms. Barata was married, to a Jose Sorzano. He *was* Cuban, involved with DGI. One of the more skilled of their weapons and martial arts specialists and intelligence gatherers. We've heard of him. He helped orchestrate the little convention we busted up. We believe he was killed in the action."

"You've taken care of their home?"

"It burned down last night. Looks like an accident. Apparently the kitchen stove and the air vents needed a lot of work. Led to some kind of fire."

"Good. ... I want to confirm who this woman is. I want proof that she is this Barata. Have you contacted Marine Corps Intelligence Activity?"

"Not yet. Am I authorized?"

"They're handling intelligence for this operation so use them. Get her prints, get a hair sample. Deal with Captain

Nordquist at MCIA and him alone. No one else."

"I understand."

"Tell Nordquist he is to report to me and me alone on this ID."

"I hear you, sir."

"I must know if she is who she says she is. Quickly. Very quickly."

"Who the fuck is this Fatima Barata? Why…"

"No need for you to know - anything. Contact Nordquist."

"Well, there are further complications…."

"Meaning…?"

"There was a child with her…."

"A … child? With Barata?"

"Yes."

"Alive?"

"Yes. Critically injured, but alive." Ellroy stopped and listened to the raspy breathing that came back to him over the phone line. "The child," he ventured at last, "she's 5 years old. She continues to hang on, sir."

"This is a … complication, Captain."

"Yes…."

"How many know that she and the child exist?"

Ellroy did a quick count in his head. "We kept her in the tent until we took her back to base. Counting me, the two soldiers with me who seized her on the ground, uh, let's see, the three in the helicopter, the three or four hospital staff and doctors who are taking care of her child, uh, the two or three lockup guards who have her on round the clock supervision…. Maybe there was 15 all told with direct, first hand knowledge that there is a mother and child…."

"Fifteen…" came the interruption. "*Fifteen*!"

"There's more you should hear."

"What?"

"She wants an attorney."

"*What?*"

"She wants an attorney, since she's considered under arrest."

"Who says she's under arrest?"

"JAG. If she's an American citizen, then we've arrested her, sir. And if we've arrested her, then she has a right to an attorney. That's the interpretation of the base's Judge Advocate who is the officer in charge for Naval Military Justice here."

"How did JAG get into this so soon?"

"We had no choice. Procedures on Guantanamo provide that anyone - be they civilian or military - anyone thrown into the base's stockade must be able to consult with the senior Judge Advocate before their incarceration. And consultation was requested and it did take place.

"That means there's 16 who know?"

"Right, 16…."

"Maybe more than that if JAG staff knows."

"Maybe more."

"I see. Captain, I want you to keep the woman and child in the stockade down there, and put the woman in solitary confinement, no privileges. Don't charge her with any crime and she won't need a damn lawyer."

"It not that easy, sir. The Judge Advocate is all over my ass. She's citing the Uniform Code of Military Justice. She says we can exercise jurisdiction over Fatima Barata, and keep her in the stockade, only if she is a prisoner of war or we've got probable cause of a crime."

"She?"

"The senior JAG is a she, sir."

"And I'm sure her little heart's bleeding all over this one. Just imagine, a mother and an injured child unjustly imprisoned by cold, unfeeling men of war. I can just hear it. … Tell the JAG officer that the prisoner is a prisoner of *war*. We're at war … with terrorists all over the globe, including Cuba. We are under siege, damn it! Why doesn't anyone see this"

"She'll want to see the declaration of war. Do we have one against terrorism? Can you fax it down to me?" Ellroy's couldn't stifle the sarcasm dripping in his voice.

"Tell her we have probable cause of a crime. Make it up. The Code says that any person within an area leased by the US pursuant to treaty can be incarcerated for probable cause, even a civilian. Last I checked we were leasing land under the Naval Base from Castro under an FDR treaty dating back to 1934."

"What are the particulars of the charge?"

"I said 'make 'em *up*,' Captain. Fatima Barata cannot, I repeat, cannot leave the base and cannot get out into the general public. We must continue to hold her there until I am able to deal with her. Her identity, her existence, must not be disclosed further."

"We got problems, then, sir. The JAG officer has informed me that the Code requires the stockade commander to report to the base's commanding officer the name of the prisoner, the charge and the name of the person who ordered or authorized the commitment of the prisoner - within 24 hours of incarceration. We've managed to stall it, until now, but the JAG says she's gonna make the report happen, and soon. Once the report goes, sir, I don't need to tell you that it's out there. It's public. It will be impossible to keep Fatima Barata's incarceration a secret. Especially," he added with a sudden smile to himself, "especially if someone's looking for her."

"Look, Captain, cite the Code back at our Miss JAG. No stockade commander or master-at-arms may refuse to keep or receive any prisoner committed to his charge by an officer of the armed forces."

"Then I'll have to furnish a signed statement, explicitly laying out the charges."

"Do it. Create probable cause. You can say that we need to keep Barata under guard until we know she will not compromise national security and is not otherwise a danger to the United States or the classified mission which resulted in her incarceration. Write it all up in a very persuasive statement and sign the statement, Captain. And then tell JAG the imprisonment is a matter of national security and is highly classified information. That she is prohibited from informing the base commander of anything having to do with this matter. By order of the Secretary of Defense. *Tell her that!* She will follow my orders or she will face immediate discharge."

"If she listens, if she believes it, that will put me right in the firing line. If this blows up, I go with it."

"You'll be taken care of."

"I am not sure that's enough. Sir."

"Consider this your *order*, then. Fuckin' *do it*, Captain!"

"This won't put an *end* to it, Mr. *Secretary*. I mean, with all due respect ... Procedures on the base say that civilians must not be detained on base for longer than is absolutely necessary, and that American citizens must be referred straightaway for arraignment to the US Federal District Court in Miami."

"Has the prisoner told the Judge Advocate that she is an American?"

He thought for a moment before answering. "Curiously, no. She's dropped it all together. She's saying very little right now other than she wants an attorney. An American attorney."

"The prisoner only wants to be an American when she's threatened and needs some *rights*, but not when she has to pay the *piper*. She's a coward as well as a traitor. She does not deserve the freedom she so desperately seeks, the freedom that the soldier - you and me, Captain - preserves at the risk of his life. She deserves to be a casualty of war. And she will be. We will see to it."

Ellroy shook his head, trying another tack. "Look, sir, you need to act now or it will all unravel. The child may not make it. She's in critical care and this hospital simply ain't fixed to deliver the kind of medical care she needs. The Judge Advocate already wants to know whether we have the obligation to transfer the kid to other facilities in the US, to the Portsmouth, Virginia, or Bethesda, Maryland, Naval hospitals where our critical cases go."

"The Judge Advocate is quite ... persistent," came the flat reply.

"Just doing her job."

"What's her name?"

Ellroy hesitated. He didn't like where this was going. "Ahhh, well.... Captain Eden Dodd, sir."

Ellroy heard rustling paper on the other line. Crombie was writing her name down. Ellroy felt a pang of loathing for what he'd done, for ratting Dodd out. But it wasn't a secret who she was. They would have found out who she was anyway, one way or the other. He only sped up the inevitable result. He squirmed in his chair. He wiped the sweat off his forehead and took a deep breath.

"One more thing, sir," he continued.

"Yes?"

"What if it ends up that she's an American citizen? How will we proceed? She will be entitled to a lawyer if we keep her locked up, she will be entitled to seek referral to the United States. Things will get much more difficult. Everything we do will be subject to stricter scrutiny."

"You initiate the investigation into her background and let Nordquist gather the data and communicate personally to me. Make no decision, engage in no documentation. Nordquist is to pass the raw data on to me by encrypted voice, and he is to contact me alone. I'll make the determination who she is and whether she's an American. And I'll let you know what you need to know."

"With all due respect, sir, is that in your job description now? Determining when someone is an American citizen? How do I sell that to JAG." Ellroy stopped. He sensed he had gone too far.

Crombie wrote another name down on his pad. Captain Paul Ellroy. OK at special ops, at executing a mission, but light in the intelligence field. And disrespectful, not a good trait for the coming, difficult days. Crombie's voice came back cracked, dry.

"In no event shall she or her child come to the United States. If she tries to escape, if she tries to communicate with the outside world, if you see her as a threat in any way, kill her. Kill her and dispose of the child, somehow. Like you should have on Juventud. That's an *order*, Captain. It's a matter of national security. Do not make another mistake."

"What do I do about her wanting an attorney?"

"Tell her that Jacoby and Myers has closed its Havana branch." A low, empty laugh filled the line.

"She already has an attorney in mind."

"Really? Who does she want? Johnny Cochran?" Another arid laugh, ending up in a wracking coughing spasm.

"Someone named John McAdams."

The coughing was stopped. "John…"

"She says he's with the U.S. Senate."

"John McAdams. He's with Senate Intelligence. Good

God…." And then a moment later "Captain..."

"Yes, sir..."

"Stand by. You will receive further orders in less than 48 hours." The line went dead.

About the Author

P. Michael Nugent is an Internet and technology lawyer in New York City. He spent 15 years in Washington, DC, as lawyer and lobbyist where he obtained an insider's view of government and Senate investigators like his protagonist John McAdams.